FROM CHRISTMAS TO FOREVER?

BY
MARION LENNOX

A MUMMY TO MAKE CHRISTMAS

BY
SUSANNE HAMPTON

Marion Lennox is a country girl, born on an Australian dairy farm. She moved on, because the cows just weren't interested in her stories! Married to a 'very special doctor', she has also written under the name Trisha David. She's now stepped back from her 'other' career, teaching statistics. Finally she's figured out what's important, and has discovered the joys of baths, romance and chocolate. Preferably all at the same time! Marion is an international award-winning author.

Married to the man she met at eighteen, **Susanne Hampton** is the mother of two adult daughters—one a musician and the other an artist. Susanne loves everything romantic and pretty, so her home is brimming with romance novels, movies and shoes. With her interest in all things medical, her career has been in the dental field and the medical world in different roles—and now Susanne has taken that love into writing Mills & Boon Medical Romance.

FROM CHRISTMAS TO FOREVER?

BY
MARION LENNOX

MILLS & BOON

Published in Great Britain 2015
by Mills & Boon, an imprint of Harlequin (UK) Limited,
Eton House, 18-24 Paradise Road, Richmond, Surrey, TW9 1SR

© 2015 Marion Lennox

ISBN: 978-0-263-24748-0

Printed and bound in Spain
by CPI, Barcelona

Dear Reader,

I was raised in a farming community, where everyone knew everyone and where our doctor seemed the linchpin of our lives. Doc—he needed no other name—was known to walk fifteen miles between clinics during wartime petrol rationing. By the time he delivered me he was in his eighties, and he worked on until I was in my teens. We never called him unless we truly needed him, but when we did he gave his all. I remember his grandson telling me what it was like at Doc's house at Christmas. You couldn't move for whisky, he said, and grateful gifts of home-baked goodies and produce were almost an embarrassment. When he died, the entire district mourned.

In a way, this book is a testament to Doc and to the caring community I was raised in. My husband and I have recently—joyously—moved back to a small town. As I write this I'm looking forward to Christmas in our new/old home, in our new/old community, and I'm wishing you the magic of belonging. I'm also wishing you the love shown by Doc, and by so many medical staff who follow his tradition of care, and I'm wishing you a very happy Christmas.

Marion Lennox

To the many people
who've already made us welcome in our new home.
To Jacky, to Gail, to Colleen, to Alison,
and to all on Fisherman's Flat, to all who welcome us
as we walk our dog, paddle our kayaks,
or simply yak over the front fence.
You're stuck with us for life, and we love it.

Books by Marion Lennox

Mills & Boon Medical Romance

The Surgeon's Doorstep Baby
Miracle on Kaimotu Island
Gold Coast Angels: A Doctor's Redemption
Waves of Temptation
A Secret Shared...
Meant-to-Be Family

Mills & Boon Cherish

A Bride for the Maverick Millionaire
Sparks Fly with the Billionaire
Christmas at the Castle
Nine Months to Change His Life
Christmas Where They Belong

Visit the Author Profile page
at millsandboon.co.uk for more titles.

CHAPTER ONE

CHRISTMAS IN THE middle of nowhere. Wombat Valley. *Hooray!*

Dr Pollyanna Hargreaves—Polly to everyone but her mother—beefed up the radio as she turned off the main road. Bing Crosby's 'White Christmas' wasn't exactly appropriate for Christmas deep in the Australian bush, but it didn't stop her singing along. She might be a long way from snow, but she was happy.

The country around her was wild and mountainous. The twisting road meant this last section of the journey could take a while, but the further she went, the further she got from the whole over-the-top celebration that was her parents' idea of Christmas.

'You can't be serious!' She could still hear her mother's appalled words when she'd broken the news that she wouldn't be spending Christmas with them. 'We've planned one of the most wonderful Christmases ever. We've hired the most prestigious restaurant on Sydney Harbour. All our closest friends are coming, and the head chef himself has promised to oversee a diabetic menu. Pollyanna, everyone expects you.'

Expectation was the whole problem, Polly thought, as she turned through the next curve with care. This road was little more than a logging route, and recent rain had gouged gutters along the unsealed verge. The whole of New South Wales had been inundated with weeks of subtropical downpours, and it looked as if Wombat Valley had borne the brunt of them. She was down to a snail's pace.

But she wasn't worried. She wasn't in Sydney. Or in Monaco, where she'd been last Christmas. Or in Aspen, where she'd been the Christmas before that.

Cute little Pollyanna had finally cut and run.

'And I'm not going back,' she told the road ahead. Enough. She felt as if she'd been her parents' plaything since birth, saddled with a preposterous name, with nannies to take care of every whim and loaded with the expectation that she be the perfect daughter.

For Polly was the only child of Olivia and Charles Hargreaves. Heiress to the Hargreaves millions. She was courted and fussed over, wrapped in cotton wool and expected to be…

'Perfect.' She abandoned Bing and said the word aloud, thinking of the tears, the recriminations, the gentle but incessant blackmail.

'Polly, you'll break your mother's heart.' That was what her father had said when Polly had decided, aged seven, that she liked chocolate ice cream, eating a family tub behind her nanny's back and putting her blood sugars through the roof. And ever since… 'You know we worry. Don't you care?'

And then, when she'd decided she wanted to be a doctor…

'Pollyanna, how can you stress your body with a demanding career like medicine? Plus you have your inheritance to consider. If you need to work—which you don't—then at least take a position in the family company. You could be our PR assistant; that's safe. Medicine! Polly, you'll break our hearts.'

And now this. Breaking up with the boy they wanted

her to marry, followed by Not Coming Home For Christmas. Not being there to be fussed over, prettied, shown off to their friends. This was heartbreak upon heartbreak upon heartbreak.

'But I'm over it,' she said out loud. 'I'm over families—over, over, over. I'm an independent career woman so it's time I started acting like one. This is a good start. I'm five hours' drive from Sydney, in the middle of nowhere. I'm contracted to act as locum for two weeks. I can't get further away than this.'

And it was exciting. She'd trained and worked in city hospitals. She didn't have a clue about bush medicine, but the doctor she was relieving—Dr Hugo Denver—had told her things would be straightforward.

'We're usually busy,' he'd said in their phone interview. 'The valley could use two doctors or more, but over Christmas half the population seems to depart for Sydney or the coast. We run a ten-bed hospital but anything major gets helicoptered out. Mostly we deal with minor stuff where it's not worth the expense of sending for the Air Ambulance, or long-termers, or locals who choose to die in the Valley rather than in acute city hospitals.'

'You provide palliative care?' she'd asked, astonished.

'Via home visits, mostly,' he'd told her. 'Most of our oldies only go to the city under duress, and it's an honour to look after them at home. I also deal with trauma, but the logging industry closes down for three weeks over Christmas and the place is quiet. I doubt if you'll have much excitement.'

'But I wouldn't mind a bit of excitement,' she said aloud as she manoeuvred her little sports car around the next bend. 'Just enough to keep me occupied.'

And then, as if in answer to her prayers, she rounded the next bend—and got more excitement than she'd bargained for.

* * *

Dr Hugo Denver was well over excitement. Hugo was cramped inside a truck balanced almost vertically over the side of a cliff. He was trying to stop Horace Fry from bleeding out. He was also trying not to think that Ruby was totally dependent on him, and his life seemed to be balanced on one very unstable, very young tree.

The call had come in twenty minutes ago. Margaret Fry, wife of the said Horace, had managed to crawl out of the crashed truck and ring him.

'Doc, you gotta come fast.' She'd sobbed into the phone. 'Horace's bleeding like a stuck pig and there's no one here but me.'

'He's still in the truck?'

'Steering wheel jabbed him. Blood's making him feel faint.'

'Bleeding from where?'

'Shoulder, I think.'

'Can you put pressure on it?'

'Doc, I can't.' It was a wail. 'You know blood makes me throw up and I'm not getting back in that truck. Doc, come, fast!'

What choice did he have? What choice did he ever have? If there was trauma in Wombat Valley, Hugo was it.

'Ring the police,' he snapped. 'I'm on my way.'

Lois, his housekeeper, had been preparing lunch. She'd been humming Christmas carols, almost vibrating with excitement. As was Ruby. As soon as the locum arrived they were off, Lois to her son's place in Melbourne, Hugo and Ruby to their long-awaited two-week holiday.

Christmas at the beach... This was what his sister had promised Ruby last year, but last year's Christmas had become a blur of shock and sorrow. A car crash the week before. A single car accident. Suicide?

Hugo's life had changed immeasurably in that moment, as had Ruby's.

Twelve months on, they were doing their best. He was doing his best. He'd moved back to Wombat Valley so Ruby could stay in her home, and he fully intended to give her the longed-for beach Christmas.

But commitment meant committing not only to Ruby but to the community he lived in. The locals cared for Ruby. He cared for the locals. That was the deal.

Lois had been putting cold meat and salad on the table. She'd looked at him as he disconnected, and sighed and put his lunch in the fridge.

'Ring Donald,' he'd told her. Donald was a retired farmer who also owned a tow truck. It was a very small tow truck but the logging company with all its equipment was officially on holidays since yesterday. Donald's truck would be all the valley had. 'Tell him Horace Fry's truck's crashed at Blinder's Bend. Ring Joe at the hospital and tell him to expect casualties. Tell him I'll ring him as soon as I know details, and ask him to check that the police know. I need to go.'

'Aren't you expecting the new doctor?' Lois had practically glowered. She wanted to get away, too.

'If she arrives before I get back, you can give her my lunch,' he'd said dryly. 'I'll eat at the hospital.'

'Should I send her out to Blinder's? She could start straight away.'

'I can hardly throw her in at the deep end,' he'd told her. 'Hopefully, this will be the last casualty, though, and she'll have a nice quiet Christmas.' He'd dropped a kiss on his small niece's head. 'See you later, Ruby. Back soon.'

But now…

A quiet Christmas was just what he wanted, he thought grimly as he pushed hard on the gaping wound on Horace's shoulder. The steering wheel seemed to have snapped right off, and the steering column had jabbed into Horace's chest.

And he'd bled. Hugo had stared in dismay into the truck's cab, he'd looked at the angle the truck was leaning over the cliff, he'd looked at the amount of blood in the cabin and he'd made a call.

The truck was balanced on the edge of the cliff. The ground was sodden from recent rain but it had still looked stable enough to hold. He'd hoped…

He shouldn't have hoped. He should have waited for Donald with his tow truck, and for the police.

It didn't matter what he should have done. Margaret had been having hysterics, useless for help. Hopefully, Donald and his tow truck were on their way but he'd take a while. The police had to come from Willaura on the coast, and he hadn't been able to wait.

And then, as he'd bent into the cab, Horace had grasped his wrist with his good arm and tried to heave himself over to the passenger seat. He was a big man and he'd jerked with fear, shifting his weight to the middle of the cabin…

Hugo had felt the truck lurch and lurch again. He'd heard Margaret scream as the whole verge gave way and they were falling…

And then, blessedly, the truck seemed to catch on something. From this angle, all he could see holding them up was one twiggy sapling. His life depended on that sapling. There was still a drop under them that was long enough to give him nightmares.

But he didn't have time for nightmares. He'd been thrown around but somehow he was still applying pressure to Horace's arm. Somehow he'd pushed Horace back into the driver's seat, even if it was at a crazy angle.

'You move again and we'll both fall to the bottom of the cliff,' he told Horace and Horace subsided.

To say his life was flashing before his eyes would be an understatement.

Ruby. Seven years old.

He was all she had.

But he couldn't think of Ruby now. He needed to get back up to the road. Horace had lost too much blood. He needed fluids. He needed electrolytes. He needed the equipment to set up a drip...

Hugo moved a smidgen and the truck swayed again. He glanced out of the back window and saw they were ten feet down the cliff.

Trapped.

'Margaret?' he yelled. 'Margaret!'

There was no reply except sobbing.

His phone... Where the hell was his phone?

And then he remembered. He'd done a cursory check on Margaret. She'd been sobbing and shaking when he'd arrived. She was suffering from shock, he'd decided. It had been an instant diagnosis but it was all he'd had time for, so he'd put his jacket across her shoulders and run to the truck.

His phone was still in his jacket pocket.

'Margaret!' he yelled again, and the truck rocked again, and from up on the cliff Margaret's sobs grew louder.

Was she blocking her husband's need with her cries? Maybe she was. People had different ways of protecting themselves, and coming near a truck ten feet down a cliff, when the truck was threatening to fall another thirty, was possibly a bad idea.

Probably.

Definitely?

'That hurt!' Horace was groaning in pain.

'Sorry, mate, I need to push hard.'

'Not my shoulder, Doc—my eardrum.'

Great. All this and he'd be sued for perforating Horace's eardrum?

'Can you yell for Margaret? We need her help.'

'She won't answer,' Horace muttered. 'If she's having hysterics the only thing that'll stop her is ice water.'

Right.

'Then we need to sit really still until help arrives,' he told him, trying not to notice Horace's pallor, deciding not to check his blood pressure because there wasn't a thing he could do about it. 'The truck's unstable. We need to sit still until Donald arrives with his tow truck.'

'Then we'll be waiting a while,' Horace said without humour. 'Donald and his missus have gone to their daughter's for Christmas. Dunno who's got a tow truck round here. It'll have to be a tractor.'

'Can you get Margaret to ring someone?'

'Like I said, Doc, she's useless.'

There was an SUV parked right where she wanted to drive.

It was serviceable, dirty white, a four-wheel drive wagon with a neat red sign across the side. The sign said: 'Wombat Valley Medical Service'.

It blocked the road completely.

She put her foot on the brake and her car came to a well-behaved standstill.

The road curved behind the SUV, and as her car stopped she saw the collapse of the verge. And as she saw more, she gasped in horror.

There was a truck below the collapse. Over the cliff!

A few hundred yards back she'd passed a sign declaring this area to be Wombat Valley Gap. The Gap looked to be a magnificent wilderness area, stretching beneath the road as far as the eye could see.

The road was hewn into the side of the mountain. The edge was a steep drop. Very steep. Straight down.

The truck looked as if it had rounded the curve too fast. The skid marks suggested it had hit the cliff and spun across to the edge. The roadside looked as if it had given way.

The truck had slipped right over and was now balanced precariously about ten feet down the cliff, pointing downward. There were a couple of saplings holding it. Just.

A woman was crouched on the verge, weeping, and Polly herself almost wept in relief at the sight of her. She'd escaped from the truck then?

But then she thought… SUV blocking the road. Wombat Valley Medical Service… Two vehicles.

Where was the paramedic?

Was someone else in the truck? Was this dramas, plural?

Help!

She was a city doctor, she thought frantically. She'd never been near the bush in her life. She'd never had to cope with a road accident. Yes, she'd cared for accident victims, but that had been in the organised efficiency of a city hospital Emergency Room.

All of a sudden she wanted to be back in Sydney. Preferably off-duty.

'You wanted to be a doctor,' she told herself, still taking time to assess the whole scene. Her lecturers in Emergency Medicine had drilled that into her, and somehow her training was coming back now. *'Don't jump in before you've checked the whole situation. Check fast but always check. You don't want to become work for another doctor. Work out priorities and keep yourself safe.'*

Keeping herself safe had never been a problem in the ER.

'You wanted to see medicine at its most basic,' she reminded herself as she figured out what must have happened. 'Here's your chance. Get out of the car and help.'

My, that truck looked unstable.

Keep yourself safe.

The woman was wailing.

Who was in the truck?

Deep breath.

She climbed out of her car, thinking a flouncy dress covered in red and white polka dots wasn't what she should be wearing right now. She was also wearing crimson sandals with kitten heels.

She hardly had time to change. She was a doctor and she was needed. Disregarding her entirely inappropriate wardrobe, she headed across to the crying woman. She was big-boned, buxom, wearing a crinoline frock and an electric-blue perm. She had a man's jacket over her shoulders. Her face was swollen from weeping and she had a scratch above one eye.

'Can you tell me what's happened?' Polly knelt beside her, and the woman stared at her and wailed louder. A lot louder.

But hysterics was something Pollyanna Hargreaves could deal with. Hysterics was Polly's mother's weapon of last resort and Polly had stopped responding to it from the age of six.

She knelt so her face was six inches from the woman's. She was forcing her to look at her and, as soon as she did, she got serious.

'Stop the noise or I'll slap you,' she said, loud and firm and cold as ice. Doctor threatening patient with physical violence... *Good one*, Polly thought. *That's the way to endear you to the locals.* But it couldn't matter. Were there people in that upside down truck?

'Who's in the truck?' she demanded. 'Take two deep breaths and talk.'

'I...my husband. And Doc...'

'Doc?'

'Doc Denver.'

'The doctor's in the truck?'

'He was trying to help Horace.' Somehow she was managing to speak. 'Horace was bleeding. But then the ground gave way and the truck slid and it's still wobbling and it's going to fall all the way down.'

The woman subsided as Polly once again took a moment to assess. The truck was definitely…wobbling. The saplings seemed to be the only thing holding it up. If even one of them gave way…

'Have you called for help?' she asked. The woman was clutching her phone.

'I called Doc…'

'The doctor who's here now?'

'Doc Denver, yes.'

'Good for you. How about the police? A tow truck?'

The woman shook her head, put her hands to her face and started loud, rapid breathing. Holly took a fast pulse check and diagnosed panic. There were other things she should exclude before a definitive diagnosis but, for now, triage said she needed to focus on the truck.

'I need you to concentrate on breathing,' she told the woman. 'Count. One, two, three, four—in. One, two, three, four—out. Slow your breathing down. Will you do that?'

'I…yes…'

'Good woman.' But Polly had moved on. Truck. Cliff. Fall.

She edged forward, trying to see down the cliff, wary of the crumbling edge.

What was wrong with Christmas in Sydney? All at once she would have given her very best shoes to be there.

CHAPTER TWO

TRIAGE. ACTION. SOMEHOW POLLY made herself a plan.

First things first. She phoned the universal emergency number and the response came blessedly fast.

'Emergency services. Fire, ambulance, police—which service do you require?'

'How about all three?' She gave details but as she talked she stared down at the truck.

There was a coil of rope in the back of the truck. A big one. A girl could do lots with that rope, she thought. If she could clamber down...

A police sergeant came onto the phone, bluff but apologetic.

'We need to come from Willaura—we'll probably be half an hour. I'll get an ambulance there as soon as I can, but sorry, Doc, you're on your own for at least twenty minutes.'

He disconnected.

Twenty minutes. Half an hour.

The ground was soggy. If the saplings gave way...

She could still see the rope, ten feet down in the back of the truck tray. It wasn't a sheer drop but the angle was impossibly steep.

There were saplings beside the truck she could hold onto, if they were strong enough.

'Who's up there?'

The voice from the truck made her start. It was a voice she recognised from the calls she'd made organising this job. Dr Hugo Denver. Her employer.

'It's Dr Hargreaves, your new locum, and you promised me no excitement,' she called back. She couldn't see him. 'Hello to you, too. I don't suppose there's any way you can jump from the cab and let it roll?'

'I have the driver in here. Multiple lacerations and a crush injury to the chest. I'm applying pressure to stop the bleeding.'

'You didn't think to pull him out first?'

There was a moment's pause, then a reply that sounded as if it came through gritted teeth. 'No.'

'That was hardly wise.'

'Are you in a position to judge?'

'I guess not.' She was assessing the saplings, seeing if she could figure out safe holds on the way down. 'But it does—in retrospect—seem to have been worth considering.'

She heard a choke that might even have been laughter. It helped, she thought. People thought medics had a black sense of humour but, in the worst kind of situations, humour was often the only way to alleviate tension.

'I'll ask for your advice when I need it,' he retorted and she tested a sapling for strength and thought maybe not.

'Advice is free,' she offered helpfully.

'Am I or am I not paying you?'

She almost managed a grin at that, except she couldn't get her sandals to grip in the mud and she was kind of distracted. 'I believe you are,' she said at last, and gave up on the shoes and tossed her kitten heels up onto the verge. Bare feet was bad but kitten heels were worse. She started inching down the slope, moving from sapling to sapling. If she could just reach that rope...

'I'd like a bit of respect,' Hugo Denver called and she held like a limpet to a particularly shaky sapling and tried to think about respect.

'It seems you're not in any position to ask for anything right now,' she managed. She was nearing the back of the truck but she was being super-cautious. If she slipped she could hardly grab the truck for support. It looked like one push and it'd fall...

Do not think of falling.

'I need my bag,' Hugo said. 'It's on the verge where the truck...'

'Yeah, I saw it.' It was above her. Quite a bit above her now.

'Can you lower it somehow?'

'In a minute. I'm getting a rope.'

'A rope?'

'There's one in the back of the truck. It looks really long and sturdy. Just what the doctor ordered.'

'You're climbing down?'

'I'm trying to.'

'Hell, Polly...'

'Don't worry. I have really grippy toenails and if I can reach it I might be able to make the truck more secure.'

There was a moment's silence. Then... 'Grippy toenails?'

'They're painted crimson.'

He didn't seem to hear the crimson bit. 'Polly, don't. It's too dangerous. There's a cord in my truck...'

'How long a cord?' Maybe she should have checked his truck.

'Twelve feet or so. You could use it to lower my bag. Horace needs a drip and fast.'

There was no way she could use a twelve-foot cord to secure the truck—and what use was a drip if the truck fell?

'Sorry,' Polly managed. 'In every single situation I've

ever trained in, triage is sorting priorities, so that's what I've done. If I lower your bag and add a smidgen of weight to the truck, you may well be setting up a drip as you plummet to the valley floor. So it's rope first, secure the truck next and then I'll work on getting your bag. You get to be boss again when you get out of the truck.'

'You've got a mouth,' he said, sounding cautious—and also stunned.

'I'm bad at respect,' she admitted. If she could just get a firmer hold... 'That's the younger generation for you. You want to override me, Grandpa?'

'How old do you think I am?'

'You must be old if you think a ride to the bottom of the valley's an option.' And then she shut up because she had to let go of a sapling with one hand and hope the other held, and lean out and stretch and hope that her fingers could snag the rope...

And they did and she could have wept in relief but she didn't because she was concentrating on sliding the rope from the tray, an inch at a time, thinking that any sudden movements could mean...

Don't think what it could mean.

'You have red hair!'

He could see her. She'd been so intent she hadn't even looked at the window in the back of the truck. She braved a glance downward, and she saw him.

Okay, she conceded, this was no grandpa. The face looking out at her was lean and tanned and...worried. His face looked sort of chiselled, his eyes were deep set and his brow looked furrowed in concern...

All that she saw in the nanosecond she allowed herself before she went back to concentrating on freeing the rope. But weirdly it sort of...changed things.

Two seconds ago she'd been concentrating on saving

two guys in a truck. Now one of them had a face. One of them looked worried. One of them looked…

Strong?

Immensely masculine?

How crazy was that? Her sight of him had been fleeting, a momentary impression, but there'd been something about the way he'd looked back at her…

Get on with the job, she told herself sharply. It was all very well getting the rope out of the truck. What was she going to do with it now she had it?

She had to concentrate on the rope. Not some male face. Not on the unknown Dr Denver.

The tray of the truck had a rail around it, with an upright at each corner. If she could loop the rope…

'Polly, wait for the cavalry,' Hugo demanded, and once again she had that impression of strength. And that he feared for her.

'The cavalry's arriving in half an hour,' she called back. 'Does Horace have half an hour?'

Silence.

'He's nicked a vein,' he said at last, and Polly thought: *That's that, then*. Horace needed help or he'd die.

She wedged herself against another sapling, hoping it could take her weight. Then she unwound her rope coil.

'What are you doing?' It was a sharp demand.

'Imagine I'm in Theatre,' she told him. 'Neurosurgeon fighting the odds. You're unscrubbed and useless. Would you ask for a commentary?'

'Is that another way of saying you don't have a plan?'

'Shut up and concentrate on Horace.' It was unnerving, to say the least, that he could see her, but then Horace groaned and Hugo's face disappeared from the back window and she could get on with…what…? Concentrating not on Hugo.

On one rope.

Somehow she got the middle of the rope looped and knotted around each side of the tray. Yay! Now she had to get back to the road. She clutched the cliff as if she were glued to it, scrambling up until her feet were on solid ground. Finally she was up. All she had to do now was figure out something to tie it to.

She had the shakes.

'Are you safe?' Hugo called and she realised he couldn't see her any more. The truck was too far over the lip. 'Dr Hargreaves?' There was no disguising his fear.

'I'm safe,' she called back and her voice wobbled and she tried again. This time her voice was pleasingly smug. 'Feet on terra firma. Moving to stage two of the action plan.'

'I thought you didn't have a plan.'

'It's more exciting without one, but I'm trying. Indeed, I'm very trying.'

Plans took brains. Plans required the mush in her brain to turn useful. To stop thinking about Hugo plunging downward...

It wasn't Hugo. It was two guys in a truck. *Take the personal out of it*, she told herself.

Plan!

She needed a solid tree, or at least a good-sized stump. She had neither.

Attach the rope to her car? Not in a million years. Her little yellow sports car would sail over the cliff after the truck.

Margaret looked kind of buxom. How would she go as an anchor?

She gave a wry grin, wishing she could share the thought with Bossy In The Truck. Maybe not.

Bossy's truck?

The thought was no sooner in her mind than she was running up the road to Hugo's car. Blessedly, his keys were in the ignition. *Yes!* A minute later, his vehicle was parked as close as she could manage to the point where the truck had gone over.

It was an SUV. She'd once gone skiing in an upmarket version of one of these—her boyfriend's. Well, her ex-boyfriend, she conceded. They'd been snowed in and the tow truck had had to winch them out.

Polly had been interested in the process, or more interested than in listening to Marcus whinging, so she'd watched. There'd been an anchor point…

She ducked underneath. Yes! She had the ends of the rope fastened in a moment.

Maybe she could pull the truck up.

Maybe not. This wasn't a huge SUV.

'Polly…' From below Hugo's voice sounded desperate. 'What are you doing?'

'Being a Girl Guide,' she yelled back. 'Prepare to be stabilised.'

'How…?'

'Pure skill,' she yelled back. 'How's Horace?'

'Slipping.'

'Two minutes,' she yelled back, twisting the rope and racking her brain for a knot that could be used.

Reef Knot? Round Turn and Two Half Hitches? What about a Buntline Hitch? Yes! She almost beamed. Brown Owl would be proud.

She knotted and then cautiously shifted the SUV, reversing sideways against the cliff, taking up the last slack in the rope. Finally she cut the engine. She closed her eyes for a nanosecond and she allowed herself to breathe.

'Why don't you do something?' It was Margaret—of course it was Margaret—still crouched on the verge and screaming. 'My Horace's dying and all you do is…'

'Margaret, if you don't shut up I'll personally climb the cliff and slap you for Polly,' Hugo called up, and Polly thought: *Uh oh.* He must have heard her previous threat. Some introduction to his new employee. Medicine by force.

But at least he was backing her and the idea was strangely comforting—there were two doctors working instead of one.

'Let's get you somewhere more comfortable,' she told the woman. She had a jacket draped over her shoulders. 'Is this Doc Denver's jacket?'

'I…yes. His phone's in the pocket. It keeps ringing.'

You didn't think to answer it? she thought, but she didn't say it. What was the point now? But if Emergency Services were trying to verify their location…

'I want you to sit in Doc Denver's truck,' she told Margaret. 'If the phone rings, can you answer it and tell people where we are?'

'I don't…'

'We're depending on you, Margaret. All you have to do is sit in the car and answer the phone. Nothing else. Can you do that?'

'If you save Horace.'

'Deal.' She propelled her into the passenger seat of the SUV and there was a bonus. More ballast. With Margaret's extra, not insubstantial, weight, this vehicle was going nowhere.

'I think you're stable,' she yelled down the cliff, while she headed back to the verge for Hugo's bag. She flicked it open. Saline, adrenaline, painkilling drugs, all the paraphernalia she'd expect a country GP would carry. He must have put it down while he'd leaned into the truck, and then the road had given way.

How to get it to him?

'What do you mean, stable?' he called.

'I have nice strong ties attaching the truck tray to your SUV,' she called. 'The SUV's parked at right angles to you, with Margaret sitting in the passenger seat. It's going nowhere.'

'How did you tie…?'

'Girl Guiding 101,' she called back. 'You want to give me a raise on the strength of it?'

'Half my kingdom.'

'Half a country practice in Wombat Valley? Ha!'

'Yeah, you're right, it's a trap,' he called back. 'You know you'll never get away, but you walked in of your own accord, and I'm more than willing to share. I'll even include Priscilla Carlisle's bunions. They're a medical practice on their own.'

Astonishingly, she giggled.

This felt okay. She could hear undercurrents to his attempt at humour that she had no hope of understanding, but she was working hard, and in the truck Hugo would be working hard, too. The medical imperatives were still there, but the flavour of black humour was a comfort all on its own.

Medical imperatives. The bag was the next thing. Horace had suffered major blood loss. Everything Hugo needed was in that bag.

How to get the bag down?

Lower it? It'd catch on the undergrowth. Take it down herself? *Maybe.* The cab, though, was much lower than the tray. There were no solid saplings past the back of the tray.

She had Hugo's nylon cord. It was useless for abseiling—the nylon would slice her hands—but she didn't have to pull herself up. She could stay down there until the cavalry arrived.

Abseiling… A harness? *Nope.* The nylon would cut.

A seat? She'd learned to make a rope seat in Abseil Rescue.

Hmm.

'Tie the cord to the bag and toss it as close as you can,'

Hugo called, and humour had given way to desperation. 'I can try and retrieve it.'

'What, lean out of the cabin? Have you seen the drop?'

'I'm trying not to see the drop but there's no choice.'

His voice cracked. It'd be killing him, she thought, watching Horace inch towards death with no way to help.

'Did you mention you have a kid? You're taking your kid to the beach for Christmas? Isn't that what this locum position is all about?'

'Yes, but…'

'Then you're going nowhere. Sit. Stay.'

There was a moment's silence, followed by a very strained response.

'Woof?'

She grinned. *Nice one.*

But she was no longer concentrating on the conversation. Her hands were fashioning a seat, three lines of cord, hooked together at the sides, with a triangle of cord at both sides to make it steady.

She could make a knot and she could let it out as she went…

Wow, she was dredging through the grey matter now. But it was possible, she conceded. She could tie the bag underneath her, find toeholds in the cliff, hopefully swing from sapling to sapling to steady her…

'Polly, if you're thinking of climbing…you can't.' Hugo's voice was deep and gravelly. There was strength there, she thought, but she also heard fear.

He was scared for her.

He didn't even know her.

He was concerned for a colleague, she thought, but, strangely, it felt more than that. It felt…warm. Strong. Good.

Which was ridiculous. She knew nothing about this

man, other than he wanted to take his kid to the beach
for Christmas.

'Never say *can't* to a Hargreaves,' she managed to call
back. 'You'll have my father to answer to.'

'I don't want to answer to your father if you're dead.'

'I'll write a note excusing you. Now shut up. I need to
concentrate.'

'Polly…'

'Hold tight. I'm on my way.'

CHAPTER THREE

IT NEARLY KILLED HIM.

He could do nothing except apply pressure to Horace's shoulder and wait for rescue.

From a woman in a polka dot dress.

The sight of her from the truck's rear-view window had astounded him. Actually, the sight of anyone from the truck's rear-view mirror would have astounded him—this was an impossible place to reach—but that a woman…

No, that was sexist… That anyone, wearing a bare-shouldered dress with a halter neck tie, with flouncy auburn curls to her shoulders, with freckles…

Yeah, he'd even noticed the freckles.

And yes, he thought, he was being sexist or fashionist or whatever else he could think of being accused of right now, but he excused himself because what he wanted was a team of State Emergency Personnel with safety jackets and big boots organising a smooth transition to safety.

He was stuck with polka dots and freckles.

He should have asked for a photo when he'd organised the locum. He should never have…

Employed polka dots? Who was he kidding? If an applicant had a medical degree and was breathing he would have employed them. No one wanted to work in Wombat Valley.

No one but him and he was stuck here. Lured here for love of his little niece. Stuck here for ever.

Beside him, Horace was drifting in and out of consciousness. His blood pressure was dropping, his breathing was becoming laboured and there was nothing he could do.

He'd never felt so helpless.

Maybe he had. The night they'd rung and told him Grace had driven her car off the Gap.

Changing his life in an instant.

Why was he thinking about that now? Because there was nothing else to think about? Nothing to do?

The enforced idleness was killing him. He couldn't see up to the road unless he leaned out of the window. What was she doing?

What sort of a dumb name was Polly anyway? he thought tangentially. Whoever called a kid Pollyanna?

She'd sent a copy of her qualifications to him, with references. They'd been glowing, even if they'd been city based.

The name had put him off. Was that nameist?

Regardless, he'd had reservations about employing a city doctor in this place that required definite country skills, but Ruby deserved Christmas.

He deserved Christmas. Bondi Beach. Sydney. He'd had a life back there.

And now…his whole Christmas depended on a doctor in polka dots. More, his life depended on her. If her knots didn't hold…

'Hey!'

And she was just there, right by the driver's seat window. At least, her feet were there—bare!—and then her waist, and then there was a slither and a curse and her head appeared at the open window. She was carefully not touching the truck, using her feet on the cliff to push herself back.

'Hey,' she said again, breathlessly. 'How're you guys doing? Would you like a bag?'

And, amazingly, she hauled up his canvas holdall from under her.

Horace was slumped forward, semi-conscious, not reacting to her presence. Polly gave Horace a long, assessing look and then turned her attention to him. He got the same glance. Until her assessment told her otherwise, it seemed he was the patient.

'Okay?' she asked.

'Bruises. Nothing more. I'm okay to work.'

He got a brisk nod, accepting his word, moving on. 'If you're planning on coping with childbirth or constipation, forget it,' she told him, lifting the bag through the open window towards him. 'I took stuff out to lighten the load. But this should have what you need.'

To say he was gobsmacked would be an understatement. She was acting like a doctor in a ward—calm, concise, using humour to deflect tension. She was hanging by some sort of harness—no, some sort of seat—at the end of a nylon cord. She was red-headed and freckled and polka-dotted, and she was cute...

She was a doctor, offering assistance.

He grabbed the bag so she could use her hands to steady herself and, as soon as he had it, her smile went to high beam. But her smile still encompassed a watchful eye on Horace. She was an emergency physician, he thought. ER work was a skill—communicating and reassuring terrified patients while assessing injuries at the same time. That was what she was doing. She knew the pressure he was under but her manner said this was just another day in the office.

'Those bruises,' she said. 'Any on the head? No concussion?'

So he was still a patient. 'No.'

'Promise?'

'Promise.'

'Then it's probably better if you work from inside the truck. If I work on Horace from outside I might put more pressure...'

'You've done enough.'

'I haven't but I don't want to bump the truck more than necessary. Yell if you need help but if you're fine to put in the drip then I'll tie myself to a sapling and watch. Margaret is up top, manning the phones, so it's my turn for a spot of R and R. It's time to strut your stuff, Dr Denver. Go.'

She pushed herself back from the truck and cocked a quizzical eyebrow—and he couldn't speak.

Time to strut his stuff? She was right, of course. He needed to stop staring at polka dots.

He needed to try and save Horace.

Polly was now just as stuck as the guys in the truck.

There was no way she could pull herself up the cliff again. She couldn't get purchase on the nylon without cutting herself. The cord had cut her hands while she'd lowered herself, but to get the bag to Hugo, to try and save Horace's life, she'd decided a bit of hand damage was worthwhile.

Getting up, though... Not so much. The cavalry was on its way. She'd done everything she could.

Now all she had to do was secure herself and watch Hugo work.

He couldn't do it.

He had all the equipment he needed. All he had to do was find a vein and insert a drip.

But Horace was a big man, his arms were fleshy and flaccid, and his blood pressure had dropped to dangerous levels. Even in normal circumstances it'd be tricky to find a vein.

Horace was bleeding from the arm nearest him. He had that pressure bound. The bleeding had slowed to a trickle, but he needed to use Horace's other arm for the drip.

It should be easy. All he needed to do was tug Horace's arm forward, locate the vein at the elbow and insert the drip.

But he was at the wrong angle and his hands shook. Something about crashing down a cliff, thinking he was going to hit the bottom? The vein he was trying for slid away under the needle.

'Want me to try?' Polly had tugged back from the truck, cautious that she might inadvertently put weight on it, but she'd been watching.

'You can hardly operate while hanging on a rope,' he told her and she gave him a look of indignation.

'In case you hadn't noticed, I've rigged this up with a neat seat. So I'm not exactly hanging. If you're having trouble... I don't want to bump the truck but for Horace... maybe it's worth the risk.'

And she was right. Priority had to be that vein, but if he couldn't find it, how could she?

'I've done my first part of anaesthetic training,' she said, diffidently now. 'Finding veins is what I'm good at.'

'You're an anaesthetist?'

'Nearly. You didn't know that, did you, Dr Denver?' To his further astonishment, she sounded smug. 'Emergency physician with anaesthetist skills. You have two medics for the price of one. So...can I help?'

And he looked again at Horace's arm and he thought of the consequences of not trusting. She was an anaesthetist. They were both in impossible positions but she had the training.

'Yes, please.'

* * *

Her hands hurt. Lowering herself using only the thin cord had been rough.

Her backside also hurt. Three thin nylon cords weren't anyone's idea of good seat padding. She was using her feet to swing herself as close to the truck as she dared, trying to balance next to the window.

There was nothing to tie herself to.

And then Hugo reached over and caught the halter-tie of her dress, so her shoulder was caught at the rear of the window.

'No weight,' he told her. 'I'll just hold you steady.'

'What a good thing I didn't wear a strapless number,' she said approvingly, trying to ignore the feel of his hand against her bare skin. Truly, this was the most extraordinary position...

It was the most extraordinary feeling. His hold made her feel...safe?

Was she out of her mind? *Safe?* But he held fast and it settled her.

Hugo had swabbed but she swabbed again, holding Horace's arm steady as she worked. She had his arm out of the window, resting on the window ledge. The light here was good.

She pressed lightly and pressed again...

The cannula was suddenly in her hand. Hugo was holding her with one hand, acting as theatre assistant with the other.

Once again that word played into her mind. *Safe...* But she had eyes only for the faint contour that said she might have a viable vein...

She took the cannula and took a moment to steady herself. Hugo's hold on her tightened.

She inserted the point—and the needle slipped seamlessly into the vein.

'Yay, us,' she breathed, but Hugo was already handing her some sticking plaster to tape the cannula. She was checking the track, but it was looking good. A minute later she had the bag attached and fluid was flowing. She just might have done the thing.

Hugo let her go. She swung out a little, clear of the truck. It was the sensible thing to do, but still...

She hadn't wanted to be...let go.

'Heart rate?' Her voice wasn't quite steady. She took a deep breath and tried again. 'How is it?'

'Holding.' Hugo had his stethoscope out. 'I think we might have made it.' He glanced into the bag. 'And we have adrenaline—and a defibrillator. How did you carry all this?'

'I tied it under my seat.'

'Where did you learn your knots?'

'I was a star Girl Guide.' She was, too, she thought, deciding maybe she needed to focus on anything but the way his hold had made her feel.

A star Girl Guide... She'd been a star at so many things—at anything, really, that would get her away from her parents' overriding concern. Riding lessons, piano lessons, judo, elocution, Girl Guides, holiday camps... She'd been taken to each of them by a continuous stream of nannies. Nannies who were chosen because they spoke French, had famous relatives or in some other way could be boasted about by her parents...

'The current girl's a Churchill. She's au-pairing for six months, and she knows all the right people...'

Yeah. Nannies, nannies and nannies. Knowing the right people or speaking five languages was never a sign of job permanence. Polly had mostly been glad to be delivered to piano or elocution or whatever. She'd done okay, too. She'd had to.

Her parents loved her, but oh, they loved to boast.

'ER Physician, anaesthetist and Girl Guide to boot.' Hugo sounded stunned. 'I don't suppose you brought a stretcher as well? Plus a qualification in mountain rescue.'

'A full examination table, complete with lights, sinks, sterilisers? Plus rope ladders and mountain goats? Damn, I knew I'd forgotten something.'

He chuckled but she didn't have time for further banter. She was swinging in a way that was making her a little dizzy. She had to catch the sapling.

Her feet were hitting the cliff. *Ouch.* Where was nice soft grass when you needed it?

Where was Hugo's hold when she needed it?

He was busy. It made sense that he take over Horace's care now, but...

She missed that hold.

'It's flowing well.' There was no mistaking the satisfaction in Hugo's voice and Polly, too, breathed again. If Horace's heart hadn't given way yet, there was every chance the fluids would make a difference.

In the truck, Hugo had the IV line set up and secure. He'd hung the saline bags from an umbrella he'd wedged behind the back seat. He'd injected morphine.

He'd like oxygen but Polly's culling of his bag had excluded it. *Fair enough*, he thought. *Oxygen or a defibrillator?* With massive blood loss, the defibrillator was likely to be the most important, and the oxygen cylinder was dead weight.

Even so... How had she managed to get all this down here? What she'd achieved was amazing, and finding a vein in these circumstances was nothing short of miraculous.

She was his locum, temporary relief.

How would it be if there was a doctor like Polly working beside him in the Valley all year round?

Right. As if that was going to happen. His new locum

was swinging on her seat, as if flying free, and he thought that was exactly what she was. *Free.*

Not trapped, like he was.

And suddenly he wasn't thinking trapped in a truck down a cliff. He was thinking trapped in Wombat Valley, giving up his career, giving up…his life.

Once upon a time, if he'd met someone like Dr Polly Hargreaves he could have asked her out, had fun, tried friendship and maybe it could have led to…

No! It was no use even letting himself think down that road.

He was trapped in Wombat Valley. The skilful, intriguing Polly Hargreaves was rescuing him from one trap.

No one could rescue him from the bigger one.

Fifteen minutes later, help arrived. *About time too*, Polly thought. Mountains were for mountain goats. When the first yellow-jacketed figure appeared at the cliff top it was all she could do not to weep with relief.

She didn't. She was a doctor and doctors didn't weep.

Or not when yellow coats and big boots and serious equipment were on their way to save them.

'We have company,' she announced to Hugo, who couldn't see the cliff top from where he was stuck.

'More polka dots?'

She grinned and looked up at the man staring down at her. 'Hi,' she yelled. 'Dr Denver wants to know what you're wearing.'

The guy was on his stomach, looking down. 'A business suit,' he managed. 'With matching tie. How'd you get down there?'

'They fell,' she said. 'I came down all by myself. You wouldn't, by any chance, have a cushion?'

He chuckled and then got serious. The situation was assessed with reassuring efficiency. There was more than one yellow jacket up there, it seemed, but only one was venturing near the edge.

'We'll get you up, miss,' the guy called.

'Stabilise the truck first.'

'Will do.'

The Australian State Emergency Service was a truly awesome organisation, Polly decided. Manned mostly by volunteers, their skill set was amazing. The police sergeant had arrived, too, as well as two farmers with a tractor apiece. Someone had done some fast organising.

Two yellow-jacketed officers abseiled down, with much more efficiency and speed than Polly could have managed. They had the truck roped in minutes, anchoring it to the tractors above.

They disappeared again.

'You think they've knocked off for a cuppa?' Polly asked Hugo and he smiled, but absently. His smile was strained.

He had a kid, Polly thought. What was he about, putting himself in harm's way?

Did his wife know where he was? If she did, she'd be having kittens.

Just lucky no one gave a toss about her.

Ooh, there was a bitter thought, and it wasn't true. Her parents would be gutted. But then... If she died they could organise a truly grand funeral, she decided. If there was one thing her mother was good at, it was event management. There'd be a cathedral, massed choirs, requests to wear *'Polly's favourite colour'* which would be pink because her mother always told her pink was her favourite colour even though it wasn't. And she'd arrange a release of white doves and pink and white balloons and the balloons would contain a packet of seeds—zinnias, she thought because *'they're Polly's favourite flower'* and...

And there was the roar of tractors from above, the sound

of sharp commands, and then a slow taking up of the slack of the attached ropes.

The truck moved, just a little—and settled again—and the man appeared over the edge and shouted, 'You okay down there?'

'Excellent,' Hugo called, but Polly didn't say anything at all.

'Truck's now secure,' the guy called. 'The paramedics want to know if Horace is okay to move. We can abseil down and bring Horace up on a cradle stretcher. How does that fit with you, Doc?'

'Is it safe for you guys?'

'Go teach your grandmother to suck eggs,' the guy retorted. 'But med report, Doc—the paramedics want to know.'

'He's safe to move as long as we can keep pressure off his chest,' Hugo called. 'I want a neck brace. There's no sign of spinal injury but let's not take any chances. Then Polly.'

'Then you, Doc.'

'Polly second,' Hugo said in a voice that brooked no argument.

And, for once, Polly wasn't arguing.

It must have been under the truck.

She'd been balancing in the harness, using her feet to stop herself from swinging.

The truck had done its jerk upward and she'd jerked backwards herself, maybe as an automatic reaction to tension. She'd pushed her feet hard against the cliff to steady herself.

The snake must have been caught under the truck in the initial fall. With the pressure off, it lurched forward to get away.

Polly's foot landed right on its spine.

It landed one fierce bite to her ankle—and then slithered away down the cliff.

She didn't move. She didn't cry out.

Two guys in bright yellow overalls were abseiling down towards the driver's side of the truck, holding an end of a cradle stretcher apiece. They looked competent, sure of themselves...fast?

Horace was still the priority. He was elderly, he'd suffered massive blood loss and he needed to be where he could be worked on if he went into cardiac arrest.

She was suffering a snake bite.

Tiger snake? She wasn't sure. She'd only ever seen one in the zoo and she hadn't looked all that closely then.

It had had stripes.

Tiger snakes were deadly.

But not immediately. Wombat Valley was a bush hospital and one thing bush hospitals were bound to have was antivenin, she told herself. She thought back to her training. No one ever died in screaming agony two minutes after they were bitten by a snake. They died hours later. If they didn't get antivenin.

Therefore, she just needed to stay still and the nice guys in the yellow suits would come and get her and they'd all live happily ever after.

'Polly?' It was Hugo, his voice suddenly sharp.

'I...what?' She let go her toehold—she was only using one foot now—and her rope swung.

She felt...a bit sick.

That must be her imagination. She shouldn't feel sick so fast.

'Polly, what's happening?'

The guys—no, on closer inspection, it was a guy and a woman—had reached Horace. Had Hugo fitted the neck brace to Horace, or had the abseilers? She hadn't noticed.

They were steadying the stretcher against the cliff, then sliding it into the cab of the truck, but leaving its weight to be taken by the anchor point on the road. In another world she'd be fascinated.

Things were a bit…fuzzy.

'Polly?'

'Mmm?' She was having trouble getting her tongue to work. Her mouth felt thick and dry.

'What the hell…? I can't get out. Someone up there… priority's changed. We need a harness on Dr Hargreaves— fast.'

Did he think she was going to faint? She thought about that and decided he might be right.

So do something.

She had a seat—sort of. She looped her arms around the side cords and linked her hands, then put her head down as far as she could.

She could use some glucose.

'Get someone down here.' It was a roar. 'Fast. Move!'

'I'm not going to faint,' she managed but it sounded feeble, even to her.

'Damn right, you're not going to faint,' Hugo snapped. 'You faint and you're out of my employ. Pull yourself together, Dr Hargreaves. Put that head further down, take deep breaths and count between breathing. You know what to do. Do it.'

'I need…juice…' she managed but her voice trailed off. This was ridiculous. She couldn't…

She mustn't.

Breathe, two, three. Out, two, three. Breathe…

'Hold on, sweetheart—they're coming.'

What had he called her? *Sweetheart?* No one called Polly Hargreaves sweetheart unless they wanted her to do something. Or not do something. Not to cut her hair. Not to do medicine. To play socialite daughter for their friends.

To come home for Christmas…

She wasn't going home for Christmas. She was staying in Wombat Valley. The thought was enough to steady her.

If she fainted then she'd fall and they'd send her back to Sydney in a body bag and her mother would have her fabulous funeral…

Not. Not, not, not.

'I've been bitten by a snake,' she muttered, with as much strength and dignity as she could muster. *Which wasn't actually very much at all.* She still had her head between her knees and she daren't move. 'It was brown with stripes and it bit my ankle. And I know it's a hell of a time to tell you, but I need to say… I'm also a Type One diabetic. So I'm not sure whether this is a hypo or snake bite but, if I fall, don't let my mother bury me in pink. Promise.'

'I promise,' Hugo said and then a yellow-suited figure was beside her, and her only objection was that he was blocking her view of Hugo.

It sort of seemed important that she see Hugo.

'She has a snake bite on her ankle,' Hugo was saying urgently. 'And she needs glucose. Probable hypo. Get the cradle back down here as fast as you can, and bring glucagon. While we wait, I have a pressure bandage here in the cabin. If you can swing her closer we'll get her leg immobilised.'

'You're supposed to be on holiday,' Polly managed while Yellow Suit figured out how to manoeuvre her closer to Hugo.

'Like that's going to happen now,' Hugo said grimly. 'Let's get the hired help safe and worry about holidays later.'

CHAPTER FOUR

FROM THERE THINGS moved fast. The team on the road was reassuringly professional. Polly was strapped into the cradle, her leg firmly wrapped, then she was lifted up the cliff with an abseiler at either end of the cradle.

She was hardly bumped, but she felt shaky and sick. If she was in an emergency situation she'd be no help at all.

'I'm so sorry,' she managed, for Hugo had climbed up after her and he was leaning over the stretcher, his lean, strong face creased in concern. 'What a wuss. I didn't mean…'

'To be confronted by two guys about to fall down a cliff. To need to climb down and secure the truck and save them. To bring them lifesaving equipment and get bitten by a snake doing it. I don't blame you for apologising, Dr Hargreaves. Wuss doesn't begin to describe it.'

'I should…'

'Shut up,' he said, quite kindly. 'Polly, the snake…you said it had stripes.'

'Brown with faint stripes.'

'Great for noticing.'

'It bit me,' she said with dignity. 'I always take notice of things that bite me.'

'Excellent. Okay, sweetheart, we have a plan…'

'I'm not your sweetheart!' She said it with vehemence and she saw his brows rise in surprise—and also humour.

'No. Inappropriate. Sexist. Apologies. Okay, Dr Hargreaves, we have a plan. We're taking you to the Wombat Valley Hospital—it's only a mile down the road. There we'll fill you up with antivenin. The snake you describe is either a tiger or a brown…'

'Tiger's worse.'

'We have antivenin for both. You're reacting well with glucose. I think the faintness was a combination—the adrenaline went out of the situation just as the snake hit and the shock was enough to send you over the edge.'

'I did not go over the edge!'

'I do need to get my language right,' he said and grinned. 'No, Dr Hargreaves, you did not go over the edge, for which I'm profoundly grateful. And now we'll get the antivenin in…'

'Which one?'

'I have a test kit at the hospital and I've already taken a swab.'

'And if it's a rare… I don't know…zebra python with no known antivenin…?'

'Then I'll eat my hat.' And then he took her hand and held, and he smiled down at her and his smile…

It sort of did funny things to her. She'd been feeling woozy before. Now she was feeling even woozier.

'We need to move,' he said, still holding her hand strongly. 'We'll take you to the hospital now, but once we have the antivenin on board we'll transfer you to Sydney. We've already called in the medical transfer chopper. Horace has cracked ribs. Marg's demanding specialists. I'm more than happy that he be transferred, and I'm imagining that you'll be better in Sydney as well. You have cuts and bruises all over you, plus a load of snake venom. You can recover in Sydney and then spend Christmas with your family.'

Silence.

He was still holding her hand. She should let it go, she thought absently. She should push herself up to standing, put her hands on her hips and let him have it.

She was no more capable of doing such a thing than flying, but she gripped his hand so tightly her cuts screamed in protest. She'd bleed on him, she thought absently, but what was a little gore when what she had to say was so important?

'I am not going back to Sydney,' she hissed and she saw his brow snap down in surprise.

'Polly…'

'Don't Polly me. If you think I've come all this way… if you think I've crawled down cliffs and ruined a perfectly good dress and scratched my hands and hurt my bum and then been bitten by a vicious, lethal snake you don't even know the name of yet…if you think I'm going to go through all that and still get to spend Christmas in Sydney…'

'You don't want to?' he asked cautiously and she stared at him as if he had a kangaroo loose in his top paddock.

'In your dreams. I accepted a job in Wombat Valley and that's where I'm staying. You do have antivenin?'

'I…yes.'

'And competent staff to watch my vital signs for the next twenty-four hours?'

'Yes, but…'

'But nothing,' she snapped. 'You employed me, Dr Denver, and now you're stuck with me. Send Horace wherever you like, but I'm staying here.'

The transfer to the hospital was swift and efficient. Joe, his nurse administrator, was pre-warned and had the test kit and antivenin ready. Joe was more than capable of setting up an IV line. Wishing he was two doctors and not one, Hugo left Polly in Joe's care while he organised an X-ray of Horace's chest. He needed to make sure a rib wasn't about to pierce a lung.

The X-ray showed three cracked ribs, one that looked unstable. It hadn't punctured his lung, though, and Horace's breathing seemed secure. If he was kept immobile, he could be taken to Sydney.

'You're not sending Dr Hargreaves with him?' Mary, his second-in-command nurse, demanded as he left Horace with the paramedics and headed for Polly.

He'd been torn… Polly, Horace, Polly, Horace…

Joe would have called him if there was a change. Still, his strides were lengthening.

'She won't go,' he told Mary. 'She wants to stay.'

'Oh, Hugo.' Mary was in her sixties, a grandma, and a bit weepy at the best of times. Now her kindly eyes filled with tears. 'You'll be looking after her instead of going to the beach. Of all the unfair things…'

'It's not unfair. It's just unfortunate. She can hardly take over my duties now. She'll need to be watched for twenty-four hours for reaction to the bite as well as reaction to the antivenin. The last thing we need is anaphylactic shock and it'll take days for the venom to clear her system completely. Meanwhile, have you seen her hands? Mary, she slid down a nylon cord to bring me equipment. She was scratched climbing to secure the truck. She was bitten because…'

'Because she didn't have sensible shoes on,' Mary said with asperity. The nurse was struggling to keep up but speed wasn't interfering with indignation. 'Did you see her shoes? Sergeant Myer picked them up on the roadside and brought them in. A more ridiculous pair of shoes for a country doctor to be wearing…'

'You think we should yell at her about her shoes?'

'I'm just saying…'

'She was driving here in her sports car. You don't need sensible clothes while driving.'

'Well, that's another thing,' Mary said darkly. 'Of all the silly cars for a country GP...'

'But she's not a country GP.' He turned and took a moment to focus on Mary's distress. Mary was genuinely upset on his behalf—heck, the whole of Wombat Valley would be upset on his behalf—but Polly wasn't to blame and suddenly it was important that the whole of Wombat Valley knew it.

He thought of Polly sitting on her makeshift swing, trying to steady herself with her bare feet. He thought of her polka dot dress, the flounces, the determined smile... She must have been hurting more than he could imagine—those cords had really cut—but she'd still managed to give him cheek.

He thought of her sorting the medical equipment in his bag, expertly discarding what wasn't needed, determined to bring him what was. Courage didn't begin to describe what she'd done, he thought, so no, he wasn't about to lecture her for inappropriate footwear.

'Polly saved us,' he told Mary, gently but firmly. 'What happened was an accident and she did more than anyone could expect. She put her life on the line to save us and she even managed her own medical drama with skill. I owe her everything.'

'So you'll miss your Christmas at the beach.'

'There's no choice. We need to move on.'

Mary sniffed, sounding unconvinced, but Hugo swung open the door of the treatment room and Joe was chuckling and Polly was smiling up and he thought...

Who could possibly judge this woman and find her wanting? Who could criticise her?

This woman was amazing—and it seemed that she, also, was moving on.

'Doctor, we may have to rethink the hospital menu for Christmas if Dr Hargreaves is admitted,' Joe told him as he entered. 'She's telling me turkey, three veggies, commercial Christmas pudding and canned custard won't cut it. Not even if we add a bonbon on the side.'

He blinked.

Snake bite. Lacerations. Shock.

They were talking turkey?

Okay. He needed to focus on medical imperatives, even if his patient wasn't. Even if Polly didn't seem like his patient.

'The swab?' he asked and Joe nodded and held up the test kit.

'The brown snake showed up in seconds. The tiger segment showed positive about two minutes later but the kit says that's often the way—they're similar. It seems the brown snake venom's enough to eventually discolour the tiger snake pocket, so brown it is. And I reckon she's got a fair dose on board. Polly has a headache and nausea already. I'm betting she's been solidly bitten.'

Hugo checked the kit for himself and nodded. He'd seen the ankle—it'd be a miracle if the venom hadn't gone in. 'Brown's good,' he told Polly. 'You'll recover faster than from a tiger.'

'I'm feeling better already,' she told him and gave him another smile, albeit a wobbly one. 'But not my dress. It's ripped to pieces. That snake owes me...'

He had to smile. She even managed to sound indignant.

'But you're nauseous?'

'Don't you care about my dress?'

'I care about you more. Nausea?'

'A little. And,' she went on, as if she was making an enormous concession, 'I might be a little bit headachy.'

A little...

The venom would hardly be taking effect yet, he

thought. She'd still be in the window period where victims ran for help, tried to pretend they hadn't been bitten, tried to search and identify the snake that had bitten them—and in the process spread the venom through their system and courted death.

Polly had been sensible, though. She'd stayed still. She'd told him straight away. She'd allowed the paramedics to bring her up on the rigid stretcher.

Okay, clambering down cliffs in bare feet in the Australian summer was hardly sensible but he couldn't argue with her reasons.

'Then let's keep it like that,' he told her. 'I want you to stay still while we get this antivenin on board.'

'I've been practically rigid since I got bit,' she said virtuously. 'Textbook patient. By the way, it's a textbook immobilisation bandage too. Excellent work, Dr Denver.'

He grinned at that, and she smiled back at him, and then he sort of paused.

That smile…

It was a magic smile. As sick and battered as she was, her smile twinkled. Her face was pallid and wan, but it was still alight with laughter.

This was a woman who would have played in the orchestra as the *Titanic* sank, he thought, and then he thought: *Nope*, she'd be too busy fashioning lifelines out of spare trombones.

But her smile was fading. Their gazes still held but all of a sudden she looked…doubtful?

Maybe unsure.

Maybe his smile was having the same effect on her as hers was on his?

That would be wishful thinking. Plus it would be unprofessional.

Move on.

Joe had already set up the drip. Hugo prepared the

serum, double-checked everything with Joe, then carefully injected it. It'd start working almost immediately, he thought; hopefully, before Polly started feeling the full effects of the bite.

'How are you feeling everywhere else?' he asked, and she gave a wry smile that told him more than anything else that the humour was an act. Her freckles stood out from her pallid face, and her red hair seemed overbright.

'I'm...sore,' she admitted.

'I've started cleaning the worst of the grazes,' Joe told him. 'She could do with a full bed bath but you said immobile so immobile it is. There's a cut on her palm, though, that might need a stitch or two.'

He lifted her palm and turned it over. And winced.

Her hand was a mess. He could see the coil marks of the rope. The marks ran along her palm, across her wrist and up her arm.

She'd come down that nylon cord...

He heard Mary's breath hiss in amazement. 'How...?'

'I told you,' he said, still staring at Polly's palm. 'She let herself down the cliff, carrying the bag with saline. Without it, Horace would probably be dead.'

'You did that for Horace?' Mary breathed, looking at the mess in horror, and Hugo thought he no longer had to defend her. Polly had suddenly transformed into a heroine.

'There's a lot to be said for elevators,' Polly said but her voice faltered a little as she looked at her palm and he realised shock was still a factor.

And there'd be bruises everywhere. He had to get that antivenin working, though, before they could clean her up properly. Joe had even left the remnants of her dress on. The polka dots made her look even more wan.

'Let's get you comfortable,' he said. 'How about a nice

dose of morphine for the pain, some metoclopramide for the nausea and a wee shot of Valium on the side?'

'You want to knock me into the middle of next week?'

'I want you to sleep.'

She gazed up at him, those amazing eyes locked to his. He couldn't make out whether they were green or brown. They were...

Um...no. She was his patient. He didn't note the colour of his patient's eyes unless there was a medical issue. Bloodshot? Jaundiced? Fixed pupils? Polly's eyes showed none of those. He needed to ignore them.

How could he ignore them?

'You promise you won't transport me to Sydney while I'm sleeping?' she demanded, and he smiled and kept looking into those over-bright eyes.

'I promise.'

'That's in front of witnesses.'

'Joe, Mary, you heard me. The lady stays in Wombat Valley.'

'Very well, then,' Polly said, her voice wobbling again. Still, she looked straight up at him, as if reading reassurance in his gaze. 'Drugs, drugs and more drugs, and then Christmas in Wombat Valley. I can... I can handle that. But turkey with three veg has to go, Dr Denver.'

'You'll get a better Christmas dinner in Sydney.'

'No Sydney! Promise?'

'I already have,' he told her but suddenly she was no longer listening. The fight had gone out of her. She had the antivenin on board. Her future was sorted.

The flight-or-fight reflex relaxed. She sank back onto the pillows and sighed.

'Okay, Dr Denver, whatever you say,' she whispered. 'I'm in your hands.'

* * *

He had Horace sorted. He had Polly comfortable.

There was still the issue of Ruby.

How did you tell a seven-year-old she wasn't going to the beach for Christmas? She'd been counting down the days for months. He'd tried to figure it out all the way back to the house, but in the end he didn't need to.

Lois, his housekeeper, was before him. News got around fast in Wombat Valley and by the time he walked in the front door, Ruby was in tears and Lois was looking like a martyr who'd come to the end of her tether.

'I'm sorry, Dr Denver, but I can't stay,' she told him over the top of Ruby's head. 'I promised my son I'd spend Christmas in Melbourne with my grandchildren and that's where I'm going. I leave in half an hour, and I've told Ruby you're not going anywhere. You can see how upset she is, but is it my fault? You went and climbed into that truck. Was Horace worth it? He's a lazy wastrel and his wife's no better. Risking your life, losing your holiday, for such a loser...' She shook her head. 'I wash my hands of you, I really do. Ruby, stop crying, sweetheart. I dare say your uncle will sort something out.'

And she picked up her handbag and headed out of the house before Hugo could possibly change her mind.

Hugo was left facing his niece.

Christmas. No beach. No housekeeper.

One fill-in doctor in his hospital instead of in his surgery.

He was trapped, but what was new? What was new was that Ruby felt as if she was trapped with him.

His niece looked as if she'd been trying not to cry, but fat tears were sliding down her face regardless. She stood silent, in her garden-stained shorts and T-shirt, her wispy blonde curls escaping every which way from their pigtails, and her wan little face blank with misery. She didn't complain, though, he thought bleakly. She never had.

He knelt down and hugged her. She held her stiff little body in his arms and he felt the effort she was making not to sob.

'We'll fix it somehow,' he murmured. 'Somehow...'

How?

Today was Monday. Christmas was Saturday.

He thought of the gifts he'd already packed, ready to be produced by Santa at their apartment by the beach. Bucket and spade. Water wings. A blow-up seahorse.

Lois had even made her a bikini.

He thought of his housekeeper marching off towards her Christmas and he thought he couldn't blame her. Lois was fond of Ruby, but he'd pushed her to the limit.

And there was another complication. It was school holidays and Ruby would need daytime care if he had to keep working. He'd need to call in favours, and he hated asking for favours.

Maybe he and Ruby should just walk away, he thought bleakly, as he'd thought many times this past year. But the complications flooded in, as they always did.

Wombat Valley was Ruby's home. It was all she knew. In Sydney she had nothing and no one but him. His old job, the job he loved, thoracic surgery at Sydney Central, involved long hours and call backs. Here, his house was right next to the hospital. He could pop in and out at will, and he had an entire valley of people more than willing to help. They helped not just because it meant the Valley had a doctor but because so many of them genuinely cared for Ruby.

How could *he* stop caring, when the Valley had shown they cared so much? How could he turn his back on the Valley's needs and on Ruby's needs?

How could he ever return to the work he loved, to his friends, his social life, to his glorious bachelor freedom?

He couldn't. He couldn't even leave for two weeks. He had patients in hospital.

He had Dr Pollyanna Hargreaves in Ward One.

Polly…

Why was Polly so important? What was he doing, hugging Ruby and drying her eyes but thinking of Polly? But the image of Polly, hanging on her appalling hand-made swing while every part of her hurt, wouldn't go away.

'Ruby, I need to tell you about one brave lady,' he told her and Ruby sniffed and swiped away her tears with the back of her hand and tilted her chin, ready to listen. In her own way, she was as brave as Polly, he thought.

But not as cute. No matter how much the Valley mums helped, Ruby always looked a waif. She was skinny and leggy, and nothing seemed to help her put on weight. She was tall for her seven years; her skimpy pigtails made her look taller and her eyes always seemed too big for her face. Her knees were constantly grubby—she'd have been mucking about in the garden, which was her favourite place. She had mud on her tear-stained face.

He loved her with all his heart.

'Is the lady why we can't go to the beach?' she quavered and he took her hand and led her out to the veranda. And there was another reminder of what they'd be missing. Hamster wasn't there.

Hamster was Ruby's Labrador, a great boofy friend. They hadn't been able to find a beach house where dogs were permitted so he'd taken Hamster back to the farmer who'd bred him, to be taken care of for two weeks.

Ruby had sobbed.

There was one bright thought—they could get Hamster back for Christmas.

Meanwhile, he had to say it like it was.

'Did Lois tell you about the truck accident?' he asked and Ruby nodded. She was a quiet kid but she listened. He'd learned early it was impossible to keep much from her.

'Well, the truck fell off the cliff, and the lady doctor— Dr Hargreaves—the doctor who was coming to work here while we were away—hurt herself by climbing down the cliff to save everyone.'

Ruby's pixie face creased as she sorted it out in her head. 'Everyone?'

'Yes.'

'Why didn't you save everyone?'

'I tried but I got stuck. She saved me, too. And then she got bitten by a snake.'

Ruby's eyes widened. 'What sort of a snake?'

'A brown.'

'That's better than a tiger. Didn't she know to make a noise? If you make lots of noise they slither away before you reach them.'

'The snake got stuck under the truck. I guess it got scared too, and it bit her.'

'Is she very sick?'

'She'll be sick for a couple of days.'

'So then can we go to the beach?'

He thought about it. *Don't make promises*, he told himself, but if Polly didn't react too badly to the antivenin it might be possible. If those cuts didn't stop her working.

She still wanted to stay in the Valley.

'I'm not sure,' he said weakly.

'Will she have to stay in hospital all over Christmas?'

That was a thought. And a problem?

Normally, snake bite victims stayed in hospital overnight for observation. She was a Type One diabetic. She might need to stay longer, but she was already having reservations about hospital food. How long could he keep her there?

He and Ruby had cleared out their best spare room. They'd made it look pretty. Ruby had even put fresh flowers in a vase on the chest of drawers. 'Girls like that.'

But he couldn't leave the moment she was released from hospital, he conceded. He and Polly would have to stay for a day or two.

He was counting in his head. Monday today. Bring Polly back here on Tuesday or Wednesday.

Leave on Thursday or Friday? Christmas Saturday.

It was cutting things fine.

Food… There was another problem. Sick and shocked as she was, Polly Hargreaves had already turned her nose up at bought pudding.

He had no food here. He'd assumed his locum could eat in the hospital kitchen.

He'd promised Ruby fish and chips on the beach for Christmas, and Ruby had glowed at the thought. Now… He might well have a recovering Polly for Christmas.

He didn't even have a Christmas tree.

And, as if on cue, there was the sound of a car horn from the road—a silly, tooting car horn that was nothing like the sensible farm vehicle horns used for clearing cattle off the road or warning of kangaroos. He looked up and a little yellow sports car was being driven through the gate, a police car following behind.

This was Polly's car. He'd seen it at the crash site but he'd been too distracted to do more than glance at it.

But here it was, being driven by one of the local farmers. Bill McCray was behind the wheel, twenty-five years old and grinning like the Cheshire cat.

'Hey, Doc, where do you want us to put the car?'

'What's the car?' Ruby breathed.

'I… It's Polly's car,' he managed.

'Polly…'

'Dr Hargreaves…'

'Is that her name? Polly, like *Polly put the kettle on*?'

'I…yes.'

'It's yellow.' Ruby was pie-eyed. 'And it hasn't got a top. And it's got a Christmas tree in the back. And suitcases and suitcases.'

There were indeed suitcases and suitcases. And a Christmas tree. Silver. Large.

Bill pulled up under the veranda. Both he and the policeman emerged from their respective vehicles, Bill looking decidedly sorry the ride had come to an end.

'She's a beauty,' he declared. 'I'd love to see how the cows reacted if I tried to drive that round the farm. And the guys say the lady doc's just as pretty. I reckon I can feel a headache coming on. Or six. When did you say you were leaving, Doc?'

'We're not leaving,' Ruby whispered but she no longer sounded desolate. She was staring in stupefaction at the tree. It was all silver sparkles and it stretched over the top of the luggage, from the front passenger seat to well behind the exhaust pipe.

Polly had tied a huge red tinsel bow at the rear—to warn traffic of the long load? It looked…amazing.

'We're staying here to look after the lady doctor,' Ruby said, still staring. 'I think she might be nice. Is she nice, Uncle Hugo?'

'Very nice,' he said weakly and headed down to unpack a Christmas tree.

CHAPTER FIVE

NIGHT ROUND. HE SHOULD be eating fish and chips on the beach right now, Hugo thought as he headed through the darkened wards to Ward One. He'd thought he had this Christmas beautifully organised.

Most of his long-termers had gone home for Christmas. He had three elderly patients in the nursing home section, all with local family and heaps of visitors. None needed his constant attendance.

Sarah Ferguson was still in Room Two. Sarah had rolled a tractor on herself a month ago. She'd spent three weeks in Sydney Central and had been transferred here for the last couple of weeks to be closer to her family. Her family had already organised to have Christmas in her room. She hardly needed him either.

But Polly needed him. He'd been back and forth during the afternoon, checking her. Anaphylactic shock was still a possibility. He still had her on fifteen minute obs. She was looking okay but with snake bites you took no chances.

Barb, the night nurse, greeted him happily and put down her knitting to accompany him.

'I'm fine,' he told her. 'I can do my round by myself.'

The scarf Barb was knitting, a weird mix of eclectic colours, was barely six feet long. Barb had told him it needed to be ten.

'Why my grandson had to tell me he wanted a Dr Who scarf a week before Christmas…' she'd muttered last night and he'd thought he'd made things easy for her by keeping the hospital almost empty.

But Barb did take her job seriously. She was knitting in front of the monitors attached to Ward One, which acted as the Intensive Care room. Any blip in Polly's heart rate and she'd be in there in seconds, and one glance at the chart in front of her told him Polly had been checked thoroughly and regularly.

'No change?'

'She's not sleeping. She's pretty sore. If you could maybe write her up for some stronger pain relief for the night…' She hesitated. 'And, Doc… She's not admitting it but I'm sure she's still pretty shaken. She's putting on a brave front but my daughter's her age. All bravado but jelly inside.'

He nodded and left her to her knitting.

Polly's ward was in near darkness, lit only by the floor light. He knocked lightly and went in.

Polly was a huddled mass under the bedclothes. She'd drawn her knees up to her middle, almost in a foetal position.

She's still pretty shaken…

Barb was right, he thought. This was the age-old position for those alone and scared.

He had a sudden urge to head to the bed, scoop her up and hold her. She'd had one hell of a day. What she needed was comfort.

Someone to hold…

Um…that wouldn't be him. There were professional boundaries, after all.

Instead, he tugged the visitor's chair across to the bed, sat down and reached for her hand.

Um… Her wrist. Not her hand. He was taking her pulse. That was professional.

'Hey,' he said, very softly. 'How's it going?'

'Great,' she managed and he smiled. Her *'great'* had been weak but it was sarcastic.

Still she had spirit.

'The venom will have kicked in but the antivenin will be doing its job,' he told her. 'Your obs are good.'

'Like I said—great.' She eased herself from the foetal position, casually, as if she didn't want him to notice how she'd been lying. 'Sorry. That sounds ungrateful. I am grateful. Mary and Joe gave me a good wash. I'm antivenined. I'm stitched, I'm disinfected and I'm in a safe place. But I've ruined your holiday. I'm so sorry.'

All this and she was concerned about his missed vacation?

'Right,' he said, almost as sarcastic as she'd been. 'You saved my life and you're sorry.'

'I didn't save your life.'

'You know what happened when they tugged the truck up the cliff? It swung and hit one of the saplings that had been holding it from falling further. The sapling lifted right out of the ground. It'd been holding by a thread.'

She shuddered and his hold on her hand tightened. Forget taking her pulse, he decided. She needed comfort and he was giving it any way he could.

'Polly, is there anyone we can ring? The nurses tell me you haven't contacted anyone. Your parents? A boyfriend? Any friend?'

'You let my family know what's happened and you'll have helicopters landing on the roof in ten minutes. And the press. You'll have my dad threatening to sue you, the hospital and the National Parks for letting the Gap exist in the first place. You don't know my family. Please, I'm fine as I am.'

She wasn't fine, though. She still had the shakes.

The press? Who was she?

She was alone. That was all he needed to focus on right now. 'Polly, you need someone…'

'I don't need anyone.' She hesitated. 'Though I am a bit shaky,' she admitted. 'I could use another dose of that nice woozy Valium. You think another dose would turn me into an addict?'

'I think we can risk it. And how about more pain relief, too? I have a background morphine dose running in the IV line but we can top it up. Pain level, one to ten?'

'Six,' she said and he winced.

'Ouch. Why didn't you tell Barb? She would have got me here sooner.'

'I'm not a whinger.'

'How did I already know that?' He shook his head, re-checked her obs, rang for Barb and organised the drugs. Barb did what was needed and then bustled back to her scarf. That meant Hugo could leave too.

But Polly was alone and she was still shaking.

He could ask Barb to bring her knitting in here.

Then who would look after the monitors for the other rooms?

It was okay him being here, he decided. His house was right next door to the hospital and they had an intercom set up in the nurses' station, next to the monitors. Ruby had been fast asleep for a couple of hours but, any whimper she made, Barb would know and send him home fast.

So he could sit here for a while.

Just until Polly was asleep, he told himself. He sat and almost unconsciously she reached out and took his hand again. As if it was her right. As if it was something she really needed, almost as important as breathing.

'I was scared,' she admitted.

'Which part scared you the most?' he asked. 'Sliding

down the cliff? Hanging on that nylon cord swing? When Joe Blake did his thing…?'

'Joe Blake?'

'You really are city,' he teased. 'Joe Blake—Snake.'

'It was a bad moment,' she confessed. 'But the worst was when I saw the truck. When I realised there were people in it.'

'I guess it'd be like watching stretchers being wheeled into Emergency after a car crash,' he said. 'Before you know what you're facing.'

'Yeah.'

'But you broke it into manageable bits. You have excellent triage skills, Dr Hargreaves.'

'Maybe.'

She fell silent for a minute and then the hold on his hand grew tighter. But what she said was at odds with her obvious need. 'You shouldn't be here,' she told him. 'You should be home with your niece. Barb tells me she's your niece and not your daughter and her name's Ruby. Is she home alone?'

'Home's next door. Her bedroom's a hundred yards from the nurses' station. Her nightlight's on and whoever's monitoring the nurses' station can watch the glow and can listen on the intercom. If Ruby wakes up, all she has to do is hit the button and she can talk to the nurses or to me.'

'Good system,' she said sleepily and he thought the drugs were taking effect—or maybe it was simply the promise of the drugs.

Or maybe it was because she was holding his hand? It seemed an almost unconscious action, but she wasn't letting go.

'Tell me about Ruby,' she whispered and he sat and thought about his niece and felt the pressure of Polly's hand in his and the sensation was…

Was what?

Something he didn't let himself feel. Something he'd pushed away?

'And tell me about you too,' she murmured and he thought he didn't need to tell her anything. Doctors didn't tell personal stuff to patients.

But in the silence of the little ward, in the peacefulness of the night, he found himself thinking about a night almost a year ago. The phone call from the police. The night he'd realised life as he knew it had just slammed to an end.

He'd been born and raised in this place—Wombat Valley, where nothing ever happened. Wombat Valley, where you could sit on the veranda at night and hear nothing but the frogs and the hoot of the night owls.

Wombat Valley, where everyone depended on everyone else.

Grace, his sister, had hated it. She'd run away at sixteen and she'd kept on running. 'I feel trapped,' she'd shouted, over and over. Hugo had been twelve when she'd run and he hadn't understood.

But twelve months ago, the night his sister died, it was Hugo who'd been trapped. That night he'd felt like running as well.

He didn't. How could he? He'd returned to the Valley and it seemed as if he'd be here for ever.

'Tell me about Ruby?' Polly whispered again, and her question wasn't impatient. It was as if the night had thoughts of its own and she was content to wait.

'Ruby's my niece.'

'Yeah. Something I don't know?'

'She's adorable.'

'And you wouldn't be biased?'

He smiled. She sounded half asleep, but she was still clutching his hand and he wondered if the questions were a ruse to have him stay.

'She's seven years old,' he said. 'She's skinny, tough,

fragile, smart. She spends her time in the garden, mucking round in the dirt, trying to make things grow, playing with a menagerie of snails, tadpoles, frogs, ladybirds.'

'Her parents?'

'We don't know who her father is,' Hugo told her. He was almost talking to himself but it didn't seem to matter. 'My sister suffered from depression, augmented by drug use. She was always…erratic. She ran away at sixteen and we hardly saw her. She contacted me when Ruby was born—until then we hadn't even known she was pregnant. She was in Darwin and she was in a mess. I flew up and my parents followed. Mum and Dad brought them both back to Wombat Valley. Grace came and went, but Ruby stayed.'

'Why…why the Valley?'

'My father was the Valley doctor—our current house is where Grace and I were raised. Dad died when Ruby was three, but Mum stayed on. Mum cared for Ruby and she loved her. Then, late last year, Grace decided she wanted to leave for good and she wanted Ruby back. She was with…someone who scared my mother. Apparently there was an enormous row, which culminated in Mum having a stroke. The day after Mum's funeral, Grace drove her car off the Gap. Maybe it was an accident. Probably it wasn't.'

'Oh, no…'

'So that's that,' he said flatly. 'End of story. The Valley loves Ruby, Ruby loves the Valley and I'm home for good. I'm not doing a great job with Ruby, but I'm trying. She loved Mum. Grace confused her and at the end she frightened her. Now she's too quiet. She's a tomboy. I worry…'

'There's nothing wrong with being a tomboy,' Polly whispered, sounding closer and closer to sleep. 'You don't force her to wear pink?'

He smiled at that. 'She'd have it filthy in minutes. What

I should do is buy camouflage cloth and find a dungaree maker.'

'She sounds my type of kid.'

'You do pretty.'

Where had that come from? He shouldn't comment on patients' appearances. *You do pretty*? What sort of line was that?

'I like clothes that make me smile,' she whispered. 'I have an amazing pair of crimson boots. One day I might show you.'

'I'll look forward to that.' Maybe he shouldn't have said that either. Was it inappropriate?

Did he care?

'So Ruby knows she's safe with you?' she whispered.

'She's as safe as I can make her. We had an interim doctor after Dad died but he left the moment I appeared on the scene. This valley could use three doctors, but for now I'm it. I've been advertising for twelve months but no one's applied. Meanwhile, Ruby understands the intercom system and she can see the hospital from her bedroom. If I can't be there in ten seconds someone else will be. That's the deal the hospital board employs me under. Ruby comes first.'

'So if there's drama…'

'This community backs me up. I'm here if, and only if, Wombat Valley helps me raise Ruby.' He shrugged. 'It's my job.'

Only it wasn't, or not his job of choice. He'd walked away from his job as a thoracic surgeon. Not being able to use the skills he'd fought to attain still left him feeling gutted, and now he couldn't even get Christmas off.

'But I've so messed with your Christmas,' she said weakly, echoing his thoughts, and he hauled himself together.

'I've told you—you've done no such thing.'

'Would it be better for you if I was transferred?'

'I...no.'

'But I'm supposed to be staying in your house. You won't want me now.'

At least he had this answer ready. He'd had the evening to think about it. Polly's tree was now set up in the living room. He was preparing to make the most of it.

'If you stay, you might still be able to help me,' he said diffidently, as if he was asking a favour. And maybe he was; it was just that his ideas about this woman were all over the place and he couldn't quite get them together. 'You'll need a few days to get over your snake bite and bruises. You could snuggle into one of our spare rooms— it's a big house—and Ruby could look after you. She'd enjoy that.'

'Ruby would look after me?'

'She loves to be needed. She's already fascinated by your snake bite—you'll have to show her the fang marks, by the way. She's also in love with your Christmas tree.'

'My tree...'

'The boys brought your car to my house. Ruby insisted we unpack it. I'm sorry but it's in the living room and Ruby's already started decorating it.'

'You don't have a tree of your own?'

'We were going away for Christmas.'

'You still should have had a tree,' she murmured, but her voice was getting so weak he could hardly hear. She was slurring her words and finally the hold on his hand was weakening. The drugs were taking over.

He should tuck her hand under the covers, he thought, and finally he did, but as he released her fingers he felt an indefinable sense of loss.

And, as he did, she smiled up at him, and weirdly she shifted her hand back out of the covers. She reached up and touched his face. Just lightly. It was a feather-touch, tracing the bones of his cheek.

'I'm glad I saved you,' she whispered and it was all he could do to hear.

'I'm glad you saved me too.' And for the life of him he couldn't stop a shake entering his voice.

'And you didn't have a Christmas tree…'

'N…no.'

'And now I'm going to stay with you until Christmas?' What could he say? 'If you like.'

'Then it sounds like I need to be helpful,' she whispered, and it was as if she was summoning all the strength she had to say something. 'Sometimes I can be my mother's daughter. December the twentieth and you don't even have a tree. And you have a little girl who likes tadpoles and dungarees. And I just know you're a very nice man. What were you doing in that truck in the first place? The snake could just as easily have bitten you. You know what, Dr Denver? As well as saving your skin, I'm going to save your Christmas. How's that for a plan?'

But she got no further. Her hand fell away. Her lids closed, and she was asleep.

He walked home feeling…disorientated. Or more. Discombobulated? There was no other word big enough to describe it.

He could still feel the touch of Polly's fingers on his face where she'd touched him.

He might just as well have been kissed…

There was a crazy idea. He hadn't been kissed. She'd been doped to the eyeballs with painkillers and relaxants. She'd had an appalling shock and she was injured. People did and said weird things…

Still the trace of her fingers remained.

She was beautiful.

She was brave, funny, smart.

She was scared and she was alone.

But what had she said? He replayed her words in his head.

'You let my family know what's happened and you'll have helicopters landing on the roof ten minutes later. And the press...'

Who was she? He needed to do some research. He'd rung her medical referees when she'd applied to do the locum. He'd been given glowing reports on her medical skills but there'd been a certain reticence...

He'd avoided the reticence. He'd been so relieved to find a doctor with the skills to look after the Valley, he wouldn't have minded if she'd had two heads. If she had the medical qualifications, nothing else could matter.

Only of course it mattered and now he was stuck in the same house as a woman who was brave, funny and smart.

And beautiful.

And alone.

He didn't need this, he told himself. The last thing he needed in his life was complications caused by a beautiful woman. A love life was something he'd left very firmly in Sydney. No complications until he had his little niece settled...

Right. Regardless, he reached the veranda, sat on the steps and typed her name into his phone's Internet app.

It took time for anything to show. His phone connection was slow. He should go inside and use his computer, but inside the door were Polly's suitcases, and in the living room was Polly's tree. For some reason he felt as if he needed to know what he was letting himself in for before he stepped over the threshold.

And here it was. Pollyanna Hargreaves.

She had a whole Wikipedia entry of her own.

Good grief.

Only child of Charles and Olivia Hargreaves. Expected to inherit the giant small goods manufacturing business built up by her family over generations. Currently practising medicine. Aged twenty-nine. One broken relationship, recent...

He snapped his phone shut. He didn't want to read any more.

What was she doing here? What was she running from? The broken relationship?

What was she doing being a doctor?

Why didn't she want to go back to Sydney?

He should insist she go back. She could no longer do the job he was paying her for. She deserved compensation— of course she did—but his medical insurance would cover it. He could discharge her from hospital tomorrow or the next day, organise a driver and send her home.

She didn't want to spend Christmas in Sydney.

He sat on the step and stared into the night. The decision should be easy, he thought. She couldn't do the job she'd come for. He and Ruby were still living in the house. She couldn't stay here, so he could send her home.

Her Christmas tree was already up in the living room. This was a big house. They had room.

What was he afraid of?

Of the way she made him feel?

For heaven's sake... He was a mature thirty-six-year-old doctor. He'd had girlfriends in Sydney, one of them long-term. He and Louise had even talked marriage, but she'd been appalled at the idea of Wombat Valley and Ruby. He couldn't blame her.

If he wanted to move on...

On to Polly?

He shook his head in disbelief. This was crazy. He'd known her for less than a day. She was an heiress and she was his patient.

She was funny and smart and brave.

And beautiful.

And he was nuts. He rose and gave himself a fast mental shake. He'd been thrown about too today, he reminded himself. He had the bruises to prove it. There'd been a moment when he'd thought there was a fair chance he could have left Ruby without any family and that moment was still with him.

He must have been hit on the head, he decided, or be suffering from delayed shock. Something was messing with his head.

Polly was a patient tonight, and tomorrow or the next day she'd be staying here as a guest and then hopefully she'd be a colleague. The jury was still out on whether she'd be well enough to take over so he and Ruby could spend a few days at the beach, but if he sent her back to Sydney he'd never know.

He could still feel the touch of her hand…

'So get over it,' he told himself. He needed Hamster. Ruby's big Labrador, given to her as a puppy in desperation on that last appalling Christmas, had turned into his confidante, someone to talk to in the small hours when life got bleak.

He'd fetch Hamster back tomorrow.

And Polly. Polly and Hamster and Christmas.

If she was still here… If he couldn't leave… He'd have to find a turkey.

He didn't know how to cook a turkey.

Turkey. Bonbons. Christmas pudding. Ruby was old enough to know what Christmas dinner should be. She'd been happy with her beach fish and chips substitute, but now…

'Maybe Dr Hargreaves will know how to cook a turkey,' he said morosely but then he glanced again at the information on his phone.

Heiress to a fortune…

'Maybe she has the funds to fly one in ready cooked from Sydney,' he told the absent Hamster.

Maybe pigs could fly.

Polly woke, some time in the small hours.

She hurt.

What was it with snake bite? she wondered. Why did it make everything ache?

Maybe she should write this up for her favourite medical journal—disseminated pain after accidental infusion of snake venom.

That sounded impressive. Her father would show that to his golf cronies.

Her mother, though…she could just hear her. 'Who are you trying to impress? You'll never get a husband if you keep trying to be clever.'

She winced. Her hand hurt.

Okay, maybe this wasn't disseminated pain from infusion of snake venom. Maybe this was disseminated pain from abseiling down a cliff with nylon cord and bare feet.

Her mother might like that better. It didn't sound clever at all.

Why did she feel like crying?

She should ring the bell. She would in a moment, she told herself. The nice night nurse would arrive and top up her medication and send her back into a nice dozy sleep. But for now…

For now she wanted to wallow.

She was missing…missing…

The doctor with the strong, sure hands. Hugo Denver, who'd sat with her until she'd slept. Whose voice was nice and deep and caring. Who looked a million dollars—tall, dark, strong.

Who made her feel safe.

And there was a nonsense. She was always safe. If she let them, her parents would have her cocooned in protective luxury, buffered from the world, safe in their gorgeous lifestyle for ever.

Marrying Marcus.

She winced and shifted in bed and hurt some more, but still she didn't call Barb. She felt as if she had things to sort, and now was as good a time as any to sort them.

She was staying here—for Christmas, at least. Hugo Denver owed her that. But afterwards... What then?

Overseas...

Maybe some volunteer organisation. Doctors were needed everywhere and heaven knew she didn't need money.

Her parents would have kittens.

Her parents were currently having kittens because she wasn't in Sydney. If they knew she was in trouble...

They'd come and she didn't want them to come. She did not want family.

Whereas if Hugo Denver walked in the door...

What was she thinking? She was falling for her boss? Or her doctor? Each was equally unethical.

So why did she want him to come back? When she'd woken, why had her gaze gone directly to the place where he'd been sitting?

Why could she still feel his hand?

Weakness, she told herself and had to fight back a sudden urge to burst into tears. Weakness and loneliness.

She had no reason to be lonely. She had her parents' world ready to enfold her, a world she'd had to fight to escape from.

It'd be so easy to give in. Her parents loved her. One

phone call and they'd be here. She'd be whisked back to the family mansion in Sydney. She'd be surrounded by private nurses and her mother would be popping in every twenty minutes with so much love she couldn't handle it.

Love…

Why was she thinking of Hugo Denver?

'Because you're a weak wuss and he has a smile to die for,' she told herself. 'And you've been battered and cut and bitten and you're not yourself. Tomorrow you'll be back to your chirpy self, defences up, self-reliant, needing no one.'

But if Hugo came back…

'Dr Denver to you,' she said out loud. 'A bit of professionalism, if you please, Dr Hargreaves.' She wiggled again and things hurt even more and she got sensible.

She rang the bell for a top-up of morphine. She didn't need Hugo Denver. Morphine would have to do instead.

CHAPTER SIX

HUGO ARRIVED IN her room at eleven in the morning, with Joe beside him. It was a professional visit: doctor doing his rounds with nurse in attendance. That was what Hugo looked—professional.

When she'd first seen him he'd been wearing casual clothes—dressed to go on holiday. Jeans and open-necked shirt. He'd been bloodied and filthy.

He'd come in last night but she couldn't remember much about last night. She'd been woozy and in pain. If she had to swear, she'd say he'd been wearing strength and a smile that said she was safe.

This morning he was in tailored pants and a crisp white shirt. The shirt was open-necked and short-sleeved. He looked professional but underneath the professional there was still the impression of strength.

Mary had helped her wash and Joe had brought one of her cases in. She was therefore wearing a cute kimono over silk pyjamas. She was ready to greet the world.

Sort of. This man had her unsettled.

The whole situation had her unsettled. She'd been employed to replace this man. What were the terms of her employment now?

'Hey,' he said, pausing at the door—giving her time to catch her breath? 'Joe tells me you're feeling better. True?'

She was. Or she had been. Now she was just feeling… disconcerted. Hormonal?

Interested.

Why? He wasn't her type, she thought. He looked…a bit worn around the edges. He was tall, lean and tanned, all good, all interesting, but his black hair held a hint of silver and there were creases around his eyes. Life lines. Worry? Laughter? Who could tell?

He was smiling now, though, and the creases fitted, so maybe it was laughter.

He was caring for his niece single-handedly. He was also the face of medicine for the entire valley.

Her research told her the hospital had a huge feeder population. This was a popular area to retire and run a few head of cattle or grow a few vines. Retirees meant ageing. Ageing meant demand for doctor's services.

Hence the hint of silver?

Or had it been caused by tragedy? Responsibility?

Responsibility. *Family.*

He wasn't her type at all.

Meanwhile he seemed to be waiting for an answer. Joe had handed him her chart. He'd read it and was now looking at her expectantly. What had he asked? For some reason she had to fight to remember what the question had been.

Was she feeling better? She'd just answered herself. Now she had to answer him.

'I'm good,' she said, and then added a bit more truthfully, 'I guess I'm still a bit wobbly.'

'Pain?'

'Down to fell-over-in-the-playground levels.'

'You do a lot of falling over in the playground?'

'I ski,' she said and he winced.

'Ouch.'

'You don't?'

'There's not a lot of skiing in Wombat Valley.'

'But before?'

'I don't go back to before,' he said briskly. 'Moving on... Polly, what happens next is up to you. We have a guest room made up at home. Ruby's aching to play nurse, but if you're more settled here then we'll wait.'

Uh oh. She hadn't thought this through. She'd demanded she stay in Wombat Valley. She'd refused to be evacuated to Sydney, but now...

'I'm an imposition,' she said ruefully, and his grin flashed out again. Honestly, that grin was enough to make a girl's toes curl.

He wasn't her type. *He was not.*

'You're not an imposition,' he said gently. 'Without you I'd be down the bottom of the Gap, and Christmas would be well and truly over. As it is, my niece is currently making paper chains to hang on your truly amazing Christmas tree. I advertised for a locum. What seems to have arrived is a life-saver and a Santa. Ruby would love you to come home. We'll both understand if you put it off until tomorrow but the venom seems to have cleared. Joe tells me your temperature, pulse, all vital signs, are pretty much back to normal. You'll still ache but if you come home you get to spend the rest of the day in bed as well. We have a view over the valley to die for, and Ruby's waiting.'

His voice gentled as he said the last two words and she met his gaze and knew, suddenly, why his voice had changed. There was a look...

He loved his niece.

Unreservedly. Unconditionally.

Why did that make her eyes well up?

It was the drugs, she thought desperately, and swiped her face with the back of her hand, but Hugo reached over and snagged a couple of tissues and tugged her hand down and dried her face for her.

'You're too weak,' he said ruefully. 'This was a bad idea. Snuggle back to sleep for the day.'

But she didn't want to.

Doctors made the worst patients. That was true in more ways than one, she thought. Just like it'd kill a professional footballer to sit on the sidelines and watch, so it was for doctors. Plus she'd had a childhood of being an inpatient. Once her diabetes had been diagnosed, every time she sneezed her parents had insisted on admission. So now… all she wanted to do was grab her chart, fill it in herself, like the professional she was, and run.

Admittedly, she hadn't felt like that last night—with a load of snake venom on board, hospital had seemed a really safe option—but she did this morning.

'If you're happy to take me home, I'd be very grateful,' she murmured and he smiled as if he was truly pleased that he was getting a locum for Christmas, even if that locum had a bandaged hand and a bandaged foot and was useless for work for the foreseeable future.

'Excellent. Now?'

'I…yes.'

'Hugo, the wheelchairs are out of action for a couple of hours,' Joe volunteered, taking back the chart and hanging it on the bed. Looking from Hugo to Polly and back again with a certain amount of speculative interest. 'It's so quiet this week that Ted's taken them for a grease and oil change. They'll be back this afternoon but meanwhile Polly can't walk on that foot.'

'I can hop,' Polly volunteered and both men grinned.

'A pyjama-clad, kimono-wearing hoppity locum,' Joe said, chuckling. 'Wow, Hugo, you pick 'em.'

'I do, don't I?' Hugo agreed, chuckling as well and then smiling down at Polly. 'But no hoppiting. We don't need to wait. Polly, you're no longer a patient, or a locum. From now on, if you agree, you're our honoured guest, a colleague and a friend. And friends wearing battle scars won on our behalf get special treatment. Can I carry you?'

Could he...what?

Carry her. That was what the doctor had said.

She needed a wheelchair. She could wait.

That'd be surly.

Besides, she didn't want one. There was no way she wanted to sit in a wheelchair and be pushed out feeling like a...patient.

She was a friend. Hugo had just said so.

But...but...

Those dark, smiling eyes had her mesmerised.

'I'll hurt your back,' she managed. 'I'm not looking after you in traction over Christmas.'

'I'm game if you are,' he said and his dark eyes gleamed. Daring her?

And all of a sudden she was in. Dare or not, he held her with his gaze, and suddenly, for this moment, Polly-anna Hargreaves wasn't a doctor. She wasn't a patient. She wasn't a daughter and actually...she wasn't a friend.

She was a woman, she thought, and she took a deep breath and smiled up into Hugo's gorgeous eyes.

He wanted to carry her?

'Yes, please.'

It was possibly not the wisest course to carry his new locum. His medical insurance company would have kittens if they could see him, he thought. He could drop her. He could fall. He could be sued for squillions. Joe, following bemusedly behind with Polly's suitcase, would act as witness to totally unethical behaviour.

But Polly was still shaky. He could hear it in her voice. Courageous as she'd been, yesterday had terrified her and the terror still lingered. She needed human contact. Warmth. Reassurance.

And Hugo… Well, if Hugo was honest, he wouldn't mind a bit of the same.

So he carried her and if the feel of her body cradled against him, warmth against warmth, if the sensation of her arms looped around his neck to make herself more secure, if both those things settled his own terrors from the day before then that was good. Wasn't it?

That was what this was all about, he told himself. Reassurance.

Except, as he strode out through the hospital entrance with his precious cargo, he felt…

As if he was carrying his bride over the threshold?

There was a crazy thought. Totally romantic. Nonsense.

'Where's your car?' she asked.

Polly's voice was still a bit shaky. He paused on the top of the ramp into Emergency and smiled down at her. The sun was on her face. Her flaming curls had been washed but they were tousled from a morning on her pillow. She had freckles. Cute freckles. Her face was a bit too pale and her green eyes a bit too large.

He'd really like to kiss her.

And that really was the way to get struck off any medical register he could care to name. Hire a locum, nearly kill her, carry her instead of using a wheelchair, then kiss her when she was stuck so tight in his arms she can't escape.

He needed a cold shower—fast.

'No car needed,' he said, and motioned towards a driveway along the side of the hospital.

At the end of the driveway there was a house, a big old weatherboard, looking slightly incongruous beside the newer brick hospital. It had an old-fashioned veranda with a kid's bike propped up by the door. A grapevine was growing under the roof, and a couple of Australia's gorgeous rosella parrots were searching through the leaves, looking for early grapes.

'This is home while you're in Wombat Valley,' he told her. 'But it won't be what you're used to. Speak now if you want to change your mind about staying. We can still organise transport out of here.'

'How do you know what I'm used to?' she asked and he grimaced and said nothing and she sighed. 'So I'm not incognito?'

'I don't think you could ever be incognito.'

She grimaced even more, and shifted in his arms. 'Hugo…'

'Mmm?'

'It's time to put me down. I can walk.'

'You're not walking.'

'Because I'm Pollyanna Hargreaves?'

'Because you have a snake-bitten ankle.'

'And you always carry snake-bite victims?'

'Oi!' It was Joe, standing patiently behind them, still holding the suitcase. 'In the time you've spent discussing it you could have taken her home, dumped her on the couch and got back here. I've work for you, Dr Denver.'

'What work?' Polly asked.

'Earache arriving in ten minutes,' Joe said darkly and glanced at his watch. 'No, make that in five.'

'Then dump me and run,' Polly said and he had no choice.

Like it or not, he had to dump her and run.

Ruby was waiting. Sort of.

He carried Polly over the threshold and Ruby was sitting on the couch in the front room, in her shorts and shirt, bare legs, tousled hair—she'd refused to let him braid it this morning—her face set in an expression he knew all too well. Misery.

He could hear Donna in the kitchen. Donna was a Wombat Valley mum. Donna's daughter, Talia, was Ruby's age, and Donna's family was just one of the emergency back-stops Wombat Valley had put in place to make sure Hugo could stay here. He stood in the living room doorway, Polly in his arms, and looked helplessly down at his niece. When she looked like this he never knew what to say.

'We have a guest,' he said. 'Ruby, this is Dr Hargreaves.'

'Polly,' said Polly.

'Why are you carrying her?'

'She was bitten by a snake. I told you.'

'She's supposed to be working,' Ruby said in a small voice. 'And we're supposed to be at the beach.'

'Ruby...'

'It's the pits,' Polly interrupted. She was still cradled against him but she sounded ready to chat. 'Sorry, sorry, sorry,' she told the little girl. 'But we should blame the snake.'

'You should have been wearing shoes,' Ruby muttered, still in that little voice that spoke of the desolation of betrayal. Another broken promise.

'Yes,' Polly agreed. 'I should.'

'Why weren't you?'

'I didn't know I was planning to meet a snake, and it didn't warn me it was coming. They should wear bells, like cats.'

Ruby thought about that and found it wanting. 'Snakes don't have necks.'

'No.' Polly appeared thoughtful. 'We should do something about that. What if we made a rule that Australian snakes have to coil? If we had a law that every snake has to loop once so they have a circle where their neck should be, we could give them all bells. How are you at drawing? Maybe you could draw what we mean and we'll send a letter to Parliament this very day.'

Ruby stared at her as if she was a sandwich short of a picnic. 'A circle where their neck should be?' she said cautiously.

'If you have a skipping rope I'll show you. But we'd need to make it law, which means writing to Parliament. How about you do the drawing and I'll write the letter?'

Ruby stared at her in amazement. In stupefaction. The desolate expression on her face faded.

'"Dear Parliamentarians…",' Polly started. She was still ensconced in Hugo's arms, but she didn't appear to notice her unusual platform, or the fact that her secretary wasn't writing. 'It has come to our attention that snakes are slithering around the countryside bell-less. This situation is unsatisfactory, not only to people who wander about shoe-less, but also to snakes who, we're sure, would be much happier with jewels. Imagine how much more Christmassy Australia would be if every snake wore a Christmas bell?'

And it was too much for Ruby.

She giggled.

It was the best sound in the world, Hugo thought. For twelve long months he'd longed to hear his niece giggle, and this woman had achieved it the moment she'd come through the door.

But the giggle was short-lived. Of course. He could see Ruby fight it, ordering her expression back to sad.

'You're still spoiling our Christmas,' she muttered.

'Not me personally,' Polly said blithely, refusing to sound offended. 'That was the snake. Put me down, Dr Denver. Ruby, can I share your couch? And thank you for putting up my Christmas tree. Do you like it?'

'Yes,' Ruby said reluctantly.

'Me too. Silver's my favourite.'

'I like real trees,' Hugo offered as he lowered Polly onto the couch beside his niece. 'Ones made out of pine needles.'

'Then why didn't you put one up?' Polly raised her brows in mock disapproval. She put her feet on the floor and he saw her wince. He pushed a padded ottoman forward; she put her foot on it and she smiled.

It was some smile.

'I know,' she said, carrying right on as if that smile meant nothing. 'You meant to be away for Christmas. That's no excuse, though. Trees are supposed to be decorated ages before Christmas. And you put all the presents for everyone from your teacher to the postman underneath, wrapped up mysteriously, and you get up every morning and poke and prod the presents and wonder if Santa's come early. It's half the fun.'

There was another fail. Add it to the list, Hugo thought morosely, but Polly had moved through accusatory and was now into fixing things.

'There's still time,' she said. 'Ruby, we can do some wrapping immediately. I'm stuck with this foot... Who's in the kitchen?'

'Mrs Connor,' Ruby muttered. 'She's cooking a Christmas cake 'cos she says if we're staying here we might need it.'

'Mrs Connor?' Polly queried.

'Talia's mum.'

'Talia's your friend?'

'Talia's at her grandma's place, making mince pies,' Ruby told her. 'She said I could come but I didn't want to. I don't have a grandma any more. My mum's dead too.'

But, despite the bleak words, Ruby was obviously fighting not to be drawn in by Polly's bounce. Hugo was fighting not to be drawn in, too. Polly was...magnetic. She was like a bright light and the moths were finding her irresistible.

What was he on about? He had work to do.

'I need to get on,' he said.

'I know. Earache.' Polly gave him a sympathetic smile. 'You could introduce me to Mrs Connor. Maybe she doesn't need to stay once her cake's cooked. Ruby and I can cope on our own. Do you have Christmas wrapping paper?'

He did get the occasional thing right. 'Yes.'

'Excellent. If you could find it for us…'

'We don't have anything to wrap,' Ruby said.

'Yes, we do. Have you ever heard of origami?'

'I…no,' she said cautiously.

'It's paper folding and I'm an expert.' Polly beamed. 'I can make birds and frogs that jump and little balls that practically float and tiny pretend lanterns. And I can make boxes to put them in. If you like I'll teach you and we can make presents for everyone in Wombat Valley. And then we'll wrap them in newspaper and make them really big and wrap them again in Christmas paper so no one will ever guess what's in them and then we'll stack them under the tree. Then we'll have presents for everyone who comes to the house or everyone in hospital or everyone in the main street of Wombat Valley if we make enough. Good idea or what, Ruby?'

'I… I'll watch,' Ruby said reluctantly and it was all Hugo could do not to offer Polly a high five. *I'll watch…* Concession indeed.

'Then find us some wrapping paper and be off with you,' Polly told him. 'Ruby and I and Mrs Connor can manage without you.' And then she hesitated. 'Though… can you find me my jelly beans? They're in my holdall. And is there juice in the fridge?'

She was a diabetic. Of course. What was he thinking, not worrying about sources of instant sugar. Hell, why hadn't he left her in the hospital? And as for telling Donna to go home…

The weight of the last year settled back down hard. Two responsibilities…

But Polly was looking up at him and suddenly she was glaring. 'Do not look like that,' she snapped.

'Like what?'

'Like I'm needing help. I don't need help. I just need things to be in place.'

'If you have a hypo…'

'If I have my jelly beans and juice, I won't have a hypo.'

'How do you know? The snake bite…'

'Is your uncle a fusser?' Polly demanded, turning to Ruby. 'Does he fuss when you don't want him to?'

'He makes me have a bath every single day,' Ruby confessed. 'And I have to eat my vegetables.'

'I knew it. A fusser! Dr Denver, I will not be fussed over. A bath and vegetables for Ruby are the limit. I will not let you fuss further.'

'He'll get grumpy,' Ruby warned.

'Let him. I can cope with a grump.' And she tilted her chin and looked up at him, defiance oozing from every pore.

His lips twitched—and hers twitched in response.

'Jelly beans,' she repeated. 'Juice. Earache. Ruby— swans, lanterns, frogs?'

'Frogs,' Ruby said, watching her uncle's face.

He wasn't grumpy. He wasn't.

Maybe he had been a bit. Maybe this year had been enough to make anyone grumpy.

'Earth to Dr Denver,' Polly was saying. 'Are you reading? Jelly beans, juice, earache. Go.'

There was nothing else for it. A part of him really wanted to stay and watch…frogs?

Earache was waiting.

He had no choice. The demands on a lone family doctor were endless, and he couldn't knock patients back.

Back in Sydney he'd been at the cutting edge of thoracic

surgery. Here, his life was so circumscribed he couldn't even watch frogs.

And he shouldn't even watch Polly.

CHAPTER SEVEN

THERE WAS A FROG, right underneath her window. Not the origami variety. The croaking sort.

She should be able to write to a Member of Parliament about that, she thought. *Dear Sir, I wish to report a breach of the peace. Surely environmental protection laws decree there shall be no noise after ten p.m....*

If she was honest, though, it wasn't the frog that was keeping her awake.

She'd given in an hour ago and taken a couple of the pills Hugo had left for her. Her aches were thus dulled. She couldn't blame her sleeplessness on them, either.

What?

This set-up. Lying in a bedroom with the window open, the smells of the bushland all around her. The total quiet—apart from the frog. Polly was a city girl. She was used to traffic, the low murmur of air conditioning and the background hum of a major metropolis.

There was no hum here. She really was in the back of beyond.

With Hugo and Ruby.

And they were both tugging at her heartstrings and she hadn't come here for her heartstrings to be tugged. She'd come here to give her heartstrings time out.

She'd had a surfeit of loving. Loving up to her eyebrows. And fuss. And emotional blackmail.

Why was it important to make a little girl happy? Emotional blackmail?

'If I'm stuck here I might as well do my best,' she told herself. 'It's the least I can do and I always do the least I can do.'

Only she didn't. She'd been trained since birth to make people happy. This Christmas was all about getting away from that obligation.

Though she had enjoyed her origami frogs, she conceded. She had enjoyed giving Ruby pleasure.

Frogs... Origami frogs...

Real frogs...

Blurring...

Uh oh.

She was light-headed, she conceded. Just a little. Sometimes sleeplessness preceded a hypo. She should get some juice, just in case.

She padded through to the kitchen in her bare feet and the cute silk pyjamas her mum had brought her back from Paris last year.

They were a funny colour. The patterns seemed to be swirling.

That was an odd thought. Actually, all her thoughts were odd. She fetched a glass of juice and then, still acting on blurry impulse, she headed out to the veranda. If she couldn't sleep, maybe she could talk to the frog.

Hugo was sitting on the top step.

He was a dark shape against the moonlight. She would have backed away, but the screen door squeaked as she swung it open.

He turned and saw her and shifted sideways on the step, inviting her to join him.

'Problem?' he asked and she hesitated for a moment

before deciding *What the heck*. She sat down. The moon was full, lighting the valley with an eerie glow. From this veranda you could see for ever.

She concentrated—very hard—on looking out over the valley rather than thinking about the man beside her.

She failed.

His body was warm beside her. Big and warm and solid. The rest of the night...not so solid.

'Blood sugar?' he asked and she remembered she was carrying juice. For some reason it seemed important not to make a big deal of it. She put it down carefully behind her.

A great blond shape shifted from the dog bed behind her. Hamster had been returned home this afternoon. Now he was headed for her juice. She went to grab it but Hugo was before her.

'Leave,' he ordered, in a voice that brooked no argument, and Hamster sighed and backed away. Hugo handed Polly back her juice—and their fingers touched.

It was a slight touch. Very slight. There was no reason why the touch should make her shiver.

She was...shivery.

It was warm. Why was she shivering?

'Polly?'

'Wh...what?'

'Blood sugar. You're carrying juice. I assume that's why you're up. Have you checked?'

'N...no.'

'Where's your glucose meter?'

'I'm okay.'

'Polly...'

'Don't fuss. I hate f...fussing.' But, even as she said it, she realised there was a reason. She was still fuzzy. Too fuzzy. Damn, she was good at predicting hypos. Where had this come from?

But Hugo was already raising her hand, propelling

the glass up, holding the juice to her lips. 'Drink,' he ordered and he made sure she drank half the glass and then he swung himself off the step, disappeared inside and emerged a moment later with her glucometer.

Yeah, okay. He was right and she was wrong. She sighed and stuck out her finger. He flicked on the torch on his phone and did a quick finger prick test, then checked the result while she kept on stoically drinking. Or tried to.

As she tried for the last mouthful her hand slipped and he caught it—and the glass.

And he kept on holding.

'Why bring this out to the veranda?' he asked as he helped her with the last mouthful. She didn't bother to answer. 'Polly? You should have drunk it at the fridge if you were feeling...'

'I wasn't feeling,' she managed. 'And I know what I should have done.'

'So why didn't you do it?'

She glowered instead of answering. This was her business. Her diabetes. Her concern.

'The snake bite will have pushed you out of whack,' he said, and she thought about that for a while as the dizziness receded and the world started to right itself. In a minute she'd get up and make herself some toast, carbohydrates to back up the juice. But not yet. For now she was going nowhere.

'Out of whack,' she said cautiously, testing her voice and relieved to find the wobble had receded. 'That's a medical term?'

'Yep. Blood sugar level, two point one. You're not safe to be alone, Dr Hargreaves.'

'I am safe,' she said with cautious dignity. 'I woke up, I felt a bit odd; I fetched the juice.'

'You have glucose by the bed?'

'I...yes.'

'Why didn't you take it?'

'You sound like my mother.'

'I sound like your doctor.'

'You're not my doctor. I'm discharged. You're my friend.'

And why did that sound a loaded term? she wondered. Friend… It sounded okay. Sort of okay.

He was sitting beside her again. His body was big. Warm. Solid.

She always felt shaky after a hypo, she thought. That was all this was.

Um…post hypo lust?

Lust? She was out of her mind. She put her empty glass down on the step beside her. Hamster took an immediate interest but Hugo was no longer interested in Hamster.

'How the hell…?' he asked, quietly but she heard strength behind his voice. Strength and anger? 'How the hell did you think you'd manage in the country as a solo practitioner when you have unstable diabetes?'

'I don't have unstable diabetes. You said yourself, it was the snake.'

'So it was. And shock and stress. And this job's full of shock and stress.'

'I'd imagine every single one of your nursing staff knows how to deal with a hypo.'

'You intended telling them you were diabetic?'

'Of course. I'm not dumb.'

'And you'd accuse them of being like your mother, too?'

'Only if they fuss.' She sighed. 'I need some…'

'Complex carbohydrates to keep you stable. Of course you do. I'll get some toast.'

'I can…'

'Dr Hargreaves, you may not be my patient but I believe I'm still your boss. Keep still, shut up and conserve energy. Hamster, keep watch on the lady. Don't let her go anywhere.'

Hamster had just finished licking the inside of the juice glass, as far in as he could reach. He looked up, yawned and flopped sideways, as if he'd suddenly used up every bit of his energy.

That was a bit how she felt, Polly conceded. Having someone else make her toast was…well, it wasn't exactly standing on her own feet but it was okay.

Especially as it was Hugo.

There she was again, doing the lust thing, she thought. The hypo must have been worse than she'd thought. She was feeling weird.

And Hugo seemed to sense it. He put a hand up and traced her cheekbone, an echo of the way she'd traced his cheek the night before. It was surely a gesture of concern, she thought, and why it had the power to make her want more…

'Sit,' he said. 'Stay. Toast.'

And she could do nothing but obey.

'Woof,' she ventured and he patted her head.

'Good girl. If you're really good I'll bring you a dog biscuit on the side.'

She ate her toast, sharing a crust or two with Hamster. Hugo made some for himself as well and they ate in silence. The silence wasn't uncomfortable, though. It was sort of…all right.

It was three in the morning. She should go back to bed. Instead, she was sitting on the veranda of a strange house in a strange place with a strange man…

He wasn't strange. He was Hugo.

Part of her—the dumb part—felt as if she'd known him all her life.

The sensible part knew nothing.

'So tell me more about you and Ruby,' she ventured into the stillness. The toast was gone. Hugo should be in bed too, she thought, but for now he seemed as content as she was just to sit. 'And you. Why are you here?'

'Do you remember me talking to you last night?'

'Yes.'

'Then you know I came back when my sister died.'

'So who was the doctor here before? After your Dad died?'

'Doc Farr. He retired here from Melbourne, thinking it was a quiet life. Ha. He intended to set up a vineyard, so he didn't want this house—my mother stayed living here. But Harry Farr felt trapped. When Mum and Grace died and I came home for good you couldn't see him for dust. I've never seen anyone leave so fast. His vineyard's still on the market but he was so inundated with work all he wanted was to get out of here.'

'You were working in Sydney. As a family doctor?'

'As a surgeon,' he said brusquely, as if it didn't matter.

'A surgeon.' She stared at him, stunned. 'Where?'

'Sydney Central.'

'Specialising?'

'Thoracic surgery. It doesn't matter now.'

'You left thoracic surgery to come here?' She was still staring. 'Your life… Your colleagues… Did you have a girlfriend?'

'Yes, but…'

'But she wouldn't come. Of course she wouldn't.'

'Polly, I don't need to tell…'

'You don't need to tell me anything,' she said hastily. 'I'm sorry. But Sydney… Friends? Surfing? Restaurants? The whole social scene of Sydney?'

'It doesn't matter!'

'I suspect it does matter. A lot. You had to leave everything to take care of Ruby. That's the pits.'

'It's no use thinking it's the pits. It's just…what it is. Ruby would know no one in Sydney, and if I stayed in my job she'd never see me. She needs me. She's my family.'

And there was nothing to say to that.

Family… The thing she most wanted to escape from.

She thought about it as the warmth and stillness enveloped them. It was a weirdly intimate setting. A night for telling all?

Hugo had bared so much. There were things unspoken, things that didn't need to be spoken. He was trapped, more than she'd ever been trapped. By Ruby… A needy seven-year-old.

'Tell me about the Christmas thing,' she ventured, and he started, as if his mind had been a thousand miles away.

'Christmas?'

'Why is it so important?'

'I guess it's not,' he said heavily. 'Except I promised. Actually, Grace promised her last year. She said they'd go to the beach for Christmas and then…well, I told you what happened. This year Ruby came out and asked— "Can we have a beach Christmas?" What was I supposed to say? I booked an apartment at Bondi and then spent three months advertising for a locum.'

'And bombed out with me.'

'There's no bombed about it. You saved me.'

'And you saved me right back, so we're quits.' She took a deep breath. 'Right. Christmas at the beach is important. Hugo, you can still go. Today's only Wednesday. Christmas is Saturday. You haven't cancelled, have you?'

He gave a wry laugh. 'An apartment at Bondi Beach for Christmas? I prepaid. Non-refundable. Somewhere in Bondi there's a two-bedroom flat with our name on it.'

'So go.'

'And leave you here?'

'What's wrong with leaving me here?'

'Are you kidding? Look at you.'

'I'm twenty-four hours post snake bite. It's three days until Christmas. Two more days and I'll be perky as anything.'

'You're an unstable diabetic.'

'I'm a very stable, very sensible diabetic who just happens to have been bitten by a snake. You told me yourself that the venom will have messed with things and you're absolutely right. Usually my control's awesome.'

'Awesome?'

'Well, mostly awesome,' she confessed. 'After the third margarita it can get wobbly.'

'You have to be kidding. Margaritas!'

'One margarita contains alcohol, which tends to bring my levels down, and sugar, which brings them up. It's a fine line which I've taken years to calibrate. I'll admit after the third my calibration may get blurry, but you needn't worry. I only ever tackle a third when I have a responsible medical colleague on hand with margarita tackling equipment at the ready. So for now I've left my sombrero in Sydney. I'm anticipating a nice and sober Christmas, with not a margarita in sight.'

He was looking a bit...stunned. 'Yet you still brought your Christmas tree,' he managed.

'Christmas trees don't affect blood sugars. Don't they teach surgeons anything?'

He choked on a chuckle, and she grinned. He had the loveliest chuckle, she thought, and she felt a bit lightheaded again and wondered if she could use a bit more juice but the light-headedness wasn't the variety she'd felt before. This was new. Strange...

Sitting beside this guy on the back step in the small hours was strange. Watching the moon over the valley...

The step was a bit too narrow. Hamster had wedged

himself beside her—something about toast—and she'd had to edge a bit closer to Hugo.

Close enough to touch.

Definitely light-headed...

'So tell me why you're not in Sydney?' Hugo asked and she had to haul herself away from the slightly tipsy sensation of sensual pleasure and think of a nice sober answer.

'Smothering,' she said and she thought as she said it, *why?* She never talked of her background. She'd hardly confessed her claustrophobia to anyone.

He didn't push, at least not for a while. He really was the most restful person, she thought. He was just...solid. Nice.

Um...down, she told her hormones, and she edged a little way away. But not very far. An inch or more.

She could change steps. Move right away.

The idea was unthinkable.

'You want to elaborate?' he asked at last and she wondered if she did, but this night was built for intimacy and suddenly there seemed no reason not to tell him.

'My parents love me to bits,' she said. 'They married late, I'm their only child and they adore me. To Mum, I'm like a doll, to be played with, dressed up, displayed.'

'Hence the Pollyanna...'

'You got it. Pollyanna was her favourite movie, her favourite doll and then, finally, her living, breathing version of the same. That's me. Dad's not quite so over the top, but he's pretty protective. They've always had nannies to do the hard work but there's no doubting they love me. I was diagnosed with diabetes when I was six and they were shattered. I'd been smothered with care before that. Afterwards it got out of control.'

'So don't tell me...you ran away to the circus?'

'I would have loved to,' she said simply. 'But there's a problem. I love them back.'

'That is a problem,' he said, softly now, as if speaking only to himself. 'The chains of loving…'

'They get you every which way,' she agreed. 'You and Ruby… I can see that. Anyway, I seem to have been fighting for all my life to be…me. They adore me, they want to show me off to their friends and, above all, they want to keep me safe. The fight I had to be allowed to do medicine… To them, medicine seems appallingly risky—all these nasty germs—but we're pretty much over that.'

'Good for you.'

She grimaced. 'Yeah, some things are worth fighting for, but you win one battle and there's always another. Two years ago, I started going out with the son of their best friends. Marcus was kind, eligible and incredibly socially acceptable. But…*kind* was the key word. He wanted to keep me safe, just as my parents did. I felt smothered but they were all so approving. I came within a hair's breadth of marrying him. He asked, and I might have said yes, but then I saw a video camera set up to the side and I recognised it. So, instead of falling into his arms, I found myself asking whether Dad had loaned him the camera and of course he had, and I pushed him further and he told me Mum had told him what kind of ring I'd like, and his parents knew and they were all having dinner together at that very moment and we could go tell them straight away.'

'Whoa…'

'You get it,' she said approvingly. 'They didn't. But I didn't just say "no" and run. Even then I had to let them down slowly. I pretended to get a text on my phone, an urgent recall to the hospital, and Marcus offered to drive me and I told him to go have dinner with the parents and then I went to a bar and risked having a very bad hypo. That was when I figured I needed to sort my life. I told them all kindly, in my own way, but since then… I've fought to take control. I need to back away.'

'Which is why you're here? Doing locums?'

'Exactly,' she said with satisfaction. 'It's five whole hours' drive from my parents' Christmas. Oh, don't get me wrong, I love Christmas, but they'll all be there, at the most exclusive restaurant overlooking the harbour, all my parents' friends, though not Marcus this year because he had the decency to accept a posting to New York. He's now going out with an artist who paints abstract nudes. He's much happier than he was with me, and his parents are appalled. Hooray for Marcus. But the rest of them... Mum will be trying to figure who I can marry now. She's indefatigable, my mum. Knock her back and she bounces back again, bounce, bounce, bounce. The rest of them will be smiling indulgently in the background, but feeling slightly sorry for Mum because she has an imperfect daughter.'

'Imperfect...?'

'Perfection has perfect teeth and skin, a toned body and designer clothes. Perfect doesn't argue, she moves in the right circles, she marries the right man and never, ever has diabetes. So here I am and I'm here to stay, so you and Ruby might as well go to Bondi because I'm a very good doctor and you've contracted me to work for two weeks and that's just what I'll do.'

'Polly...'

'Go,' she said. 'Enough of this guilt stuff. If I have this right, you've left a perfectly good career, I suspect a perfectly satisfactory girlfriend, a perfectly acceptable lifestyle, all because you love Ruby. That's some chains of loving.'

'And you've left a perfectly good career, a perfectly satisfactory boyfriend, a perfectly luxurious lifestyle all because you want to cut the chains of loving?'

'Exactly,' she said.

'So why encourage me to break away?'

'Because if you stay I'll feel guilty and I'm over guilt. Go.'

'I don't think I can.'

'Hugo,' she said, figuring a girl had to make a stand some time and it might as well be now. She was full of toast. Her blood sugars had settled nicely. She was back in control again—sort of. 'This is nuts. You're a surgeon, and a thoracic surgeon at that. I'm trained in Emergency Medicine. If a kid comes in with whooping cough, who'd be most qualified to cope?'

'Whooping cough's lung…'

'Okay, bad example. Itch. In he comes, scratch, scratch, scratch. Is it an allergy or is it fleas? What's the differential appearance? Or could it be chickenpox? Some kids don't get immunised. And if it's chickenpox, what's the immunisation period? Then the next kid comes in, sixteen years old, cramps. How do you get information out of a sullen teenager? Do you suspect pregnancy?'

'Not if it's a boy. Is this an exam?'

'Do you know the answers?'

'I've been working as a family doctor for twelve months now.'

'And I've been training as an emergency doctor for five years. I win.'

'Did you know you look extraordinarily cute in those pyjamas?'

'Did you know you look extraordinarily sexy in those jeans? Both of which comments are sexist, both beneath us as medical professionals and neither taking this argument forward. If you can't come up with a better medical rebuttal then I win.'

'You can't.'

'I just have. Give me one more day to get my bearings and you leave on Thursday.'

'Friday,' he said, sounding goaded. 'Tomorrow's another rest day and I spend Thursday watching you work.'

'That's ridiculous, plus it's discriminatory. I have diabetes, not gaps in my medical training. Tell you what, for the next two days we work side by side. That'll give you time with Ruby and it should set your mind at rest. If at the end of Thursday you can truthfully say I'm a bad doctor then I'll leave.'

'Go back to Sydney?'

'That's none of your business.'

'No,' he said. 'It's not. Polly, it's not safe.'

'Go jump. Ruby's Christmas is at stake. You're leaving, I'm staying, Dr Denver, and that's all there is to it. I have a nice little Christmas pudding for one in my suitcase, and I'm not sharing. Go away.'

'I can't.'

'You have no choice. Ruby needs you.'

'Everyone needs me,' he said, sounding even more goaded.

'I don't need you,' she retorted. 'I don't need you one bit. So get used to it, and while you're getting used to it, you might like to pack and leave.'

CHAPTER EIGHT

HIS STIPULATION WAS that Polly stayed in bed until noon. She agreed, but reluctantly. She also didn't like it that Hugo had pulled in yet more help.

His housekeeper was away. Ruby was on school holidays. He needed to care for Ruby, but Polly figured she could at least do that.

But she'd got tired of arguing last night. She'd fallen back into bed and when she woke it was nine o'clock. Okay, Hugo had a point. As a childminder she was currently less than efficient.

She snagged her glucose meter and took a reading. Six point three. *Nice.* 'I've won, Snake,' she said out loud and settled back on her pillows feeling smug.

Or sort of smug. She was still sore. She'd made origami gifts with Ruby the day before, but in truth it had been a struggle. Maybe Hugo was right with his two days of rest.

He looked like a man who was used to being right, she thought. Typical surgeon.

But the thought didn't quite come off in her head. It sounded a bit…lame.

Hugo wasn't typical anything, she thought.

There was a scratch on the door.

'Yes?'

Ruby's head poked around. Looking scared. She'd relaxed a little the day before when she'd been engrossed in origami frogs, but tension was never far from this little one.

'Hi.' Polly smiled, hoping for a smile in return.

'Are you awake?' she whispered.

'Yes.' She edged over on the bed. 'Want to come and visit?' The bedspread was pretty—patchwork. Had Ruby's grandma made it?

The house was cosy. A family house. Home of Hugo and Grace and their mum and dad.

She found herself hoping Grace had had a happy childhood and suddenly she thought she bet she had. Depression usually didn't strike until the teens. She looked out of the window at the valley beyond. A tyre swing was hanging from a huge gum nearer to the house.

Hugo would have used that swing…

She was still feeling odd. How bad had that hypo been last night? She shouldn't be feeling weird now.

Ruby was still by the door, still looking nervous, but she was obviously on a mission. 'I have to find out your blood sugar level before you get up,' Ruby quavered and Polly pulled herself back to the here and now.

Blood sugar level. It was six point three; she'd just taken it. She went to say it but then she paused. Something made her stop.

I have to find out your blood sugar level…

'Did your Uncle Hugo tell you to find out?'

'He says you're d…diabetic and your blood sugar has to be under ten and above four and if it's not I have to ring him and he says I have to make sure you still have juice on your bedside table.'

Polly glanced at her bedside table. There was a glass of juice there.

Hugo must have brought it in last night or early this morning. He must have come into her bedroom while she was asleep.

Creepy?

No. Caring.

But she didn't like caring. She didn't like fuss. She'd been swamped with fuss since childhood.

Ruby was patiently waiting for an answer.

'Can you help me with my glucose meter?' she asked and motioned to the small machine beside her.

'What does it do?'

'If you hold it out, I put my finger in it and it takes a tiny pinprick of blood. It tests the blood and gives a reading.'

'Does it hurt?'

'Not if you hold it still.'

Ruby looked fascinated. Still a bit scared, though. 'I don't want to hurt you.'

'I can do it myself,' Polly confessed. 'But I have to be brave, and now I have a sore hand. It would help if you do it for me.'

And Ruby tilted her chin and took a deep breath. 'Like doctors do?'

'Exactly.'

'My Uncle Hugo is a doctor.'

'Yes.'

'He could do it.'

'Yes, but he's not here. It's lucky I have you.'

'Yes,' Ruby said seriously and picked up the glucose meter and studied it. She turned it over and figured it out.

'That's the on switch?'

'Yes.'

'Then I think you have to put your finger in here.'

'Yes.'

'Do we have to wash your finger first?'

'You're practically a real doctor,' Polly said with admiration. 'Wow, how do you know that? Ruby, I would disinfect my finger if this wasn't my meter, but I'm the only person ever to use this. There are only my germs in there. I take a chance.'

Ruby raised one sceptical eyebrow. 'But it'd be safer if I did wash your finger,' she declared and who was Polly to argue?

'Yes,' she conceded, and Ruby gave a satisfied nod and fetched a damp facecloth and a towel and a tube of disinfectant.

She proceeded to wipe Polly's finger, dry it and then apply disinfectant cream. A lot of disinfectant cream.

'Now it's done its job, maybe we need to use a tissue to wipe most of it off,' Polly offered. 'Otherwise, we'll be testing the disinfectant instead of my blood. You'd be able to tell your Uncle Hugo that your tube of disinfectant is safe, but not me.'

And Ruby stared down at the ooze of disinfectant, she looked at the meter—and she giggled.

It was a good giggle. A child's giggle, and Polly guessed, just by looking at her, that for this child giggles were few and far between. But the giggle died. Ruby was back in doctor mode. She fetched a tissue and wiped the finger with all the gravitas in the world.

'Put your finger in,' she ordered Polly, and Polly put her finger in and the machine clicked to register the prick and seconds later the reading came out.

'Six point eight,' Ruby said triumphantly. 'That's good.'

'That's excellent,' came a gruff voice behind them and Ruby whirled round and Polly looked up and Hugo was standing in the doorway.

How long had he been there? How much had he heard? He was smiling. *Oh, that smile...*

'That's really good,' he reiterated and he crossed to the bed and ruffled Ruby's pigtailed hair. Which was easy to do because the pigtails looked very amateurish—blonde wisps were escaping every which way. 'Thank you, Ruby.

How's our patient? Was she brave when you did the finger prick?'

'Yes,' Ruby said. 'She moved a little bit when it went in, but she didn't scream.'

'I didn't,' Polly said, adding a touch of smug to her voice. 'I'm very brave.'

'It's all about how you hold the meter.' Hugo was talking to Ruby, not her. 'You must have very steady hands.'

'Yes,' the little girl said, and smiled shyly up at her uncle but there was anxiety behind the smile. 'I did. Are we really still going to the beach for Christmas?'

'We're going to try,' Hugo told her. 'I told you this morning, and I mean it. If we can get Dr Hargreaves better…'

'I'm Polly,' Polly said fast, because it seemed important.

'If we can look after Polly,' Hugo corrected himself. 'If we can make her better, then she can be the doctor and we can still have our holiday.'

'She doesn't look like a doctor,' Ruby said dubiously.

'She doesn't, does she? Those are very pretty pyjamas she's wearing.'

'They are,' Ruby conceded. He and Ruby were examining her as if she were some sort of interesting bug. 'I'd like pyjamas like that.'

'I think I can find some like these on the Internet in your size,' Polly ventured. 'If it's okay with your uncle.'

'Doctors don't wear pyjamas.' Ruby seemed distracted by Polly's offer but not enough to be deflected from her main purpose, which was obviously to find out exactly how qualified Polly was to take over here and thus send Ruby to the beach.

'Does your uncle have a white coat?' Polly demanded, and Ruby nodded.

'He has lots. They're hanging in the airing cupboard.'

'If you put one of those on me, I'll look just like a doctor.'

'But your hair's too red,' Ruby told her. 'Doctors don't have red curly hair.'

'You've been moving with the wrong type of doctor. The best doctors all have red curly hair. If the medical board discovered your Uncle Hugo's hair was black and almost straight he'd be sent to the nearest hairdresser to buy a wig.'

'A wig…' Ruby's eyes widened.

'You can get wigs on the Internet too. You want to help me look?'

'No!' Hugo said, and both girls turned and stared at him. At his hair. It was thick and short. It only just qualified as wavy—definitely not curly—and it was definitely black.

'A red wig would be perfect,' Polly decreed, and Ruby giggled and giggled some more and Hugo's face creased into a grin and Polly lay back on her pillows and smug didn't begin to describe how she was feeling.

She'd been in some tight situations before this. Lots of tight situations. As an emergency physician she'd even saved lives. It had felt great, but somehow this moment was right up there. Making Hugo and his niece smile.

'Ruby, Mrs Connor's just asked if you'd like to go to the pictures in Willaura,' Hugo said, almost nonchalantly. 'Three girls from your class will be there. Talia and Sasha and Julie. Mr Connor will pick you up in ten minutes if you want to go.'

And he picked up the glucose meter and studied it as if it was really interesting instead of something doctors saw all the time—and Polly realised that this was important.

How many times did Ruby accept this kind of invitation? She suspected seldom. Or never?

'Don't I have to look after Polly?' Ruby asked dubiously.

'She's awake now and she's been tested and her blood sugar's good. We'll give her breakfast and then she needs to go back to sleep. We can ask Hamster to snooze under her bed to look after her.'

'We could put a white coat on Hamster,' Ruby said and giggled again. 'He could be the doctor. And I could maybe teach the girls how to make frogs.'

'That's a grand plan,' Hugo told her and Ruby swooped off to get ready.

And Hugo was left with Polly and Polly was left with Hugo and suddenly there were no words.

What was it with this woman?

What was it that made him want to smile?

She should be just another patient, he told himself, or just another colleague.

She was both. She was neither.

She lay in the too big bed in her cute swirly pyjamas, pink and orange and crimson and purple. They should have clashed with her red hair but they didn't. She looked up at him and she was still smiling but her smile was tentative. A bit uncertain.

She looked…vulnerable, he thought, and suddenly he realised that was how he was feeling.

Vulnerable. As if this woman was somehow edging under his defences.

He didn't have defences. What sort of stupid thought was that?

'Lorna will bring you breakfast,' he told her.

'Lorna?'

'My housekeeper for this morning. Our usual housekeeper, Lois, has taken Christmas off.'

'And because of me you're having to find fill-ins.'

'I told you. Yes, because of you, Ruby and I are stuck here, but if it wasn't for you I wouldn't be here in the worst sense of the term. So lie back and get better without qualms. What would you like for breakfast?'

'Toast and marmalade,' she said, almost defiantly, and he raised an eyebrow in exactly the same way she'd just seen Ruby do it.

'Don't tell me.' The corner of his mouth quirked upward. 'Plus coffee with three sugars.'

'If you're about to lecture me...'

He held up his hands as if to ward off attack. 'You're a big girl, Dr Hargreaves. You manage your own diabetes. And we do have sourdough, which has a low...'

'Glycaemic index. I know.' She glowered. 'If you turn into my mother I'm out of here.'

'For the next two days I'm your doctor and I have a vested interest in getting your diabetes stable.'

'I like sugar.'

'You had enough last night to keep you going for a week.'

And she knew he was right, he thought. Her protests were almost instinctive—the cry of a kid who'd been protected since diagnosis, told what to eat and when, who'd not been given a chance to make her own choices.

'I'm not silly and I'm not a child,' she muttered, confirming what he'd thought.

'I know you're not. And of course you can have marmalade.'

'Your generosity overwhelms me.'

'Good,' he said cheerfully. 'Let me look at your hand.'

She held it out for inspection. He lifted a corner of the dressing and nodded.

'It's looking good. If you stay here and work you'll need to be extra careful. Glove up for everything.'

'Yes, Grandpa.'

'The correct term is *Doctor*. Say, "*Yes, Doctor*".'

'Won't,' she said and grinned, and he looked down into her face, that smattering of freckles, at those gorgeous auburn curls and...

And he had to get out of here.

She was messing with his equilibrium.

'Call Lorna if you need anything,' he said and she glowered.

'Why is Lorna staying? Ruby's going to her friends. Hamster and I are fine.'

'Humour me,' he told her. 'Lorna will stay until after lunch, just until I'm sure that you're...safe.'

'I don't like being safe,' she snapped and he grinned and patted her head as if he was patting Ruby's head.

Except it wasn't like that at all. It felt...different. Intimate.

Okay?

'Says the woman who's just been playing with snakes,' he told her. 'You don't like being safe? You know, Dr Hargreaves, I'm very sure that you do.'

Polly slept on and off for the rest of the day. She woke late afternoon and looked at the time and nearly had kittens. Five o'clock? Where had the day gone? She must have been more shocked than she'd realised.

Lorna had brought in sandwiches around midday. She'd eaten two. The other plus her untouched mug of coffee still sat on her bedside table.

Two days' rest. 'That's enough,' she told herself and headed across to the bathroom and showered—just a little grateful for the hand rail—and then tugged on jeans and a T-shirt and pulled a comb through her curls.

Hamster was still under her bed. The rest of the house was in silence.

She ate her remaining sandwiches—yeah, she did have

to be careful—checked her blood sugars and felt smug again and then headed to the kitchen.

No one.

There was a note from Lorna on the kitchen table.

I've had to go, Dr Hargreaves, but Dr Denver thinks you'll be okay. My number's on the pad by the phone if you need me. Ruby's staying at Talia's for a sleepover. Dr Denver has some emergency over at the hospital. He says help yourself to what you need and he'll see you as soon as he can. Fridge is full. Good luck.

She hardly needed good luck. She opened the fridge and stared in and thought it would take a small army to eat their way through this.

She meandered through the empty house feeling a bit intrusive, a bit weird. It was still very much Hugo's parents' home, she thought, furnished and decorated over years of raising a family. There were pictures of Hugo and a girl who was evidently Grace as babies, as they grew up. There were pictures of high school graduations, Hugo's medical graduation. Happy snaps.

Though Polly could see the telltale signs of early depression on Grace's face as soon as she reached her teens. Hugo smiled obediently at the camera. Some of his smiles said he was long-suffering but Grace's smiles seemed forced.

As were the smiles Grace produced in later photos, taken with Ruby.

Depression... *Aagh.* It was a grey fog, thick sludge, permeating everything and destroying lives.

And now it had destroyed Hugo's.

But had it been destroyed? He'd had to leave Sydney, commit himself to his family.

It'd be the same if Polly had to stay in Sydney, commit herself to her family.

'He has the bigger load to bear,' Polly said out loud, though then she thought of Hugo ruffling Ruby's hair and saw there would be compensations. And this did seem like an awesome place to live.

'But people probably think that about the six-star places my parents want to cocoon me in,' she muttered and thought: *enough*.

What she needed was work. Or at least an introduction to work.

She thought back to the note:

Dr Denver has some emergency over at the hospital...

Work. *Excellent.*

She found one of Hugo's white coats. It was a bit too big—okay, it was a lot too big, but with the sleeves rolled up she decided she looked almost professional.

'See you later,' she told Hamster but Hamster heaved himself to his feet and padded determinedly after her.

'Are you my minder?' she demanded and he wagged his tail and stuck close.

'Has he told you to bite me if I'm not sensible?'

Hamster wagged some more and she sighed and gave up and headed across to the hospital, her minder heading after her.

CHAPTER NINE

SURGEONS WEREN'T TRAINED to cope with human conflict. Surgeons operated.

Yes, surgeons consulted pre-operatively. Yes, they visited their patients at their bedsides, but consultations were done within the confines of appointments, and patient visits were made with a nurse hovering close by, ready to whisk away all but the closest of friends or family.

Death, however, observed no such restrictions. Max Hurley had passed away peacefully in his sleep, aged ninety-seven. He'd been in the nursing home section of the hospital for the last twelve months, during which time his daughter Isobel had been a constant visitor, having nursed him at home for years. His wife had died ten years back. Hugo had assumed there was little other family.

Two hours after his death, he'd learned how wrong he was. A vast extended family had descended on the place like a swarm of locusts. Isobel, seventy years old and frail herself, was jammed into a chair at the edge of the room while her family railed around her.

One of the older men in the group looked almost ready to have a medical incident himself. He was red in the face and the veins on his forehead were bulging. 'I can't believe it!' he was shouting. 'He's left her the whole blasted farm. She's seventy. A spinster. What the hell…? It's a family farm. It's hard up against my place. The old man always intended the farms to be joined. We'll be contesting…'

'There's no need!' another man snapped. 'Isobel will be reasonable, won't you, Isobel?' The men were standing over her, obviously furious. 'But, as for your farms being joined… We'll split, fair down the middle. You get half, Bert, and I'll get the other half. Isobel, we can organise you a nice little retirement unit in town…'

Isobel was surrounded by her family, but what a family! She had a buxom woman sitting on either side of her. One was even hugging her, but she looked…

Small. He could think of no better adjective. Her father's death seemed to have shrunk her.

Any man's death diminishes me… It was a quote from John Donne and, looking down at the helpless Isobel, he thought, even though her dad had been almost a hundred, that diminishment was just as powerful.

'Do you want everyone to leave?' he asked Isobel, thinking she needed time to be alone with her father, but she shook her head.

'N…no. These are my family.'

Family. This was her call, but oh, he felt for her. Trapped by loving…

But then, suddenly, standing at the door was Polly. Her white coat reached her knees, with the sleeves rolled up two or three times. Her freckles stood out in her still pale face, accentuating the flame of her curls, but her green eyes were flashing professionalism—and determination.

She was wearing a stethoscope around her neck. A red one. It was inscribed, he thought, fascinated. *What the heck…?*

Who had a personally inscribed stethoscope?

'I'm sorry but I need you all to leave,' she said and

he stopped thinking about personalised stethoscopes and stared at her in amazement.

He'd thought of her as small, frail, ill.

She sounded like a boom box with the volume turned up full.

'I'm Dr Hargreaves and I'm here to organise the death certificate,' she said so loudly that she cut across arguments, squashing the gathering that was threatening to become a riot. 'Dr Denver has asked me to confirm his diagnosis and I have limited time. I need the immediate next of kin. Who's that?'

After a moment's stunned silence Isobel put up a timid hand.

Polly nodded. 'You can stay. Everyone else must leave.'

'Why?' the oldest of the arguing men demanded. 'What the…?'

'If you wish to avoid a coroner's inquest and possible autopsy then this is what has to happen.' Polly glanced at her watch. 'My time is precious. Could you leave now?'

'You're the doc who got bitten by a snake.'

'Yes, which has pushed my workload to crazy limits before Dr Denver leaves on vacation. Go now, please, or I'll be forced to request an independent assessment from Sydney.'

'When can we come back?'

'When I've made my assessment and, since I've never treated this patient, it may be a while. I suggest…' She hesitated and looked at Isobel, and then at Hugo.

'This is Isobel,' Hugo told her, starting to enjoy himself.

'I suggest Isobel will tell you when it's possible,' Polly continued smoothly. 'Meanwhile, my apologies for the inconvenience but you have two minutes to say your goodbyes before I must start work.'

'We're family,' the closest guy muttered and Polly nodded.

'I can see that, and my condolences, but I'm afraid Isobel needs to face this alone.'

And then she stood back and crossed her arms and waited.

She was superb, Hugo thought. If he didn't know she was talking nonsense—in truth he'd already signed the death certificate—he'd have been totally taken in.

'Why do you need to worry about a death certificate?' one of the men demanded. 'He just died of old age.'

'That's nonsense,' Polly snapped. 'How old are you?'

'I…seventy-two.' There was something about Polly that said *Don't mess with me*, and the guy clearly got it.

'So you're older than your prescribed three score years and ten. If you drop dead now, surely you'd expect us to dignify your death with a diagnosis. Not just dismiss it as old age.'

'Yes, but…'

'But what? Do extra years mean fewer rights, less respect?'

'No, but…'

'Then please leave and let me get on with my work.' And, to Hugo's further astonishment, she stared at her watch and started toe tapping. Less than one minute later the room was clear and the door closed behind them.

As the door closed Isobel gave a muffled sob and crossed to the bed and hugged her father.

How had Polly understood this? Hugo thought, stunned. How had she figured so fast that Isobel desperately needed time alone? That sometimes family wasn't wanted.

'We'll come back in an hour,' he said gently and touched Isobel's shoulder. 'Or earlier, if you want. The bell's here. Just press it if you need it.'

Isobel's tear-stained face turned up to them. 'Thank

you. I didn't think… When I got the call to say he was going I rang Henry to ask him to feed the dogs and suddenly they were all here. I didn't even know they knew the contents of the will. And…'

'And it doesn't matter,' Hugo said gently. 'All those things can be sorted later. I think it'd be a good idea if we got Ron Dawson—he's your dad's lawyer, isn't he?— to take responsibility for any questions. If anyone asks, just say Ron's in charge. No more questions, Isobel. No more worry. For now it's simply time to say goodbye to your dad.'

And he ushered Polly out of the room and closed the door behind them.

Wherever Isobel's obnoxious family were, they were no longer here. The silence after the din was almost tangible.

Joe came round the corner from the nurses' station, his arms above his head in a gesture of triumph. 'You're a champ, Doc Hargreaves,' he boomed. 'A clean knockout. You can come and work here any day.'

'Did you set that up?' Hugo asked faintly and Joe grinned.

'All I did was tell Polly that you and Isobel were surrounded by a rabid pack of mercenary relatives and she went off like a firecracker. I listened from out in the corridor. Did you ever hear anything like it? A couple of them asked how long before they could go back in and I said our Doc Hargreaves is known for thorough work. A detailed examination, pathology, maybe even scans. It could take until tomorrow.'

'Scans…' Hugo managed and Polly grinned happily up at Joe and Joe high-fived her with her good hand and suddenly Hugo was left feeling a bit…

Jealous? Jealous of his fifty-year-old head nurse high-fiving his colleague? He had to be kidding.

'Of course, scans,' Polly said happily. 'You have to scan

a patient very thoroughly when you're looking for cause of death.' She tugged up her jeans and held up her still swollen foot. 'If you hadn't scanned me you might have missed the snake bite. See? Two little holes. Scans are vital and they can take as much time as Isobel needs.'

Hugo choked. Joe guffawed and high-fived Polly again then a bell rang down the corridor and Joe took himself off and Hugo was left with Polly.

She was amazing.

She was gorgeous!

'So,' she said, turning brisk again. 'Are you going to show me your hospital?' And she was back to being a colleague, purely professional, except her coat was too big and her hair was too red and her toenails were crimson and…

And she was a colleague.

'Sure,' he said and managed to do a decent professional tour of his hospital without once—or maybe once but that was professional, as she bumped her leg on a trolley and he had to make sure the swollen ankle was still okay—looking at those amazing toenails.

And she was terrific. Any doubts he might have had about her ability to care for the medical needs of Wombat Valley were put to rest fast. She was just…right.

He now had four patients in his nursing home beds—yes, Max had just died, but over the last twenty-four hours he'd had two new admissions. Christmas often did that. The family was heading away for the holiday, Dad couldn't cope on his own and the easiest solution was respite care. Or a lonely senior citizen was suddenly overwhelmed with the memories of Christmases past and got chest pain or stopped eating, or even forgot normal care and fell…

Hazel Blacksmith was one such lady. She'd fallen chopping her firewood last night. Her hip had proven to be badly bruised rather than broken but she lay in bed, a ball of misery, refusing to be comforted.

But Polly didn't acknowledge misery. 'Hey, how lucky are you?' Polly demanded as Hugo introduced her and explained the diagnosis. 'Just a bruised hip? If someone made me chop wood I'd probably end up suffering from amputation from the knee down.'

'I've chopped wood all me life,' Hazel told her in a firmer voice than Hugo had heard since her neighbour had brought her in. 'I don't cut meself.'

'And you don't get bitten by snakes either, I'll bet,' Polly said. 'Wise woman. Look at this.' And she stuck her leg in the air for Hazel to see her snake bite.

'I heard you got bit,' Hazel said cautiously.

'It was Dr Denver's fault.' Polly cast a darkling look at Hugo. 'He trapped the snake with his shenanigans in the truck, so when I went to rescue them it was ready to attack.'

And Hazel's lips twitched. 'Shenanigans…'

'Men,' Polly said. 'You can't trust them to do anything right. Holding snakes by the tail is the least of it. Would you mind if I had a look at your bruise? I've much gentler hands than Dr Denver.'

They were gentle. Hugo watched as Polly performed a careful examination of the old lady—a scan? She gently probed and teased and by the end of the examination the old lady was smitten and Hugo was getting close himself.

What a gem! He would be able to go away for Christmas and leave the hospital in her charge.

But…why did going away for Christmas suddenly not seem as desirable?

'Are you staying in for Christmas?' Polly asked cheerfully as she tucked Hazel's bedclothes back around her and Hazel looked brighter than she had since Hugo had admitted her.

'Dr Denver thinks I should.'

'Then I concur,' Polly said warmly. 'But I need to

warn you, the Christmas dinner menu here is looking a bit dodgy. However, we have three more days. I'll see what I can do. I'll ring my mother's chef and get some advice.'

'Your mother has a chef?' Hazel sounded stunned.

And Hugo was stunned as well. Not only did this woman come from a privileged background, she was happily admitting it.

'Doesn't everyone's mother?' Polly said happily. 'Left to my own devices, I'm a beans on toast girl, but this is Christmas. We all have to make some sacrifices, and ringing Raoul might be the least of them. Just as long as he promises not to tell my mother where I am.'

She wasn't making sacrifices at all, Polly thought happily as she sat on the veranda that evening. She was about to have a very good time.

Her ankle still hurt. Her hand ached, but not so much as to mess with her equanimity. This was a beautiful little hospital, full of easy patients, and she was pretty sure she could cope.

Her silver tree was up in the living room, surrounded by origami gifts and a few real ones as well.

Hamster was lying by her side on the top step. He was due to head back to his temporary carer's but she intended to have a word with Hugo about that. She wouldn't mind Hamster staying here for Christmas as well.

She'd do a bit of online shopping, she decided. If she paid enough for express postage, she could get heaps of good stuff here. Lots of treats for her coterie of oldies in the hospital.

Would Isobel like to come too? Maybe she could take her tree over to the hospital and have Christmas dinner over there?

Maybe she could wear her little red alpine dress and

the wig with the blonde pigtails. And her crimson boots and the Santa hat. She just happened to have packed them.

She grinned. Three suitcases… A girl could never be prepared enough.

The screen door opened behind her and Hugo emerged carrying two mugs of tea. She nudged over on her step, heaving Hamster to the side as well, and he sat down beside her.

Ma and Pa Kettle, she thought, and the feeling was sort of…okay.

More than okay. Good.

She liked this man.

Actually…

Um…don't go there. He'd be gone before Christmas. He'd come back in the New Year, she'd do a quick handover and then she'd have no reason to see him again.

Her bounce faded a little as she took the offered mug and she gave herself a swift inward kick. What was she thinking? Having fantasies about a man who was so steeped in domesticity he couldn't get out of this valley?

Falling for a man who was committed to love?

Love was what she was running from, she thought dryly. Love was why she'd packed her car and headed for the hills.

Love was chains, blackmail, guilt. Love was your mother watching every mouthful you ate and mentally counting insulin dosages. Love was catching your boyfriend phoning in to report how you were— 'She's great, Mrs Hargreaves, and of course I'm looking after her. No, of course I won't let her get tired…'

Toerag. She glowered at the absent Marcus and took her tea and stared morosely out into the dark.

'Hamster been annoying you, then?' Hugo asked mildly and she caught herself and managed a rueful smile.

'Not so much.'

'Are you hurting? How's your…?'

'Don't you dare fuss!'

'Okay,' he said cautiously.

Silence.

It wasn't bad tea. Good and hot.

It was very hard to appreciate tea when Hugo was sitting beside her.

'Where would you be now?' she asked, suddenly needing to know. 'If it wasn't for Ruby.'

'Sydney.'

Of course. 'Working?'

'Possibly. If I wasn't on call, though, I'd be in a supper club around the corner from the hospital. It has a roof top bar that overlooks the harbour. Most of my friends use it.'

'And you miss it?'

'What do you think?'

'And your work? Your surgery?'

'Almost more than I can bear,' he said and she flinched at the sudden and honest sound of gut-wrenching loss.

'So why don't you take Ruby back to Sydney?'

'If I had Ruby in Sydney, do you believe for a moment that I'd be in the supper club?'

'You could get a housekeeper.'

'Yes, I could. The problem is that I love Ruby.'

'She's prickly.'

'Tough to love. She is. She lets me, though. Inch by inch.'

'Is it worth it?'

'What, hoping for Ruby's love in return?'

'I guess,' she said, doubtfully though, because she wasn't quite sure where she was going with this.

'I don't have a choice,' Hugo said gently. 'And I can't count its worth. I met Ruby when she was two days old. My sister was in a mess. I was called to a hospital up in Darwin because Grace was drug addicted and unable to cope. She went into rehab. I took four weeks off work, then my parents took over. But for those four weeks... I held Ruby in the palm of my hands—literally—and she's been there ever since.'

And what was there in that to make her tear up? Nothing, she thought, frantically sniffing, and Hugo handed her a tissue and she thought this was just the sort of man who walked round with spare tissues in his pocket because something about him made you...made her...

Back off. She needed to back off. She'd been here for less than three days and suddenly it seemed as if a fine gossamer web was closing around her. The web she'd run from.

A trap, every bit as claustrophobic as the one Hugo found himself in.

She stood up, so suddenly she splashed tea on Hamster, who looked up reproachfully and then started licking the tea from his paws.

Hugo looked up too, but not reproachfully. It was as if he understood where she was coming from.

And that was a scary thought all by itself.

'I should go to bed,' she said a bit shakily and he nodded.

'You should.'

And then his phone rang.

He answered it, listened, then clicked it closed and rose as well.

'Work?'

'What do you think?'

'Anything I can help with?'

'You're going to bed.'

'Is that an order?'

'Um...no.'

'So tell me.'

'Groin and knee injuries,' he said. 'Terry Oakshot.

Local farmer and amateur footy player. Late twenties. This sounds like a party prank gone wrong. His mates are bringing him in now.'

'I'll stay up until I see what the problem is.'

'No need. If I can't handle it I'll send him out.'

'Evacuate when you have two doctors?'

'If I need to evacuate, I'll evacuate.'

'Of course you will,' she said warmly. 'But if it's not too complicated, don't forget I'm not just a pretty face.' She grinned and took his mug. 'Okay, Doc Denver, you go see what the problem is, but yell if you need me. I'll go put my feet up and garner strength for the onslaught to come. Ooh, I wouldn't mind a good onslaught. I'm a wee bit bored.'

CHAPTER TEN

ONE LOOK AT the mess that was Terry Oakshot's knee confirmed that he needed a surgeon skilled in reconstruction. The blood supply wasn't compromised, though. There was no need for immediate intervention for his knee. He needed decent pain relief and transport as soon as possible to the experts in Sydney.

Unfortunately, it wasn't his knee that was causing Terry to whimper. He was clutching his groin in agony.

It would be agony too, Hugo thought, as Joe helped examine him.

A fast conversation with the mates who'd brought him in had given him all the information he needed. The boys had been having a pre-Christmas party in the footy ground's stadium. After a few beers someone had shouted for Terry to come down to ground level to kick the footy. After a beer or six, Terry had decided there was a faster way than the stairs and he'd tried to slide down the banister.

It hadn't been a good idea. Terry had smashed groin first into the bottom post, then toppled onto the wooden stairs. The knee was bad. His groin was worse. One side of his scrotum was swollen and cut, and one testicle was higher than the other. The less injured side didn't look too good either, and Terry was retching with pain.

'What's going on?' he moaned as his wife arrived.

Maree was in her early twenties and seemed terrified. She looked as if she'd been baking. Her face was streaked white with flour, and it was whiter still with shock.

'You seem to have given yourself a testicular torsion,' he told him. 'Terry, your knee's broken and it'll need special- ist surgery in Sydney, but what's happened to your groin is more urgent. The spermatic cord running to your testicles has been damaged. The cord's a blood vessel, so the blood supply's been cut. We need to work fast to get it sorted.'

'Fast'd be good, Doc,' Terry moaned. 'Fast like now?'

And, with that, Polly's presence came slamming back at him, bringing a wash of relief. He had an anaesthetist.

'You know I have another doctor working here?'

'The one that got bit by the snake?' Terry demanded.

'She's recovered.' Or almost recovered. She could still do with an early night but this needed to take precedence. 'Terry, you and Maree don't have any kids yet, do you?'

'No!' And Maree had understood the inference faster than Terry. 'But we want them. The spermatic cord... Doc, you're not saying...?'

'I'm thinking we need to operate fast,' Hugo told them both. 'I'll get Joe to ring Polly. She can do the anaesthetic.'

'Polly...' Maree managed. 'What sort of name is that for a doctor?'

'It's short for Pollyanna. It's a great name for a fine doc- tor,' he told her. 'Wait and see.'

Polly didn't see the wound until they were in Theatre. Terry declared he 'wasn't going to get looked at down there by a female'.

'You'll get looked at by anyone who can fix you,' Maree snapped and clutched Polly as soon as she saw her. 'We want kids,' she stammered. 'You get him right, no matter what.'

'We'll do our best,' Polly told her. She'd arrived at the

hospital fast, she was heading to scrub, and she had no time to waste.

Once in Theatre she could focus, and she needed to. Terry was a big man, he was deeply shocked and he'd been drinking. In an ideal world she'd wait for him to sober up, but there wasn't time.

She ran through the options in her head, talked them through with Hugo. Then they went for it. With Terry safely asleep and intubated, Joe started disinfecting the injured area. For the first time she saw the extent of the damage.

'Ouch,' she said and Hugo cast her a look that could almost be amused.

'You might say that.'

But he was calm. She watched him assess the wound carefully. She watched as he started the procedure as if he'd done it a thousand times.

He was a thoracic surgeon. This was a job for a trained urologist.

He didn't look concerned. He looked…competent.

He's good, she thought, and then she relaxed a little, although not very much because her anaesthetic skills were basic, but they were good enough to spare her time to watch Hugo work.

No highly skilled urologist could do a better job than this, she thought. Repairing a damaged spermatic cord was tricky at the best of times, and that was in a large hospital with every piece of modern gadgetry. Large hospitals had magnification, monitors showing exactly what was happening. Large hospitals had skilled backup.

Hugo had a semi-trained anaesthetist, Joe and himself.

If she hadn't been here…

What then?

Hugo would have needed to send him to Sydney, she

thought, and by the time Terry reached Sydney, he and his wife would be fated to be childless or needing a sperm donor.

What if this had happened when she was here by herself?

For the first time, her bold foray into bush medicine looked less than wise. She would have failed this couple.

How could Hugo work here by himself?

'If you hadn't been here I would have talked Joe through the anaesthesia. We've done it before,' Hugo said.

She glanced up at him in shock. 'How do you know what I'm thinking?'

'You have an entirely readable face. You were concentrating, concentrating, concentrating, and suddenly you looked petrified. I checked the monitors, saw you had nothing patient-wise to be petrified about and figured you had to be projecting yourself into the future.'

'He has eyes in the back of his head.' Joe was grinning. 'You'll get used to it.'

'She won't,' Hugo said. 'We'll work together tomorrow and then I'll be gone.'

But he'd be back, Polly thought as his skilled fingers continued their fight to repair the appalling damage. In the New Year he'd be back here being a solo doctor with his little niece. He'd be on his own and she'd be...

Where?

She hadn't figured that out yet. One locum at a time. Wandering...

She'd thought she'd quite like to do a stint for an aid agency, working overseas, getting right away from her parents.

Her diabetes was the killer there. No aid agency, working in Third World conditions, would accept a Type One diabetic.

Maybe that was one of the reasons she wanted it so much. Maybe the locum thing was part of it.

Locum to locum to locum? Never settling? Never doing family?

That was what she'd decided. No more fuss. She couldn't bear it.

Doing things despite her diabetes…

Was this another way her diabetes was controlling her?

'I'm thinking…' Hugo's voice was a lazy drawl but there was satisfaction behind it and it drew her attention back to where it should be. 'I'm thinking we might just have succeeded in repairing this mess. The left one's possible and the right one's looking certain. We'll transfer him to Sydney for his knee and get him checked by the urologist while he's there but I'm thinking we've done the thing.'

'Yes!' Joe said, but Polly didn't say anything at all.

Locum to locum to locum…

That was what she'd dreamed of. Why did it suddenly seem so bleak?

And why did what she'd thought of as a dream suddenly seem like running away?

There was no more time for introspection. Polly reversed the anaesthetic, Terry started to come round and Hugo sent her out to talk to Maree.

'She won't believe Joe. Something about the beard. Polly, go tell her Terry's okay.'

'So she'll believe a whippersnapper who came on the scene in polka dots with snake bite instead of a beard?' Joe demanded.

'Absolutely. If Polly, who's hung upside down with snakes, decrees someone's safe, then…'

'Then she'll think Polly has a weird definition of safe,' Joe retorted and he and Hugo chuckled and Polly looked from one to the other and thought that even though Hugo was trapped in this little hospital there were compensations.

It was like family...

Family... There was that word again.

'I have drips to adjust and you deserve to be the bearer of good tidings,' Hugo told her. 'How's the hand?'

She hadn't even noticed her hand. She'd double gloved because she couldn't scrub the dressing and then she'd forgotten about it.

Her ankle wasn't hurting. She couldn't feel a bruise.

She felt...a mile high.

Successful surgery... There was nothing like it.

She thought suddenly of her parents' recriminations when she'd decided on medicine and she knew, without doubt, that medicine at least wasn't running from her parents' world. Medicine was what she most wanted to do.

She met Hugo's gaze and he was smiling and once again she got that blast of knowledge that told her he understood what she was feeling.

'Good, isn't it?' he said softly and he smiled at her—and he might as well have kissed her.

It felt like a kiss. A caress from four feet apart.

And Joe was smiling at them, beaming from one ear to the other, and Polly stepped from the table a bit too fast and could have tripped, but she didn't. She wasn't that stupid.

She felt pretty stupid. She backed out of Theatre feeling totally discombobulated.

Terry's wife was waiting outside, sitting huddled on the room's big couch. There were people around her, two older couples who looked as if they'd come in a hurry. One of the women was wearing a crimson-smeared apron—very smeared. Her husband had matching crimson smears on his gingham shirt.

They all looked up at her as she emerged and Maree moaned and put her face in her hands.

'Hey, it's all right, love.' The bigger of the two men put a rough hand on her shoulder. He was watching Polly's face. 'The Doc's smiling. You're smiling, aren't you, Doc? You wouldn't do that if our Terry was bad.'

'I'm smiling,' Polly told them, smiling even more just to prove the point. 'Dr Denver's operated and everything went as smoothly as we could hope. Everything's been put back together. Terry's not quite recovered from the anaesthetic yet but as soon as Dr Denver's set up the drips—he'll be administering pain relief, fluids and antibiotics—you'll be able to see him.'

'Oh.' Maree put her face behind her hands and burst into tears. The crimson lady knelt down and gathered her into her arms.

'There, dear, what did I tell you? Terry always bounces back.' And then she glared up at her husband. 'I told you. Now we have a pot full of burned toffee and a hundred uncoated toffee apples for nothing.'

There was uncertain laughter, the beginnings of relief, and then Maree put her head up again.

'And he will…we will be able to have babies?' she whispered.

Polly heard the door swing open behind her. She didn't have to turn to see it was Hugo—she was starting to sense this man.

Why? What was it between them?

He didn't say anything, though—it seemed this was her call.

'Maree, Dr Denver's done everything we can to make sure that can still happen. We think we've succeeded. I've just watched him operate and I don't think any city surgeon could have done better.'

'Excellent,' the toffee apple lady said. 'And will he be home for Christmas?'

'He won't be, Lexie.' And Hugo took over, putting a

hand on Polly's arm as if to signal that he was about to impart medical advice from the team. It was a solid way to go, Polly thought, presenting a united front, and why it made her feel…

Um, no. She wasn't going there. Right now, she couldn't.

'Guys, we're going to send him on to Sydney,' Hugo said, firmly now. 'The operation I just performed was to his groin and, as far as I can tell, it's successful. But his knee needs a competent orthopaedic surgeon. I'd also like him checked by a specialist urologist. We'll send him on to Sydney Central as soon as possible. It'll take about an hour to get the chopper here for transfer. Maree, if you'd like to go with him, I'll tell the hospital you'll need accommodation—they have self-contained flats for just this purpose.'

The group had been starting to relax. Now, as one, they froze.

'But it's Christmas,' Maree whispered. 'We can't go to Sydney for Christmas.'

'You don't have a choice,' Hugo said, still gently, and Maree burst into tears again.

'Hey.' The toffee apple lady still had her in her arms. 'Hey, sweetheart, it's okay. We'll manage.'

'But what about Grandma?' Maree lifted a woebegone face to Hugo. 'What about you, Mum?'

'We'll manage.'

'You can't. Grandma's got Alzheimer's,' Maree explained, looking wildly up at Hugo. 'She's so confused and she gets angry with Mum, but if Terry and I are there she calms down and Mum relaxes and enjoys Christmas. If we're not there…'

'We'll take care of things.' The other woman spoke then, a woman who by her looks had to be Terry's mum. 'We'll look after everyone.'

'But we'll be by ourselves for Christmas.'

'With a recovering husband. Surely that's the most

important thing?' It was Terry's dad, glancing back at the door into Theatre, but all three women turned and glared at him.

'Christmas with family...' Maree snapped. 'What's more important than that?'

'Now you know very well that health comes first,' her mum said. 'But you know what? Terry'll be recovering. And you know Aldi Baker? She moved to her son's big house in the centre of Sydney and now her son's gone to Paris for Christmas. She's gone with him and she said if ever we want a base in Sydney we can use that house. So why not now? Why not pack all of us up and we can go to Sydney?' She looked up at Terry's parents. 'You too. Aldi says there's six bedrooms—can you believe that? It's as if it's meant. We can pick up everything—except the toffee apples—they might be well and truly stuffed and they were just for the Christmas Eve fete at the school anyway. We can take everything down there tomorrow morning. If needs be, I bet we could have Christmas in Terry's hospital room.'

'The specialists might even let him out by then,' Hugo conceded, smiling as the despair in the room turned to tentative excitement. 'He'll still need tests but if he stays in Sydney... No promises, but it's possible...'

'There you go then,' Maree's mum said and before Hugo could protect himself she'd flung her arms around him and planted what was probably a very sticky kiss on his cheek. She hugged Polly for good measure and then headed back to hug each and every one of her family.

Family...

And Polly was suddenly staring at them all thinking... *family.*

She was running away.

Why was she running?

Enough. She was tired, she decided. She was overwrought. Her emotions were all over the place. What she needed right now was bed. Hugo was right—bed rest.

Somewhere away from Hugo.

Why did the presence of this man unsettle her so much? A week ago she'd never met him.

Why was the concept of family suddenly everywhere?

'I'll see you back at the house,' she mumbled and Hugo took her arm and led her to the door.

'I'll take you.'

'It's two minutes' walk.'

'I'll take you,' he said more firmly, and then he turned back to Terry's family. 'I'll be back in a few minutes. Joe's looking after Terry. He'll let me know the minute he's awake enough for you to see him. But, Maree, that chopper lands in an hour so it might be better to grab some clothes now…'

'We'll all be in Sydney by midday tomorrow,' her mum said. 'We can bring everything she needs.'

'And I don't need toffee apples, Mum,' Maree managed and everyone laughed and Hugo's arm tightened around Polly's shoulders and he led her to the door.

'I do need to take Polly home,' he said. 'She's still suffering after-effects…'

'From the snake bite.' Terry's dad finished the sentence for him and came forward and took her hand—her bad hand—and gripped it and didn't even notice her wince. 'You're amazing. Thank God you came to the Valley, girl. If you'd like to stay for ever, you'd be very, very welcome.'

Her hand hurt. The grip had been hard.

Her ankle hurt.

Actually, all of her hurt. The aches and bruises that had been put on the backburner by adrenaline now started to make themselves known.

She really was wobbly. She really did need Hugo's arm

around her as they headed across the path from hospital to house.

Or she told herself that. Because somehow it felt…okay.

It felt as if his hold was somehow linking her to…reality?

That was a nonsense thought, but then her head was producing a lot of nonsense at the moment.

It was his skill, she told herself. His surgeon's fingers had been amazing to watch. Skill was always a turn-on.

Skill had nothing to do with it.

Hugo was a turn-on.

She was so aware of him. She was behaving like a teenager with a crush, she decided, but the thought was fleeting because the sensation of being held, being cared for, was so infinitely sweet…

They reached the veranda steps. He took her arm and she let herself lean on him as she climbed.

She hated being cared for. Didn't she?

'I need to go back,' he said, and she heard a reluctance in his voice that matched hers. 'I need to organise transport.'

'Of course you do.'

'Polly…'

'Mmm?'

'Thank you.'

'There's no need to thank me,' she said, whispering suddenly although there was no need to whisper because there was no one to hear but Hamster, who'd wagged his tail once when they'd reached the top of the steps and then gone back to sleep. He was a dog obviously used to the comings and goings of his master. 'I believe I'm being paid.'

'Not enough,' he said and she turned and smiled. She knew her smile was shaky. She knew she was too close and she knew what she was doing was unwise—but she was doing it anyway.

'I'd do it for free,' she murmured and his smile suddenly faded and so did hers. And his hands came out to take hers and almost unconsciously—as if she had no say in what was happening at all—she tilted her chin in a gesture that meant only one thing.

That meant he had nothing to do but lower his mouth to hers.

That meant he had nothing to do but kiss her.

She'd never been kissed like this.

She must have been, she thought dazedly. She'd had boyfriends since her early teens. Her mum had been matchmaking for ever, and Polly wasn't exactly a shrinking violet. Boyfriends were fun. Kissing was nice.

This kissing wasn't nice. This kiss was…

Mind-blowing. There were no other words big enough, for from the moment his mouth met hers she seemed to be melting. It was as if his body was somehow merging into hers, supporting her, warming her, becoming part of her.

Her senses were exploding.

His mouth enveloped hers and all she could do was taste him, feel him, want him. She was kissing with a fierceness that almost frightened her.

She'd never been out of control with her boyfriends. She dated 'nice' boys.

This was no nice boy. This was a man who was as hungry as she was, as demanding, as committed…

Hungry? Demanding? Committed? That described her. She could be none of those things, yet right now she was all three. She surrendered herself to his kiss and she gloried in it. Her fingers entwined themselves in his hair, tugging him closer. She was standing on tiptoe but his arms were around her waist, pulling her up, so the kiss could sink deeper...

She was on fire.

Hugo... His name was a whisper, a shout, a declaration all by itself. Pollyanna Hargreaves was right out of her comfort zone. She was right out of control.

If he picked her up and carried her to his bed right now, would she submit?

There was no *submit* about it. If she had her way it'd be Polly who'd be doing the carrying. She wanted him!

She couldn't have him. Even as the crazy idea hit, the need to carry this straight through to the bedroom, he was putting her back.

It was a wrench like no other. Their mouths parted and she felt...lost.

'I need to go.' His voice was ragged. 'Terry needs...'

'Y...yes.'

He took a step back, turned away and then paused and turned back. 'That wasn't a casual kiss.'

'You could have fooled me,' she managed and he gave a twisted smile.

'Polly, what I'm feeling...'

And suddenly it was out there, this thing between them. Lust, love—whatever. Only it couldn't be love, Polly thought dazedly, because they'd only known each other for three days and no one fell in love that fast.

Lust, then. The way she was feeling...certainly it was lust.

'Yeah, I'm feeling it, too,' she managed. 'So it's just as well you're going away soon because I'm just over a possessive boyfriend. And I don't do casual affairs, or family either, for that matter, and you have a daughter...'

'A niece.'

'A niece.' She closed her eyes as she corrected herself.

A waif-like kid who Hugo loved. Why did that make him seem more sexy, not less?

Why was Ruby suddenly in the equation?

'Hugo, I don't do family,' she said again and surprisingly her voice sounded almost calm. 'That's why I'm here—to get away from ties.'

'This isn't some kind of trap.' He said it fast.

Trap? How could she ever think of a kiss as a trap?

'Of course it's not,' she agreed. 'It was a kiss, simply that. Excellent surgical skills always turn me on, Dr Denver.'

'So if I had warts on my nose, a sagging middle and a disinclination to wash, but I removed an appendix with style, you'd still turn into a puddle of molten passion?'

He was smiling, making things light, and she had to too. 'You'd better believe it.'

'So, on a scale of one to ten…speedy repair of ingrown toenail?'

'Ooh, don't talk dirty,' she managed and scraped up a grin. 'Next you'll be talking laparoscopic gallstone removal and I have no defences.'

He chuckled but it sounded forced. He was as shaken as she was, she thought.

But they were apart now. Work was waiting and they both knew it.

'Bed,' he said and she blinked.

'Is that an order?'

'I guess it is.'

'You're not my doctor.' It suddenly seemed important—incredibly important—to make that clear.

'I know.' He hesitated. 'And in two weeks I won't be your colleague.'

'And I'll be on the other side of the world.'

'Really? Where?'

'Sudan, maybe. Ethiopia.'

'With Type One Diabetes?' He sounded incredulous.

'I can cope.'

'Polly...'

'Don't fuss.'

'I'm not fussing.' Except he was, she thought, and she also thought, with a modicum of self-knowledge, that she'd driven him to fuss. It was like someone with one leg declaring they intended to be a tightrope walker.

She could probably do it.

Her parents would worry.

This man might too, and by making such a declaration...it had been like a slap. *Fuss if you dare; it'll give me an excuse to run.*

It wasn't fair.

'Go,' she told him. 'Work's waiting. The chopper should be here soon.'

'Yes.' But still there was hesitation.

'The kiss was a mistake,' she said. 'An aberration.'

'We both know it was no such thing, but I can't push. I have no right. Polly...'

'Go,' she said. 'No such thing or not, I'm completely uninterested.'

Hugo headed back to the hospital feeling...empty. Gutted?

What had just happened?

He'd been knocked back. He'd kissed her. She'd responded with passion but that passion had given way to sense. She was fiercely independent and wanted to be more so. He had a commitment that would tie him here for life.

He was trapped here. How could he possibly ask a woman to share this trap?

Maybe he could move back to Sydney. Maybe he could pick up the strings of the life he'd known before. He moved in the circles Polly moved in...

Except she wasn't going back to Sydney. She was escaping family and he had Ruby. The life he had in Sydney was over.

The thought of Sydney was like a siren song. He could go back to performing the surgery he'd trained for. He was picking up his family medicine skills here, but the surgical skills he'd fought to gain…to let them fade…

He had no choice but to let them go. Ruby had lost far more than he had. He could take Ruby back to Sydney—of course he could—but apartment life wouldn't suit her or Hamster. He'd be back working twelve-hour days. Ruby wouldn't be surrounded by people who cared about her.

His trap had firmly closed.

He sighed and squared his shoulders and headed up the ramp to the hospital entrance.

A wallaby was sitting by the door.

'Popped in for a check-up?' he asked the little creature. The wallaby seemed to be admiring her reflection in the glass door. 'Or is there anything more urgent I can help you with?'

The wallaby turned and gazed at him, almost thoughtfully. They stared at each other for a long moment and then the helicopter appeared, low and fast, from the east. The wallaby looked up at the sky, looked again at Hugo and then bounded off, back down the ramp and into the bush.

Back to freedom. No ties there.

'I'm not jealous,' Hugo muttered as he headed through the doors and made his way to the waiting Terry. 'I can make a life here.'

Without Polly?

'And that's a stupid thought,' he told himself. 'You made that decision well before Polly came on the scene. How one red-headed, flibbertigibbet doctor can mess with your equanimity…'

'A flibbertigibbet?' he demanded of himself and he

must have said the word too loud because Joe was waiting for him and he raised his brows in enquiry.

'The wallaby,' he explained. 'She was looking at her reflection in the glass door. She's headed back to the bush now. I thought she might have a medical issue, but she was probably just checking her mascara. Flibbertigibbet. Wallabies are like that.'

'Yes, Doctor,' Joe said cautiously. 'Mate, are you... okay?'

'Never better,' he murmured. 'One more day of work and then I'm off for Christmas holidays. Bring it on.'

'You can't wait to get out of here?'

'How can you doubt it?' he demanded, but he thought of Polly standing on the veranda looking after him and he knew that doubt was totally justified.

Polly stayed on the veranda for a very long time.

The kiss stayed with her.

She sank into one of the big cane chairs and Hamster licked her hand and put his big boofy head on her knee. It was almost as if he knew she needed comfort.

Why did she need comfort? What possible reason was there to feel bereft?

Just because someone had kissed her...

Just because someone was impossible.

She should leave now. That was what part of her felt like doing—packing her little sports car and driving away, fast.

That was fear talking—and why was she fearful?

Where was the new brave Polly now? The intrepid Polly who'd walked away from her family, who'd vowed to be independent, who'd hankered after a life free of the obligations of loving?

It had all seemed so simple back in Sydney. Toss in her hospital job. Declare her independence to her parents. Start treating herself as a grown-up.

She wasn't feeling grown-up now. She was feeling... just a little bit stupid.

'Which is stupid all by itself,' she told Hamster. 'Here I am, less than a week into my new life, and I'm questioning everything. I haven't given it a chance. And if I left here...where would I run to? Back to my parents? Not in a month of Sundays. Off to Ethiopia? We both know that's not going to happen. No, all I need to do is stay here, keep my feet firmly on the ground, keep lust solidly damped and get on with my work. And I'll work better if I sleep now.'

But the kiss was still with her, all around her, enveloping her in its sweetness.

'Hugo's back at work and he's probably forgotten all about it,' she told Hamster. 'Men are like that.'

Hamster whined and put a paw on her lap.

'With one exception,' she told him generously. 'And by the way, if Hugo thinks he's taking you back to that boarding place while he's away, he has another think coming. You're staying with me for Christmas.'

Because she didn't want to be alone?

The question was suddenly out there, insidious, even threatening.

She did want to be alone, she told herself. That was what this whole locum bit was about. She'd been cloistered since birth. She needed to find herself.

She didn't need Hugo.

'And he doesn't need me,' she told herself, rising and heading indoors, not because she wanted to but because it was sensible and a woman had to be sensible. She had the remnants of a snake bite and a cut hand to take care of. Medicine... That was what she was here for, and that was what she needed to focus on.

'And nothing else,' she told herself as she passed the tree in the living room with Ruby's stack of origami gifts.

She hoped Ruby was having a happy sleepover with her friend tonight.

'But that's nothing to do with me either,' she told Hamster and she took a couple of deep breaths and poured herself a glass of juice for her bedside, because a woman had to be sensible.

'That's the new me,' she told Hamster as she headed for her bedroom. 'Sensible R Us. I'm Dr Pollyanna Hargreaves, with the frivolous name, but there's nothing else frivolous about me. I'm here to focus on medicine and nothing else. I will not think about Hugo Denver. Not one bit.'

She lied.

She went to bed and lay in the dark and all she could think of was Hugo. All she could feel was Hugo. His kiss enveloped her dreams and she tossed and turned and decided that snake bite venom was insidious.

It had turned one sensible doctor into an idiot.

CHAPTER ELEVEN

POLLY WOKE AND rain was thundering on the roof. It wasn't a shower. This was a deluge.

In Sydney—in fact in any house or hotel she'd ever stayed in—she hardly heard the rain. At most it was a hushed background whisper. Here it was crashing so hard on the iron roof she figured she could sing Christmas carols out loud and no one would hear.

Why not? She did.

Ruby heard her. Two bars into 'Silent Night' there was a scratching on the door. She called, 'Come in,' and Ruby flew in to land on the bed beside her. Hamster arrived straight after. He was wet. Very wet. He leaped onto her bedcovers and shook and Polly yelped and Ruby gave a tentative giggle. A very tentative giggle.

'Is he…is he okay?' she stammered.

Polly surveyed the dog with disgust. He appeared to have taken a mud bath or six.

'He appears okay. Is there a problem?'

'He's scared of thunder. He was outside jumping in puddles when the last bit of thunder came. We got scared.'

'Where's your uncle?' Hamster's wetness was soaking her feet. So much for a nice invalidish sleep-in, she thought, and resigned herself.

'He's over at the hospital.'

'Why are you home?'

'There was thunder in the night. I got scared too, so Talia's mum rang Uncle Hugo and he came and got me.'

So even if they'd indulged in a night of molten passion they would have been hit by kid-interruptus, Polly thought, and then snagged her errant thoughts and shoved them in the place in her brain marked 'Inappropriate'.

'It's raining a lot,' Ruby said, snuggling into Polly's bed as if she had every right to be there. 'Uncle Hugo says it's raining even in Sydney but it'll stop by Christmas so that's okay. And we're leaving first thing in the morning as long as you're better. But he says you're almost better anyway. He says I can stay here with you this morning. He says you have to stay in bed until at least ten o'clock. He says Hamster and I can make you toast but we can't make you coffee because I'm not allowed to use the kettle yet.'

'Your Uncle Hugo is bossy.'

'Yes,' Ruby said happily. 'I like it. My mum wasn't bossy. One day I had to make her a cup of tea and I burned myself. See my scar?' She held up a wrist, where a scar showed the burn had been small but significant. 'Uncle Hugo said Mum shouldn't have asked me but he said she only did 'cos she was sick. But he's not sick so he's allowed to be bossy.'

'And he's at the hospital?'

'Mr Millard's cow got bogged.' Ruby was right under the covers now, nudging Hamster's rear end with her feet. The dog was heaving up and down but grinning his dopey Labrador smile, thunder forgotten. 'And Mr Millard pulled it out with a rope but he fell over when it came out fast. He broke his arm and Uncle Hugo has to put plaster on it. But Polly, I've been looking at our presents and worrying. We won't have a Christmas tree at the beach. Uncle Hugo says it doesn't matter but I think we need one.'

'You definitely need one. You can take mine,' Polly offered.

'But what will you and Hamster have?'

'We'll chop down a gum tree.'

'With an axe?'

'Yes.'

'Uncle Hugo won't let you use an axe.'

'Uncle Hugo's not the boss of me.'

'He just doesn't want us to get burned,' Ruby said worriedly. 'You might hurt yourself.

'I can take care of myself. I'm a grown-up.'

'My mum was a grown-up and she didn't take care of herself. She died.'

There was no answer to that. Another clap of thunder rumbled across the valley. Hamster turned into a quivering mess; Polly and Ruby had to hug him and then the whole bed was pretty much a quivering and soggy mess and Polly decided convalescence had knobs on and she might as well get up.

'You would like to take my Christmas tree?'

Ruby looked through to the living room where the sparkling silver tree shimmered with its party lights on full. 'I don't want you not to have one,' she said longingly, 'but you aren't allowed to use the axe.'

'I'll let Uncle Hugo wield the axe,' Polly conceded. 'But we need more decorations. You're not going to leave me with nothing.'

'We could buy more tinsel.'

'Nonsense.' She was in her element here. Interior decorating had been bred into her—her mother had been making hotel rooms into Christmas-themed fantasies for ever. 'Let's leave the silver tree as it is—we'll pack it tonight for you to take. Then we'll concentrate on Tree Two. Plus making this house Christmassy for me and Hamster. Let's go.'

By two in the afternoon the inhabitants of Wombat Valley were mostly hunkered down. The weather forecast was dire. Leaving the house meant a soaking. Most minor ailments could be put in the worry-about-it-after-Christmas basket, so the population mostly stayed put.

Which meant Hugo didn't call on Polly for help.

Though maybe he should have, he thought as the day went on. The agreement was that she'd join him in the afternoon so she'd get used to the place and he could assess her work…

Except he had assessed her work and it was excellent. She'd given last night's anaesthetic with skill. On her tour of the place she'd moved seamlessly between patients, chatting happily, drawing them out without them realising it. Underneath the chat there were carefully planted medical queries, and skilled responses to the replies. She was good.

More, Polly's reputation had already spread through the Valley. She was the Doc-Who'd-Been-Bitten-Saving-Horace. Horace wasn't particularly popular but he was a local, and Wombat Valley looked after their own.

So she was already accepted. She already knew her way round the hospital. She could have another full day of rest.

Minding Ruby?

He did feel a bit guilty about that, but he'd assumed Ruby would stay at Talia's until midday so he hadn't worried about calling anyone in. And Ruby was quiet. She did her own thing. The monitor was on. He could be home in a heartbeat if he was needed.

He just sort of happened to wander past the monitor a lot.

'They sound like they're having a ball,' Joe told him. Joe was catching up on paperwork at the nurses' station.

The whole hospital seemed as if it was snoozing, and in the silence Polly and Ruby's voices could be heard clearly.

He'd told Polly about the monitor. She'd know whatever she was saying could be overheard but it didn't seem to be cramping her style.

'The flour looks great. No, sprinkle some more on, Ruby, it looks like snow. Hamster, no! It's snow, you idiot, not flour. Oh, heck, it's on your nose—no, don't lick it, it'll turn to paste—no, Hamster, noooo...'

'Uh oh,' Joe said, grinning. 'When my kids sound like that I go in armed with a mop. You want to go home and check?'

'I should...'

'Should what?' Joe said, and eyed him speculatively. 'Think of something else to do? You've been thinking of other something elses to do for the past two hours. Don't you need to pack?'

'I've packed.'

'Then don't you need to go home and spread a little flour?' His brows went up. 'But Dr Hargreaves is there, isn't she? A woman in your living room.'

'With my niece,' he snapped.

'She's gorgeous,' Joe said.

'Ruby's cute.'

'I didn't mean Ruby and you know it. Polly's gorgeous. We're lucky to have her.'

'Yes.'

'But you're going away tomorrow.' His nurse administrator's eyebrows were still raised. 'Not having any second thoughts about going?'

'Only in as much as Polly needs care.'

'Care?'

'She's diabetic.'

'And I have a bung knee. We can commiserate.' Still the speculative look. 'So why don't you want to go home now?'

Because I might want to kiss her again.

Because I do want to kiss her.

Neither of those thoughts he could say aloud. Neither of those thoughts he should even admit to himself.

Polly…a wealthy socialite, a woman who was here for two weeks while he was away, a woman who…

Made Ruby chuckle.

A woman who made him want to pick her up and carry her to his bed.

A woman who he wouldn't mind protecting for the rest of her life.

Whoa… How to go on a hundred-mile journey in four days. He didn't know her. She was so far out of his league…

But he was there. He wanted her.

'Go home,' Joe said, watching his face, and Hugo wondered how much of what he'd been thinking was plain to see. 'Go and spend some time with her. Heaven knows, you could use a friend.'

'I have friends.'

'None like Polly,' Joe retorted. 'And isn't that just the problem? I'd go nuts without my Hannah, but for you… My Hannah's already taken and there's a limited dating field in the Valley. And now you have Pollyanna right in your living room.' He paused as Polly's infectious chuckle sounded through the monitor. 'Hannah or not, wow, Doc, I'm almost tempted to head over there myself.'

'I'll go when it stops raining.'

'Like that'll happen,' Joe said morosely. 'Forty days and forty nights… This is setting in bad. But it's not raining women, not on your parade…'

'Joe…'

'I know; it's none of my business.' Joe held up his hands as if in surrender. 'But she's there, she's gorgeous and you have no reason not to be there too. Go on, get out of here. Go.'

* * *

He went. Of course he went—there was no reason not to.

It was wet and it was windy. He opened the front door and was met by a squeal of protest.

'Uncle Hugo, noooooooo!'

'Uh oh,' said another voice and he stared around in amazement. The other voice said, 'Maybe you could shut the door?'

The door opened straight into the living room. The living room was…white.

Very white.

'We may not have thought this through,' Polly said.

She was sitting on the floor threading popcorn onto string. Or she had been threading popcorn. She was now coated in a cloud of flour. It was all over her hair, over her face and nose, over the floor around her.

Over Hamster.

Ruby was closest to the door. She seemed to have escaped the worst of the dusting.

'You made it blow,' she said accusingly as he finally closed out the gale.

'Flour?' he said, and his niece sent him a look that put him right in the dunce's corner.

'It's snow. We made a nativity scene. See, we've made everything out of pods from the banksia tree, even the camels, and we got really wet looking for the right banksias, and then we spent ages getting everything dry so we could put them up along the mantelpiece and we put flour over the bottom to look like snow only Polly said I probably put too much on, but it looked *beeeyootiful* but now you've opened the door and you've ruined it.'

And her voice wobbled.

She really was fragile, Hugo thought, bending down to

give her a hug. Last year had been tragedy for Ruby, and it still showed. She expected calamity.

'This isn't ruined,' he said gently. 'It's just flour.'

'It's snow to make Polly feel better when we're not here.'

'And Polly loves it,' Polly said and then she sneezed as if she needed to accentuate the point. 'Ruby, it's still great. Look what we've done, Dr Denver. All we need you to do is chop down a tree.'

'With an axe,' Ruby added. 'I wouldn't let Polly do it on her own.'

'Very wise,' Hugo said faintly, looking round his living room again.

At chaos.

His mother had kept this room perfect. 'The Queen could walk in unannounced and I'd be ready for her,' his mother used to say and she was right. His mother might even have made Her Majesty remove her shoes and leave the corgis outside.

'It was wet,' Ruby said, noticing his sweep of the room and getting in first with her excuse. 'Polly needed something to do.'

'And now she has something else to do,' Polly decreed, using Hamster as a lever to push herself to her feet. 'In case you haven't noticed, Dr Denver, you seem to be dripping on our snow and our type of snow, when dripped upon, makes clag. So I suggest you stop dripping and start helping thread popcorn while I clean up your mess...'

'My mess?'

'Your mess,' she said and grinned. 'Walking in on artists at work...you should know better.'

'I'm glad I didn't,' he said faintly and he looked around at the mess and he thought for the first time in how long... this place looked like home.

What was better than this? he thought.

What was better than Polly?

* * *

He chopped down a Christmas...branch?...while the girls admired his axe technique. They all got wet, but what the heck; he was beyond caring. The branch dripped as he carried it inside but there was so much mess anyway that a little more wouldn't hurt. Then he cooked while they decorated.

He cooked spaghetti and meatballs because that was his speciality. Actually, he had three. Macaroni cheese was another. He could also do a mean risotto but Ruby didn't like it, so to say their menu was limited would be an understatement. But Ruby munched through raw veggies and fruit to stop him feeling guilty and Polly sat down in front of her meatballs and said, 'Yum,' as if she meant it.

They now had two Christmas trees. Ruby had declared Polly's silver tree was too pretty to take down until the last minute so there was a tree in each corner of the living room. There was 'snow' on every flat surface. There were strings of popcorn and paper chains and lanterns and Polly's amazing gift boxes, plus the weird decorations and nativity figures they'd fashioned out of banksia pods.

Polly ate her dinner but every now and then he caught her looking through to the sitting room and beaming.

She'd dressed for dinner. She was wearing another of her retro dresses. This one had splashes of crimson, yellow and blue, and was cinched at the waist with a shiny red belt. The dress had puffed sleeves and a white collar and cuff trim.

Her curls were shining. Her freckles were...freckling. She did not look like a doctor.

She looked adorable.

He didn't want to leave tomorrow.

How could he fall for a woman called Pollyanna?

How could he not?

'We've done good,' Polly was saying to Ruby and Ruby looked where Polly was looking and nodded her agreement.

'Yes. But you'll be here by yourself.' She sounded worried.

'Me and Hamster,' Polly reminded her. 'I'm glad your uncle agreed to let him stay. I might be lonely without him.'

'Won't you be lonely without your mum and dad?' Ruby asked and Polly's smile died.

'No.'

'Won't they be lonely without you?'

There was an uncomfortable silence. Polly ate another meatball but she suddenly didn't seem so hungry.

'They have lots of friends,' she said at last. 'They've booked a restaurant. They'll have a very good party.'

'It won't be much fun if you're not there.'

'They'll hardly miss me,' Polly said stoutly. 'Whereas if I wasn't here Hamster would miss me a lot. Plus Hazel Blacksmith's promised to teach me to tat.'

'Tat,' Hugo said faintly. 'What on earth is tat?'

'You come back after Christmas and I'll show you. Whatever it is, the house will be full of it.'

'That'll make a nice change from soggy flour.'

'Bah! Humbug!' she said cheerfully and got up to clear the dishes. Instead of getting up to help, he let himself sit for a moment, watching her, watching Ruby jump up to help, feeling himself…wanting.

It wasn't fair to want. He had no right.

To try and saddle her with Wombat Valley and a needy seven-year-old? And…

And what was he thinking?

He was trapped. He had no right to think of sharing.

At Ruby's request, Polly read her a bedtime story while Hugo did a last fast ward round. The hospital was quiet. The rain had stopped, the storm was over and what was left was peace. The night before Christmas? Not quite, but it might just as well be, he thought. The whole Valley seemed to be settling, waiting…

Waiting? There was nothing to wait for.

Of course there was, he told himself as he headed back to the house. He was heading to the beach tomorrow. Ten glorious days of freedom.

With Ruby.

He wouldn't have it any other way, he told himself, but he knew a part of him was lying. His sister's suicide had killed the part that enjoyed being a skilled surgeon in a tight-knit surgical team. It had killed the guy who could head to the bar after work and stay as late as he wanted. It had killed the guy who could date who he wanted…

And it was the last thing that was bugging him now.

Dating who he wanted…

Polly.

He wanted Polly.

And she was waiting for him. The light was fading. She was sitting on the old cane chair on the veranda, Hamster at her side. She smiled as he came up the steps and he had such a powerful sense of coming home…

He wanted to walk straight to her, gather her into his arms and claim her as his own. It was a primitive urge, totally inappropriate, totally without consideration, but the urge was so strong he held onto the veranda rail, just to ground himself.

Do not do anything stupid, he told himself. *This woman's ethereal, like a butterfly. You'll be gone tomorrow and when you return she'll flit on. Life will close in on you again. Accept it.*

'Ruby's asleep,' Polly said, leaning back in the rocker and rocking with satisfaction. 'I read her to sleep. Boring R Us.'

Nothing about this woman was boring, he thought, but

he managed to make his voice almost normal. 'What did you read?'

'*The Night Before Christmas*, of course,' she told him. 'I just happen to have a copy in my luggage.'

'Of course you do.'

'My nannies read it to me every Christmas.' She sailed on serenely, oblivious to his dry interruption. 'I started asking for it to be read about mid-November every year. I can't believe you don't own it.'

'My mother didn't believe in fairy tales.'

And her eyes widened. 'Fairy tales? What's fairy tale about *The Night Before Christmas*? Next you'll be saying you don't believe in Santa.'

And Hugo thought back to the Christmases since his father died—the struggle to stay cheerful, Grace's depression—and he thought… *All we needed was a Pollyanna. A fairy tale…*

His parents had been down-to-earth, sensible people. He thought of his sister, crippled by depression. He thought of his father, terse, impatient, telling the teenage Grace to snap out of it.

Grace might still be alive, he thought suddenly, if she'd been permitted a fairy tale.

And… Life might be good for him if he could admit a fairy tale?

A fairy tale called Pollyanna?

'Polly…'

'I need your help,' she told him. 'You're leaving at crack of dawn and we need to pack the silver Christmas tree without making the living room look bereft. I don't intend to have a bereft Christmas, thank you very much.' She rocked her way forward out of the rocker and it was all he could do not to step forward and…

Not!

Somehow he managed to calmly follow her into the

house and start the demolition process, following instructions as to which decorations would stay and which would go.

'I wonder if I could make a tatted angel for your tree next year,' she mused as she packed golden balls into a crimson box. It seemed even the crates she stored things in were a celebration. 'What do you reckon? If you get an angel in the post, will you know what to do with it? Will you value it as you ought?'

She was kneeling by the tree. The Christmas tree lights were still on, flickering multi-coloured patterns on her face. Her eyes were twinkling and a man wouldn't be human...

He didn't go to her. There was a mound of tinsel and a box of Christmas decorations between them. It had to act like Hadrian's Wall.

To stop himself scaring this butterfly into flight.

'Polly, I'd like to keep in touch,' he ventured and she went right on packing decorations as if what he'd said wasn't important.

'I'd like that too,' she said. 'But you're behind the times. Ruby and I already have it planned. We're going to be pen pals—real pen pals with letters with stamps because that's cooler than emails. Ruby will send pictures of herself, and of Hamster too, because I'm starting to think I'll miss him.'

Pen pals.

'That's good, as far as it goes,' he said cautiously. 'But it's not what I had in mind.'

'What did you have in mind?'

'The kiss,' he said and her head jerked up and the atmosphere in the room changed, just like that.

'The kiss...'

Stop now, the sensible part of him demanded, but there was a crazy part that kept putting words out there. 'It meant something,' he said. 'Polly, I'd like to keep seeing you.'

'That might be hard if you're in Wombat Valley and I'm in Ethiopia.'

'You're really thinking of Ethiopia?'

'No,' she said reluctantly. 'I can't.'

'Then how about an extension of your time in Wombat Valley?'

The question hung. It had been dumb to even ask, he thought, but he couldn't retract the words now.

'Stay here, you mean?' she said cautiously.

'We could…just see.'

'See what?' Her eyes didn't leave his face.

'If you and I…'

'I don't do family.' She stumbled to her feet and a crimson ball fell onto another and shattered. She didn't appear to notice.

'Polly, this isn't a proposal.' What had he done? He was appalled at the look of fear that had flashed across her face. 'I'm not asking for permanent. It's far too soon…'

'It's not only too soon,' she snapped. 'It's stupid.'

'Why is it stupid?' He knew, but he still found himself asking. Did she know what a trap his life was?

But it seemed she was worrying about a different kind of trap. 'Hugo, it's true, I kissed you and I felt…like I might be falling for you,' she managed. 'But it scared me. I don't want to go there. I can't. You worry about me, and Ruby hugs me, and even Hamster wriggles his way round my heart like a great hairy worm. But I came here to get away from family, not to find myself more.'

Her words cut, but they were no more than he'd expected.

To hope for more was stupid.

So now what? There was a strained silence while he tried to find a way forward. He'd thought he'd put away his love life when he'd left Sydney, but somehow Polly had hauled it front and centre. He wanted…a woman like Polly?

No. He wanted Polly herself, yet he had no right to haul her into his own personal drama. How could he possibly think of adding his constraints to hers? There was no way through this tangle to a happy ending.

So now? Now he had to get this situation back to a relationship that could go forward as it should. Employer and employee, nothing more.

'You don't think you might be propelling things forward just a tad too fast?' he ventured. 'I'm not asking you to commit to Wombat Valley for life.' He tried smiling, aching to ease her look of fear, but the fear stayed. It seemed she wasn't good at pretending. The employer, employee relationship was finished.

'Hugo, I know what I felt—when I kissed you.' She put her hands behind her and took a step back. 'When I'm with you I feel like someone else. It would be so easy to fall into this place, become your lover, become Ruby's best friend, become Hamster's third favourite cushion, but you'd tie me down. You'd fret—you already do—and before I know it you'd be watching what I eat and checking my long-term sugar levels and making sure I wear warm coats and boots when it's raining and not letting me do the hard medical cases because it might upset me. And I'm sick of cotton wool; I'm just…over it.'

'Polly, of all the things I'm offering, cotton wool isn't one of them.'

'You're saying you wouldn't fuss?'

'Warm coats, boots, the Hamster cushion thing…all those things are negotiable,' he said evenly. 'But if we ever tried it…maybe you couldn't stop me caring.' He had to be honest. 'I'd hope you could care back.'

'I don't do caring.'

'I've watched you for days now. You care and you care and you care.'

'Not with you.'

There was nothing to say to that. Nothing at all.

He'd been stupid to ask. This place—his life—had nothing a woman like Polly would wish to share. How could he ever have imagined otherwise?

He looked at her for a long moment and then, because he couldn't think of anything else to do, he started untangling tinsel. And Polly knelt again to put decorations into boxes.

'There's broken glass by your knee. Be careful.'

'I know,' she snapped, but she hadn't noticed—he knew she hadn't. She looked and saw the shattered Christmas bauble. 'Thank…thank you.'

'I'll get the dustpan.'

'I broke it. I'll fix it.'

'Fine,' he said and then his cellphone rang and he was almost relieved. He went outside to answer it because he needed space.

He felt like smacking himself over the head. For one brief moment he'd tried to prise open the doors that enclosed him. All he'd done was frighten her.

Where to take it from here?

Nowhere.

She was an idiot.

She gathered the shards of glass and then got the vacuum cleaner because you could never be too careful with glass on carpet and she wasn't stupid…

She was stupid, stupid, stupid.

For heaven's sake… He wasn't asking her to marry him, she told herself. He was simply asking her to extend her time here as a locum.

Ruby would love it. Hamster would love it.

Polly would love it?

Love... The word echoed round and round in her head. She hit the power switch to the vacuum cleaner so it faded to silence and she gazed round at the mess that was the living room.

Mess. Christmas.

Family.

She didn't do family. She hated Christmas.

But still she was staring around the room. One intact Christmas branch, gaily decorated. One lopsided silver tree, semi naked. Hugo saw this place as a trap, she thought. A prison. Oh, but if she let herself care...

If she cared, he'd care right back, and the cotton wool would enclose her.

'It's a mess,' she muttered to herself and suddenly she found herself thinking of her parents' Christmases. They were perfection in planning and execution. Exquisite. Her mother employed party planners.

There'd be no soggy flour on her mother's carpet. The only thing missing from her family's perfect Christmas this year would be her.

And, stupidly, she felt tears well behind her eyes. She dashed them away with an angry swipe. *What the heck*... She didn't cry. She never cried.

She'd walked away from her family Christmas without a second glance. She'd felt joyful to be escaping.

And here was Hugo offering her another family Christmas. Not yet, she thought, not this Christmas, but she knew his offer was like an insidious web—*'Come into my parlour,' said the spider to the fly*...

Only it wasn't like that. What fly had ever thought the spider doing the inviting was gorgeous? What spider was ever kind, skilled, gentle, loving, awesome...?

Stop it, stop it, stop it, she told her spinning head. *You've refused him and there's an end to it. You don't want to be caged. Get your head in order and get on with cleaning up this mess.*

And then Hugo walked back into the room and one look at his face told her cleaning had to be put onto the backburner.

CHAPTER TWELVE

'TROUBLE?' POLLY DIDN'T have to ask but she did anyway. Vacuum cleaning was forgotten.

'I need to go out.'

'Tell me.'

'If you could look after Ruby…'

'Tell me,' she snapped again and he paused at the door and looked at her—really looked—and she could almost see the struggle to transform her from a ditzy woman in a rainbow dress to someone who might just be a colleague.

She dropped the vacuum cleaner to help the transition. She thought about white coats but there was hardly time.

'There's been a landslide,' he said.

A landslide…

The rain had stopped now, but it had been torrential. With the steepness of this valley, landslides had to be an ever-present danger.

'I need to go…'

'Tell me,' she said for a third time and he got it then. She wasn't a ditzy redhead. She was an Emergency Medicine specialist and she was demanding facts.

And he switched, just like that. As unlikely a setting as this was, in that moment they joined forces.

A medical team.

'On the road to the south,' he told her. 'We already

have trouble. The north road's still cut where Horace's truck went over. Everyone's been using the south road. But Ben Smart's cow got out and wandered down the road this morning in the rain. A petrol tanker came through and wiped the cow. That wasn't a problem—apart from the cow. The tanker had bull bars. But Ben's cow was left dead on the side of the road and Iris and Gladys Freeman live right where it was hit and they don't want a dead cow smelling up their Christmas.'

He headed for his bedroom as he spoke, hauling on his jacket, speaking to her through the open door.

'Ben's not all that addicted to hard work,' he threw at her. 'But Iris and Gladys were insistent, so Ben got his brother and they looked at the dead cow and thought how hard it would be to bury her. They're Smart by name but not by nature. They looked at the nice soggy side of the cliff face and thought they could just dig a bit and shove her in.'

'Uh oh.' Polly was heading into her bedroom too. Jeans, she thought. Jacket. And shoes. Sensible shoes would be important.

Did snakes come out after rain?

'So...' she called out from the bedroom. 'Situation?'

'The whole side of the hill's come down. Ben's brother, Doug, seems to have a broken leg but he got himself out. Ben was completely buried for a bit. Amy and Max Fraser were there first—they're sensible farmers. Amy's an ex-nurse. She says Ben's in a bad way. Oh, and Iris and Gladys are there too, but Iris has fallen over and Gladys has hurt her back. I might be a while.' And then she emerged from her bedroom and he was in the living room and he looked at her jeans and jacket and boots. 'What the...?'

'I'm coming too. Incident with multiple casualties. Why question it?'

'Ruby?'

'Excuse me? Am I here as a childminder?'

'No, but...'

'Isn't Ruby asleep?'

'Yes...'

'And isn't your normal child care system working?'

'Polly, you can't. You're three days post-snake-bite.'

'Yeah and you'll be post-kick-on-the-shins if you fuss for no reason,' she snapped. 'Do what you must to let the hospital know Ruby needs monitoring. Then let's go.'

What confronted them could have been a tragedy. It was bad, but by the time they got there Ben was sitting up, retching mud and wheezing. He was still gasping but at least he was conscious.

Iris and Gladys, two very elderly ladies, were fussing over him and berating him at the same time.

'We had to do CPR for ages.' Iris, an indomitable lady who looked to be in her nineties, was sitting back on her heels, glaring as if she wanted to punch Ben again. 'I hit him so hard to get him breathing before Amy and Max arrived that I've hurt my wrists, and then he threw up on my dressing gown. And I'll never get it dry in this weather.'

All this and she was complaining about the weather? Polly and Hugo shared a grin as they set to work.

Ben was indeed all right. He'd been momentarily buried in the mud. Luckily, Amy and Max had had a shovel on their truck and had done some fast digging. Amy was now tending to Doug, who lay beside his brother, moaning in pain.

Doug's leg was fractured. His patience with his brother had snapped completely.

'That's the last time I'm gonna agree to one of his harebrained schemes. "It'll be easy," he said. "Just dig a bit into the cliff and shove her in and we won't even have to move her".'

The cow, thankfully, was now buried, but at what a cost?

'You've succeeded, you idiots,' Max said dourly. 'You've also succeeded in cutting the road. The north road's still impassable so we're stuck. The town'll have your guts for garters, guys. Just saying.'

But while he was talking, Hugo and Polly had moved into triage mode, figuring what needed to be done and doing it with the ease of a team that had worked together for years. Polly was wiping the mud from Ben's face, checking his mouth, his nose, his neck. She was preparing an oxygen mask. Ben was breathing but his colour was poor. Assuming his breathing had stopped, even for a moment, it was important to get his oxygen levels up.

Hugo was administering morphine to Doug, then slitting his pants leg to expose the leg break. Polly glanced over and saw no exposed bone, no break in the skin.

They might be lucky, she thought. Doug looked well into his seventies, maybe early eighties. Even a simple fracture would take time to heal but a compound fracture could be disastrous.

'I think you've been lucky,' Hugo told him, confirming what she was thinking. 'Okay, without moving anything—head, neck, arms or legs—let's do a bit of wiggle checking.'

She did the same for Ben, carefully checking each limb. She fitted a neck brace as a precaution—if the dirt had come down on his head she wanted an X-ray before she let him move.

'We'll need to get everyone to hospital,' Hugo told her. 'I want a proper examination.' He turned to Gladys who looked, if anything, even older and more withered than her sister. 'Max said you hurt your back.'

'It's a twinge,' Gladys said with dignity. 'We had to pull to try and get this idiot's head out. Iris fell over—look at her first.'

Iris had indeed fallen over. She had a long graze, the length of her shin.

There was another exchanged glance between Hugo and Polly. Iris's skin was old-age-dry, scarred from years of bumps and bruises and varicose veins. It'd be a miracle if her leg didn't ulcerate. And Gladys's hands were surreptitiously going to the small of her back. Pain was obvious and both she and Hugo could see it.

'Right,' Hugo said. 'Let's get you all into the hospital where we can look at you properly. We need to do it carefully. Amy, Max, are you happy to help? Great. Can you take Iris and Gladys—they're both good to go sitting up, but drive slowly. Try not to bump. Ben and Doug, though, need to be transported flat. I have matting in the back of my van. Polly, can we do a three-way shift? Max, can you help?'

'But we're not going to the hospital,' Gladys said, astounded, and Hugo put a hand on her shoulder and met her frightened gaze with compassion.

'Gladys, how long did Iris's leg ulcer take to heal? Let's try and prevent one forming. And Iris, you can see that Gladys has hurt her back. Do you really not want me to see what the damage is? Won't you let me see if I can stop it hurting for Christmas?'

And, put like that, heading to the hospital for each other, there was no choice.

'We need to ring a couple of local farmers.' Hugo had been carrying lanterns in his truck. So had Amy and Max, so the scene they were working in was lit, but to the north there was a sea of mud where the road should be. 'We'll need to set up road blocks and warning lamps.'

'Can't we get the ambulance?' Polly asked. 'Surely it'd be better to wait.' The ambulance had proper stretchers—a much safer way of carrying patients with potential spinal injuries. To put them in Hugo's van…

'We can't do it,' Hugo said grimly. 'We share the ambulance service with Willaura. They're fifteen miles down the road, on the far side of the land slip. Given that the south road's cut and now the north road... Sorry, guys, the truck it is.'

They worked solidly for the next few hours. Each of the four, although not dangerously injured, had their own urgent needs. Ben had swallowed—and inhaled—dirty water and mud. He needed intravenous antibiotics. Doug's leg needed setting. Luckily, it was a simple tibial break but he was a pack a day smoker. He coughed and wheezed and the decision was admission, oxygen and observation.

They admitted Gladys and Iris, too. Gladys's back showed little damage apart from osteoarthritic change but she was more shaken than she'd admit. Iris's leg needed scrupulous cleaning and dressing, and once they'd got over their first protests the elderly ladies seemed content to be fussed over.

'And you do need to let us fuss over you,' Polly declared as she tucked them in for the night. 'You're both heroes.'

'I agree.' Hugo must have finished at the same time as she did. He was suddenly standing at the ward door, smiling warmly at the two old ladies. 'Heroes, both of you. Max tells me even though you didn't have a spade, by the time he got there you'd already got Ben's head clear.'

'We're gardeners,' Iris said as if that explained everything.

'But we're tired gardeners,' Gladys whispered and snuggled down a bit further on her pillows. Polly had given them both pain relief and they seemed dozily content. 'Thank you, dear.'

And Hugo grinned and crossed to each of them and planted a kiss on each elderly cheek.

'No. Thank you. You've saved Ben's life.'

'Well, we're much happier being kissed by you than by Ben,' Gladys said and she giggled, and Hugo and Polly slipped out of the ward and left them to sleep.

Drama over. They could go home.

They walked in silence across the small distance that separated house from hospital. The silence between them was strained. Almost as soon as the hospital doors closed behind them they seemed no longer colleagues.

What then? Friends?

Ha.

But that was how they had to act, Polly thought, at least until tomorrow.

And with thought came another...

'Hugo... If the roads are cut in both directions... You won't be able to leave.'

Hugo didn't break stride. 'You think I don't know that?' The surge of anger in his voice was almost shocking. 'That road can't be made safe until it dries out, and the engineers have already assessed the other road. They need to blast further into the cliff to make it safe.'

'So that would be...after Christmas?' She could hardly make herself say it but it had to be said. 'Ruby will break her heart.'

'She'll understand.' But the anger was still in his voice. 'I'll show her the roads.'

'And she'll be stoic,' Polly whispered. 'I don't think I can bear it.'

'So how the hell do you think it makes me feel?' His words were an explosion. He stopped and closed his eyes and she could see the pain, the fury that fate had once again messed with his plans for his little niece's Christmas. 'How am I going to tell her?'

'Oh, Hugo...'

'I meant the Valley to be her base, her one sense of continuity. Now it's like a trap.'

'A trap for you both?' she ventured and he stared at her for one long baffled moment and then dug his hands deep in his pockets and started walking again.

Polly didn't move on. She stood and watched his retreating back.

She couldn't help him. Not without…

No. She couldn't help him.

Or could she?

Her parents' money… Her parents' power and resources…

They could get a chopper here first thing tomorrow, she thought. Hugo and Ruby could be at the beach long before they could ever have driven.

But how could she ask that of her parents? She thought of the look on her parents' faces as she'd told them she wouldn't spend this Christmas with them. They'd been gutted. So now…

How could she tell them where she was, ask them for such a favour and then tell them to leave her alone?

Family… Love…

She stood stock-still in the darkness while her thoughts headed off in so many tangents she felt dizzy.

She should be home for Christmas.

She wasn't home. She was here. And so was Hugo because he'd chosen this place—because of love.

'Polly? What's wrong?' Hugo had reached the gate into the house yard and had turned back to see what was keeping her.

'Nothing,' she said in a small voice. 'Just…recalibrating. I guess this means…Christmas together.'

'Can we keep our hands off each other until the roads clear?' He tried to say it with humour but she heard the strain.

'I'll do my best.' She walked towards him in the darkness, but there was a part of her that said she should retreat.

She was as trapped as he was. But…define trap? Some traps you had to walk right into.

'Polly…' She was too close now, she thought, but she couldn't retreat. She was close enough to…close enough to ask for what she wanted?

'If you kiss me,' she managed, 'I think I might crack.'

'I've already cracked,' he said roughly, still with that edge of anger. 'Because all I want to do is kiss you.'

'And where will that leave us?'

'Together until after Christmas? Time for one mad passionate affair?' He snapped the words as if she'd been taunting him. 'Crazy.'

But what if it's not so crazy? It was her heart doing the thinking, not her head. *What if I want to stay? What if I don't think this is a trap at all?*

The thought was almost terrifying. How could she think of staying? She'd railed around the confines of her parents' loving. How much more would she hate the confines of being here?

Of being loved by Hugo?

'You're looking scared,' he said, suddenly gentle, and she wished he wouldn't say things gently because it was almost her undoing. His voice made things twist inside— things she seemed to be unable to untwist.

She wanted him.

They were between house and hospital—no man's land. Medicine and home.

She'd used her career to escape from home, Polly thought with sudden clarity. Maybe that was driving her nuts now. In her world of medicine, she could forget the confines of her parents' worry, her parents' overwhelming adoration. She could be Dr Hargreaves, known for her over-the-top dress sense but respected for her medical skills.

Here, between hospital and home, nothing seemed clear.

Hugo was standing beside her. He was her colleague, except he wasn't a colleague. He was just... Hugo.

How could a heart be so twisted?

How could he be so near and not reach for her?

And in the end, because the silence was stretching and she didn't know how to step away and it seemed that he didn't either, it was Polly who reached for Hugo.

She put her hands up to his face and she cupped his bristled jaw.

'You are the nicest man, Dr Denver...'

'Polly, I can't...'

'One kiss before bedtime,' she whispered and she raised herself on tiptoe. She tugged his head down, her lips met his and she kissed him.

She kissed him, hard and sure and true. She kissed him as she'd never kissed a man before and doubted if she could ever kiss a man again. It was a kiss of aching want. This was a kiss that came from a part of her she hadn't known existed.

But he didn't respond. His arms didn't come around her. He didn't kiss back.

He didn't push her away, but the heat she'd felt before was now under rigid control. She could feel his tension, his strength, the power of his boundaries. She sank down to stand on firm ground again, feeling the first sharp shards of loss.

'Whatever I said... Polly, a short affair over Christmas is never going to work,' he managed. 'We both know that. Bad idea.'

'It is a bad idea,' she conceded.

'So we need to figure the ground rules now. No touching.'

'None?'

'Don't push me, Polly.'

And it was all there in his voice. He wanted her as much

as she wanted him, but this man had already learned what it was to give up what he loved. How much had he hated to give up his surgical career, his friends, his lifestyle? He'd done it for love.

How could she ask him to give up more? An affair and then walk away? It'd hurt her. How much more would it hurt Hugo, who had no power to follow?

She had to be very sure…

'Okay, no touching,' she managed. 'I might… I might as well go to bed, then.'

'That's a good idea.' He touched her cheek—which was breaking the rules but maybe they didn't start until morning. He traced the line of her face with a gentleness she found unbearably erotic. But then, 'Sleep well, Polly,' he told her. 'Tomorrow's Christmas Eve, the night Santa comes. Maybe the old gentleman will bring sense to the pair of us.'

He didn't follow her inside. Instead, he stood where she'd left him, staring into the darkness.

He wanted her so badly it was a physical pain. She'd kissed him and the control it had taken not to sweep her into his arms and claim her had left him dizzy.

Hell, he wanted her.

'Yeah, and Ruby wants Christmas at the beach,' he told himself. 'And I want my career back. We can't all have what we want—you're old enough to know that.'

He knew it but it didn't stop him wanting.

He wanted Polly.

Sleep was a long time coming, and when it did it was full of dreams she had no hope of understanding.

She woke to the dawn chorus. Stupid birds, she thought, lying in her too-big bed listening to the cacophony of parrots, kookaburras and bellbirds. She wouldn't have had to put up with this in Sydney.

Christmas Eve. Her mother would be up by now, doing the flowers—a task undertaken with care for every important occasion. Then there'd be the hair salon, nails, a massage, lunch with her friends, then a nap...

Then there'd be the final gift-wrapping, followed by drinks with more friends and dinner.

And, at every step of the way, her mother would miss her.

Polly lay in bed and listened to the birds and thought about her parents' demands. Why was she suddenly feeling guilty? Her parents smothered her with love and they were constantly disappointed. Last year she'd managed to juggle leave so she could join them in Monaco on Christmas Eve, but her mother had been gutted that Polly hadn't arrived early enough to get her nails done.

'And when did you last get your hair done?' she'd demanded. 'Polly, how can you bear it?'

She smiled then, remembering her father rolling his eyes, and then she thought of her father demanding she tell them the results of her last long-term blood sugar test and telling her he'd researched a new diabetic regime being tested by a clinic in Sweden and he'd fly her there in the new year...

She was right to get away. She knew she was.

It was just...they were her parents. And somehow, looking at Hugo and Ruby, she thought...she thought...

Maybe behaviour had boundaries but love was different? Maybe running away couldn't lessen that.

She sighed and rolled over and tried to sleep a bit more and she must have succeeded because the next thing she knew there was a scratch on her bedroom door. The door flew open and Hamster landed with a flying thud, right across her stomach.

He'd left the door open and from the living room she could hear every word Hugo was saying.

'Ruby, I'm so sorry.' She could almost see Hugo. He'd be crouched in front of his little niece, she thought. Ruby would have flown up as soon as she woke, letting Hamster inside and then bounding to find her uncle. The beach. They were supposed to be leaving right now.

'There's been another accident,' Hugo was telling her. 'Ruby, the roads out of here have been cut. The storm's caused a landslide. We're just going to have to put the silver tree up again and have a two-Christmas-tree Christmas.'

There was no sound. She could have borne it better if Ruby sobbed, Polly thought, but Ruby didn't cry.

If enough was taken away from you, you expected nothing.

Like Hugo... So much had been taken away from him.

How could he expect her to love him?

Would he want her to love him?

She'd only known him for four days. Ridiculous. How could she feel this way about a man after four days?

How could she fall in love with Ruby after four days?

She could still hear Hugo's muffled voice. Maybe he was hugging. Maybe he was holding, trying to comfort...

Beach for Christmas... It was a little thing. A minor promise. Kids got over things.

Last Christmas Ruby had lost her grandmother and then her mother.

Beach for Christmas...

She heard one sob, just the one, and somehow she knew that'd be it. This kid didn't rail against fate.

Polly did, though. She put her pillow over her head and railed.

There had to be a way.

She could still ring her father, ask him to send a chopper to get them to the beach. The idea was still there but she knew it wouldn't work, or not like she hoped. Her father would be incapable of carting away Wombat Valley's permanent doctor and leaving his daughter on her own.

What would he do? Cart her away by force? Not quite, but he wouldn't leave her here.

And with that thought came another. It was a thought so ridiculous… So over the top…

She was trying to escape her parents. She was trying to escape loving.

But if she let loving have its way…

The more she thought about it, the more she started to smile. And then to chuckle.

It was crazy. It'd never work. Would it?

It might.

Hamster wriggled down beside her, trying to nose his way under the covers. 'Don't you dare,' she told him. 'You're needed in the living room. Your mistress needs all the hugs she can get, and you're just the Hamster to give them to her.'

And Hugo? How would he take to hugs?

Ridiculous, ridiculous, ridiculous.

But a girl had to try. She reached for her phone.

'Nothing ventured…' she whispered and then she took a deep breath and finished the thought with force. 'Nothing gained. Okay, Hamster, listen in. My parents have spent their lives wanting to do things for me that I've thought unreasonable. In return I'm about to ask them to do something that is the most unreasonable thing I can think of. Watch this space, Hamster. We're about to push the limits of loving to outer space.'

CHAPTER THIRTEEN

CHRISTMAS EVE AND Wombat Valley Hospital was almost full. None of last night's injured were ill enough to require evacuation but each needed care, pain relief and reassurance.

They also needed sympathy; indeed, with the road closure, sympathetic ears were required everywhere. Many of the Valley residents had been expecting guests for Christmas or had intended going elsewhere. Now everyone was stuck.

However, most accepted the situation with resignation. The Valley had been cut off before, by fire or by flood. The population moved into planning mode. Those who'd been expecting guests shared provisions with those who'd been going away, and some of them swapped Christmas plans, so by mid-afternoon it seemed to Hugo that everyone seemed to have planned an alternative.

As the day went on and he heard more and more rearranged plans he felt...

On the outer?

He and Ruby could be included in any Christmas in the Valley—he knew that. He only had to say the word. But the Valley assumed that he and Ruby could have a very merry Christmas with Polly. There'd been offerings of food but no offers of hospitality. The Valley was collectively stunned by Pollyanna Hargreaves and the assumption was that he was a lucky man.

'Make the most of it, Doc,' Joe growled. 'There's mistletoe growing over by the church—you want me to cut you a trailer-load? You could string it up in every room. By Christmas night…hmm. Do you have brandy sauce? I could get my girls to make some for you. Add a bit more brandy, like…'

'Joe…'

'Just saying,' Joe said placidly. 'You gotta enjoy Christmas.'

But how could he enjoy Christmas when Ruby was simply…flattened? Her life had been full of broken promises. She'd almost expected this, he thought, and it broke his heart.

And Polly… How could he spend Christmas not thinking about kissing her?

How to spend Christmas avoiding her?

Polly, however, was almost infuriatingly cheerful. She was wearing another of her amazing dresses—hadn't anyone advised her on appropriate dress for a working doctor? She'd appeared this morning in crimson stilettoes, for heaven's sake, and had only abandoned them when Joe pointed out the age of the hospital linoleum.

'Not that I don't love 'em,' he'd said, looking wistfully at her patent leather beauties. 'They're an artwork all by themselves.'

So the compromise was that a pair of crimson stilettoes brightened up the desk of reception, while Polly padded round the wards in her harlequin dress, her reindeer earrings with flashing lights and a pair of theatre slippers.

There wasn't one disapproving comment. She went from ward to ward, she helped in his routine clinic and, wherever she went, chuckles followed.

She'd offered to take over his morning clinic and, the

moment people knew, it was booked out. 'Where's she come from?' a normally dour old farmer demanded as he emerged after consulting her for an allergy he'd had a while but had suddenly deemed urgent this morning. 'No matter. Wherever she came from, let's keep the road blocked. She's a keeper.'

A keeper. Right. As if that was going to happen.

Polly headed back to the house at lunch time. By mid-afternoon there was nothing else to do. It was time for Hugo to go home.

He wasn't looking forward to it.

Ruby had spent the morning at Talia's, but she was home again too. She was sitting on the veranda with Hamster on one side and Polly on the other. She looked despondent and didn't manage a smile as Hugo reached them.

Polly might have cheered the Valley up, but she was having less luck with Ruby. The promise of the beach had held the little girl in thrall for months.

'Hey.' Polly smiled, rising to greet him. 'All finished?'

'I…yes.' He was watching Ruby, thinking how impossible this was. Polly had cheered her up for a while with her laughter and her origami and her crazy flour snow, but that was surface stuff. What really mattered was trust.

Hell, he was giving up so much by being here and he couldn't even get this right. No logic in the world could get through this kid's sense of betrayal.

'So everyone's tucked up for Christmas?' Polly was still smiling, but he thought suddenly her smile seemed a bit nervous.

'Yes.'

'Then…' She took a deep breath. 'Hugo, I know this is an impertinence, and I really hope you don't mind, but I've invited guests for Christmas.'

Guests…?

He thought of all the Valley's oldies. The Valley had

its share of lonely people but he'd thought they'd all been catered for. Who'd been left out? Polly was just the sort of woman who brought home strays, he thought. Which particular strays had she chosen?

'For Christmas dinner?' he asked, his mind heading straight to practicalities. 'Polly, our turkey's tiny.' It was the turkey Polly had brought—or rather a turkey breast, cryo-packed, enough for a couple at most.

'Our turkey's rubbish,' she told him. 'A minnow. I gave him to Edith and Harry Banks.'

'You gave away our turkey?'

'It was actually my turkey,' she reminded him. 'I bought it from home when I thought I'd be alone here, but now a bigger one's coming.' She tried to beam but there was uncertainty behind it. 'I… If it's okay with you… It's not too late to call it off, but…'

'But what?' he said and if he sounded goaded he couldn't help it. Ruby was on the sidelines, looking just as confused as he was. He didn't need any more confusion.

This woman had blasted her way into their lives and knocked them both off-kilter, he thought, but then…maybe they'd been off-kilter since Grace died. Maybe their foundations had been blasted away and the force of Polly's enthusiasms was simply making them topple.

That was pretty much how he was feeling now. As if there was no solid ground under his feet.

'My parents…' she said. 'I've invited my parents.'

The ground didn't get any more solid. Confusion, if anything, escalated.

'You don't get on with your parents. Isn't that why you're here?'

'I ran away from home.' She looked down at Ruby and smiled. 'How dumb was that? I didn't figure it out until I saw how much your Uncle Hugo loves you that running away was crazy. And cruel. But it seems too late to run back now, so I thought I'd bring them here.'

'You ran away?' Ruby asked and Polly nodded.

'My mum and dad treat me like a little girl and I was trying to make them see I was a grown-up. But grown-ups don't run away.' She took a deep breath and looked directly at Hugo. 'They stay with those they love.'

'Do you love us?' Ruby asked, still puzzled, and Polly gave a wavery smile.

'I might. I don't know yet. But I do know I love my mum and dad, so this morning I rang them and invited them for Christmas.'

'Didn't you say they've booked out a Harbour restaurant?' Hugo demanded.

'That's just the thing,' she told him, still trying to keep her smile in place. 'Yes, they've booked out the restaurant. They have fifty of their closest friends coming, but most of those friends have been moving in the same social circles for years so if Mum and Dad aren't there they'll hardly be missed. We were in Monaco last year and our Australian friends seemed to get on fine without us. It's me who they will miss. So I thought…'

'You'd invite them here? I thought…they don't even know you're here.'

'They do now,' she confessed. 'Wow, you should have heard the screech on the phone. And I even had to confess about the snake bite. I figured, seeing I'm referred round here as The Doc the Snake Bit, it'd be about two minutes before they found out.' She sighed. 'But I can handle it. I'll just square my chest, tuck in my tummy and face them down.'

There was a moment's stunned silence. He wanted to smile at the vision of Polly with her chest out and tummy in, but he was too…what? Hornswoggled?

Focus on her parents, he thought, because focusing on

Polly was far too discombobulating. Her parents, cancelling their amazing Christmas. The best restaurant in Sydney…

'Won't your parents be paying for the restaurant?'

Polly nodded, and then her smile faded.

'They will, but they won't mind, and that's something I need to talk to you about. My parents are over-the-top generous and also over-the-top extravagant. They have the money behind them to back that up. Hugo, if that's likely to be a thing between us…if you mind…then maybe you'd better say so now.'

What was she saying? There were undercurrents everywhere. The question from Ruby, and Polly's answer, kept reverberating in his head.

Do you love us?

I might. I don't know yet.

And now…

If her parents' wealth was likely to be a problem, say so now? Was she thinking future?

'Polly…'

'Because they're coming and they're bringing Christmas with them,' she said, more urgently now. 'I rang them and said I'd love to have them here, but we have a few specific requirements. So Mum's taken it on as a personal challenge and she's loading the choppers as we speak…'

'Choppers?' he said faintly.

'A truck would be better but if the residents of Wombat Valley insist on destroying all roads, you leave us with no choice. So, are my parents welcome or not?'

'Yes,' he said, even more faintly because there was no choice.

'Great.' She gave him a wobbly smile and then she turned to Ruby. 'Ruby, if you really want—if you really, really want—then my mum and dad can put you and your Uncle Hugo into one of their helicopters and take you to the beach. That'll be fine with me. But can I tell you… My mum and dad organise some of the most exciting Christmases I know. One year I even woke up and there was a snowman in my bedroom.'

'A snowman...' Ruby breathed and Polly grinned.

'I know. Ridiculous. Ruby, I don't know what they'll do this year but I know it'll be a Christmas to remember. And it'll be a family Christmas. It'll be you and your Uncle Hugo, and me and Hamster, and my mum and dad. And presents and lovely things to eat and more presents and Christmas carols and fun. And family. You and your Uncle Hugo can go to the beach after Christmas because I'll stay on until you can, but I'd love you to stay at least until tomorrow. I'd love you to share my Christmas.'

And then there was silence.

The whole world seemed to hold its breath—and Hugo held his breath even more.

The generosity of this woman...

She'd come here to escape. She'd been bruised and battered and bitten and yet she was staying. More, she'd now invited the very people she was running away from.

She was doing this for him, he thought. The helicopters could be an escape for him and for Ruby—or they could mean something more. So much more.

A family Christmas...

'How did they put a snowman in your bedroom?' Ruby sounded as shell-shocked as he was but the fact that she required more information was encouraging.

'It was made with packed ice. We were in Switzerland. Christmas was stormy so we couldn't get out, but that didn't stop Mum getting me the Christmas snowman she'd promised me. It sat in a little paddling pool so it could melt without damaging the hotel's carpet. It had a carrot for a nose and chocolates for eyes and it was wearing my dad's best hat and scarf. Dad got crabby because they got soggy. But there won't be a snowman this year.

Mum never repeats herself. There'll be something just as exciting, though. But you don't need to be here, Ruby. You can still have fish and chips on the beach with your Uncle Hugo—if you want.'

And Ruby looked at Hugo. 'What do you want to do?' she whispered and there was only one answer to that.

'I want to stay with Polly.'

'Then so do I,' Ruby whispered and then she smiled, a great beaming smile that almost split her face. 'As long as it's exciting.'

'If Polly's here, I think we can guarantee excitement,' Hugo said gravely, although there was nothing grave about the way he was feeling. He was feeling like a kid in a toyshop—or better. 'Christmas with Polly can't be anything else but excitement plus.'

The Hargreaves senior arrived two hours later, two helicopters flying in low and fast from the east. They landed on the football oval and it seemed half the town came out to see. The Christmas Eve service had just come to an end in the Valley's little church. The locals were wandering home and they stopped to look.

They saw Polly being enveloped.

Polly's mother was out of the chopper before the blades stopped spinning. Olivia was wearing a bright, crimson caftan with gold embroidery. She had Polly's auburn hair—possibly a more vivid version. Her hair was piled in a mass of curls on top of her head, and her huge gold earrings swung crazily as she ran.

Charles Hargreaves was small and dapper and he didn't run, but he still covered the distance to his daughter with speed.

Polly simply disappeared, enveloped in a sandwich hug which looked capable of smothering her.

Hugo and Ruby stood on the sidelines, hand in hand, waiting to see if she'd emerge still breathing.

For Hugo, whose parents had been…restrained, to say the least, this display of affection was stunning.

Ruby's jaw had dropped and was staying dropped. The combination of helicopters, Polly's over-the-top parents and the effusiveness of the greeting left them both awed.

But eventually Polly did break free, wriggling from her parents' combined embrace with a skill that spoke of years of practice. She grabbed a parent by each hand and drew them forward.

'Mum, Dad, this is Dr Denver. And Ruby.'

Charles Hargreaves reached forward to grasp Hugo's hand but Olivia was before him. She surged forward and enveloped him in a hug that matched the one she'd given her daughter.

'You're the dear, dear man who saved our daughter. Snake bite. Snake bite! And us not even knowing. Of all the places… And you saved her. Putting herself at such risk… We knew she shouldn't leave Sydney. Never again, that's what we said, Charles, isn't it? Never again. And what about her blood sugars? What if she'd died out here? I don't know how we can ever…'

Enough. He was enveloped in silk and gold and crimson and he had a feeling if he didn't take a stand now he'd stay enveloped for Christmas. He put his hands on her silk shoulders and put her firmly away from him.

'Mrs Hargreaves, I'm not sure what Polly's told you, but your daughter's made a very good job of saving herself.' He said it strongly, forcibly, because a glance at Polly said that this was important. Her face had sort of…crumpled?

Never again, her mother had said. What sort of strength had it taken to tear herself from these two? But she'd voluntarily brought them back—so he and Ruby could have Christmas.

'Polly's the strongest woman I know,' he continued, and he reached out and took Polly's hand. It seemed natural. It also seemed important and Polly's hand clung to his and he thought: he was right. These two were like bulldozers, and their daughter stood a good chance of being crushed by their force.

'But don't accept my word for it,' he continued. 'The whole Valley agrees. Polly came to this town as the fill-in doctor. She saved two lives the day she arrived. She looks after her own health as well as everyone else's, and she spreads laughter and light wherever she goes. You must have brought her up to be a fiercely independent woman. Her strength is awesome and the whole of Wombat Valley is grateful for it.'

They were taken aback. They stared at him, nonplussed, and then they stared at Polly. Really stared. As if they were seeing her for the first time?

'She has diabetes,' Olivia faltered and Hugo nodded.

'We have three kids with Type One diabetes in the Valley. Polly's already met one of them. Susy's a rebellious thirteen-year-old and Polly knows just what to say. If Susy can get the same control Polly has, if she can make it an aside to her life as Polly has…well, I'm thinking Susy's parents will be as content and as proud as you must be.'

And it sucked the wind right out of their sails. It seemed they'd come to rescue and protect their daughter, but their daughter was standing hand in hand with Hugo and she was smiling. She had no need of rescue and her armour was reforming while he watched.

'Polly said… Polly said you might bring a snowman.' Until now, Ruby had been silent. She was on the far side of Hugo, quietly listening. Quietly gathering the courage to speak. 'Polly says you make Christmas exciting.'

And it was exactly the right thing to say. Hugo's arm came around Polly. She leaned into him as her parents shifted focus.

From Polly to Ruby. From Polly to Christmas. He felt Polly sag a little, and he knew it was relief. Somehow energy had been channelled from saving Polly to saving Christmas.

Olivia looked down at the little girl for a long minute, and then she beamed.

'So you're Ruby.'

'Yes,' Ruby said shyly.

'Pollyanna said you wanted to go to the beach for Christmas.'

'We did,' Ruby told her. 'But now… Uncle Hugo and I want to stay with Polly.'

There was a sharp glance at that, a fast reassessment. Hugo expected Polly to tug away, but she didn't. Which was a statement all by itself?

'That's lovely,' Olivia said after a moment's pause. 'Can we stay too?'

'Yes,' Ruby said and smiled and Polly smiled too.

'We have spare bedrooms,' Polly said and Hugo thought *we?*

Better and better.

'Then I guess we need to get these choppers unloaded so the pilots can get back to Sydney for their own Christmas,' Polly's father said, moving into organisational mode. 'Can we organise a truck, Dr Denver?'

'A truck?'

'For the Christmas equipment my wife thought necessary.' Charles gave an apologetic smile. 'My wife never travels light.'

'Excellent,' Polly said and moved to hug her parents. 'Mum, Dad, I love you guys. Ruby, welcome to my parents. My parents are awesome.'

* * *

At two in the morning Hugo finally had time to sink onto the veranda steps and assess what had happened over the last few hours.

Polly's parents were overwhelming, overbearing, and they loved Polly to distraction. He could see why she'd run from them. They were generous to the point of absurdity and he could see why she loved them back.

They were also used to servants.

Right now he'd never been more physically exhausted in his life. Polly, on the other hand, didn't seem the least exhausted. She was happily arranging potted palms around a cabana.

There was now a beach where his yard used to be.

The centrepiece was a prefabricated pool it had taken them the night to construct. They'd started the moment Ruby had gone to bed. That had been six hours ago—six hours of sheer physical work. Because it wasn't just a pool. The packaging described it as *A Beach In Your Backyard*, and it was designed to be just that.

A motor came with the pool, with baffles that made waves run from one side to another. Hugo had shovelled a pile of sand—almost a truckload had emerged from the chopper—to lie beside it. A ramp ran up the side—it could be removed to keep the pool child-proof and safe. A life-buoy hung to the side. Seashells were strewn artistically around. Polly had done the strewing, making him pause to admire her handiwork. There were also sun umbrellas, deckchairs and a tiny palm-covered cabana.

'Because Christmas isn't just for children,' Olivia had decreed as she'd handed over a sheaf of instructions and headed to bed herself. 'There needs to be somewhere to store the makings of martinis. And margaritas. Polly loves margaritas but she's only allowed to have one.'

His eyes had met Polly's at that and laughter had flashed between them, silent but so strong it was like a physical link.

'Don't say a word,' Polly had said direfully and he hadn't.

Charles had helped for the first hour but at the first sign of a blister he, too, had retired. Since then Hugo and Polly had laboured non-stop.

For Ruby's joy was in front of them. In the hope of Ruby's joy he'd even allowed Polly to override his own concerns.

'I want to play Santa as much as you do,' she'd decreed when he'd tried to send her to bed. 'If you fuss, Hugo Denver, I'll throw a tantrum big enough to be heard in Sydney.'

So they'd worked side by side, by torchlight and by the help of a fortuitous full moon. It was hard. It was fun. It was...wonderful.

Six hours of working with Polly was somehow settling things. There were promises being made, unspoken yet—it was much too soon—but working side by side felt right.

It was a promise of things to come? The disintegration of the walls of two different traps?

Whatever it was, now he had a beach in his front garden.

'We've taken over.' Polly had arranged her last palm to her satisfaction. Now she settled onto the step beside him and gazed at the scene before them in satisfaction. 'Goodness, Hugo, are you sure you want us here?'

For answer he reached out and took her grimy and blistered hand. It matched his grimy and blistered hand. He didn't reply. He simply held and the silence settled around them with peace and with love.

They didn't need to say a thing.

'They didn't bring buckets and spades and surfboards,' Hugo said at last, and Polly cracked a guilty grin.

'I checked the back of your wardrobe,' she admitted. 'Hugo, it pains me to admit it but I'm a Christmas snooper from way back. Let me tell you that you're very bad at hiding. The shapes of buckets and spades and surfboards take skill to be hidden and the back of your wardrobe is chicken feed in the hiding stakes.'

'So you told your parents what not to bring?'

'I told them what I thought the bumpy presents were. Mum might be over the top, but she never tries to outshine anyone.'

'Really?'

She giggled. 'Well, she never tries but sometimes she's very, very trying.' She hesitated. 'Hugo, I try not to,' she confessed, 'but I love them.'

'They're hard not to love.'

'You wait until they decide to decorate your bedroom to look like a Manhattan chic hotel...'

'They wouldn't.'

'Only if they love you.' She sighed. 'And they'll probably make you do the painting. Mum'll drink martinis and boss you as you paint. Love doesn't get boundaries.'

'It doesn't, does it?' he said softly and his hold on her hand tightened. 'Polly...'

'Hey, I didn't mean anything by that,' she said hurriedly, as if it was important that she said it. 'I wasn't hinting...'

'You don't need to hint.' He hesitated a moment more, but why not say it? It was all around them anyway.

'Polly, I'm falling in love with you,' he said softly. 'I may have already mentioned it but I'll mention it again now. I have so much baggage I'm practically drowning in it but...'

'By baggage do you mean Ruby?' She sounded incensed.

'I can't leave her.'

'I'd never expect you to. But you think you have baggage! I have Mum and Dad and I've already figured there's no use hiding from them. Wherever I am, they'll be hovering. The term "helicopter parents" takes on a whole new meaning when you're talking about my parents.'

'They love you. They worry.'

'Which infuriates me. It makes me claustrophobic.'

'Are you feeling claustrophobic now?'

'I guess I'm not.' She smiled tentatively. 'You seem to have set new boundaries. They're recalibrating their position but they won't stop worrying.'

'Maybe it's natural.' His hand held hers, gently massaging her fingers. He wanted her so much, and yet he had to say it. There was no space here for anything but truth. 'Polly, I'd worry too.'

She turned and looked at him, square-on. 'When would you worry?'

'If you let me close. As close as I want to be. And Polly, this Valley constricts your life.'

'Like my diabetes.'

'I guess…'

There was another long silence. The night seemed to be holding its breath. There was so much behind the silence, so much it was too soon to say or even think, and yet it was undeniably there.

'If you worried,' she said at last, 'then I might react with anger. I've had enough worry to last me a lifetime.'

'So you might never worry about me?'

He'd been running the hose into the pool. It was now almost full. The moonlight was glimmering on its surface. A wombat had been snuffling in the undergrowth as they worked. Now it made its way stealthily up the ramp and stared at the water in astonishment. It bent its head and tentatively tasted.

'Happy Christmas, Wombat,' Hugo whispered and Polly's hand tightened in his and she smiled.

'It is a happy Christmas. And Hugo, okay, maybe I would

worry. Maybe I already do worry. You're a surgeon with amazing skills. You've uprooted yourself, buried yourself...'

'Is this what this is? Burying myself?'

She looked out again, at the pool, at the wombat, at the lights of the little hospital and at the moon hanging low over the valley. 'Maybe not,' she whispered. 'But I would still worry. And you'd have the right to tell me it's none of my business.'

'We're moving forward,' he said gently. 'Into places I hardly dare hope...'

'Me too,' she whispered. 'But maybe we're allowed to hope? Maybe we even have grounds for hoping?'

'Maybe we're stretching our boundaries,' he said softly. 'Figuring they can be stretched. Figuring how to see them as challenges and not chains.'

'I thought I was trapped by family,' she whispered. 'And you're trapped with family too. Maybe the way not to feel trapped is...to combine?'

'Polly...'

'Hush for now,' she whispered. 'Think about it. Just know that I'm thinking about it all the time.'

And it was enough, for now. They sat on, in silence, the stillness of the night enveloping them. It was too soon, too fast, there were too many things ahead of them to even think this could be a beginning, but somehow hope was all around them.

'It's almost full,' Polly ventured at last, almost inconsequentially. 'The pool...'

'That's why I'll stay sitting out here. To turn the hose off.'

'Really? I thought you were sitting because you're too exhausted to move?'

He grinned, and then he kissed her because it seemed okay. No, it seemed more than okay. No touching? *Ha!* Rules were made to be broken. The kiss was long and lingering, insidious in its sweetness and an affirmation of the future all by itself.

And then the first splash of water hit the ground and if a flooded garden was to be avoided they had to pull apart. So Hugo went to turn off the tap while Polly looked at the water, and looked up at the stars and made a decision.

'You should always trial Christmas gifts before the day,' she said as he returned to her. 'What if it's faulty?'

'The wombat already tried it.'

'And then he waddled away. What if he thought there was something wrong? He could hardly have reported it.'

'So you're suggesting…what?'

'A swim,' she said promptly. 'Just to make sure.'

'Me?'

'Both of us. It'd be kind of cool.'

'This water comes straight from the creek. It hasn't had any warmth from the sun yet. You can bet it'll be cool.'

'Chicken.' She rose. 'I'm putting on my bikini.'

'You have a bikini?'

'With polka dots. You want to see?'

'Yes,' he said fervently.

'Only if I get to see you in boxers.'

'How do you know I don't wear budgie smugglers?'

She grinned. 'You're not that type of man. I know it.'

'How do you know?'

'Intuition,' she said happily, heading up the steps to the front door. 'But it's not infallible. Will I still love you if you turn out to be a man who wears budgie smugglers? Watch this space, Dr Denver. In the fullness of time, all will be revealed.'

But he didn't follow. 'Polly, wait.' He hesitated, not because he wanted to, but because things were suddenly moving with a speed that made him dizzy. Boundaries seemed about to be crossed, and if he was to ask Polly to step over them then honesty was required. She needed to see the things he'd railed against for the last twelve months for what they were.

She turned and smiled back at him, but her smile faded as she saw his face. 'What? Are you about to tell me you've two wives and nineteen children in Outer Mongolia?'

'Only Ruby.'

'Then what's the problem?'

'Polly, there's no ER here. We have no specialists on call. There's no three hat restaurant or even a decent curry takeaway. Everyone knows everyone and everyone knows everyone else's business. If you dive into the pool in a polka dot bikini it'll be all over the town by morning.'

'Really?'

'The wombat's reporting it to the grapevine this very minute.'

She didn't smile. 'Do you hate it?' she asked and the question caught him off guard.

Did he hate it?

There'd been times in the past year when he had. There were still times when he longed for his old life, his old job, his friends. But now...

He'd learned to love this little hospital, he thought. Joe and his teasing. Barb and her incessant knitting. Mary and her worries. And his patients... He was becoming part of the lives of the Valley and he was finally starting to see why his father had worked here for so long.

But would he still escape if he could?

Not if Polly was here.

And suddenly he thought that even if she wasn't, things had changed. Polly had brought him laughter. She'd brought smiles to his little niece. She'd brought him Christmas.

But more. She'd brought him courage and, no matter what happened now, something of her would stay.

Did he hate Wombat Valley? Suddenly it was like asking: Did he hate life?

'I did hate it,' he said slowly. 'But I hadn't figured that all it needed was a dusting of polka dots.'

'And flour,' she said and grinned. 'Flour's important. And tatted angels. I'm learning fast. By next Christmas you could have tatted angels from one end of the house to the other.'

'That sounds okay to me,' he said, and it felt okay.

Actually, it felt more than okay. It felt excellent.

'But you?' he asked, because he had to be fair. He had to know. 'Polly, I will not trap you.'

And in answer she walked back down the steps and she took his hands. 'I'm not walking from one trap into another,' she said softly. 'Eyes wide open, I'm stepping into magic.'

Christmas *was* magic, he thought, as finally they broke away and he headed inside for his board shorts. Kiss or not, decision or not, Polly was still insisting on a swim and Polly was bossy and he had the gravest forebodings of bossiness to come.

He couldn't wait.

But for now they were heading for a swim and maybe it wouldn't even be cold.

For magic happened. It was the night before Christmas and the night was full of promise of magic to come.

CHAPTER FOURTEEN

HUGO HAD SLEPT for three hours or maybe a bit less before a squeal broke the stillness of dawn.

Polly had tied a balloon to the end of Ruby's bed, with a red ribbon stretching across the floor and out of the open window. Ruby had obviously found the ribbon.

There was another squeal, longer than the first, and then a yell of pure joy.

'Uncle Hugo! Polly! Hamster! Everyone! Santa's been and he's left a…a pool! There's sand and umbrellas and it's just like the beach. And there's presents piled up beside it and *ohhhhhh…*'

They heard a thud as she jumped out of her window and then hysterical barking as Hamster discovered the enormous intruder in his yard.

'I'd better sneak back to my bedroom before she finds me,' Polly murmured, laughing, and he rolled over and smiled down into her dancing eyes.

'Why would she come and find you when she has a beach?'

'Uncle Hugo!' The yell from outside was imperative. 'Come and see!'

He had to come and see. He had no choice, he thought, as he hauled on his pants and headed for the door, giving Polly time to work out a decorous strategy for her appearance.

He had no choice at all, he thought, as he walked through the front door and was hit by the world's biggest hug from the world's most excited seven-year-old.

'How wonderful!' He emerged from the hug to find that somehow Polly had made it back to her bedroom and was leaning out of her window, smiling and smiling as she called to them both, 'Happy Christmas, Hugo. Happy Christmas, Ruby. Yay for Santa.'

He had no choice at all, Hugo thought as Ruby dragged him forward to inspect every aspect of this amazing transformation of his yard.

He hadn't had a choice twelve months ago and he didn't have a choice now.

And the strange thing was, no choice at all seemed wonderful.

Polly lay on her sunbed beside the swimming pool and thought about dozing but the world was too big, too wonderful, too full of magic.

Around her was the litter of Christmas. Ruby had woken to little-girl magic, to gifts she loved, to excitement, to fun. She was now asleep on a daybed, cuddled between Olivia and Hamster. Charles was asleep on the next bed.

Weird, wonderful, somehow fitting together...
Family.

She wouldn't run again, Polly decided. She didn't need to.

For Hugo was coming towards her, striding up the slope from the hospital. He'd gone across to check Bert Blyth for chest pain. It'd be indigestion, Polly thought. Hospitals the world over would be filling with indigestion after Christmas dinner.

'All clear?' she asked as he reached her. She stretched

languorously, deliciously, and he sat down beside her and tugged her into his arms.

'All done.' He kissed her nose. 'If you stay out in the sun you'll get more freckles.'

'I have cream on.'

'I'm not complaining. I like freckles. Polly, I don't have a gift for you.' He hesitated and then kissed her again, more deeply this time. And when he put her away his smile had faded.

'It's okay,' she told him. 'I don't have a gift for you either.'

'We could take a raincheck until the roads are open. We could buy each other socks. Socks are good.'

'I don't have a lot of time for socks.'

'Really?' He was holding her shoulders, looking down into her eyes. 'Then I have another suggestion.'

'Wh… What?'

'What about a partnership?'

Her eyes never left his face. 'A partnership?'

'Polly, you know the partnership I'm thinking of,' he said, and he smiled, his best doctor-reassuring-patient smile. And it worked a treat. She loved that smile.

'But I know that's too soon,' he told her. 'So I thought… what's not too soon is a professional partnership. Wombat Valley has only one doctor and that leaves me on call twenty-four seven. That's more than enough to keep me busy. The Valley could easily cope with a doctor and a half.'

'A half,' she said dubiously. 'So you're offering…'

'Three-quarters.' He was smiling again but there was anxiety in his smile. He wasn't sure, she thought, but then, neither was she. 'Three-quarters each,' he said softly. 'A medical practice where we have time to care for our patients but we also have time to care for ourselves.'

'If this is about my diabetes…'

'It's nothing to do with your diabetes. It's everything to do with Ruby and Hamster and swimming and enjoying the Valley and making origami frogs and maybe even, in time, making a baby or two...'

'A...what?'

'Given time,' he said hastily. 'If things work out. I don't want to propel things too fast.'

'Babies! That's propelling like anything.'

'I'm sorry,' he said hastily, but he kissed her again, lightly at first and then more deeply, making a liar of himself in the process. 'No propelling,' he repeated as the kiss came to a reluctant end. 'A professional partnership first and then, if things go well...maybe more?'

'Wow,' she breathed. 'Just...wow.'

'What do you think?'

What did she think? 'If we're not propelling... I'd need somewhere to live.'

'So you would. There are a few Valley folk who could be persuaded to take in a boarder. Or,' he suggested, even more tentatively, 'we might be able to split this house. We could put a brick wall or six between us.'

'It wouldn't work.'

'No?'

'Not now I've seen you in boxers.' And without boxers, she thought, and she felt her face colour. She looked up at him and she couldn't help but blush, but she managed to smile and he smiled back.

She loved him so much. How could she love someone so fast?

How could she not?

'So you think it's too soon?' he asked.

Define too soon, she thought. Too soon to love this kind, gentle man who'd given up his world for his little niece? This skilled and caring surgeon who had the capacity to twist her heart?

This gorgeous, sexy man who had the capacity to make her toes curl just by smiling?

Too soon?

She forced herself to look away, around at her parents, at Ruby, at Hamster, then at the little hospital and the valley surrounding them.

Too soon?

'It's Christmas,' she whispered. 'Christmas is magic. Christmas is when you wave a wand and start again, a new beginning, the start of the rest of your life.'

'Isn't that New Year?'

'Maybe it is,' she said as the last lingering doubts dissipated to nothing. She tugged him back into her arms and felt him fold her to him. If home was where the heart was, then home was here. 'So we have New Year to come.'

'What could possibly happen in the New Year that could be better than right now?' he murmured into her hair, and she smiled and smiled.

'Well,' she whispered, 'if we sign for a professional partnership on Christmas Day, what's to stop another type of partnership occurring in the New Year?'

And it did.

EPILOGUE

Christmas, one year on. Dawn...

POLLY STRETCHED LANGUOROUSLY in her enormous bed, and Hugo's arm came out to tug her close. Skin against skin was the best feeling in the world, she decided. She closed her eyes to savour the moment. The dawn chorus would soon wake the house. Ruby and Hamster would burst in at any minute, but for now she could just *be*...

With Hugo.

'Happy Christmas, my love,' he murmured, and she snuggled closer.

'Happy Christmas to you too.' But as his hold tightened and she felt the familiar rush of heat and joy, she tugged back. 'Oi,' she said in warning. 'Ruby and Hamster will arrive at any second.'

'So let me announce number one of my Christmas gifts,' he told her. 'One lock, installed last night. Eight years old is old enough to knock.'

'Really?'

'Really.' His arms tightened and he rolled her above him so she was looking down into his eyes. 'So it's Happy Christmas, my love, for as long as we want.'

'Hooray!'

But the house was stirring. There were thumps and

rushing footsteps and then whoops as one small girl spotted what was under the Christmas tree. And then they heard Polly's mum's voice...

'We've hidden a gift for Hamster in the backyard,' Olivia called. 'Let's go help him find it. We'll give those sleepyheads a few more minutes' rest.'

'Sleepyheads?' Polly murmured. 'Who's she calling a sleepyhead?'

'That would be you.' And it was true. For the last few weeks Polly had seemed to doze any time she had to herself.

The first trimester often did that. She must have fallen pregnant on the first week of their honeymoon.

It had been...that sort of honeymoon.

'But I'll defend you,' Hugo offered. 'If I can just hold you first...'

And who could resist a bargain like that?

It was good to hold. No, it was truly excellent, Polly decided some time later. She was curved against her husband's body, feeling cat-got-the-cream smug, nowhere near sleep.

Thinking *Christmas*.

Thinking *family*.

How had she ever thought family could be a trap? It had freed them all.

It had even given Hugo back his career.

For two doctors in Wombat Valley had transformed the medical scene. No doctor had wanted to practice here, knowing it meant isolation and overwork. But, with two doctors already committed, more followed.

A couple wanting to escape the rat race of Sydney had looked at Wombat Valley six months ago with fresh eyes. Doctors Meg and Alan Cartwright had bought Doc Farr's vineyard, but the vineyard was a hobby and they needed income to support it.

That meant the Valley now had four doctors, which meant there was cover for holidays. They could go to the beach. What was more, the locals no longer had to go to Sydney for thoracic surgery. A new, stable road meant Hugo could operate twice a week at Willaura. Meg's specialty was urology so she spent a couple of days in Willaura too. The rotation of surgical medical students through Willaura had increased. Hugo could even teach.

It was all Hugo wanted.

No. It wasn't all he wanted.

He wanted Polly and Ruby and Hamster. He even wanted Polly's parents, which was just as well, as Charles and Olivia were constant visitors.

They'd backed off, though. From that first day when Hugo had set the boundaries, they'd accepted them. There was even talk of them building a 'small granny flat', though Polly and Hugo had almost choked when Olivia had explained what she meant by 'small'.

That was for the future, though. For now, for this Christmas, Charles and Olivia were once again staying in their house. 'For how can we not be there on Christmas morning to share the joy?' they'd asked and who could say no? Definitely not Hugo. Definitely not Polly.

For joy was here in abundance. This morning they'd tell them about the baby. They'd already told Ruby. 'It's a secret,' they'd told her, and Ruby was almost bursting with excitement.

'Happy?' Hugo asked. They could hear Olivia and Charles, Hamster and Ruby, heading back to the house. Lock or no lock, their peace was about to be blasted.

'Can you doubt it?'

'I don't doubt it,' he murmured. 'Not for a moment.' He kissed her deeply and then swung out of bed—and paused. Polly's Christmas outfit was hanging by the window, ready for her to slip on. Red and white polka dots. A sash with a huge crimson bow. Crimson stilettoes.

'Wow,' he breathed. 'I thought we'd lost the polka dots for ever.'

'Mum had this made for me,' Polly told him. 'Seeing the snake got the last one.'

'And stilettoes…' He looked at the gorgeous dress with its tiny waist and then he looked at the high stilettoes. He grinned. 'You know, Dr Hargreaves, you may need to consider slightly more staid dressing as our baby grows.'

'Bah! Humbug!' Polly said and chuckled up at him. 'Our baby will love polka dots. Polka dots are delicious, life's delicious and so are you.'

'Package deal?'

'You got it,' she said serenely. 'I have polka dots, life and you, all tied up in one delicious Christmas package. Happy Christmas, Dr Denver. Who could ask for more?'

* * * * *

A MUMMY TO
MAKE CHRISTMAS

BY
SUSANNE HAMPTON

Published in Great Britain 2015
by Mills & Boon, an imprint of Harlequin (UK) Limited,
Eton House, 18-24 Paradise Road, Richmond, Surrey, TW9 1SR

© 2015 Susanne Panagaris

ISBN: 978-0-263-24748-0

Harlequin (UK) Limited's policy is to use papers that are natural, renewable and recyclable products and made from wood grown in sustainable forests. The logging and manufacturing processes conform to the legal environmental regulations of the country of origin.

Printed and bound in Spain
by CPI, Barcelona

Dear Reader,

In this Christmas story my heroine, Dr Phoebe Johnson, declares that 'all men are the same' as she leaves her old life behind, choosing to focus on her career and forget about love. A cheating fiancé gives her no choice but to leave Washington or spend her life reliving the humiliation and heartbreak.

Many have experienced disappointment or heartbreak and muttered the very same words—although few have discovered on the eve of their wedding that their fiancé has slept with both bridesmaids! But poor Phoebe has, and it sends her packing to Australia in search of a quiet place to mend her heart and pride, burying herself in work with an older surgical mentor Dr Ken Rollins.

But the universe has other plans…and those plans materialise into the very handsome Dr *Heath* Rollins, who has stepped in to replace his injured father for one month. Despite Phoebe and Heath feeling an attraction, neither is looking for a relationship or anything close to it.

Phoebe and Heath's journey to happily-ever-after is about:

• The need to bend rules and occasionally break them completely—particularly when true love is at stake

• Not judging all people on the actions of just one person

• Accepting that Christmas is a magical time and about so much more than tinsel and baubles…it's about love and family

I hope you enjoy Phoebe and Heath's love story, and I wish you all a very Merry Christmas filled with love!

Warmest regards,

Susanne

As I was putting the final touches to this book I was given the news that my amazing editor Charlotte was moving along her career pathway and would no longer be working with me. So this will be my final dedication to her and my last written recognition of her guidance, patience, much needed honesty and unwavering belief in my work. However, what I have learnt from her over the last five books will travel with me on my writing journey, so in many ways all of my books and writing success in the future will be a dedication to Charlotte Mursell.

Thank you, Charlotte.

Books by Susanne Hampton

Mills & Boon Medical Romance

Unlocking the Doctor's Heart
Back in Her Husband's Arms
Falling for Dr December
Midwife's Baby Bump
A Baby to Bind Them

Visit the Author Profile page
at millsandboon.co.uk for more titles.

CHAPTER ONE

DR HEATH ROLLINS momentarily looked away from the emails on his laptop computer, across the living room of the family home, to see his father sitting by the lace dressed bay window in his favourite armchair. With the mid-morning sunlight streaming into the room, he was intently reading the paper. Heath smiled a bittersweet smile as his gaze roamed to the old oversized chair, upholstered in green and blue tartan. It was a piece of furniture his mother had tried to have re-covered or removed from their home for many years but Ken Rollins had been adamant that it stayed. And stayed exactly as it was. It was a Clan Sutherland tartan, of the Highland Clans of Scotland, Heath would hear his father tell his mother, and it had direct links to the maternal side of his family. She would tell him that family connections or not, it was an extremely unattractive chair that looked out of place in their new French provincial decor. Frankly, it was hideous and it just didn't belong.

His mother and father had argued about very little except that chair. But, unlike all those years ago, now his father was stuck in that now slightly worn chair for hours on end, his leg elevated and his knee freshly dressed after surgery. And there were no more arguments about the chair as Heath's mother had passed away twenty years ago.

Heath then caught sight of his own suitcases, stacked against the hall wall, with the airline tags still intact. He would shortly be taking them to the room that would be his for the next month. His attention returned to the email he was drafting to the Washington-based podiatric surgeon travelling to Australia to work with his father. As he perused her résumé to find an email address, he couldn't help but notice her impressive qualifications and certifications. A quizzical frown dressed his brow as he wondered why she had chosen to relocate to Adelaide and consult at his father's practice. Then he dropped that line of thought. It was not his concern.

'I hope you don't mind the last-minute change in plans, Dr Phoebe Johnson,' he muttered as he pressed 'send' on the keyboard, hoping that even if she had turned off her computer she would receive the notification via her mobile phone. 'It looks like you'll be working with me not my father. At least until he's back on his feet again.'

Phoebe Johnson had switched off her cell phone an hour earlier. There was no point in having it on as there was only one person who would try to reach her and she would go to any lengths to avoid another conversation with her mother.

Unfortunately her mother had found her.

'Why on earth are you leaving Washington? It's been over three months since you postponed the wedding, Phoebe. It's time you set a new date.'

'I *cancelled* the wedding, Mother. I didn't postpone it.'

Completely dumbfounded, and shaking her head, Phoebe stood on the steps of her rented brownstone apartment, her online printed boarding pass and her passport both gripped in one leather-gloved hand while the other searched for keys in her oversized handbag. The second of her matching tweed suitcases was balanced precariously by her feet, and her heavy woollen coat was buttoned up against the icy December wind that was howling down the narrow car-lined street.

She found her keys and, aware that the meter was running on the double-parked cab, hurriedly locked the front door. She was in no mood for another confrontation and frustrated that at the eleventh hour it was happening again. Her mind was made up. She was not looking back.

'How can you work things out if you go rushing off to another country? Surely you've punished Giles enough for his indiscretion?' her mother continued, not at all deterred by anything Phoebe had said, nor by her imminent travel plans. 'I'm certain he's learnt his lesson.'

Phoebe tugged down her knitted hat, at risk of blowing away in a chilly gust, then made her way down the snow-speckled steps with her last suitcase and handed it to the cab driver, who had been tapping his foot impatiently on the kerb.

'It isn't a punishment, Mother. I ended it. I gave the ring back, returned the wedding presents and told Giles that I never want to see him again. It's about as final as it gets. And I've thought this through until I've gone almost mad. You don't seem to understand—I no longer love Giles and I don't want to see him again. *Ever*. To be honest, I'm surprised that after everything he's put me through you'd want him to have any part in my life.'

She paused as she looked long and hard at her mother, completely bemused that they saw the situation so very differently.

'He's not the man for me. I don't know if there even *is* a man for me, but right now I'm not looking. I want to put all my energy into my work and I refuse to waste another second on Giles.'

With that said, Phoebe headed to the waiting cab. The headlights of the oncoming traffic were reflected on the icy road as night began to fall.

'That seems so harsh. He really does regret his behaviour. His mother told me so over our bridge game yesterday,' her mother continued as she followed Phoebe, her pace picking up with each step. 'Please see reason, Phoebe. Giles is committed to making it up to you. He's apparently not at all his usual jovial, outgoing self at the moment. He's taken the postponement very seriously. Esme said he's quite sullen, and that's not like him. She thinks he's turned over a new, more responsible leaf. He's sown his last wild oat.'

She placed her gloved hand over Phoebe's as her daughter reached for the door handle of the cab. Stepping closer, she dropped her voice almost to a whisper.

'Darling, you could do worse. Giles is so very handsome—and let's not forget his family tree. His ancestors arrived on the *Mayflower*.'

Phoebe rolled her eyes in horror that her perfectly coiffed mother, dressed in her favourite New York designer's latest winter collection, was pulling out both the looks *and* the ancestry cards. She watched the driver close the trunk, walk to his door and climb inside.

Pulling her hand free, she responded in an equally low voice. 'Let me see… My sulking but extremely good-looking ex-fiancé, with his impeccable lineage, is apparently committed to me but isn't averse to sleeping with other women. Please, Mother, let's not try to paint him as something he isn't. I don't think he is capable of loving anyone but himself, and I don't believe for a minute that he's turned over a new leaf. And, frankly, I don't care. He ruined any chance of us being husband and wife when he chose to cheat on me.'

She kissed her mother goodbye and climbed into the cab, then dropped the window to hear the last of her mother's not so wise words.

'Darling, as your grandmother always said, every man is entitled to one big mistake in life.'

'He slept with both of my bridesmaids the weekend before our wedding—that's not one big mistake…that's two enormous, deal-breaking mistakes!' Phoebe's voice was no longer soft or controlled and she didn't mind if the cab driver heard. Her frustration had limited her ability to care.

'If you want to be *technical*, it's two….but couldn't you see fit to consider it Giles's one weekend of poor judgement and call it the same mistake?'

The cab pulled away and Phoebe slumped back into the cold leather seat. Over the rattling of the engine she heard her mother's parting words.

'Darling, don't forget—Christmas is a time for forgiveness.'

Phoebe was abruptly stirred from her unpleasant recollection of the pointless argument that had occurred less than twenty-four hours previously. An impeccably groomed flight attendant was standing beside her seat, accompanied by a young girl in a lime-green sweater and matching pants, with a mass of golden curls, a red headband and a big smile. Everything about her was a little too bright for Phoebe at the end of a long-haul flight.

The little helper reached across to Phoebe with a basket of cellophane-wrapped candy. 'If you chew something it will stop your ears getting blocked when we land. Would you like one?'

Phoebe wasn't sure what she wanted, but politely smiled and accepted a sweet. She would never hurt a child's feelings. She had no idea what Phoebe had been put through, and she envied her innocence just a little. The young girl had no idea that boys grew into cads.

'Thank you,' she said, and as the pair moved on to the

next passenger Phoebe unwrapped the candy and slipped it into her mouth.

She wasn't sure of anything. She should be a happily married woman back from an eight-week honeymoon in Europe, but instead she was a single woman about to arrive in the land Down Under. And this trip was probably the first of many she would make on her own.

Midway over the Pacific Ocean she had looked out of her tiny window into complete darkness. It had represented her life…the huge unknown.

The very thought of ever trusting a man again was ludicrous. She would more than likely see out her days as a spinster, she'd told herself as she had flicked through the choices of inflight entertainment when the rest of the passengers had been sound asleep. Her head had been much too busy thinking about things that she knew she couldn't change, and her thoughts had been as unrelenting as they'd been painful.

All men were the same—well, except for her father, she had reminded herself, as she'd realised there was nothing she'd wanted to watch on her personal screen and pulled down her satin night mask to try and shut out the world. He was one of the last decent men and then they broke the mould.

Susy, her best friend since junior college, who had left Washington two years previously to work as a barrister for the Crown Prosecution Service in London, agreed with her. She had sworn off relationships after her last disastrous rendezvous three months prior.

Men were not worth the effort or the heartbreak, the two friends had decided over a late-night international call before Phoebe's flight. They'd both eaten copious amounts of ice cream in different time zones as they'd commiserated. Susy had been devouring her feel-good salted caramel treat after returning home from a long day in court, while Phoebe had been scraping the melted remnants of her cookies and cream ice cream at just past midnight, Washington time.

'They're just not worth it,' Susy had said into the phone as she'd dropped her empty bowl and spoon on the coffee table, kicked off her shoes and reached for a throw.

'Absolutely not worth even a second of our time,' Phoebe had agreed. 'They are full of baloney—and I'm not talking about the good Italian mortadella. I'm talking the cheap and nasty supermarket kind of baloney.'

'My sentiments exactly.'

'Men and women shouldn't even be on the same planet.'

'Not even the same universe,' Susy had replied, reaching for the bowl of luxury candies her mother had sent over for her recent birthday. She'd still been suffering from post-break-up sugar cravings. 'I think the entire male race should be banished. Except for your dad, though, Phoebs— John's a real sweetie, so he can stay. Mine hasn't called since my birthday, so he can take a jet to another planet for a while with the rest of them.'

Not long after their decision to relocate the earth's male population Phoebe had felt her eyes getting heavy and had said goodnight to her friend. She was glad she had such a wonderful friend, but very sad that they had both been hurt by callous men. She had no clue why they had both been dealt bad men cards, but she was resolute that it would never happen again.

Because neither of them would ever date again.

From that day forward it would be all about their careers.

The plane dropped altitude to land. The sun was up and Phoebe looked from the window to see varied-sized squares of brown and green crops making a patchwork quilt of the undulating landscape. It was nothing like landing in Washington, where she lived, or New York, where she had undertaken her medical studies. Australia couldn't be further from either, in distance or in landscape, and for that reason she couldn't be more relieved.

She was a little anxious, but she was a big girl, she kept reminding herself. It would be a healing adventure. A time to bury the past and focus on furthering her career in podiatric surgery. And time away from her mother. As much as Phoebe loved her, she doubted she would miss her while she was still clearly on Team Giles.

Phoebe did, however, have a strong bond with her father John, and would miss him and their long chats about local and world politics, theology, and to which particular rat species Giles belonged. Susy was right—her father *was* one of the last good men. Over the years he had taught Phoebe to seek out answers, to find her path and not to be afraid to experience life and the joys the world had to offer. He had told her always to demand in return the same good manners and consideration that she gave to others, and most importantly to smile….even if her heart was breaking. There were always others far worse off.

And, much to the chagrin of his wife, John had agreed that time away from Washington and the wedding debacle was the best idea for Phoebe.

'We are now commencing our descent into Adelaide. Please ensure your tray table is secured and your seat is in the upright position. We will be landing in fifteen minutes and you will be disembarking at gate twenty-three. The current time in Adelaide is eleven-thirty. Your luggage will be available for collection on Carousel Five. Adelaide is experiencing a heatwave and expecting an extremely hot forty-three degrees for the fifth day in a row. For our overseas passengers, that's a hundred and nine degrees Fahrenheit—so shorts and T-shirts would be the order of the week, since the hot spell is not ending for another few days! We hope you enjoyed your flight and will choose to fly with us in the future.'

Phoebe rested back in her seat and her mind drifted back to the snow-covered streets of Washington that she had left behind. And to her cheating fiancé and quite possibly the world's worst bridesmaids… She thought of her position at the university hospital…and of how, after the flight attendant's announcement, she might quite possibly die of heat stroke on her first day in a new country…

Fifteen minutes later, a disembarked and ever so slightly dishevelled Phoebe looked around the sea of strangers waiting with her in line at Customs and questioned herself for heading to a country where she didn't know a soul. But then reason reminded her that the alternative would be crazier.

Staying with the very charismatic but totally insincere Giles. Accepting his pathetic 'last fling' excuse and her mother's unrelenting need to defend his abominable behaviour due to his impressive family tree… Giles's womanising would have his notable ancestors with their seventeenth-century Pilgrim morals turning in their graves.

She shook her head as she moved one step closer to the booth where a stern-looking official was scrutinising the passports of the very weary long-haul travellers wanting to enter the country.

Despite her stomach churning with nerves at the prospect of being so far from home, particularly at Christmas, she knew she had done the right thing. Remaining in her home town wasn't an option as the two families were joined at the hip, and that closeness wasn't allowing her to heal and move on. Thanksgiving had gone a long way to proving her right, with both families and a supposedly contrite Giles gathering and expecting her to join them. She'd refused, but she had known immediately that Christmas gatherings would be no different.

If she'd stayed it would have given her mother a glimmer of hope that she would rekindle her relationship with Giles. That an ensuing wedding of the year in Washington might be on the cards again, and that the wedding planner would once again ask Phoebe's father to check the diary of the Vice-President to ensure he could attend.

In Phoebe's mind there was absolutely no chance that she would wed a man who had been unfaithful. She couldn't turn the other cheek and ignore his indiscretions. It was the twenty-first century and she had choices. She wanted to be a man's equal partner in life. That was what she needed and if she never found it then she would not take second best. She would rather spend her life alone.

For better or worse with Giles would mean Phoebe always hoping his behaviour would get better, but knowing he'd more than likely get worse. The further away she stepped from her ex-fiancé the more she suspected he had done her a huge favour by showing his true nature before the wedding. No doubt, she surmised, having a wife who wouldn't ruffle feathers but would instead add value to his reputation by having her own medical career, and whose father was a Presidential advisor, had all been part of Giles' political game plan.

It had become painfully clear once she'd broken up with him that Giles had manipulated her for his own benefit. She thought she had fallen in love, but now she wasn't so sure. Perhaps it had been a little rushed, and she'd been caught up in the idea of happily-ever-after once the wedding momentum had started. All of her friends except for Susy were engaged or married and it had seemed a natural progression.

The wedding had been set up so quickly by her mother

who, along with Washington's most popular wedding planner, had had everything moving at the speed of light.

Susy had accepted the role of her maid of honour, and the two young women had been excited about seeing each other after so long, but the day before she'd been due to fly out Susy had called and broken disappointing news. She was unable to leave London as the jury had not returned the verdict on a very prolonged case. In her own words, she'd said she'd have to miss the wedding of her best friend in the world in order to see some bad guys locked away for a very long time in an English prison.

Deflated and disappointed, Phoebe had understood, but it had left her with only two distant cousins in her bridal party. She had agreed to include the young women, who were both twice removed on her mother's side of the family, because she had been secure in the knowledge that Susy would be beside her for the days leading up to her wedding and with her at the altar of the Cathedral Church of Saint Peter and Saint Paul.

She barely knew the girls. She hadn't seen them in over five years and from what she had heard they were party girls who were living on the west coast and their antics in social media were a constant source of embarrassment to their respective families.

It had been decided that it was time they returned to Washington and settled down. They were both single and in their early twenties, and the families' combined strategy had been to use the wedding as their wayward daughters' entrée into the right circles. They'd hoped that a society wedding would help the girls meet potential husbands and leave their wild life behind them.

Unfortunately that had never happened. They'd flown in a few days before the final dress fittings and managed to ruin Phoebe's life in the process.

Looking back, Phoebe realised that everything about

that day had been wrong, but at the time she hadn't been able to step back far enough to see it for what it really was. But now she could. The three months since the scheduled wedding day that never happened had given her time to see Giles for the man he was. Controlling, calculating and ambitious. There was nothing wrong with ambition, but, fuelled by his other character flaws and good looks, it made for a man who would do whatever he wanted, whenever he wanted—and apparently with whomever he wanted. A misogynist, with a lot of family money and connections.

Phoebe would be eternally grateful to the best man, Adrian, who had delivered the bad news the day before their nuptials. She appreciated that it had been a difficult call for him, but knew he had spent a number of months working closely as a political intern with her father and respected him enormously. Adrian had told Phoebe that he cared too much for her and her family to stand by and let Giles hurt her. He'd broken the boys' club rules and she knew he would no doubt pay the price with his peers. She also knew that her father would do his best to support him, but Adrian was not motivated by professional gain and that made his act even more admirable. Honesty in the political arena was rare, and Phoebe and her father were both grateful.

Phoebe's head was spinning as she was finally called up to one of the immigration booths. She dragged her hand luggage behind her and handed over her passport. Then, with everything in order, her visa was stamped and she was waved through to collect her luggage.

'Enjoy your stay, Miss Johnson.'

Phoebe's lips curved slightly. It was an attempt at a smile but she was still not sure how she felt and whether she had just made another of life's bad calls—a huge error she would live to regret almost as much as accepting the first date with Giles and, six short months later, his proposal in the opulent wood-panelled and chandelier-filled dining room of that five star hotel in Washington.

The ring was a spectacular four-carat diamond, set in platinum, and it had been served on a silver platter alongside her *crème brûlée* dessert. A single strategically placed violin had played as Giles had fallen to one knee. But it had only been a fleeting kiss on the forehead he'd given her when she'd agreed to be his wife.

It hadn't been a passionate relationship, but she had still believed their life together could be perfect. He wasn't one to show public displays of affection and she had accepted that. In hindsight, she suspected he preferred to look around at all the enamoured faces in the room rather than at hers. He had enjoyed the attention the proposal had focused on him. In person and in the media.

As she shuffled through the airport to collect her checked baggage Phoebe drew a deep breath and thought about the irony of his reticence in showing any public display of affection with her while enjoying very *private* displays of affection with other women. And she felt sure there had been more than the two she knew about. It was all about appearances. And what happened behind closed doors seemed inconsequential to him.

She shuddered with the thought of how close she'd come to being his wife. And the lies that would have been the foundation of their marriage.

No matter what lay ahead, her life *had* to be better than that.

CHAPTER TWO

THE MOMENT PHOEBE saw the sign *'Welcome to Adelaide'* she decided she would quiet her doubts. There was no room for second-guessing herself. She was already in her new home. *This is it,* she said to herself silently as she collected her luggage and then made her way to the cab rank. *No turning back now.*

The airport was only twenty minutes from the centre of town, where she would be living. The town she would call home for six months. Six months in which she hoped to sort out her life, her head, and if possible her heart—and forget about the man who had seduced her bridesmaids.

'You were supposed to meet potential husbands—not hump the groom!' she muttered under her breath.

Phoebe noticed the cab driver staring at her strangely in the rear vision mirror. His eyes widened. She realised that her muttering must have been audible to him and she bit her lip and looked out of the window in silence.

Phoebe paid the driver, giving him a generous tip. She had been told it was not necessary in Australia, but it was second nature. He placed her suitcases on the pavement and tucked the fare into his pocket. She was left standing in the heat.

It was a dry heat, like the Nevada desert, and it engulfed her like a hot blanket dropped from the sky. She was grateful that she had changed on the two-hour stopover in Auckland, and was now wearing a light cotton sundress and flat sandals. She lugged her heavy suitcases, one at a time, up the steps to the quaint single-fronted sandstone townhouse that she prayed had air-conditioning. The suitcases were so heavy it would have cost a small fortune in excess baggage if her father hadn't insisted on paying for her first class flight.

On Phoebe's personal budget, post hand-beaded wedding dress, along with the purchase of the maid of honour's and the bridesmaids' dresses, beautifully crafted designer heels for four, three pearl thank-you bracelets and half of a non-refundable European honeymoon, she could only have managed a premium economy flight. But she'd been so desperate to leave Washington for the furthest place that came to mind she would have rowed to Australia just to get away from the drama of the cancelled wedding and her desolate mother.

Phoebe drew another laboured breath. A week ago she'd known little of Adelaide, save the international bike race and the tennis that took over the city in January. Her career as a podiatric surgeon specialising in sports-related conditions made her aware of most large-scale sporting events worldwide. She hoped that her skills would be utilised in Adelaide, a city ten thousand miles from home. She was there with no clear plan for the future. She did, however, have a job.

Her father had been wonderful. It was fortunate for Phoebe that his role at the White House gave him the knowledge and connections to assist her, which meant that her application to practise in Australia had been fast-tracked. She met all of the criteria, and her credentials were impeccable, so approval had been granted.

She'd had the option of a small practice in Adelaide or a much larger practice in Melbourne that focused entirely on elite sportsmen and women. While the second option was her dream job, it was still a few weeks off being secured, and Phoebe had liked the idea of leaving town immediately. She had also done some research around the sole practitioner, Dr Ken Rollins, a podiatric surgeon in his early sixties with an inner-city practice and the need for an associate for six months. The position sounded perfect. His research papers were particularly interesting and Phoebe looked forward to working with him.

So she was more than happy with her decision. They were two very different opportunities, but she felt confident she had made the right choice.

Opening the door to her leased townhouse was heavenly. It was like opening a refrigerator. The air-conditioning was on high and the blinds were half closed, giving a calm ambience to the space. There was a large basket of fruit and assorted nibbles on the kitchen bench. Her father, no doubt, she mused.

She dropped her bags, closed the front door and wandered around the house for a moment before she found the bedroom and flung herself across the bed. Embarrassed at remembering what she'd said to herself in the cab, she kicked off her shoes and then reminded herself that the driver would have witnessed far worse than a jet-lagged passenger's mutterings. The pillow was so cool and soft against her face as she closed her heavy eyes. Exhaustion finally got the better of her and she fell into a deep unexpected sleep.

It was nearly four hours before Phoebe stirred from her unplanned afternoon nap. Her rumbling stomach had woken her and she remembered the basket she had spied on her arrival. The fruit was delicious, and she had opened the refrigerator door to find sparkling water, assorted juices, a cold seafood platter, two small salads and half a dozen single serve yoghurt tubs.

Thanks, Dad.

She smiled. She knew her father must have called the landlord and arranged for the house to be stocked. She knew, despite what she said, that he felt to blame for the way everything had turned out as *he* had introduced to her young, 'going places' political intern fiancé.

John Johnson had thought Giles was a focussed young man with a huge career ahead of him and he'd had no hesitation in introducing him to Phoebe. He'd been polite, astute, with no apparent skeletons in the closet, and from a well-respected Washington family. But they had all been hoodwinked.

There was no way that John could have foreseen the disaster. And he had done everything in his power to get her away from the situation when it had turned ugly. Phoebe would never blame him for anything.

After eating, Phoebe showered and sent her father a text message to let him know she was safe and sound and to thank him for everything he had arranged. Then she raised the air-conditioning temperature enough to ensure that she didn't freeze during the night before setting the alarm on her phone and climbing back into bed.

She just wanted to be fresh and not suffering the effects of jet-lag.

Eight hours later, as Phoebe lifted the blinds and looked across the Adelaide parklands, she felt refreshed. She had never flown such a distance and had expected to be exhausted, but she was feeling better than she had in months. It was as if a weight had been lifted from her shoulders.

The view from her bedroom window was picturesque. The morning sun lit up the large pinkish-grey gum trees towering over the beautifully manicured gardens. The flowers were in bloom in the garden's beds and it was like a pastel rainbow. It was a new beginning.

She reached for her phone and took a snapshot, sent it to her father in a quick text, then headed for the shower. She wasn't about to be late for her first day on the job. She wanted to get there early and learn the ropes before the patients arrived. Working with an older, more experienced specialist would be a learning experience for Phoebe, and she was excited by the prospect. It would keep her mind off everything she had been through.

Ken Rollins's papers focussed on his holistic and conservative approach in treating lower limb conditions, using a variety of modalities such as gait retraining, orthotic therapy, dry needling and exercise modification. Phoebe had printed the most recent before she'd left Washington and she'd read it on her flight over. He would be a great mentor.

It was going to be a much-needed change and Phoebe couldn't be more optimistic. After all, she had heard Adelaide was the place to raise children or retire, and it had the highest aging population of any other capital city, so she assumed there would be a lower than average population of single men. Single, arrogant, self-serving men, all incapable of remaining faithful. There truly couldn't be a better city in the world for her at that moment, but for the fact that she knew she would miss Christmas with her family. It was her favourite time of year. But it was the price she had to pay for her sanity.

As Phoebe stepped out of her house half an hour later the heat of the day was already building. She felt glad she had chosen a simple cream skirt that skimmed her knees, a black and cream striped blouse and black patent Mary Jane kitten heels with a slingback, so she didn't need to wear stockings. Her shoulder-length chestnut hair was pulled into a high ponytail and she had applied tinted sunscreen, a light lip gloss and some mascara.

She hoped the practice rooms would be as cool as her

townhouse. Her previous address at this time of the year was freezing cold at best and icy on bad days. She knew she wouldn't cope in the heat for too long, but felt confident that the inner-city practice would be cool as a cucumber.

Unfortunately, as she discovered five minutes later, she couldn't have been more wrong. The air-conditioning at the practice had been working overtime during the heat-wave. Phoebe had arrived when the city had been sweltering for close to a week. The infrastructure of the old building was buckling and clearly the air-conditioning had been the first thing to succumb. It was like a sauna as she entered, and she wondered if it wasn't cooler outside than inside the old building.

A bell above the door had chimed as she'd walked in but the waiting room was empty and it appeared no one had heard her enter. Standing alone in the uncomfortable, stifling air she felt sure that in minutes she would be reduced to a melting mess. Not a great first impression, she surmised as she looked around anxiously, all the while hoping that Ken Rollins would appear at any minute and take her into the air-conditioned section of the practice. There *had* to be an air-conditioned part.

Then, in the distance, she heard a noise and saw a very tall male figure walking down the corridor towards her. She blinked as she saw that he was bare to the waist with a white hand towel around his neck. She pinned her hopes on the fact this man was working on the air-conditioning and that he was good at his job, because she was wilting quickly. And she doubted her more senior boss would enjoy working in these conditions either.

She couldn't help but notice as he drew near that the man was wearing dress pants and highly polished shoes. Although nothing covered his very chiselled, sweat-dampened chest.

'I'm looking for Dr Ken Rollins. I'm Dr Phoebe Johnson from Washington.'

'*You're* Phoebe Johnson?' the man said, with a look of surprise on his handsome face and doubt colouring his deep voice.

'Yes, I am. Did he tell you I was arriving?'

The man wiped his forehead and then his hands on the towel he was carrying, then stretched out his free hand. 'I'm Heath Rollins, Ken's son, and I've been expecting you.'

His voice was sonorous and austere. And the frown on Phoebe's face did little to mask her confusion. *Why on earth was he expecting her and why was he half naked?*

'So are you here to repair the air-conditioning for your father?'

'Not exactly. I'm attempting to repair the air-con, but I'm not a repairman—not even close as you can tell by how hot it still is in here. I'm a podiatric surgeon from Sydney.'

Phoebe was more confused than ever. Why did Ken Rollins have his *podiatric surgeon* son trying to fix the air-conditioning unit? And why wasn't Ken there to meet her?

'Is your father in with patients already?' she asked as she looked around her surroundings, hoping that the older surgeon would suddenly appear and clear up the confusion. And bring his son a shirt so he could cover up.

'No, he's not...'

'Is he running late?'

'No he's not,' he replied without any hint of emotion in his reply. 'I'm actually standing in for him for the next four weeks.'

Phoebe quickly realised as she shook his hand that the man standing before her was potentially her new boss. She took a few steps back from the very warm handshake and looked warily at him. She had signed on to work with *Ken* Rollins. *This* Dr Rollins was definitely not in his sixties. *Disastrous*, was the first thought that came to her mind. The second thought, as she looked at his lightly tanned physique, was not in any way ladylike and nothing she wanted to be considering with this man. Or *any* man, now that she had sworn off the species. It was not what she needed. In fact this was close to a catastrophe.

She had envisaged an older, established and experienced mentor to work closely with for five days a week over the next six months. This was supposed to be a professional development opportunity. And the man standing before her stripped to the waist was anything but professional development. He was not what she wanted and nor did she have the capacity to deal with him either. With the combination of Heath Rollins's half-naked physique and the heat in the room Phoebe knew she had stepped into the fire—literally.

'Where exactly *is* your father?' she asked. 'And why are you stepping in for him?'

As she spoke she was doing her best not to be distracted by his very toned body or his equally gorgeous eyes. But it was a struggle, and she faced the prospect that the cruel hand of the universe had just replaced her playboy fiancé with someone even more handsome, if a comparison was to be made. And she had to work with him until almost the middle of the following year. Six long months.

She settled her eyes on the stubble-covered cleft in his chin, then moved them to his soft full lips, framed by dimples and slightly smiling, and then finally she looked up and discovered his brilliant blue eyes.

She had to admit that he was a very different type from Giles. This man had more cowboy good-looks, while Giles was the Wall Street slick type. But she didn't want *any* type of good-looking and she was far from happy with the arrangement. Good-looking men were all the same, and a long-haul trip to the other side of the world only to find that fate had ordered her another one was not what she had wanted.

Suddenly she felt a little dizzy. The heat was closing in by the minute. She mopped her forehead with a tissue as she reached for a seat and promptly sat down with a sigh. Her plans had gone terribly awry and the added lack of air-conditioning made it unbearable. This was nothing close to the first day she had planned in her mind.

'I sent you an email outlining the changes,' he said, his lean fingers rubbing his chin. 'You shouldn't be surprised.'

'What email?' she managed as she looked around for something to use as a fan and grabbed a magazine, which she moved frantically through the air in front of her face in the hope that it would cool her down.

'The one that clearly explained my father was in an accident two days ago, fractured his patella and had to undergo surgery, so you'll be working alongside me until he returns.'

'So he's coming back?' she asked, with a little relief colouring her voice. 'When, exactly?'

'In about a month, if his rehabilitation goes as planned. It wasn't a complete reconstruction, so he should be back on deck a lot sooner than after a full recon.'

Phoebe nodded and bit the inside of her cheek as she considered his response. At least it was four weeks, not six months. She felt a little better about the time frame but the confirmation that Heath was going to be her boss, for however short or long a time, was still not news she needed to hear.

She kept her improvised fan moving through the thick air, trying to bring some relief to the situation. Against the oppressive heat it was little use; against news of the working arrangements it was no use at all. For the next four weeks she would be working with a man too hand-some for his own good and definitely for the good of all the women who fell victim to his charm. But, thinking of what she had just escaped, she knew she would never fall for a man like Heath. Not that she was on the market for anyone anyway.

She loosened the belt cinched at her waist to allow her to breathe a little more easily in the mugginess that was wrapping around her.

'You're looking extremely pale,' he said, with something she thought sounded like a level of concern. 'I'll get a glass of water for you.'

Phoebe swayed to and fro in her seat, watching as Heath crossed back to her with a plastic cup he had filled from the water cooler. She took a few sips, then shakily handed him back the cup. Just as the polished wooden floor became a checked pattern that surged towards her in waves. As she fought the swirling focus that made her feel more disorientated by the minute, she wondered why any of this had happened to her.

Was there any way she could escape the heat? Why did Ken have to wreck his knee *now*? Why did she have to work with *this* man for the next few weeks?

Suddenly there were no more questions. The stifling heat finally claimed her. And Dr Phoebe Johnson fainted into Heath's strong arms.

CHAPTER THREE

'GOOD, YOU'RE BACK with us.'

Phoebe heard the deep timbre of a male voice very close, and when she opened her eyes she realised just how close. She was facing some well-defined and very naked male abdominal muscles, only inches away from her. Her brow formed a frown as she realised she recognised the distinctly Australian accent. It was her temporary boss—and in her direct line of vision was his bare tanned stomach.

Still lying down, she attempted to let her eyes roam her surroundings—until she was finally forced to look up and see Heath looking down at her. She couldn't read his expression. He wasn't frowning, but nor was he smiling. His look was serious. Concerned. And the concern appeared genuine. She discovered her resting place was an examination table. And soon realised there was a cool towel on her forehead and that a portable fan was stirring the heavy air and moving the fine wisps of hair that had escaped from her ponytail.

'She's lucky you were there to catch her. Sorry—I stepped out to get a cool drink and missed her.'

Phoebe heard a second voice. It belonged to a female but she couldn't see anyone from her vantage point. It made sense to her, even in her disorientated state, that for him to have set so much in place so quickly, such as the cool towel and the fan, he had to have had some assistance.

'I must apologise, Phoebe. I'd hoped to have the air-con up and running before you arrived,' Heath said, in a serious, professional tone that belied his appearance. He looked more like a private dancer than a stoic doctor. 'I'm not surprised you passed out. Aussie summers can be tough if you're not used to them.'

Phoebe was so embarrassed when she realised what had happened. She stirred from her horizontal position, but still felt light-headed so didn't attempt to sit completely upright immediately. But while she slowly moved she remembered a little of the conversation they had shared—including the news he had imparted to her. *'You'll be working alongside me.'* Silently she begged the universe to tell her it wasn't true.

The last thing she needed was a man like Heath. She needed to be thinking about her career as a podiatric surgeon and she wanted to be taught by an experienced older practitioner. This new arrangement was not a dynamic she had even considered as a possibility when she'd agreed to work in Adelaide. She'd thought it would be six months of respite. An emotionally healing time packaged as a working sabbatical.

'Here's some water,' the young woman said as she stepped into view, and she handed Heath a glass with a plastic concertina straw. 'It's not too cold.'

Phoebe squinted as she tried to focus. The woman looked to be in her mid-twenties. Blonde, quite tall, very pretty, with a lovely smile. Phoebe suddenly felt Heath's strong arm lift her upright, yet there was no warmth in the way he held her. It was as if she was an inanimate object.

'Hold on to your cold compress and sip this,' he said as he curved the straw to meet her lips.

He held the drink steady with one hand while the other still supported her. His bedside manner she would have described as 'reserved' at best.

Phoebe held the cold towel in place as she slowly sucked the water through the straw and felt immediately better for it. But the sight of her skirt no longer demurely skimming her knees did not make her feel good at all. Most of her legs were bare, for the world and Dr Heath Rollins to see, and she was horrified.

'I've had enough, thank you,' she said as she moved her mouth away from the drink and then, struggling to keep the towel on her head, she tried to lift her bottom slightly and release the hem of the skirt.

There was little covered at all. Fainting and baring parts of her anatomy that should be saved for the beach, or more intimate encounters, was definitely *not* a great start to this already less than desirable working relationship. She had secured the job purely on her references, and now she could only guess what he was thinking as she reached down to gain some dignity.

'Here—let me help you.'

His hands lifted her gently and with ease. Her heartbeat suddenly increased with the unexpected touch of his hands on her bare skin. Suddenly she did not feel like an inanimate object. And this time her giddiness wasn't from the heat of the room. His closeness while he held her up made the job of adjusting her clothing difficult. She finally wriggled the skirt into place and swung her legs around, subtly encouraging Heath to release her and step back.

Clearing her throat, and raising her chin a little defensively, Phoebe looked at Heath as if he were almost the perpetrator of the incident. 'How exactly—?' she began and then paused for a moment. 'How did I get here? I don't remember leaving the reception area. I do remember feeling very hot, then light-headed, but where was I when I fainted?'

'You passed out on a chair in the waiting room, and I carried you in here and put you on your side. You were out for less than a minute. As soon as your head was level with your body you came to.'

The way he spoke was quite clinical and detached, but she still managed to feel uneasy at the mental picture of him scooping her up in his arms and carrying her to the examination bed with little or no effort.

Her eyes briefly scanned his firefighter physique before she blinked and turned away. Ken Rollins would be back before she knew it, she told herself. Then all would be right in her world again. This was just a hiccup in her plans. And if Heath's attitude was anything to go by she had nothing to worry about. His body might have been created for sin but his manner certainly hadn't.

'Thank you. I'm sorry I created such a fuss.' Her tone quickly mimicked his coolness.

'These things happen, but you seem fine now,' he said as he stepped back further and turned to face the other woman.

'Tilly, you can finish up. I think we're fine here. Thanks for cancelling the next two days' patients. The air-con should be repaired by Thursday. You can pick up the twins from childcare early and stay home for a couple of days.'

'Are you sure, Heath? I can come in and do some accounts and general office catch-up work tomorrow.'

'No,' he replied firmly, wiping his brow with the back of his hand. 'It's like a sauna today and it will be worse tomorrow. It's a health and safety issue to be working in these conditions.'

'All right—have it your way,' Tilly said as she reached over and kissed him on the cheek. 'See you at home tonight, then. Oh, and Dr Johnson? I hope you feel better soon.'

'Thank you, but please call me Phoebe.'

Phoebe looked down at the young woman's hand as she left the room and saw a wedding band and stunning solitaire diamond. They were married. And they had twins. Of course they did. They were perfect for each other. Two stunning blonde Aussies, sun-kissed and fabulous. She could only guess how gorgeous their children would be.

Phoebe wondered if she had read Heath incorrectly. Perhaps he *wasn't* a Giles clone. Perhaps he was an austere but loving husband who just happened to be very good-looking and in Phoebe's still emotionally raw state that had incorrectly translated to him being a potential cad. All good-looking men had been tarnished by Giles. And she had clearly been scarred.

She suddenly felt very self-conscious, and a little sad at her own ability to jump to conclusions. Perhaps all men were not the same... Just the one she had chosen. And Susy's recent choice too.

Moving awkwardly on the examination table, she tried to inch her skirt down further to cover her knees.

He shook his head. 'You don't have to rush to cover up. I'm not looking at your legs, if that's what you're worried about.'

Phoebe felt instantly embarrassed. She began fidgeting nervously and smoothing the rest of her clothes into place, and then tidying her hair in an attempt to gain composure without saying a word. There was nothing that came to mind that wouldn't make her appear even sillier and more self-conscious, so she stayed silent.

Heath watched the way she was fussing. He found her behaviour so far from the image he had created in his mind of a podiatric surgeon from Washington with impeccable references, who was triple board certified in surgery, orthopaedics, and primary podiatric medicine. She was also a Fellow of the American College of Foot and Ankle Surgeons, the American Academy of Podiatric Sports Medicine and the American College of Foot & Ankle Orthopaedics & Medicine. All of those qualifications had had him picturing someone very different. He'd thought she would be brimming with confidence, more than a little aloof. And definitely nowhere near as pretty.

Dr Phoebe Johnson had taken Heath by surprise...

Phoebe's blood pressure had slowly returned to normal and she felt more steady physically.

'So, what would you like me to do? I guess if you've cancelled the patients there's probably no point me being here. I can take some patient notes back to my house and read over them.'

She looked around and ascertained where she was in relation to the front door and the reception area, where she assumed her bag would be, and headed in that direction. His wife, she assumed, had already left.

'There's definitely no point you staying here, and to be honest your first two days' patients are post-op and quite straightforward,' he told her as he followed her out to where her bag was resting by a chair. 'Here is probably the worst place to be. We don't want a repeat performance.'

The waiting room and reception area was even hotter as it faced the glare of the morning sun on the huge glass panes.

'If you're sure I can't do anything here, then I'll see you on Thursday.'

She reached for the front door and he stepped closer to her to hold the door open. Her face looked angelic, and he was intrigued by her. He momentarily wondered why, with all her experience and qualifications, she wanted to work in Adelaide, of all places? Suddenly he felt curious. She was just nothing like he had imagined. He could work out most people, and he prided himself on being able to know what made them tick. But not her. Not yet.

When he'd glanced over her résumé in search of her contact details he had worried that she would not find the practice enough of a challenge, with her interests and her extensive experience in sports podiatry, but then had conceded that she had made her professional choice and it was none of his concern. And if she did grow bored and move on before the six months were up—again, it was not his concern. He wouldn't be there long enough for it to have any impact on him. His father could find a replacement if she did.

'Okay, I'll see you on Thursday.'

'Yes. I'll see you then,' Phoebe responded as she walked past him into a wall of warm, dry air.

She wasn't sure if it was warmer outside than in, but it felt less humid—although she quickly realised neither was particularly pleasant. It was still early, but the pavement held the heat from the day before and she could tell it would be blisteringly hot in a few hours.

'I hope you find a way to stay cool.'

Without much emotion in his voice, but clearly being polite, he said, 'I think I'll take my son to the pool later on today. Maybe you should hit the beach or a pool—there's quite a few around. There are some indoor ones too. Oscar's looking forward to finding some other children to play with.' Before he turned to walk inside he added, 'I hope you find a way to stay cool too.'

Phoebe stopped in her tracks. 'I thought you and your wife had twins?' she called back to him from the bottom step, with a curious frown dressing her brow.

'No, my sister Tilly has twin girls, but they're only two and a half years old. Oscar's five,' he told her, with a little more animation. 'Tilly's like a mother to Oscar while we're in town, and it's been good for him since it's just the two of us the rest of the time. I'm sure as they grow up the cousins will all be great friends, but right now Oscar really doesn't find them much fun at all.'

He looked back at Phoebe with an expression she

couldn't quite make out as he paused in the doorway, as if he was thinking something through before he spoke.

Phoebe turned to leave.

'It's ridiculously hot out there,' he remarked, catching her attention. 'If you have time perhaps we could pop round to the corner café and grab a cool drink. I wouldn't want you fainting on the way home. I can answer any questions you have about the practice.'

Phoebe could see he was a very serious man—nothing like Giles, with his smooth flirtatious manner. But there was something about Heath that made her curious. She reminded herself that she would never be interested in him in any way romantically, but with his demeanour she didn't flag him as a threat to her reborn virginal status. And she did want to know about the running of the practice so she decided to accept his invitation. He was her boss after all.

'I have time.'

Phoebe had decided on the quick walk to the café that she did not want to discuss her personal life and that she would not enquire about his. She knew enough. He was Ken Rollins's son. He was filling in for a month, and he was the single father of a five-year-old boy. That was more than enough. Whether he was divorced or had never been married was none of her business and immaterial.

She wasn't going to be spending enough time with Heath for his personal life to matter. Four weeks would pass quickly and then he and his son would be gone. She wasn't sure if she would ever even meet the boy. It wasn't as if a medical practice dealing with feet would be the most interesting place for a child to visit, she mused, so their paths might never cross.

'Thank you,' she said as she stepped inside the wonderfully cool and thankfully not too densely populated coffee shop.

'They make a nice iced coffee,' Heath told her as they made their way to a corner table and he placed his laptop containing patient notes beside him. 'It's barista coffee, and they add ice-cold milk and whipped cream. They do it well.'

'Sounds perfect—but perhaps hold the cream.'

'Looking after your heart?' he enquired as he pulled out the chair for her.

In more ways than one, she thought.

It was a surprise to Phoebe how easy she found it to talk with Heath. While he was still reserved, and borderline frosty, he was attentive and engaged in their discussion. He asked about her work at the hospital in Washington and their conversation was far from stilted, due to their mutual love of their specialty. With Giles, she had not spoken much about her work as he hadn't seemed to understand it and nor had he wanted to. It had been plain that he wasn't interested and he'd never pretended to care. It had been all about *his* career aspirations and how they could achieve them together.

'I've seen your résumé—it's impressive, but definitely geared towards sports podiatry. My father's practice is predominately general patient load along with the occasional sportsman or woman—not the focus I assume you're accustomed to. How do you think you will adjust to that?'

'Sports podiatry is a passion of mine. I've been working in a fantastic unit within a large teaching hospital, where we offer a full spectrum of services for the athlete—including physical therapy and surgery, with an emphasis on biomechanics. My focus outside of essential surgical intervention was primarily on orthotic treatment directed to correct structural deficiency and muscular imbalance. But in general my goal is to return any patient, regardless of their profession, to their maximum level of function and allow them to re-engage in an active life.'

Heath agreed with all she was saying, but added, 'I understand—I just hope you don't begin to feel that this practice is not what you signed up for.'

'No, I love what I do—and feet are feet, no matter what the owners of them do.'

Heath found her answer amusing, but he didn't smile. He rarely did, and those moments were saved for his son. And there was still that unanswered question…

'So tell me, Phoebe, if you love the hospital back in your hometown, you enjoy your work and your colleagues, why did you want to leave?'

Phoebe nervously took a sip of the icy drink. It was rich and flavoursome, just as good as he had promised…and she was stalling. 'I needed a break from Washington,' she finally responded.

'A Caribbean cruise or skiing in Aspen would have been easier than relocating to the other side of the world. And if you were looking for alternative employers I'm sure there must be loads of options for someone of your calibre in the US. It's a big country.'

'I wanted more than a quick vacation or a new employer. It was time for a sea change.'

'Like I said, there are a lot of places that would fit that bill on your own continent—and I'm sure with a lot less red tape than it must have taken for you to work Down Under.'

'I suppose,' she said nonchalantly, trying to deflect his interest in her reasons for being there, which did not seem to be abating easily with anything she said.

It wasn't the Spanish Inquisition, but it felt close. Phoebe did not want to go into the details of her failed engagement to Giles. Nor her desperate need to escape from him and her mother to a place neither would find her. And there was no way he would ever hear from her the tale of the bridesmaids from hell bedding the groom. It was all too humiliating. And still too raw.

Heath was her temporary boss and he would be leaving once his father's knee had healed. The less he knew the better. In fact the less everyone in the city knew about her the better.

'Your father's interest in harnessing the power of biomechanics and advanced medical technology to challenge convention and his ensuing breakthrough results were huge draw cards for me to come and work with him. And I wanted to know more about his collaborative approach to co-morbidities. Your father wrote a great paper on the subject of the co-operative approach to treating systemic problems.'

Heath sensed there was more, but he took her cue to leave the subject alone. He appreciated she had a right to her privacy on certain matters. Just as he did to his own. And there was no need for him to know too much, he reminded himself, as they would be working together for a relatively short time and then he would be leaving. Theirs would be a brief working relationship. Nothing more.

But, stepping momentarily away from being her very temporary boss, he had to admit Phoebe was undeniably beautiful.

Phoebe shifted awkwardly in her seat, not sure if Heath had accepted her response and they could move on. Unaware that her glass was empty, she casually took another sip through her straw. Suddenly the loudest slurp she had ever heard rang out. To Phoebe's horror, apparently it was the loudest the people at an adjacent table had ever heard too, as they shot her a curious stare.

The sound echoed around the café. Phoebe's eyes rolled with embarrassment. Only half an hour before she had passed out in his arms, revealed far too much of her legs, and now her manners were more befitting a preschooler.

She wanted to find an inconspicuous hole and slink inside. Heath had such a serious demeanour she could only imagine what he was thinking. It was, without doubt, the worst first day on the job of anyone—ever.

'I told you they make the best iced coffee. There's never enough in my glass either,' Heath said, his mouth almost forming a smile.

It was the first time, in the hour or so since they'd met, that she had seen him show anything even vaguely like a smile. And it was the most gorgeous almost-smile she had ever seen. Her heart unexpectedly skipped a beat.

Giles would have been mortified, she thought. He would have shot her a glare that told her she had embarrassed him. His body language would have reminded her that it was unladylike without saying a word. She would have felt his displeasure while those around would have had no idea. But Heath didn't appear to react that way, and it surprised her. Apparently in his eyes it was *not* cringeworthy behaviour—or if he thought it was he certainly masked it well.

She felt her embarrassment slowly dissipate. Maybe it wasn't the worst day ever after all. And that was confirmed when he continued the conversation as if nothing had happened.

'So, how do you see this working arrangement? Are you happy to split your time with taking half of my father's post-operative patients and the remainder to be new patients, along with a surgical roster?'

'That sounds great to me. I'm fairly flexible—not a hard and fast rules kind of woman—so we can just see how it all works out, and if we need to move around within those parameters we can discuss it as it unfolds.'

Heath didn't feel the same way at all. 'You'll learn quickly that I'm a rules kind of a man. I live by a number of them, and if I set something up then I like to stick by it. So I'd rather we made up our minds and set up now the way it will play out.'

'I guess…' Phoebe replied, a little taken aback by his rigid stance on their working arrangements. She had heard that Australian people were laid-back. Heath didn't fit that bill at all. 'But in my opinion most situations have both a teething period and a grey area. There's generally room to manoeuvre and move around with some degree of compromise if you're willing to look for it.'

'Not with me. Once I've made a decision, it's rare that I'll shift my viewpoint. In fact it would take something extraordinary to make me change my mind.'

While she appreciated Heath's honesty upfront, she thought she would pity whoever lived with him if they got the bathroom roster wrong. 'Well, then, since it's only for a month let's go with your way. You undoubtedly know the practice and the patient load better than I do, so I'm happy to carve it in stone right now if that's how it's done around here.'

Heath appreciated her wit, but made no retort.

An hour later they were still at the café. Once they had agreed to their working arrangements Heath had dropped all other lines of questioning and given Phoebe the low-down on the city she would call home for a few months.

Despite the ease with which they spoke, Heath had still not had his questions answered about Phoebe's motives for relocating. But he did know she was a lot more adaptable than he was. It made him curious, although he didn't verbalise it.

With her academic record the surgical world was quite literally her oyster. There would be few, if any, practices or teaching facilities that would not welcome her into their fold with open arms. There was no ring on her finger, but he would not be arrogant enough to assume that there was no man in her life. If there was then he too must be as adaptable as Phoebe, and willing to compromise and let her travel to the other side of the world for work. *He* was not that type of man.

'Adelaide is very quiet, I assume?' she asked as she relaxed back into her chair and admired the artwork on the café walls.

'Yes—a little too relaxed in pace for me. It's very different from Sydney, which I prefer. I grew up here, but moved to Sydney about ten years ago when I finished my internship. I was offered a position on the east coast and I took it.'

'I'd like to see Sydney one day, but I think Adelaide will be lovely for the next six months.'

'Adelaide's like a very large country town,' Heath replied. 'And that's the reason I never stay too long.'

'A large country town suits me. It isn't the size of the town but more the attitude of the people that matters.'

Heath watched Phoebe as she studied the eclectic collection of watercolour paintings and charcoal sketches on the wall. She was smiling as she looked at the work of novice artists and he could see her appreciation of the pieces. There was no sign of the big town superiority that he had thought she might display, and she didn't launch into a spiel about comparisons with Washington, as he had expected.

'That's what my father keeps telling me when I try to get him to relocate to Sydney. He won't budge. He likes the growing medical research sector in Adelaide, even if it's a small city by comparison.'

'From all reports he's one of the finest podiatric surgeons in the southern hemisphere. I look forward to meeting him when he's up to it.' While Heath had not enquired more about her reasons for relocating, to cement that line of questioning shut she added, 'Your father's work is revolutionary in its simplicity, and I respect his conservative

approach of proceeding, where possible, with surgery as
the second not the first option. His expertise in soft tissue
manipulation and trigger point therapy is impressive. A lot
of practitioners routinely go for surgery, but your father is
quite the opposite, preferring to view his patients through
a holistic filter and follow a slightly more protracted but
less invasive treatment plan.'

Heath could see that his father's work had made quite
an impression on Phoebe. 'I hope you're not disappointed
that you'll be working with me. It's like ordering Chinese
takeout and having pizza arrive on your doorstep.'

Phoebe liked his quirky analogy, although it seemed
at odds with his less than lighthearted nature. He was
far from a poor second, and she silently admitted that
pizza was a favourite of hers. Heath was charming and
knowledgeable, and his reserved demeanour was a pleasant change.

Although his rigid viewpoint might possibly test her
reserves of patience in the long term, she was very much
looking forward to working with him in the short term.
She doubted he would disappoint on any level, but professional was the only level she was interested in exploring.

Heath considered the woman sitting opposite him for a
moment. She was a highly regarded surgeon in their mutual field, but there was a mixture of strength and frailty
to her. It was as if she was hiding, or running away from
something. And he wasn't sure *why* he wanted to work her
out, except that it was as if she was second-guessing herself on some level. He had no idea why she would.

Heath knew that she was an only child, that her father
was a Presidential advisor and her mother a Washington
socialite, and that she'd spent her high school years at a
prestigious private school in Washington. She had openly
chatted about that. He also knew that she had graduated
top of her class from her studies at the New York College

of Podiatric Medicine, and had done her three-year residency at the university hospital.

It would appear she had the makings of someone who could be quite consumed with their own self-importance, but she wasn't. She was, he'd realised quickly, very humble—because Heath knew of her Dux status from his father, not from her. Phoebe hadn't brought it up. It was a huge honour and she was omitting it from her abbreviated life story over morning coffee.

In that way she was not unlike his wife, Natasha—a former model and fashion designer who had also been very humble about the accolades she'd been given both on and off the runway.

Natasha had not been at all what Heath had imagined a model would be like the night he'd met her at a fundraising event. He'd been thirty and she only twenty-three. After a whirlwind courtship they'd married, and Natasha had fallen pregnant soon afterwards. They'd both been so excited and looking forward to growing their family.

Heath had come to learn that she worked actively and tirelessly for many causes—including one to support research into a cure for the disease that had eventually claimed her life. And from that day, Heath's purpose in life—his only focus outside of his work—had been raising their beautiful little boy, Oscar, who had been given life by the only woman Heath had ever loved.

And nothing and no one would ever come between them.

Not his work and not a woman.

It was a promise he'd made to himself five years earlier. The day he lost his wife. The day he'd walked away from the hospital without her and realised he would never again hold her in his arms or wake next to her in the bed they had shared. He'd vowed that day that he would dedicate his life to being the kind of father to their son that Natasha would have wanted.

And he would never wake with another woman in his arms.

He had been true to both promises.

Oddly, sitting with Phoebe, he felt almost comfortable, more at ease than in a long time, and he suspected their mutual professional interests had a lot to do with that. He couldn't remember the last time he had spoken in depth to a woman about his chosen career and engaged in a meaningful conversation. He had taken lovers over the years, but nothing more than a shared night. He left before dawn, and conversation was at the bottom of the list of his needs on those occasions.

'I'd better let you go and I'll head back to the practice and sort out the air-con, or we'll have melted patients for the next few months,' Heath told her in a matter-of-fact tone as he stood. 'It's only December, and both January and February are hotter months in general.'

Phoebe was taken aback by the way Heath ended their time together. He had invited her to go for a drink and now he was excusing himself quite abruptly. Not that she minded at all. In fact she was relieved, as it gave him no further opportunity to quiz her about her personal life.

'You mean hotter than this?' Phoebe asked.

'Not hotter, but hot for longer stretches.'

Phoebe shrugged. 'Well, then, I *really* hope you get the air-conditioner working.'

He paid the tab and walked Phoebe to the door and then out into the street. His body language was stiff and distant again. Any hint of being relaxed had evaporated.

'I'll see you in a few days. Take some downtime to recover from your trip and I'll see you on Thursday morning at eight. If you get a chance, try to head to the beach or a pool. It will do you the world of good.'

Phoebe nodded. 'Okay, thanks—maybe I will.' She walked away, then suddenly turned around and called out. 'Heath, we never discussed Thursday's patients.'

Heath turned back and looked at Phoebe for the longest moment, then glanced at the laptop tucked loosely under his arm. 'We didn't, didn't we?'

CHAPTER FOUR

'DADDY!'

Heath was welcomed home by tiny arms that wrapped around his knees and hugged him ferociously. He bent down and returned the hug before he picked up his son in his strong arms and swung him around like a carousel ride. Oscar was his reason for living. He had been the beacon of hope during his darkest days. Heath would never let Oscar down. No matter what the future held, he would be his son's anchor through life. He was the only thing that brought a smile to Heath's face and love to an otherwise broken heart.

'How's my favourite little man?' he asked, kissing his tiny son's chubby cheek.

'I'm good, Daddy.'

Heath lowered him to the ground, then sat on the sofa. Oscar climbed up next to him.

'Can we go to the pool tomorrow—can we, please?'

Heath considered his son for a moment. He had his mother's deep brown eyes and he was the apple of his father's. There was nothing Heath wouldn't do for him, but he did like to have fun and tease him a little sometimes.

'I thought you hated the pool? You distinctly told me the other day that you never, *ever* wanted to go swimming again. You said that you would rather eat live worms than go to a swimming pool!'

'Don't be silly, Daddy. I *loooooove* the pool!'

Heath picked Oscar up and put him on his lap and held him tightly. 'Then it looks like tomorrow we're off to the pool, my little man.'

Phoebe enjoyed a lazy sleep-in the next day. It would end, she knew, when the air-conditioning at the practice was repaired, so she made the most of it. Then she had a quick shower, put on shorts, sandals and a T-shirt, and went out to buy a newspaper. While she enjoyed a light breakfast she planned on reading local stories of interest and about the issues affecting the town she would call home for the near future.

When she arrived home there was a delivery man on her doorstep, holding a medium-sized box, which she signed for and carried into the kitchen.

She discovered it was filled with Christmas gifts. All wrapped in colourful paper and equally pretty ribbons. And every one had her name on it.

She rang her father, but it went to voicemail. 'Hi, Dad. I know you're probably busy, but thank you so much for my gifts. By the way, how did you get the presents here the very day after I arrived?'

A few minutes later, as she was putting the presents away in her wardrobe, she received a text message.

I posted them a week before you left. Hope you like them. PS I would have been in trouble if you'd cancelled the trip! Xxx

Although she would miss her family, knowing they were only a call or a text away made her feel less lonely.

After breakfast and a thorough read of the newspaper, in a small cobblestoned patio area that had an outdoor table setting for two under a pergola covered in grape vines,

Phoebe felt even more positive about her temporary stay in Australia. She was actually enjoying this time to herself, and she decided after completing the crossword and finishing her freshly squeezed orange juice that Heath's suggestion of spending some time swimming wouldn't be so bad.

She could do with some sun. A long, relaxing swim at the beach or in a pool was just what the doctor ordered. With no preference, but also no idea where to go, she looked up some local beaches and public pools on the internet.

The beach, she discovered, would mean a thirty-minute tram trip to Glenelg, or there was a pool about a ten-minute cab ride away in Burnside. She opted for the pool.

Searching in her suitcase, she found her floral bikini, sarong and sunblock. She slipped on the bikini, stepped into her denim shorts and popped a white T-shirt over the top. Then, with a good book, a towel, a wide-brimmed hat and a bottle of water in her beach bag, she called for a cab.

Phoebe had found a perfect spot on the lawn area, adjacent to a huge shade cloth and overlooking the pool. She surmised the sun would get intense later, and she would shift into the shade, but she wanted to enjoy a few minutes of the warm rays and assist her vitamin D intake.

The pool was picturesque, with huge gum trees and parklands surrounding the fenced area. There were quite a few families and some small groups of young mothers with babies enjoying the peaceful ambience of the late morning. Children were laughing and splashing in the crystal water of the wading pool and more serious swimmers were head down, doing lengths of the main pool.

Phoebe had spread out her large blue towel and set up camp. She had spied the fruit in the refrigerator before she'd left home, so she had packed an apple and some strawberries in with her water. Slipping out of her shorts and T-shirt, and putting her hair up atop her head, she strode across the lawn and climbed into the water for a long, relaxing swim.

She was right—it was just what the doctor had ordered. Quite literally.

She lay on her back, lapping the pool slowly and looking up at the stunning blue sky through the filter of her sunglasses. Her worries seemed to dissipate—not completely, but more than she had imagined they would when she had alighted from the plane just a day earlier.

Fifteen minutes later she climbed from the pool and dried herself off with her sun-warmed towel before she spread it out and sat down. With her sarong beside her, in case she needed to cover up, she put on her floppy straw hat, pulled out her book and flipped the lid on her sunblock. She thought of how if she was back in Washington she would be trying to get the ice off her windscreen—instead she was about to cover herself in sunscreen. Perhaps there was justice in the world—or at least a little compensation in the form of sunshine.

She poured a little lotion into her palm and began to rub it over her shoulders.

'Phoebe?'

Phoebe spun around to see Heath standing so tall he was blocking the sun. His chest was bare and his low-slung black swimming trunks left little to her imagination. Beside him was the cutest little boy, with the same blond tousled hair, dinosaur-patterned swim trunks, and a very cheeky smile. But very different eyes. While Heath's were the most vivid blue, his son's huge, twinkling eyes were a stunning deep brown.

'Hello, Heath,' she managed, a little shocked to find him in front of her, and a little more shocked by how gorgeous he looked in even less clothing than the day before.

'I didn't expect to see you here. I didn't think you'd actually take my advice about getting some sun and a swim.'

'It sounded like a good idea,' she replied, trying not to show how embarrassed she felt in choosing the same outdoor pool as Heath. He had described the city as a large country town, but now she wondered how small Adelaide was to have found them in the same place. 'And I do need to get some vitamin D.'

As she said it Phoebe realised she was wearing only a string bikini, and suddenly felt very self-conscious. She hadn't thought twice about it with the other pool guests, as she didn't know them, but for some reason she felt more exposed in front of Heath. She wanted to reach for her sarong and bring it up to her neck, but realised how silly she would appear.

Heath sensed that Phoebe was feeling awkward in that very brief and very stunning bikini. He had witnessed her discomfiture the previous day, when she had been so intent on tugging her skirt into place. But suddenly his eyes just naturally began to roam her body. Every curve was perfect, he thought, before he quickly slipped on his sunglasses, then turned his attention back to his son. Where it had to stay.

'Oscar.' Heath began ruffling the little boy's hair with his hand. 'This is Phoebe—she'll be working with me for the next month, while Grandpa gets better.'

'Hello, Phoebe,' the little boy responded. 'You're pretty—like Aunty Tilly.'

Phoebe felt herself blush. 'Thank you, Oscar, that is a very nice thing to say.'

'It's the truth,' he replied. 'My kindy teacher isn't as pretty as you, but she can sing really well. Can you sing?'

'No, I'm afraid I can't.'

'That's okay. Don't feel bad. My grandpa can't sing either—he tries in the shower, but it sounds terrible and the dog next door barks. He barks a *lot*. I don't know if Daddy can sing. I've never heard him try to sing. Even when there's Christmas carols he never sings along.'

'That's because my voice is worse than Grandpa's,' Heath added, knowing his inability to sing Christmas carols had nothing to do with the quality of his voice. There was much more to it than that. 'It's best I don't try or the dog next door might run away.'

'You're silly, Daddy. The dog can't open the gate.'

Phoebe smiled at their happy banter. It was the first time she had seen a full smile from Heath. The other time there had been only the hint of a smile. She thought he should do it more often.

'Can I go in the pool now? Can I? Can I? Please, Daddy?' Oscar's words became faster and louder as they came rushing out.

'Sure can.' Heath said, eager to move away from Phoebe in her skimpy bathing suit. 'I hope you enjoy your time here today, Phoebe,' he added before he took his son's hand. 'If you need anything we're not too far away.'

'Thanks, I'm sure I will be just fine.'

Heath positioned his sunglasses on the top of his head, nodded in Phoebe's direction and then reached for his son's hand and walked towards the water's edge.

Phoebe suddenly felt a little shiver run all over her body. She ignored it. She had no intention of asking Heath for anything or paying any attention to her body's inappropriate reaction to her boss. It was her hormones, simply out of sorts after the emotional rollercoaster of the last few months, she decided. Perhaps jet-lag was playing a part too.

She had worked with some very attractive medics over the years and he was just another one—nothing more, she thought as she reached for her book. Once Heath Rollins exited from the practice she would never see him again. And that was how she wanted her life to remain. No men and all about her career.

Heath loved being with his son. He always gave him one hundred per cent of his attention when they were together. Oscar was his reason for getting up every day, although he never let the little boy feel that pressure or carry that load. He didn't want his family to attempt to change that dynamic or to question his reasons for still being alone five years after Natasha's death. His choices were no one else's business. He would cover for his father at the practice and then return to Sydney, where he and Oscar would live life the way he wanted. With no interference or futile attempts at matchmaking.

Heath knew that no woman would ever replace Natasha. And, even more than that, he thought every day of how Natasha had been denied the joy of watching her child grow into a man. Some days were harder than others. The sadness, the guilt, the emptiness... Aside from Oscar, Heath's work was his saviour. It was a distraction that gave him purpose.

But today he felt as if someone else was pulling his thoughts away momentarily. Someone who was not only academically and professionally astute, and beautiful from head to toe, but whose humility appeared genuine. But, he reminded himself as he took Oscar to the bigger pool for a father-son swimming lesson, he barely knew her and he was happy with his life just the way it was. He had Oscar and he had his career and that had been enough for him for five years.

He slipped small brightly coloured goggles over his son's eyes and held him securely, encouraging him to take big strokes and put his head under the water, and he didn't look back in Phoebe's direction. Not once.

* * *

Despite her best efforts, Phoebe couldn't concentrate on her book. Initially she thought it was tiredness that made her read and reread the same sentence until there was no point continuing. But then she realised it was curiosity, or something like it, that drew her to glance back at Heath and his son. Through her sunglasses Phoebe could see how the two were incredibly close, and the love between them was palpable. Heath looked to be the perfect father, and watching them made Phoebe smile just a little.

She had never thought too much about having children. She'd assumed she would, and had looked forward to being a mother one day, but it hadn't been a driving force in her life. Unlike some of her friends, who had set a date by which they wanted to have the picket fence and three children, Phoebe liked to live her life as it unfolded and had never been one to over-plan. She had spent so long studying, achieving her career goals through long hours at the hospital and in surgery, and then she had got caught up in the wedding...

She blinked away memories that needed to be forgotten and decided, sitting on her damp towel in the sticky heat and looking up at the towering gum trees, that this would be the day she packed them away for good. The pain, the disappointment and the humiliation had no place in her life. She didn't know what did have a place exactly, but the sadness seemed to be fading in the warmth of the Australian sun and Phoebe finally felt good about life. Three months in the same cold town hadn't helped, but the distance and the glorious summer weather appeared to be working. Her decision to set sail was one she felt a little surer she would not regret.

With her mind wandering, she hadn't noticed the two handsome men walking towards her. Both dripping wet, they stood at the bottom of her towel and she came back to the present with a jolt. But a very pleasant one.

'I hope we didn't scare you. You looked like you were a million miles away.'

'About ten thousand, to be exact.'

'You're homesick for Washington already?' Heath asked, almost hoping she would confirm his thoughts and tell him she was planning on returning immediately to the US. That would be fortuitous news for him, because he had a gut feeling that Phoebe's presence might bring complications into his otherwise contained life.

'Not at all,' she replied honestly and, being completely clueless to his hopes, she had lightness in her voice. 'I was just thinking about how lucky I am to be melting rather than freezing.'

'If you were a chocolate bar you wouldn't say that!' Oscar told her with a big smile, before he scampered back to the wading pool and signalled to his father to follow.

Phoebe watched Oscar run in and out of the pool for the best part of an hour, and she found it difficult not to occasionally look at Heath, who stood watch over his son. She walked to the far end of the pool, as she didn't want to infringe on Heath and Oscar's time together. He was a single father, who no doubt worked long hours like most medical professionals, so their time together as father and son was precious. She was surprised that a man who said he didn't like to compromise certainly appeared to let his son make the rules.

Sitting on the pool edge, she dangled her legs into the water and thought for the first time in her life she had no future plans. Past these next six months in Adelaide she had no clue where she would go. Perhaps back to Washington—perhaps not. There was a newfound security in having no security in place. Nothing set in stone. And no one to let her down since she only had herself to rely upon. No man to break her heart and shatter her dreams. She had a temporary job and an income and that was all she really needed for the time being.

Phoebe Johnson was finally sailing her own ship and she liked it. She hoped that in this town, so far from everyone she knew, she might possibly find herself. But not for a very long time did she want to share her heart, her bed or potentially her future with a man—if indeed she ever did.

She pulled her legs out of the water and headed back to her towel, where she ate her apple and her strawberries and then felt her stomach rumble. It was time to go back to her house for lunch, she decided, and began to pack up her belongings. Heath and Oscar were lying in the shade, eating ice cream, so she waved and quietly headed out to the main road. She planned on hailing a passing cab.

After five minutes, with no sign of any passing cabs, she reached into her bag to dial for one.

'Daddy, look—there's Phoebe. Is she waiting for her daddy to pick her up?'

'I don't think so, Oscar. She just arrived in town and her father lives in another country a long way from here.'

'Then we need to take her home. That would be a nice thing to do.'

Although part of him knew extending an invitation to share a ride home was close to the last thing he should do, given his desire to stay away from Phoebe when she had so little clothing on, Heath knew it was the right thing to do. Phoebe knew no one, and she was stranded at the pool after she'd taken him up on his suggestion. She had at least now put shorts on.

There was only one thing to do, he knew, as he took Oscar's hand and walked slowly over to Phoebe.

'Can we offer you a ride home?'

* * *

Phoebe had accepted the ride back to her home with a still mostly serious Heath and his very excited and happy little boy. She assumed Oscar had inherited his outgoing personality from his mother. The conversation came predominantly from the back seat, where Oscar was recalling his swimming prowess, until they drew near to her house.

'I'm here on the left—well, I think I am,' she said, then paused as she questioned the accuracy of her directions. 'I tried to notice the way the cab driver took me and reverse it in my head.'

'It's two down on the right, actually. I have your address,' he told her as he ignored her directions and kept driving. 'I noted it from your personal records, which were transferred with the immigration form. It's listed as your residence for the next six months.'

Phoebe could sense he was being a little condescending, and while he wasn't exactly rude she still didn't take kindly to it. She had only been in the country two days, and she thought even to be in the close vicinity of her new home was quite good. She doubted *he'd* do any better if the tables were turned and he was dropped into Washington.

'Well, maybe it was transcribed incorrectly and maybe it was the street you just passed—on the *left*.'

Heath sensed she was being petulant and he found it almost amusing. He had grown up in Adelaide and knew the street she was referring to was home to a food market and some restaurants—not houses.

'Fine, then I'm happy to turn around and drop you back in the street you think is yours.'

Phoebe knew he had called her bluff, and on such a hot day he had won.

'No, let's do it your way and see if you're right.'

'Let's.'

'You sound like Aunty Tilly and Uncle Paul,' Oscar suddenly announced from the back seat. 'They talk like that all the time, but in the end Aunty Tilly always wins.'

Heath froze, and so did Phoebe. Heath knew he was talking about his sister and brother-in-law—a married couple—and that Phoebe would suspect as much. They both went silent, and the rest of the short trip was dedicated to Oscar's chatter about the pool.

It wasn't long before Phoebe found herself waving goodbye and thanking her travelling companions before making her way inside her house. Oscar's comment still resonated with her long after she'd closed the front door. *They'd sounded like a married couple bickering.*

Initially, looking over at her handsome, almost brooding chauffeur, with his wet hair slicked back and his shirt buttoned low over his lightly tanned chest, she'd felt herself wondering what might have been had they met under different circumstances…before she had been hurt so terribly by Giles.

But as she tried to forget that heartbreak she couldn't deny that her heart beat a little faster being so close to Heath. His nearness had made her play self-consciously with loose wisps of her hair and swallow nervously more than once as she had looked away from his direction and to the scenery outside of the car during the trip home.

But she wasn't interested in men and particularly not pompous men who took enjoyment in proving they were right. And romance only brought anguish into her life, she reminded herself. After Oscar's bombshell she'd realised she had to step back. Right away from any contact with Heath outside of work arrangements, she decided as she dropped her bag of wet things into the laundry.

Pushing the child's observation out of her mind, Phoebe made some lunch. What could Oscar really know about married couples? Nothing, she told herself, and decided to call her father. It was late in Washington, but he had left a message on her phone so she knew he was still awake.

'So, what do you think of Adelaide?'

Phoebe wasn't sure what to tell her father. She hadn't seen much of the city, save for the airport, a coffee shop, a stifling hot podiatric practice and of course the pool, so her experience was limited. Her view of the parklands was lovely, but she had kept inside a small radius since arriving so thought she wasn't yet placed to give a great evaluation. And when it came to the people of Adelaide she had spoken to the customs official, her cab drivers, Heath, Oscar and momentarily Tilly.

Not really enough to gauge a whole town, she thought. Immigration had been pleasant, the cab drivers were polite, Tilly seemed sweet, Oscar was cute—and then there was Heath. She really didn't want to spend time thinking about him. Particularly after Oscar's comment.

She was confused, but pushed thoughts of him to the back of her mind. He was a conundrum that she wasn't sure she cared to solve. It could be another woman's problem, she decided. One good-looking man had already taken too much of her time and energy with no reward. And she was definitely not looking for a replacement. No matter how handsome.

'It's super-hot,' she finally replied.

'That's it?' Her father laughed heartily. 'You fly to the other side of the world and all you can tell me about the city is that it's super-hot? Wouldn't want *you* to be the only witness for the prosecution any time soon.'

Phoebe realised how vague it had sounded, and she also knew she didn't need to have her guard up. Her father knew the worst that had happened.

'I met Dr Rollins, and the practice is great, but the air-conditioning has broken down so we just had coffee yesterday, and today I went for a swim since I have the day off while it gets repaired.'

'So Ken Rollins is a good man? Do you think you'll enjoy working with him?'

Phoebe drew breath. She wished she could answer in the affirmative to both questions but she couldn't. She hadn't met Ken.

'Ken's undergone emergency knee surgery, so his son is looking after the practice.'

'It's fortunate for him that he has a son to take over,' her father replied, then added thoughtfully, 'But I know you were looking forward to working with Ken after you read his papers. I hope you're not disappointed?'

It was the second time she had been asked that question. And her answer still stood. She wasn't disappointed. Confused about the man, and definitely not interested beyond their working relationship, but not disappointed.

'Working with Heath will be a learning experience.'

'I hope you enjoy it, then,' he told his daughter.

'I hope so too, and if nothing else I've got a few months of warm weather ahead,' she said, trying to remind herself of the only benefit she should be considering.

'Try feeling sorry for your father. I'll be shovelling snow at some ungodly hour in the morning. Perhaps you should get some sleep, sweetie. Your flight would have been taxing, and the high temperatures will add to that.'

'It was a little tiring, but I think…' Phoebe paused as she heard the beeping of a text message come through. 'Can you hold for one minute, Dad? I think I got a message…'

'Sure, honey.'

Phoebe pulled the phone away from her ear and saw a number she didn't know. She recognised it as local and read the message.

Phoebe, it's Tilly. I know it's late notice, but would you be free for dinner tonight around seven at my place? Dad will be here and he'd love to meet you. And I would love to chat properly. Heath can pick you up.

An invitation to have dinner with the family was something Phoebe hadn't expected and she felt her errant heart race a little with the prospect of seeing Heath again. She knew it was crazy but her response to seeing him again made it obvious she may have a battle ahead. It clearly wasn't going to be as easy as telling herself the facts. She couldn't look out of a car window and ignore her reaction. She had to look inside of herself and face the fact that Heath was awakening feelings that she thought she had packed away when she had decided to focus on her career. Suddenly butterflies began to quicken in her stomach.

She didn't answer the text immediately as she quickly made plans in her head. She couldn't decline as that would be rude. And she wanted to meet Ken. With her breathing still a little strained, she resolved to get a taxi there on the pretext of saving Heath the trip—when she was only too aware it was to avoid the closeness of him in the confines of his car.

'I'm back,' she said, trying to concentrate once again on the conversation with her father. 'How's Mother?'

'She's fine. At her yoga class and then off to have a manicure, I think—or maybe it's to have her hair done. I can't remember. My day's been taken up with a new healthcare bill that the President wants to pass through Congress. It's a struggle, but you know me, I'm always up for a challenge.'

'Always—and you're so good at it.'

'Thanks, but the apple didn't fall too far from the tree. Look at you. Going to the other side of the world after what you've been through is quite the challenge too.'

'Hardly going to change the world here—and you did all the work. I really do appreciate you arranging everything. The house is wonderful, and it's stocked for a hungry army. Thank you so much.'

'You are more than welcome—but, speaking of an army, I'd better go, honey,' her father cut in. 'Urgent briefing with the Secretary of Defence at six a.m. tomorrow, so I'd better get some sleep before I head out in the wee hours of the morning with salt and a shovel to clear the driveway.'

'Okay, Dad. Love you.'

'Back at you—and I hope you have fun, whatever you do.'

Phoebe went into her room and collapsed into the softness of her bed, dropping the mobile phone beside her. She decided to take a shower and think logically about the invitation before rushing in. Perhaps she should decline and meet Ken another time. Perhaps she should avoid Heath in a social situation. Keep it purely professional the way it should be. Stepping under tepid water, Phoebe washed her hair, and by the time she had rinsed out the conditioner she had come to the conclusion that she had to stop overthinking the situation.

Oscar's remark had thrown her, and Heath's attitude had been a little patronizing, but he was right—he had known the way to her home. And she hadn't. Perhaps she had been a little defensive for no reason other than to push him away.

Her head was spinning and it wasn't the heat. Her house was wonderfully cool.

'Get a grip, Phoebe Johnson. Stop creating false drama where there is none. Heath Rollins is not interested in you. It's dinner with Ken's family and that's it. Almost business. And Oscar was way off the mark. He's only a child, and no judge of what married couples *really* sound like. You

have nothing to worry about. Heath Rollins is not looking
for love any more than you.'

So she accepted the invitation…with the proviso that
she would catch a cab.

CHAPTER FIVE

'PHOEBE SEEMS LOVELY,' Tilly said as she placed a large bowl of homemade potato salad on the dining table, where Heath, Oscar, Ken, her husband Paul and her two daughters were seated, waiting for Phoebe to arrive.

Heath watched as Paul, a tall man with an athletic build, by trade an engineer who directed huge construction teams, struggled to keep his tiny girls from climbing down from their booster chairs and heading back to their toys. He was clearly losing the battle, and one of them took off across the room, so he surrendered and set the girls up with a picnic blanket on the floor, added some toys and invited Oscar to join them.

Tilly was a wonderful cook, who never liked to see anyone leave hungry, so she had grilled a selection of chicken shashlik, vegetable patties and gourmet sausages from her local butcher, along with her famous potato salad and a Greek salad.

'Can someone please remind me why she's coming to dinner? She's here to work—not join family gatherings, surely?'

'It's called being hospitable to a stranger in town, Heath. And she's lovely, as I said.'

'Yes, she's nice.' Oscar seconded his aunt's opinion of

Phoebe as he stood up and strained to reach for a slice of bread from the table.

Smiling, his grandfather slid the plate closer to him to make the task easier.

'You met her too, Oscar?' Tilly asked as she brought cold drinks to the table.

'Yes, at the pool,' Oscar responded as he sat down with his twin cousins again, a big slice of bread in his hand. 'And we drove her home and she and Daddy talked a lot.'

'So you all went to the pool together, then?' Tilly addressed her question to Heath, her eyes smiling.

'I took Oscar to the Burnside pool and Phoebe happened to be there,' he responded defensively.

He had experienced more than a few attempts by his sister to matchmake over the years, and he intended to quash this attempt immediately. He wasn't buying into her supposedly casual conversation that would no doubt lead to something more like an interrogation over his love-life if he allowed it.

'So, of all the pools in Adelaide, a woman who knows nothing of Adelaide just happened to choose that one?'

Heath's silence was his answer.

'So everyone has met the doctor I hired except me?' Ken asked. 'Well, at least I'll get to meet her tonight and judge for myself.'

'*I* haven't met her yet,' Paul said. 'But then I didn't know you'd even hired anyone—I thought Heath was filling in for you.'

'He is. But the practice is growing, and I needed help, and Dr Phoebe Johnson was highly recommended. I had made arrangements for her to work with me before the accident. From all accounts she's a brilliant young podiatric surgeon looking for a change of scenery, so I jumped at the chance. Pardon the pun,' he said as he looked down at his bandaged knee.

'Very pretty too,' Tilly remarked.

'I hadn't heard that part, but it never hurts to have a pretty doctor in the practice,' said the older Dr Rollins. 'So, Heath, do you think you two will get along?'

Heath considered the question and answered in his usual guarded tones. 'I've read her transcripts and she has an impressive record—and the reports from the Washington hospital are great. We chatted yesterday morning at the café for a while, and she seems suited to the role.'

'Yesterday morning? You mean you took her out after she fainted? Quick work, Heath. I'm impressed,' said Tilly.

'Phoebe fainted? Is she okay?' Ken asked.

'I didn't *take her out*—we had a cool drink to talk about work and, yes, Dad, Phoebe's fine. The heat just got to her but I'm sure we won't have a repeat once the air-con is up and running again. You might like to consider renovating the building in the not too distant future.'

He'd added that to change an obvious subject direction that he didn't like.

'I could do you a rebuild,' Paul chipped in. 'Bulldoze and start again. Prime real estate there, and I've been saying for years the old building has had its day.'

Ken looked stony-faced at his son-in-law, to end that line of conversation, and then turned back to Heath. 'So, when my newest employee is conscious and upright, *is* she pretty?'

Heath looked around the table and realised they were all poised for his reply. 'Yes, she's pretty.'

Tilly smiled a self-satisfied smile, while Ken nodded to himself and Paul winked at his wife.

Heath saw the looks they gave each other and lowered his voice so that Oscar wouldn't hear the adults' conversation. 'Just because I made mention of Phoebe's appearance, don't think for a minute that I'm interested in her. It was a response to a direct question. Don't try and set us up. I don't need anyone in my life, and if you try anything you'll be short one staff member. *Me*. I'll be on a plane back to Sydney faster than you can blink. Neither Oscar or I need anyone else in our lives.'

'Are you sure about that?' Tilly asked with a brazen look.

'Yes. You know how I feel. It's been just Oscar and me for the last five years. No woman has come into our lives.'

'I know, but now Phoebe has. And you've already broken one of your unbreakable rules with her. *No woman shall meet your son*. Well, she has and he seems to like her.'

Just then the doorbell rang, and Heath stood up and walked briskly past the Christmas tree that Tilly had decorated that morning. It was the second time he had walked past it that evening, and both times he had looked at it only briefly and then looked away without making mention of it. He was still not able to face Christmas and all the trimmings. He doubted he ever would again. There was nothing that could make him enjoy the holiday season. He had tried and failed. Christmas was just too painful.

As he opened the door Oscar ran over to join him.

'Hello, Phoebe!' Oscar called out excitedly before Heath had a chance to greet her. 'Aunty Tilly has cooked lots of food, so I hope you're hungry.'

'Hello, Oscar,' she replied, and smiled at his toothy grin and cheeky smile before he ran off, allowing her to lift her gaze to greet Heath. 'Hello.'

Heath drew a deep breath. Phoebe looked gorgeous. She wore a deep blue halter dress. Her skin was pale against the fabric and looked like delicate porcelain, and her hair was falling in soft curls around her shoulders. Her beauty was not lost on him.

'Hi, Phoebe—come in.'

He moved back from the doorway and as she stepped inside he couldn't help but notice as she brushed past him that the back of her dress was cut low and revealed even more of her bare skin. His pulse instantly, and against his will, picked up speed.

'Phoebe,' Tilly said as she opened her arms to greet her dinner guest. 'So lovely you could make it. It's only casual, but I thought you could meet Dad and chat over a bite to eat since he was feeling a little left out.'

'It's my pleasure—thank you so much for inviting me,' she said, and then, spying the huge Christmas tree, she couldn't help but comment. 'That is a *gorgeous* tree, Tilly. Christmas truly is my favourite time of year.'

The two women walked into the dining room and on their way Phoebe gave her hostess some chocolates she had brought as a thank-you gift. Heath followed, and after hearing the Christmas comment realised that he and Phoebe had less in common than he'd first thought. She was a professional woman, and he had hoped she wouldn't be the nostalgic type. Apparently, he'd been wrong.

He couldn't deny to himself that Phoebe was stunning, and in that dress desirable, but he wasn't looking for a woman to share his life the way his family thought he should. And one night with Phoebe in his bed wouldn't work any way he looked at it. It would only complicate his life on so many levels, and that was something he didn't need.

As they entered the dining room, Ken was chatting with Paul.

'The simple joy of enjoying a pale ale any time I like is my compensation for not being able to operate. But believe me, I would prefer to have the use of my gammy knee than to be sitting around all day,' Ken said, then paused as he caught sight of Phoebe. 'Please excuse my bad manners and not standing to meet you,' he continued with an outstretched hand. 'I'm Ken Rollins, and you must be Dr Phoebe Johnson.'

Phoebe stepped closer to Ken and met his handshake. 'Yes, I'm Phoebe, and I'm very happy to finally meet you.'

Ken was impressed with the grip in her handshake. 'For a slender woman you have a strong handshake. But then you're a surgeon, so a strong and steady grip is a prerequisite for our shared field of medicine.'

Phoebe wasn't sure how to react, so she smiled.

'Please—sit down, I didn't mean to embarrass you. And sit next to *me*. I want to hear everything about you that wasn't written down on your incredibly impressive résumé. I'm sure there's lots to know.'

'Fire away,' she managed to return as she took her seat at the table, hoping his questions would be broad enough to avoid the awkward moments in her recent history.

Tilly began handing the platters of food around and soon everyone was filling their plates, while Paul put the children's food on their picnic blanket for them to share, then returned to join the adults.

'So why Adelaide?' Ken asked as he took a serving of Greek salad, ensuring there was plenty of feta cheese and olives on his plate.

'The chance to work with you,' Phoebe replied. 'I read your most recent paper on improvements to prescribed orthotic devices to control motion and position of the leg during locomotion and I think your work is outstanding. The chance to have you mentor me was too good to pass up.'

'Well, I must say that is lovely to hear, and I look forward to working with you once my knee is tickety-boo again,' he told her, with a hint of pride in his expression. 'So tell me about your family. I picked up from our correspondence that your father works at the White House.'

Ken reached for another shashlik and held the plate so that Phoebe could take one as well.

'Yes, he's an advisor to the President. He's been in the

world of politics for over nineteen years. He was in international banking before that.'

'And you weren't tempted to follow him into the political arena?' Heath cut in.

'Not at all. You see, you're right—it's an arena, and that's why I wouldn't do it. Sometimes it's great, but at other times it seems like a fight to the death. I'd rather be repairing bodies than ripping apart political opponents and their policies.'

'Touché,' Ken replied with a huge smile.

'Still, it must be an interesting lifestyle,' Tilly commented. 'Do you visit the White House often?'

'Now and then. But my place is the other side of town, nearer to the hospital. I just hear about it when I visit or call my parents.'

'I suppose it would be a little like the emergency department of a hospital—with everyone rushing frantically and everything code blue,' Tilly replied.

Phoebe smiled at her. 'You're not too far wrong with that analogy. It's like everything needs to be delivered or decided yesterday. I would most certainly go mad. My father, however, loves a challenge—he sees the big picture and the changes that need to be made for the disadvantaged and most particularly those with intergenerational problems.'

'And your mother? What does she do?' Ken asked between bites.

'Anything and everything social. Fundraising committees, women's political auxiliaries—pretty much anything that she believes helps with my father's career. Along with her bridge club.'

'So why did you choose medicine?' Ken asked. 'With a father in politics and, for want of a better word, a socialite mother, why did you choose to specialise in podiatric surgery?'

'My best friend Susy's mother had an accident driving us to school when I was fourteen…' Phoebe began.

Feeling a little parched from answering all the questions, took a sip of her cold drink before she continued.

'Anyway, she broke her heel and I was there when the paramedics took her by ambulance to the hospital. Susy and I had both been strapped in the back of the car and didn't suffer even a scratch. I visited her mother in hospital a few times with Susy, and I became curious and started asking the nurses questions. Then one day her podiatric surgeon came in. I asked him all about the operation and he went into great detail with me and that was it. I knew what I wanted to do with my life.'

'I'm impressed that you knew at such a young age—'

'I think that we should let poor Phoebe eat,' Tilly cut in. 'She's been grilled and she's passed with flying colours, Dad, so now she gets fed and watered.'

They all smiled, and then chatted about themselves so Phoebe could enjoy the delicious dinner Tilly had prepared and also get to know the family.

Everyone but Heath told her something about themselves and their lives. Heath stayed quiet, and Phoebe noticed his jaw clench more than a few times as they talked about Oscar as a baby. It was obvious to Phoebe that it had been a difficult time for him. But why exactly she wasn't sure, and they all clearly avoided the topic of Oscar's mother.

'Do you want to look at the stars?' Oscar suddenly asked Phoebe as she sat waiting for Heath to bring a drink out to the patio, where everyone had moved after dinner to enjoy the balmy evening.

'Do you have a telescope?'

'No, but we can lie on the grass and look up and see

them. That's one of my favourite things to do at night. Grandpa knows lots about stars.'

Phoebe thought it was a lovely idea, and very sweet of Oscar to extend the invitation for her to join him. She stepped out of her shoes and followed him to a patch of lawn just near the patio, where they both lay down on the grass and looked up at the stars twinkling in the ebony sky. The cool ground beneath her bare skin felt wonderful.

'That's the saucepan. Can you see it? You have to draw a line between the big star—up there—and the others—just there—and it looks like a saucepan,' he said, pointing his tiny finger straight up in the air. 'And it has a handle too.'

'I can see it,' she responded as she looked to where he pointed.

They both lay staring at the perfect night sky and Oscar talked with lightning speed about everything his grandfather had told him. Phoebe was impressed with all he had retained, and his interest in astronomy.

'Perhaps you might grow up and study the stars,' she said. 'That would make you an astronomer.'

'I think I might visit them instead.'

'So you want to be an astronaut?'

'Yes. That would be more fun than just looking at them.'

Heath stood in the doorway to the patio and looked out at the two of them, lying in the dark on the lawn, talking. He had no idea what they were saying but he could hear their animated chatter. He felt a tug at his heart, thinking that his wife had missed out on doing just that. And that Oscar had missed out on those important long talks with his mother.

They had both been cheated. And even though his pain lessened with every passing year he wondered if Oscar's would grow as he realised what he had lost.

"You know, Phoebe's nothing like I imagined,' Ken

said softly when he saw Heath in the doorway with Phoebe's drink.

Heath agreed with his father's sentiments but he would not let him know. He wouldn't let any family member know, for fear of them trying to make a spark ignite between them. He had found her to be sweet when they'd first met, sexy at the pool, and looking at her now, lying beside his son, he was discovering she was apparently maternal—but that wasn't a combination he wanted. He preferred sexy with no strings attached, for one-night stands that could never break his heart. Or impact on his son.

'I think we should probably get going,' he said to his father. 'I need to get Oscar to bed—and you as well, Dad.'

'Don't fuss about getting me to bed, son,' Ken told him as he watched Oscar and Phoebe. 'I'm quite enjoying the company and I'm not that old yet. But, having said that, I imagine young Oscar might be getting tired after a day out.'

'Let him spend the night with us,' Tilly offered as she stepped outside and was pleasantly surprised to see her nephew relaxing on the lawn with Phoebe. 'Then we can get up early and have a swim before it gets hot. I think he's a little lonely over at Dad's. I can do some things with him that you—'

'That I can't do because they are things only a mother can do?'

'No, Heath. Not even close,' Tilly replied in a gentle tone. 'You're doing an amazing job with Oscar. He's adorable and polite and I love him to bits—you know that. But it's hard with you working long hours, and Dad can't do anything while he's laid up, so I thought I'd help out and do something fun while you're stepping in for Dad. Stop being so hard on yourself.'

'I'm not being hard—I'm a realist, and I think Oscar is out of his routine over here. He probably misses his nanny and preschool. Once he gets back to Sydney he'll be fine again.'

'I'm sure you're right. But in the meantime let me have him for a day.'

'Tilly's enjoying having you both in Adelaide,' Paul added. 'And I'm sure she wants to make the most of it. It doesn't happen often enough.'

'Absolutely,' Tilly agreed. 'Check with Oscar and see if he's up for it…'

'Up for what?' Oscar and Phoebe had left their observation spot on the lawn and walked up quietly without the others noticing.

'A sleepover and a day with us tomorrow.'

'Sure am—then I can go swimming with Aunty Tilly in the morning. Can I, Daddy, *please*?'

'Well, I guess the decision has been made,' Heath said, not having expected Oscar to jump at the idea of a sleepover so quickly. He'd thought they were joined at the hip, but perhaps that tie was loosening. And maybe he did need to let Tilly mother him now and then.

'Do you want to sleep over too, Phoebe? And Daddy could too?'

Heath's eyes widened in surprise at Oscar's invitation to both of them.

Phoebe smiled. 'That's very kind of you, but I have to go home to my own bed and my pyjamas.'

'I sleep in my T-shirt and jocks in summer,' Oscar cut in, with a serious tone in his little voice. 'You could do the same.'

They all smiled at Oscar's matter-of-fact response— well, everyone bar Heath. He was still thinking about the void in his son's life that was becoming more and more obvious. It was one that he'd thought he had managed to fill.

'Perhaps another time,' Phoebe said politely, thinking

that there was no way she would be stripping down to her underwear for a sleepover with Heath.

Tilly tried not to laugh as she hugged her nephew and, looking at his food-stained T-shirt, she directed a request to Heath. 'Could you drop off some fresh clothes tomorrow morning in case we want to go out?'

Still deep in thought, he responded, 'Sure—as long as you're sure it's not too much trouble for him to stay?'

'Not at all,' Tilly said as she picked up Oscar and put him on her lap. 'Early-morning swim for you and me, Oscar—and, Phoebe, if you're not doing anything please come over and join us for a swim.'

Phoebe was surprised at how warm and welcoming the family was, and was very quickly feeling at home, but she declined, thinking that perhaps the offer was Tilly just being courteous.

Heath looked at his sister and then back at Phoebe without saying a word, then he kissed his son goodnight and walked out to the car. He was glad Phoebe had not accepted. She was becoming too close to his family too quickly. And starting to get under his skin a little too. He understood why she was a perfect fit for his family, with her down-to-earth personality, quick wit and sense of fun. He was also very aware that those same traits combined with her beauty were making her far too desirable to him. And he didn't like it.

She could leave at any minute, and that wouldn't be fair to Oscar. He didn't want him to grow close to a person who would walk away. He needed to protect his son from that pain. And, more than that, he didn't want their life to change.

'I will see you in the morning,' he called out before he drove away, with his father and Phoebe in the car.

The sun was setting as the three of them drove through the city to Phoebe's home. Each one was thinking about the same thing. How quickly and naturally Phoebe was seeming to fit into their lives. Ken was thrilled; Phoebe was surprised—Heath was more worried than he had been in a very long time...

CHAPTER SIX

HEATH WOKE AT four and lay staring out his window to the
dark sky that was softly lit by a haze-covered moon. He
knew the warm air outside would be heavy and still. He
rolled onto his back and lifted his arms above his head and
thought back over the previous two days, since Phoebe had
fallen into his arms.

He didn't want to be thinking about her—and especially not at four in the morning, lying in bed—but her face
wouldn't leave his mind. When Phoebe had been close to
him—close enough for him to smell the scent that rested
delicately on her skin and close enough to see the sparkle
in her beautiful green eyes—he had struggled to remember why he didn't want a woman in his life on any permanent basis.

But that was something he had to remember. Particularly now.

His life had begun to change since he'd arrived back
in Adelaide.

He had worried for a little while that the life he had built
with his son, just the two of them, might not be enough
for Oscar one day. And he feared now that that day was
almost upon him. But he didn't want to lose control. Once
before he had lost control of a situation—lost his wife and

almost lost his mind. He wouldn't let it happen again. He needed to remain in control and not blindly accept change.

And he couldn't accept Phoebe as the catalyst for that change.

He was more than concerned after seeing how comfortable the family had been with her. It was moving too fast for him. He had to put the brakes on the level of intimacy he thought they were all building with her. It needed to stop immediately. The air-conditioning repairman had notified him that the work was completed at the practice and while there were no patients booked in until the next day, he would send Phoebe a message just after nine and ask her to call into the practice to go over the patient notes. That would serve his purpose.

He needed to remind her why she was there—and it wasn't to grow close to any member of his family, and particularly not his son. It was a relationship he didn't want to see develop and risk it being torn apart when they headed back to Sydney and Phoebe headed back to her home country.

Phoebe woke early, picked up the paper and was halfway through the crossword when she got the call just after eight.

'Hi, Phoebe—it's Tilly. Would you like to jump in a cab and have breakfast by the pool with us? I'd pick you up, but by the time I load the diaper gang you could already be here.'

'I'm not sure…' She hesitated to accept the invitation. 'This is your time with Oscar. I don't want to infringe on that.'

'Nonsense. I would love to chat to another adult. Away from the surgery my days are filled with nursery rhymes and potty-training, and Oscar could do with another set of eyes on him while he's in the pool. It is hard with three of them, and my stomach is in a knot trying to keep a watch over them all. At their age it's a bit like herding cats.'

'Well, if you're sure I can help, I'd love to.'

'It's settled, then,' Tilly said. "See you soon—and don't forget your swimsuit.'

Half an hour later Phoebe was alighting from a cab at Tilly's home and a very happy little boy was opening the front door before she'd even reached the doorbell. He was wearing his swimsuit, dry flippers and goggles on the top of his head.

'Hi, Phoebe! Have you got your bathers?'

'Bathers?' she asked as she walked up the paved entrance towards him.

'He means swimsuit,' Tilly said as she invited Phoebe inside. 'In Australia we call a swimsuit bathers. You'll get used to our funny expressions soon enough.'

Phoebe smiled at her hostess, then turned her attention to Oscar, 'Yes, I have my bathers—so I hope you're wanting to swim, because in this weather *I* do!'

Phoebe didn't hear the three text messages from Heath because she was splashing in the pool with his son, and Melissa and Jasmine were excitedly screaming from the sidelines behind the child-safe fence, blocking out all other sounds. Oscar's floating armbands were in place but Phoebe didn't let him go for even a second. They'd had a lovely morning, stopping only for some juice and freshly cut fruit, after which Oscar walked Phoebe around the garden, collecting insects in his bug catcher.

'I only keep them for a few hours, then I let them go back to their daddies…and their mummies. I think some of them have mummies too.'

'I'm sure some of them have both, and some just have

a mummy or a daddy,' Phoebe said, then fell silent as he continued walking, collecting and talking.

Oscar suddenly seemed very deep in thought for a five-year-old, and it worried Phoebe a little.

'My mummy died when I was very little.'

Phoebe felt herself stiffen as he delivered this news. 'I'm sorry to hear that, Oscar.' She paused to gain some composure as her heart went out to the little boy. 'I'm sure she's looking over you every day.'

Phoebe had not considered the prospect that Heath might be a widower. She wasn't sure why it hadn't occurred to her, but now she knew it did go part way to explaining why he was such a serious man, who appeared only to lighten up around his son. Losing his wife and the mother of his child would have been a life-altering tragedy.

'I was very little. I couldn't talk or walk and I don't remember her. But I know her name was—'

'Hello, you two.'

Heath's deep voice suddenly called from the back door, interrupting their conversation and making them both turn abruptly.

Phoebe felt her stomach drop. Then it lifted, and then spun as her heart fluttered nervously. She'd thought she had her reactions to Heath under control, but suddenly she discovered she didn't.

But she had to.

Somehow.

'Hello, Daddy!'

'Hi, Heath.'

Heath quickly crossed to them and dropped to his knees. 'I'm sorry, Oscar, but I'm going to have to take Phoebe to work with me.'

'But we're having *fun*, Daddy, and I want her to stay. She showed me how to swim like a bug and...'

'Swim like a bug?' Heath asked, turning to Phoebe with a curious look on his face.

'The butterfly stroke,' Phoebe said as she looked at this man whom she now knew had suffered the tragedy of losing his wife. It did put a different filter on the way she saw him, but she didn't want him to know that. He seemed too stoic to want pity—in fact she suspected pity would drive him into a darker place.

Despite what she now knew she didn't want it to colour her feelings towards him. She wasn't looking for love and he was obviously still grieving. Although she *was* grateful for the insight, as she would understand his motives a little better and make their working relationship easier. She just had to get her emotions under control. And he was dressed again, as he had been the night before, so it made it easier to concentrate.

'How did you know I was here?' she asked, trying to mask how sad she felt for them both. And how equally drawn she was to the father and son.

'Well, you didn't answer your phone, so on the off-chance that my sister had convinced you to visit I called her and she said you were swimming with Oscar. Unfortunately I'll have to cut that short and ask you to head back to the surgery with me.'

'Like this?' She looked down at her swimsuit covered by a sarong. She had chosen not to wear her bikini that day, and had slipped the one-piece swimsuit under her sarong before she'd left her house. 'But if the air-conditioning isn't running maybe this is the right thing to be wearing.' She tried to be lighthearted. Friendly. At ease. Everything she wasn't feeling.

Heath had tried not to look at her body, but he couldn't help but notice how stunning she looked. He definitely didn't want to be alone with her at the practice in the outfit she was barely wearing.

'Perhaps not,' he replied, trying to avert his eyes from her petite curves. 'I can drop you home to change, if you'd like.'

A little while later, after a quick stop at her house for a change of clothes, they sat reading through the patient notes in the cool surgery. The newly repaired and efficiently running air-conditioner was working perfectly, but Phoebe had the distinct feeling that this activity wasn't really essential. They were straightforward records that could easily have been read through prior to her meeting with each patient.

She wondered if it wasn't so much her being at the practice that was important but perhaps more her *not* being at Tilly's house with Oscar. She wasn't sure why but she said nothing, and continued to concentrate for the next two hours on the records that Heath was explaining in great detail.

Occasionally she would glance at the man across from her. His chiselled jaw, with a light covering of stubble, was tense. There was no half-smile. She realised there was no chance of a full smile and she knew why. Despite her resolve to keep it professional, still she felt her heart pick up speed a little when their eyes met by accident. And at that time, they both paused for only a moment in silence. She didn't know how he was feeling or what he was thinking but there was something Heath was keeping to himself.

And she suspected it was his heart.

Finally she left to go home. It was a short walk, and she wanted the time to clear her head. She now knew that Heath was still suffering from the loss of his wife and although she also knew that Oscar had been little when his mother had died she wasn't sure exactly how long ago it had happened. Three years? Four years? Even five?

But there was one other thing she knew. Heath must have loved his wife very much, and if it had been half as much as he clearly loved Oscar then, although her life had been cut short, his wife had been a very lucky woman to have known that deep a love and commitment. It was something that Phoebe knew she had never experienced. And probably never would.

'Why don't you guys move here permanently?' Tilly asked, sitting down and pouring herself a cold soft drink after dropping Oscar back at her father's later that day. Paul had arrived at her home to mind the twins for a little while. 'I adore Oscar, and I'd love Mels and Jazzy to grow up with their big cousin to keep the boys at bay. I think it makes complete sense.'

'My thoughts exactly,' Ken agreed, while admiring the stunning violet and red hues of the setting sun. The lighting provided a canvas for the silhouettes of the towering gum trees that surrounded his home and the scent of eucalyptus floated in the night air.

But Heath didn't notice anything. He could still remember the scent of Phoebe, sitting so close to him at work, could see her beautiful face, and nothing he did was successful at pushing those images from his mind. He could vaguely hear the mutterings of his father and his sister, but none of it registered. His mind was consumed by thoughts of Phoebe and he felt uneasy. Her sweetness. Her sincerity. She had stumbled into his world and into his arms quite literally, and for some inexplicable reason he couldn't shake her from his thoughts. But he wouldn't break another rule. He had to ignore this fleeting infatuation.

Heath came back to the conversation to see two sets of eyes on him, seeking answers. He didn't like the fact that a family inquisition was developing on the back porch because there was another one going on in his mind and one was more than enough to endure. Two would certainly send him crazy.

'The air-con is now working and that's all that matters. Let's leave it at that. Phoebe is a surgeon, in town to meet the terms of her employment contract. And, by the way, Tilly, she can't be your babysitter.'

'My babysitter? That's a little unfair. She knows no one, and she was alone in her house, and I thought she'd enjoy a swim and a chat. And, FYI, Oscar totally commandeered her for the better part of two hours and that was not my plan—it was his.'

'Well, I'm here only until Dad's knee mends. End of story. So I hope Oscar doesn't get comfortable with the current arrangements. It's all only temporary.'

With that Heath stood up and went inside to find his son. Reading him a story was always a highlight of his day, but that night it would also serve as his avenue of respite from the barrage of questions about Phoebe.

And for a short while it might also silence those inside his head.

'I like Phoebe,' Oscar told his father as he went to turn out the light. 'She's neat.'

'As in tidy?'

'Daddy, you're being *silly*. Not tidy. She's fun—and she makes you happy too.'

Heath was taken aback by his son's words. 'What do you mean by that?'

'Well, I saw you smile. You don't smile very much. I always thought you were sad, but now that Phoebe comes over you're happy more. That makes me happy too. It's almost like we're a family—like Aunty Tilly and Uncle Paul.'

Phoebe called London after she'd eaten her takeaway dinner. She wanted to chat with Susy and hoped with the time difference that while it was evening in Adelaide she would catch her young barrister friend before she left in the morning for court in London.

'Phoebs, how are you?'

'I'm great—how are you, Susy? And how's work? Anything interesting that you can talk about?'

'I'll put you on loud speaker—trying to finish my make-up before I rush out the door.'

'If it's not a good time I'll try another day,' Phoebe said as she rested back into the three soft white pillows on her bed.

The ceiling fan was moving the air above her and Phoebe had opened a window on the approaching darkness. She knew she would be in air-conditioning all of the next day and she wanted to sleep with fresh air, even if it *was* a little warm.

'No, I'm good to talk. Nothing to report. There was a guilty verdict in the grand theft case, which I was thrilled about, and today I'm selecting the jury for a new IT case. Possession of data with intent to commit a serious offence. Same old, same old.' Susy laughed. 'I *do* love my job. We've been securing a high percentage of convictions lately, so it makes it all worthwhile. Unfortunately there's never a shortage of bad guys needing to be put away. But let's forget about me—how are you on your adventure Down Under?'

'It's hot—melting hot, to be accurate.'

'Well, I don't feel even a teeny bit sorry for you, if that's what you're hoping for. I spent last night in my Wellingtons, overcoat and scarf, shovelling snow off my car in case I need it in an emergency. I'll take the Underground into London again today. So, my sister from another mother, stop complaining—'cos while you're over there, getting a suntan, I'm warding off frostbite!'

Both women laughed.

Then Susy's voice became momentarily stern. 'Seriously, Phoebs, has the creep left you alone? And your mother—is she finally coming to terms with the fact that Niles won't be a member of the family?'

'It's Giles...'

'I know...but I prefer to disrespect him at every opportunity, and forgetting his name is a start.'

'I promise he's out of the picture completely. Mother is still not convinced, but I've given up on telling her that cheating is a deal-breaker.'

'Absolutely,' Susy agreed, in her prosecuting barrister tone. 'Guilty, charged and dumped. I do wish there was a way to lock him *and* those tarts away. Pity there's no legal avenue to put the lot of them behind bars and throw away the key.'

'In a perfect world there would be, but I'm trying not to think about him any more. Just onwards and upwards. I'm starting work tomorrow with... Heath.' Phoebe stumbled over his name.

'I thought you were working with Ken Rollins? Who's Heath?'

'His son, actually. Ken needed emergency knee reconstruction. His son's a podiatric surgeon too, so he's stepped in to help out for the next few weeks.'

'I hope you're not disappointed? I know you were really excited to be working with Ken.'

This was now the third time she had been asked and still her answer remained the same. Disappointed, no... confused, yes...and now she was feeling a little melancholy about what had made Heath the man he was.

'I was looking forward to working with Ken, but I'm sure Heath will be an equally good operator.'

'So good to hear you back to your old optimistic self, Phoebs. I'd love to chat and hear all about Heath, but I have to dash. The Underground waits for no one,' Susy said.

'Hope sonny-boy is not too nerdy or dull—but it's only for a few weeks. Talk tomorrow. I'll call you.'

With that, Suzy hung up.

Nerdy? *I wish*… Dull? *Not in anyone's book.* In fact she had to admit that Heath seemed perfect…if a little battle worn.

Heath arrived at the practice early the next morning. He had a surgical list beginning at one, with two post-operative patients and two new patients in the morning. Phoebe's day was light—three morning patients and two in the afternoon. Heath had arranged it that way to allow her to settle in.

Generally December was not busy, as most patients delayed non-urgent treatment, particularly surgery, until after the busy holiday season. By the time her patient numbers increased Heath knew he would be back in Sydney and his father would be back on deck.

'Good morning,' Tilly greeted her brother as she dropped her bag behind the desk. 'Loving the cool air in here.'

'It's great, isn't it? Not sure the landlord will be thrilled when he sees the invoice, but it's worth every penny.'

'*Dad* owns the building. *He's* the landlord.'

Heath laughed. 'Yes—and hopefully I'll be back in Sydney when he gets the bill in the mail. I had it completely overhauled and replaced the motor.'

'I think he can cover it.'

'Not sure about that, since he has the most expensive receptionist in the country.'

Tilly rolled her eyes and smiled. 'You're in fine form today, Heath. Be nice to your sister or I'll walk out—and then you'll be lost without my administrative wizardry.'

Heath headed back to his consulting room, and on the way checked that everything had been prepared for

Phoebe. Her patient list was all in order. He had set up her log-in details for the computer and given her access to the database with the patient notes. The room was spotless. Although he refused to admit it to himself, he wanted to impress her.

'Hi, Phoebe,' Heath heard his sister say cheerily from the other end of the practice.

'Hi, Tilly,' Phoebe replied. She stepped inside, feeling apprehensive and nervous, as if it was the first day at school. 'It's a lot cooler than a couple of days ago in here.'

'Hopefully we can avoid doctors and patients fainting,' Heath said as he walked briskly down the corridor and into the waiting room.

'Good morning, Heath.'

'I'll show you to your consulting room.'

Phoebe could sense that he had slipped back into his cool demeanour again, but he wasn't quite as cold and she did not take it personally.

'I'll try not to faint on the way,' she said, in an attempt to lighten the mood.

Heath smirked, but because he was leading the way Phoebe didn't see. Her view was his broad shoulders, slim hips and the long stride he was taking. And, despite not wanting to notice, it was the best damn view she had seen in days. In fact the last time she had seen anything so impressive was in the very same man at the pool.

'Nancy Wilson?' Phoebe called into the waiting room.

A young woman stood up and followed Phoebe into her consulting room, hobbling a little and clearly in pain.

Phoebe closed the door. 'Let me introduce myself, Nancy. I'm Dr Phoebe Johnson and I've stepped in to help Dr Ken Rollins for the next few months. Please take a seat.' Phoebe had briefly read the patient's notes and was aware of her medical history of chronic heel pain. 'I see

you have undergone some reconstructive treatments with
Dr Rollins.'

'Yes, but it hasn't made a permanent improvement.'

'I see. Did you find any of them had long-lasting benefits? I know it was more invasive, but was the plasma
therapy successful from your perspective? Or did you prefer the low-intensity shock wave treatment?'

'Both were good—but only short term. I'm an ice skater.
I hope to compete for Australia in Switzerland in nine
months, so I need to be back on my feet and out of pain to
train in Europe and then compete. At the moment it feels
like there's a pebble in my left shoe when I walk. On really bad days it's like a shard of glass.'

'They are common descriptions of the problem. Please
come over to the examination table and I'll have a look,'
Phoebe said, and assisted the young woman to the narrow table against the far wall. She moved a small step into
place with her foot to help Nancy climb up onto the bed. 'I
appreciate you've tried the conservative approach, and to
be honest, Nancy, sometimes after all else fails there's no
choice but to choose corrective surgical treatment.'

Phoebe eased the soft boot and sock from the woman's
left foot and then, slipping on surgical gloves, began her
examination. Although the conservative restorative treatments to increase blood flow and break up scar tissue had
assisted temporarily with pain management, Phoebe decided that surgery was the only option.

'Unfortunately your plantar fasciitis has not improved
with past treatments, and your ice skating training has,
according to your notes, been compromised for a number
of months now.'

'Yes, I do train, but only for short periods, and then I require ice, cortisone, and when all else fails codeine to manage the pain—and then I lie in bed for hours some days.'

'Heavy doses of pain relief or cortisone are not long-term options for anyone, but particularly not at your age, Nancy. Nor is being incapacitated in bed an option for an athlete. Your condition is almost epidemic in the United States, with one in ten people suffering from varying degrees of heel pain from scar tissue, and it appears this approach is no longer viable for you, considering your lifestyle. We'll need to proceed to the next level on your treatment plan, so you can move forward with your career.'

'Surgery is fine by me. I just want to get it over and finished and get back on my feet—literally.'

Phoebe gently put the sock and soft boot back on the young woman and helped her down from the examination table. She explained the risks of surgery, confirmed that Nancy was in general good health and a suitable patient for surgery, and then walked her out to the front desk for Tilly to make the hospital arrangements and for Nancy to sign the consent forms.

Heath had just seen off his first patient for the day, and was at the reception desk checking up on a late arrival.

'Were you part of the medical team assisting the disabled athletes at the international games last year?' Nancy asked Phoebe as they waited for Tilly to check the surgical roster at the Eastern Memorial, where Phoebe would be operating.

'Yes, I was—but how did you know? The games weren't held in Australia.'

'My older brother Jason's a weightlifter. He lives in Detroit with his wife and baby daughter,' Nancy continued as she offered Tilly her credit card for the consultation payment. 'He suffers from congenital amputation of his left leg below the knee, and he had a similar issue to me with his right heel the night before his heat. I remember he told me about a consultation he had with Dr Phoebe Johnson, the podiatric surgeon with the American team. Once I heard your accent I assumed that there couldn't be two of you in the same specialty.'

'No—not that I'm aware of anyway,' Phoebe replied as she finished signing the notes so Tilly could book surgery the following week. She turned back to Nancy. 'Being involved with the teams was a wonderful experience. Can you please give my best to Jason? If I remember correctly he won a medal—was it silver?'

'Yes, and he was thrilled to win it. He swore that if it wasn't for you and the treatment you provided to alleviate the pain he would have pulled out and wasted almost four years of training.'

Heath walked back to his office, unavoidably impressed with this experience that Phoebe had kept close to her chest and not put on her CV. She was even more unforthcoming than him!

He wondered what else he didn't know about his temporary associate. And he still wondered if this small inner-city practice would prove enough of a challenge for her...

The morning was steady, and by lunchtime Heath was preparing to leave for his afternoon surgical list at the Eastern Memorial. Aware that Phoebe's last patient for the morning had left, he knocked on the open door of Phoebe's consulting room.

'Come in, Tilly.'

Heath paused. 'It's not Tilly.'

Phoebe turned from her computer screen, where she was reading through the notes for her first afternoon patient.

'Sorry, Heath—come in.'

With only fifteen minutes before he had to leave for the hospital, he wanted to catch up and see how her morning had progressed. And he just wanted to see her but couldn't admit that even to himself.

Before he had a chance to open his mouth, Tilly knocked on the door.

'This time it has to be Tilly,' Phoebe remarked as she watched Heath cross his arms across his broad chest.

'Yep, you're running out of alternative suspects now.'

Phoebe smiled, then asked Tilly to join them.

'Sorry to interrupt, Phoebe, but your afternoon patients have both cancelled due to the extreme weather,' Tilly told her. 'So it looks like you've got the afternoon off.'

'Oh, no. That's disappointing,' Phoebe said, slumping into her chair and not masking her feelings. 'I feel so guilty, being here and doing nothing.' She had a strong work ethic and that made sitting around seem a complete waste of time for her and a waste of money for the practice. 'I've had more time off since I arrived than I've worked.'

Heath considered her for a moment and then came up with a suggestion. 'I have an idea to appease your misguided sense of guilt. Why don't you assist me in Theatre over at the Eastern Memorial this afternoon? I have three on the surgical list and I could do with an extra set of hands—but we'd need to leave immediately.'

Phoebe sat bolt-upright and answered with an unhesitating, 'Yes!' as she reached for her bag. 'Let's go... I'm all yours.'

Heath nodded, but his body abruptly reminded him that if his life had played out differently and Phoebe really was *all his* there would be far more pleasurable things he would do with her that afternoon.

CHAPTER SEVEN

THE SCRUB NURSE greeted Heath as he prepared for the first patient.

'Abby, we have Phoebe Johnson, a podiatric surgeon from Washington, joining us this afternoon,' Heath announced as he turned off the tap with his foot and shook the water from his hands into the scrub room trough.

'Hi, Phoebe, welcome aboard.'

'Pleased to meet you, Abby.'

Phoebe slipped her freshly scrubbed hands inside some surgical gloves. Her long dark hair was in a flat bun and neatly secured inside a floral cap, and like the other two she was already dressed in sterile blue scrubs. They entered the theatre just as the patient was drifting off under anaesthesia.

'So, today's patient is a thirty-five-year-old professional skateboarder. He's here for a lateral ankle ligament reconstruction. The ankle has not responded to non-surgical treatment and has been unstable for over six months,' Heath informed the surgical team, including two observing third-year medical students as he began marking the stained sterile area. 'Would you like to lead on this one, Phoebe?'

Phoebe was both flattered and pleased to be asked. Heath was a complex man, but a man who treated her as his equal, not only in words but in actions.

Quietly she declined. 'I'd prefer to assist today. We can switch it around another time, perhaps.'

'Certainly.' Heath looked over his surgical mask at Phoebe for slightly longer than required before he averted his eyes back to the patient. 'I routinely use the modified Brostrom procedure.' He confidently made a J-shaped incision over the outside of the patient's left ankle with his scalpel, identified the ankle ligaments and began the process of tightening them, using anchors that he placed on to the fibula bone.

Phoebe appreciated the way he led the students through the procedure by describing the steps clearly and precisely.

'I'm stitching other tissue over the repaired ligaments to further strengthen the repair,' he said as he continued, with Phoebe holding the incision open with forceps.

Phoebe had done many of these operations over the years. 'That looks great, Heath. Very clean and tidy. I've had a few when I've needed to use tendons to replace the ligaments. I've woven a tendon into the bones around the ankle and held it in place with stitches, and occasionally a screw in the bone. I've utilised a patient's own hamstring tendon before. But it made it a much longer operation as I had to take the hamstring tendon through a separate incision on the inside part of the knee.'

Heath nodded in agreement. 'On more than one occasion I've needed to use a cadaver tendon and had to weave it into the fibula bone. There's many ways to solve a problem like this, and as we know each has its merits.'

Phoebe and Heath worked together as if they had been operating as a team for years—or at the very least months. Their effortless collaboration would be deceptive to any external observers, who might not think that this was their first time together in the operating theatre. Phoebe was able to pre-empt Heath's next move, and neither of them could deny their natural synchronisation.

'That went well.'

Phoebe nodded her agreement with Heath's statement as they scrubbed in for the second operation. Each was exceptionally happy with how well they'd worked together but not wanting to state the obvious.

They made a great team.

The afternoon progressed well, with the other two patients' procedures completed successfully and on time. Phoebe felt a great deal of satisfaction working with such a skilful surgeon as Heath. His dexterity and knowledge in the field was second to none and, while she was confident in her own abilities, she felt there was still much she could learn from him.

After only a short time in the operating theatre with Heath she could see that he had a level of skill that must come close to his father's. The knowledge Heath had casually and without ceremony imparted to her already was amazing, and she was excited for the next few weeks until he left for Sydney.

'I really hope we can do this again.' The words rushed from her lips with unbridled honesty as she removed her surgical gloves and cap.

Heath watched as her long dark hair tumbled free and fell over her shoulders. In the harsh theatre lights she still looked gorgeous, and he knew that in any lighting her stunning smile and sparkling eyes would bring a glow to the room.

'I'd like that,' he said, and again kept his eyes focused on her for a little longer than a casual glance.

Phoebe flinched and felt something tug at her heart. Was it pity for the man? Or desire? She wasn't sure, but there was something stirring inside.

'Would you like to grab some dinner? My way to say thank you for assisting in there this afternoon.'

Heath had surprised himself with the invitation, but he enjoyed spending time with Phoebe and it seemed a natural progression for the day. They had a professional connection, and he told himself it was nothing more than a dinner invitation to a colleague.

'I'll have to go out and eat anyway. Oscar will be eating at Tilly's, and Dad will more than likely defrost a TV dinner, so I will need to pick up something or eat alone at a restaurant. You'll be doing me a favour by sharing a table with me.'

'If you put it that way...' she replied.

'That's settled, then,' Heath said as he left to change into his street clothes. 'As you know, I have your address, so what say I pick you up at seven?'

'Sounds perfect.'

'I'll put Oscar to bed early, since last night was a late one for him, then you and I can have a nice dinner somewhere—maybe even in the foothills. I'll show you something of Adelaide. It should be a little cooler out tonight, so I'll find a good alfresco restaurant.'

Phoebe walked into the female change room. There were two other young doctors also changing from their scrubs to day clothes, but they didn't notice Phoebe and continued their conversation.

'Did you know he's back in town?' an attractive redhead asked the other woman. 'He's been here for a week already.'

'The doctor with the *no second date* rule?' the blonde doctor replied as she ran a brush though her short bobbed hair, then put it back on the shelf and closed her locker. 'Yes, I heard he came back last week and that he's here for a month.'

'I wonder how many hearts he'll break in that time, with his hard and fast rules. And don't forget the *never meet his son* rule. There was another one too, but I can't think of it now.'

'I think it's to *leave before the sun comes up.*'

'That's right. Pity he's so damned gorgeous—if he wasn't he'd never get away with it.'

They both slammed shut their lockers. 'But despite all that he doesn't hide the rules. I hear he's upfront with all the women he intends to bed. They all know what they're getting into and not one has ever met his precious son. Dr Rollins is a player, but he's an honest one.'

Almost two hours later there was a knock on Phoebe's front door.

Thank God, she thought as she sprayed a light fragrance on her neck and wrists, that this wasn't really a date. It had the makings of a date, and to others observing it might even look like a date, but to Phoebe it most certainly *wasn't* a date. She wasn't ready for anything close to a date. And after what she'd heard in the locker room she never would be. They would only ever be friends—because she had already met his son, so clearly he wasn't thinking about bedding her.

Deep in thought, she smoothed her hands over her long white summer dress as she made her way from her room. The halter-style dress, cinched at the waist by a thin gold belt, was made of soft cotton that flowed as she moved. She wore simple flat gold sandals to match. Her hair fell in silky curls around her bare shoulders.

'Hi, Phoebe,' Heath greeted her as she opened the door.

'Hi, Heath. Let me grab my bag and I'll be right with you.' She picked up her purse and keys and locked the door behind her as they left.

'It's a little cooler this evening, like I predicted, so I've left the top down to enjoy the fresh air on the drive but if you'd prefer I can put it up again.'

Phoebe looked past him to see his silver convertible sports car parked by her front gate. Then her gaze quickly returned to him. His white T-shirt was snug across his toned chest and he wore khaki trousers. A single, handsome medic with a sports car would be every woman's dream. But not hers—not after what she'd heard.

She reached into her purse for a hair tie. 'You can leave the top down,' she said and she pulled her hair into a high ponytail.

Heath had to remind himself that he was doing the right thing and providing dinner for a colleague who had done a great job in Theatre that afternoon. And not that she was a woman whose company he was very much beginning to enjoy.

'So, I thought we'd head up to Hahndorf for dinner. It's a German town in the Adelaide Hills.'

'Sounds lovely,' she said as they walked to his car.

Heath held open the car door and, after lifting the flowing hem of her dress safely inside, closed and patted it, as if he had secured precious cargo. It did not go unnoticed by Phoebe and it made her feel torn—almost like jumping back out and telling him that it was a mistake and she wasn't hungry.

The car suddenly felt a little like a sports version of a fairytale carriage, and she was *not* looking for Prince Charming—and by reputation he was far from that gallant. But he was in the car and the engine was running before she could muster an excuse.

'Hahndorf—is that how you say it?'

'Yes,' he said, and moments later had pulled away from the kerb and into the traffic. 'It's about twenty minutes up the freeway. Something different—I hope you like it.'

As he said this he turned momentarily to see Phoebe look back at him with her warm brown eyes. She was a conundrum. He sensed so many layers to the woman who sat beside him, and one layer appeared to be a lack of trust. He wondered why. What had caused Phoebe to be outwardly happy and yet as distant as himself on a personal level?

Except around his son. She seemed to let her guard down around him very easily.

Had her heart been broken? he wondered as he entered the freeway and picked up speed.

The drive in the warm evening air was wonderful and their chatter was intermittent as Phoebe admired the scenery of the foothills.

'It was a pity you didn't bring our work to Tilly's the other morning. We could have gone over the patient notes by the pool,' Phoebe suddenly announced as he slowed a little to take the turn-off to Hahndorf.

Guilt slammed into Heath. 'I thought it would be easier at the office,' he said, clearing his throat. He had to keep it simple, when in fact it was so far from that.

Phoebe surveyed the scenery, dotted with massive gum trees that enveloped them as they drove into the quaint town. This evening would be a no-strings-attached walk in the park—or in this case a walk in a German town.

'I'm looking forward to visiting this town and to eating authentic German cuisine. I've never had the opportunity to travel to Germany—or the time, to be honest—so this is my chance to sample it.'

Heath pulled into a restaurant car park. The breeze had picked up but there were no rain clouds, so he left the top of his car down. 'There are great reviews about the food here, although I've not been. Tilly says it's very nice.'

Heath looked down at his watch. Their dinner reservation was not until seven forty-five, so they had fifteen minutes to spare.

'Would you like to walk for a few minutes? Take in the sights of the town? It's not quite the size of New York, so fifteen minutes should have it covered.'

Phoebe turned to catch what she thought was a smile from Heath.

They walked along the narrow footpath and stepped inside the small antiquity shops still open for the tourist trade and window-shopped at those that had closed.

Heath was enjoying the time with Phoebe.

'I think we can head back to the restaurant, if you're ready,' he told her as they stepped from a bric-a-brac shop where Phoebe had been admiring the vintage hand-embroidered tablecloths and runners. 'The sauerkraut is probably primed to go.'

Phoebe laughed and followed his lead to the casual eatery, where the *maître d'* showed them to a table outside and provided them with menus. There were lights strung up high across the alfresco dining area, and their small table had a lovely street view. She felt more relaxed the more she thought of Heath as a colleague. A very handsome colleague, who bedded other women but would never bed her.

'I love that all the speciality dishes are served with creamy mustard potato bake, sauerkraut, red wine sauce and German mustard. It seems so authentic. Hahndorf really is Adelaide's little Germany,' Phoebe said as she looked over the menu.

Heath ordered a crisp white wine and some iced water while Phoebe tried to focus on the menu. It all looked wonderful, and there was a varied selection within the list of traditional German fare. Her mouth twisted a little from side to side as she carefully considered her options. Her finger softly tapped her bottom lip as she weighed up her decision.

Heath fell a little further under the spell she didn't know she was casting—one he was finding it almost futile to ignore.

'I think…' She paused to reread, and then continued. 'I think I would like the smoked Kassler chops, please.'

'Sounds great. I'll go with the Schweinshaxe—crispy skin pork hock is a favourite of mine.'

With that he signalled the waiter and placed their order. The waiter returned moments later with the drinks, before leaving them alone again.

Phoebe was staring at the people walking by and at the cars slowly moving down the single-lane road that meandered through the town. She was thinking about Washington, covered in snow, while she was enjoying a balmy evening in the foothills on the other side of the world.

'A penny for your thoughts?'

'It will cost you a quarter.'

'A quarter of what?'

'A quarter of a dollar.'

Heath rubbed the cleft in his chin and considered her terms. 'Tell me honestly—are your thoughts right now worth twenty-five cents?'

'I guess unless you pay up you'll never know,' Phoebe returned with a cheeky smile.

Heath decided to call her bluff and, reaching for his wallet, found a twenty-cent and a five-cent coin. He placed both on the table and pushed them towards her with lean strong fingers. 'Well, your thoughts are officially mine now.'

'I was thinking about Washington…'

'International thoughts are always more expensive, so I can see why there was a price-hike from a penny to twenty-five cents,' he teased. 'So go on.'

Phoebe bit the inside of her lip. 'That's it.'

'That's it?'

'Yep. I'm afraid you probably didn't get your money's worth after all,' Phoebe said with her head at a tilt. 'It was always going to be a gamble. When the stakes are high and you play big…sometimes you lose.'

Heath's lips curved a little at her response. He suddenly had the feeling that spending time with Phoebe would never be a loss.

'That was delicious—thank you so much.'

'You're most welcome,' he replied as they made their way along the now darkened street.

Street lamps lit their way, but the sky was dark and dotted with sparkling stars. The breeze had picked up a little over the almost two hours they had spent eating and conversing, but it was refreshing, not cold, and it carried along with it the gentle wafts of eucalyptus and other native bushes.

Phoebe filled her lungs with the beautiful fresh air. Both had purposely steered the conversation away from their personal lives and discussed issues aligned to their careers.

'We can head to my father's home, if you like, to have a coffee with him.' Heath wanted to prolong his time with Phoebe, but in a way that was safe for both of them.

'Isn't it a bit late to be calling on your father?' she asked as they left the freeway and headed towards the city residence.

'My father is a night owl. He has been for many years. He was always the last to bed. I remember coming home in the early hours of the morning sometimes, maybe from a pub crawl with uni friends, and he would still be up reading.'

'And your mother didn't mind?'

Heath drew a shallow breath. Although it had been a long time since his mother had died he still felt the loss.

'My mother was killed in a light plane crash returning from Kangaroo Island. She was a social worker and had been over there consulting about issues with the high rate of school truancy. She was working on strategies to keep the children on the island engaged, and she called my father just before she boarded, very excited with the outcome. She told him that they had made significant progress and that she would tell him all about it when she arrived home. The plane went down ten minutes after take-off from Kingscote, in bad weather that had come in quickly.'

'I'm so sorry to hear that.' Phoebe's hand instinctively covered her mouth for a moment. She felt her heart sink with the news he had just broken. That meant he had lost two women he had loved. That was a heavy burden to carry for any man.

'How old were you at the time, Heath?'

'Sixteen—so it will be twenty years this July since she was killed.'

The desolate expression on Phoebe's face told Heath how she was feeling. She knew she had no words that could capture the depth of his sadness so she didn't try to speak.

'I think, to be honest, he has no reason to go to bed early any more. There's no one waiting so he stays up late—unless he has an early surgery roster…then he goes to bed at a reasonable hour.'

'And he's never wanted to remarry?'

'No. He and my mother were soul mates. He didn't think he would find that again, so he never looked.'

'That's sad. There might have been someone just perfect…' Phoebe replied—then realised that she was overstepping the mark, by commenting about someone else's love-life when her own had been a disaster, and stopped.

'Perhaps. But he's never recovered from losing my mother. Some people never do. They just can't move on.'

Phoebe wondered if Heath was the same as his father. Cut from the same cloth and faithful to the woman he had lost. Never having healed enough to be with someone else.

They travelled along in silence after that, until Heath

pulled up at the front of the beautiful old sandstone villa that his father had called home for so many years, and where he was staying for just a few weeks. Standard white roses, eight bushes on each side, lined the pathway.

Someone must have been watering them in the extreme weather, Phoebe mused as she walked past them, tempted to touch the perfect white petals. Their delicate perfume hung in the night air. The front porch light was on and the home had a welcoming feel to it. It was as if there was a woman still living there, Phoebe thought as she made her way to the front door with Heath.

He unlocked it and they both stepped inside.

'Hi, Dad, we're home. I hope you're decent. I have Phoebe with me, and you don't need to scare her in your underwear, or worse.'

Phoebe felt a smile coming on at the humour in his greeting and it lifted her spirits. She looked around and was very taken by the beautiful stained glass around the door of the softly lit entrance hall. And she felt comforted by the lighthearted side of their father-son relationship. It was not unlike the way she related to her own father. The warmth, respect and humorous rapport were very similar.

'I'm outside on the patio.'

Heath dropped his keys onto the antique hall stand and then led the way down the long hallway, through the huge country-style kitchen, complete with pots and pans overhanging the marble cooking island, to the back veranda. From what she could see of the house in the dim lighting it was pristine, and she wondered if it was the work of Ken or if perhaps he had a cleaning service to keep it looking so picture-perfect. It didn't look like two men were living there.

Phoebe excused herself to visit the bathroom while Heath walked through the French doors to the patio.

'There you are,' he said to his father, who was sitting in the light of the moon.

'Yes, just sitting alone with my thoughts. And here's one of them. Don't look at me as a role model—look at me as a warning… It's not a real life without a woman to share it. Don't leave it too long to look for love again.'

CHAPTER EIGHT

THE NEXT DAY Phoebe was sitting in the cool of her house. It was the weekend, and the previous days had gone by quickly. She had been busy consulting at the practice, but she was a little disappointed that the opportunity to operate with Heath had not arisen again. The way they had preempted each other's needs during surgery still remained in her mind and she looked forward to the opportunity to do it again.

Heath had been at the hospital, presenting some tutorials for the third-year medical students, but they'd caught up at the practice briefly, and talked over any questions that Phoebe had had about her patients. She had reminded herself that with his *rules* they would never be more than friends, but despite her still simmering feelings that she needed to ignore, he was still a fascinating friend to have.

Phoebe was enjoying her work, but the jet-lag had finally caught up with her and she'd wanted to have plenty of rest to ensure she didn't compromise her patients, so she had enjoyed a couple of early nights.

Wondering what to do on a Saturday, she put on a load of washing, did some yoga and although she considered calling her father, it was still Friday in the US. No doubt he would be busy, dealing with some political emergency, so she decided to leave it until the end of his day—which would be just after lunch for her. She didn't dare call her mother, to hear yet another sales pitch about her repentant ex-fiancé, so she decided not to make any calls.

It was much too hot to head to the park or the Botanic Gardens so, while the washing was on its spin cycle, she picked up a magazine that she had purchased at the airport and left on the coffee table and thought perhaps later she would visit the museum or an art gallery.

Suddenly the doorbell rang. With a puzzled expression she looked through the window to see a delivery truck parked outside her home. She tentatively opened the door. Surely there wouldn't be another delivery? It would be the second since she'd arrived in town.

'Phoebe Johnson?'

'Yes.'

'Great,' the man replied, lifting his baseball cap slightly and handing her an electronic device with a signature pad. 'I have a delivery for you. Sign here, love, and I'll bring it in.'

Phoebe signed, then watched as the man disappeared back to his truck. He opened the large double doors and stepped up inside. There were some loud banging and dragging sounds coming from the back of the truck and Phoebe's brows knitted in confusion. She had no clue who would be sending her something. And how big *was* this delivery?

Suddenly the delivery man emerged and jumped down from the truck. He pulled a huge box out onto the road. Then another two smaller packages. He also pulled down a trolley, and piled everything on top and headed back in Phoebe's direction.

'Are you sure all of that is for me?'

'Dead sure, love,' he said, as he waited for her to step aside so he could wheel it inside.

Phoebe followed him and told him to leave it to the side

of the living room, near the kitchen doorway. He offloaded all the items and then left, closing the front door behind him.

Phoebe scratched her head as she searched for the delivery note and discovered it was from a local department store. She headed into the kitchen, found some scissors and began to cut open the largest of the three packages.

A moment later she squealed in delight. It was a Christmas tree. But as she pulled it gently from the oversized box she could see it was a very special type of tree.

The branches were the deepest forest-green, and looked so real. She moved closer and smiled as she could smell pinecones. It was just like the tree she'd had back home when she was very young. It was still her favourite Christmas tree of all time, and she had looked forward every year to her mother and father bringing it down from the attic and spending the night decorating it, with tinsel and lights, and baubles with their names handwritten on them in gold. Even the dog had had a personalised bauble...

But the branches had broken one by one over the years, and eventually the tree had had to be replaced. They hadn't been able to find the same one. And the new one had been nice but it was a slightly different green and it didn't smell like pinecones. It just hadn't been the same...

She heard her phone ringing in the other room and raced to pick it up.

'Do you like it?' the very recognisable voice asked. 'I asked them to text me when they'd delivered it. In the catalogue it looked like the one we had when you were a little girl.'

'It is—it's just the same! Thank you so much, Dad. I love it, and it was so sweet of you.'

'Well, I couldn't have my little girl the other side of the world and all alone for her favourite time of the year without a tree,' he told her.

'But there are two more boxes.'

'You can't have a tree without decorations.'

Phoebe felt a tear trickle down her cheek. 'I miss you.'

'Miss you more—but I have to head back in to deal with another crisis. Middle East is on the agenda again today,' he said, then added, 'I want to hear all about work and your new home. I'll call you again soon.'

'Thank you again, Dad. Love you!'

'Ditto, sweetie.'

Phoebe had planned on putting up her Christmas tree that night, but she got a call from Tilly, inviting her to dinner. It was Ken's birthday.

They were such a social family, and it was stopping her from feeling lonely, so she accepted. It meant spending time with Heath but she hoped that with the family around and by catching yet another cab, she would keep that professional distance between them. But as it was Ken's birthday she realised she would need to race into the city for a gift.

She closed the giant box and dragged it across the polished floorboards into the second bedroom, and then put the boxes of decorations in with it. She looked forward to putting it up another day.

As she closed the door she felt a little ache inside. This should have been her first Christmas with Giles, in their own home as husband and wife. She didn't miss him, but she still felt sad that she was spending it so far from home.

The birthday dinner was lovely. It was the whole family again, and Ken loved the astronomy book Phoebe gave him. Heath was pleasant, but he seemed a little preoccupied as he sat at the end of the table with Oscar by his side.

Knowing what she did about his past, she didn't press him to be anything more than he could be, but she enjoyed his company and found that during the evening that he seemed to grow less guarded, and even smiled once or twice at her stories of growing up in the US. And she managed, with a concerted effort, to keep her butterflies at bay.

The next few days sped by. The weather had thankfully cooled slightly—enough that Phoebe felt the need for a light sweater one night. She had planned on putting up the tree over the weekend, but on Sunday she had slept in and read some patient notes to prepare for Monday's surgical schedule, so it was still packed away.

Ken invited her over on Wednesday for 'hump day take-out'. This time it was just the four of them. And that night Heath took the seat next to her.

Oscar smiled at his grandpa.

And his grandpa hoped Heath was taking his advice on board.

They chatted about work, and then about their lives outside of work. The conversation between Heath and Phoebe continued on the patio as a light breeze picked up and Oscar was tucked up in bed.

'Does it feel like second nature, being in Adelaide now?' he asked.

'It does. In fact this whole experience is strange in that it feels almost like déjà-vu in familiarity. Your family are wonderful—so down-to-earth and welcoming.'

Phoebe looked out across the garden from the wicker chair where she sat. The landscaping wasn't modern and manicured, like Tilly's, it was more like a scene from *The Secret Garden*. The flowerbeds were overflowing with floral ground cover, large old trees with low-hanging branches lined the perimeter of the generous-sized property, and there was an uneven clay brick pathway leading to an archway covered in jasmine.

It was beautiful and timeless and she felt so very much

at home in Ken's house. All that was missing, she thought, was a Christmas tree and a hearth in the living room. The hearth would never happen in temperatures over one hundred degrees, but perhaps she could work on bringing a little bit of Christmas to the three men who lived there.

'My family have their moments,' Heath told her.

'Don't they all? But yours don't appear to interfere in your life, which is great.'

Heath shook his head. 'Believe me, they try—but I put a stop to it quickly.' Then he paused. 'The way you said that sounded a little Freudian. Am I to gather that your family *does*?'

Phoebe ran her hand along the balustrade next to her. 'Sometimes.'

Heath sat down in the armchair next to hers. 'Did they try to interfere in your decision to come to Australia?'

Phoebe rolled her eyes and sipped her soda and lime as she recalled the last conversation she'd had with her mother, by the waiting cab.

'I'm taking your expression to be a yes,' Heath commented.

'Well, a yes to my mother—but my father was supportive from the get-go,' she said, putting the glass down on the table.

'Why was that?'

'He knew I needed a break from Washington and he wanted to help.'

'But your mother didn't think you needed a break?'

'Hardly...' she lamented. 'She wanted me to stay and work it out.' Phoebe instantly realised that she had said too much, but the words were already out.

'Work what out?' he asked, leaning forward in the chair with a perplexed look on his face.

'Oh, just things... You know—things that she thought

needed to be worked through and I thought needed to be walked away from.'

'No, I can't say I do know what you mean, Phoebe.'

She sighed. She knew she had to elaborate, but she had no intention of going into all of the detail. 'Relationship issues. Some of those just can't be sorted out.'

'With another family member?'

'No, thank God—he never made it into the family.'

'Ah…so an issue with a man, then?'

'Yes, with a man.'

'So you ran away to the colonies of Australia to get away from a man?"

'Uh-huh…' she mumbled, and then, looking at the question dressing his very handsome face, she continued, 'Now you know everything there is to know about me, it's your turn. What is Heath Rollins's story? Have *you* ever run away from anything?'

As she said it she wanted to kick herself. She knew his story, and it was a sad one that begged not to be retold. He had lost both his mother and his wife. And Phoebe suddenly felt like the most insensitive woman in the world to be asking that question.

'I'm sorry, I shouldn't have asked. Please ignore me.'

Heath considered her expression for a moment. There was sadness in her face, almost pity. 'You know about my wife?'

'Yes.'

'Well, you know I did run away from something, then. From overwhelming grief and a gaping hole so big that I never thought it would heal.'

She closed her eyes for a moment. 'I can't begin to know what that feels like.'

He sat back in his chair again in silence, with memories rushing to the fore. 'Did my father let you know or was it Tilly?' His voice was calm—not accusing, but sombre.

'Neither,' she answered honestly. 'It was Oscar. He told me the other day, when we were in the garden at Tilly's. He said that he was very little when his mother died and doesn't remember anything. I assume he must have been a toddler.'

Heath was surprised that Oscar had opened up about it to Phoebe. He rarely spoke of his mother, and particularly not to anyone he didn't really know.

'He was five months old, actually—when Natasha died. He never had the chance to know his mother. To walk beside her or even to hold her hand.'

'Oh… I don't know what to say except that I'm so sorry, Heath.' As she sat on the chair next to him she felt her heart breaking for him. 'After a loss as devastating as that it must have been so hard for you to even begin to find your way through the grief and cope for the sake of your son.'

'It was hard for all of us, watching her die. Knowing there was nothing we could do. It was the hardest time of my life and I was powerless to stop it. I felt guilty for allowing it to happen, for not making her have treatment earlier.'

Phoebe didn't ask what had taken his wife's life. It wasn't for her to know. But she could see he was still wearing the guilt. 'You can't make a person do what you want if it's not their wish. They have to do what is right for them, even if it's not what we see as right. I'm sure she had her reasons for not starting treatment.'

'Yes—Oscar was the reason. She was twenty weeks pregnant when Stage Three breast cancer was diagnosed, and although she could have safely undergone modified chemotherapy during the pregnancy she refused. She wanted to wait until she had given birth, then start the treatment but with the hormones surging through her body she understood there was a chance it would spread. But it was a risk she wanted to take. In my mind, with the oncologist's advice, it was one she never needed to even consider. They took Oscar four weeks early, but the cancer had already metastasised. She underwent surgery and chemo but she knew it was useless. She had done her research and was aware that there was little chance of her surviving.'

'What an amazingly selfless woman.'

'More than you can know. But at the time I was angry with her, for leaving me with a baby to raise and no wife to love.'

Phoebe watched Heath wringing his hands in frustration.

'I can understand your feelings, but I guess I can also understand your wife had a right to do what she thought was best. Sometimes what two people in love want is not the same, and it's not that either is wrong, or not respecting the other, it's just that they see things differently. Their life experience and values alter their perspective. And she was a mother. I can't say it from any experience, since I have never had a child, but I am sure carrying a baby would change everything about how you see the world.'

'But she was so young, and she had so much to live for—no matter how I try I will never understand. I love Oscar so much, and I'm grateful every day for him being in my life, but it was a huge and difficult choice she had to make. And I feel guilty for what happened because it means Oscar is growing up without a mother.'

Phoebe was puzzled at his feelings of remorse. She understood the sadness, but not the guilt. 'I don't know why you would say that. Your wife made the decision—not you.'

'But I should have made her have the chemo. I should have never let her delay it. And perhaps I shouldn't have married her so young. If she hadn't married me then she wouldn't have rushed into having a child, and when she was diagnosed she would have gone ahead with treatment.'

'Heath, you can't know that for sure. Natasha might not have been diagnosed until it was too late anyway. A young woman in her twenties wouldn't have been having mammograms, so it might have gone undetected for a long time—by which time she might have faced the same fate. It's something you will never know. But you have a very special little boy. And you can't harbour any blame—it's not good for Oscar.'

Heath nodded, but Phoebe could see his thoughts were somewhere else, struggling with his memories.

He was thinking back to the day Natasha had died.

It had been Christmas Day.

The next day Phoebe woke early, still thinking about everything that Heath had told her. While the heartbreak Giles had inflicted on her had been soul-destroying at the time, she knew now that it had been for the best. But nothing about Heath's heartbreak was for the best. His wife had died and left behind a little boy who would never know her. And a man who couldn't fully understand or accept her reasons.

She felt a little homesick for the first time, and called her father.

'I assisted in surgery last week, and I'm heading in today to the practice, and then tomorrow I'm in Theatre again,' she told him as she ate her muesli and fruit breakfast with her mobile phone on speaker. 'And I finally met Ken Rollins.'

'That's great. I bet you quizzed him about his papers.'

'I did and he was so generous with his knowledge.'

'How long will his son be filling in before he leaves and heads back to his old position?'

Phoebe's mood suddenly and unexpectedly fell as she listened to her father and was reminded that Heath and Oscar were only transient in her life. She had enjoyed spending time with Heath out of work hours. No matter how much she was looking forward to working with Ken, she knew she would miss Heath. He was charming company when he lifted his guard, and he had managed to make her feel important with the way he listened to her and engaged in their conversations.

He was a far cry from the distracted man who had once held the title of her fiancé. And she suddenly felt a little sad that Heath would be gone in a few short weeks. She knew she wanted more. What that was, she wasn't sure—but she knew even after such a short time there would be a void in her life when he left.

'Um... I'm not sure, exactly,' she muttered, trying not to think about exactly how much she would miss him as she washed her bowl and spoon and put them in the dish drainer. 'I think another four weeks, unless Ken's recovery takes longer.'

Phoebe realised she wouldn't be disappointed in any way if the older Dr Rollins chose to recuperate at home for a little longer than originally planned. She would be more than agreeable to holding down the fort with his son. In fact she knew it was something she wanted very much.

But that was in the hands of the universe and Ken's doctor.

'Well, I miss you, honey, and so does your mother.'

'Miss you too, Dad. How is Mom?'

'Rushing about, keeping herself busy with her charity work as always.'

'Maybe you could both head over for a short vacation in sunny Australia in a few months? By then I will know my way around and I can be your tour guide.'

'That sounds like a wonderful idea—but don't book any accommodation for us yet. With the presidential election only eleven months away I can't see sleep on my agenda, let alone a vacation any time soon.'

'Of course—how silly of me. I guess I was caught up with my life here and I forgot about everything happening back in Washington.'

'And that's a *good* thing. I'm proud of you, honey, and you deserve this time away. Just don't come home with an Australian drawl or I'll need to hire an interpreter!'

He laughed, then said goodbye, promising to call again that week, and left Phoebe free to get ready for work.

The morning was filled with a few post-operative checks and one new patient.

Phoebe loved working with Tilly. She was funny and sweet and made the workplace even more enjoyable. And she made her feel almost like part of the family.

She just wished that there was a way she could make Heath feel whole again. But she doubted it. And she had limited time. His guilt was not allowing him to move on. Perhaps it also framed his *rules*. For those rules would protect him from getting too close to a woman again.

'Evan Jones?' she called, to the man she assumed was her next patient.

'That'd be me.'

The man in his early thirties stood, and with a strained expression on his suntanned face, using crutches, he crossed the room to Phoebe.

'We can take it slowly,' she said as they walked the short distance to her consulting room.

As she passed Heath's room she felt compelled to look, even though she knew he wasn't there. He hadn't been in all day. He had ward rounds at the hospital, then a short surgical roster to keep him occupied at the Eastern Memorial. She missed seeing his face, and wanted to believe that their current working arrangement could remain in place for a longer time.

Heath was everything she wanted in a colleague, a mentor and a friend. And perhaps even a lover, her body told her, before she quickly brought herself back to the task at hand. She should not be thinking about anything other than work. And definitely not thinking about Heath Rollins.

'Is that an American accent?' the man asked.

'Yes, East Coast,' she told him. 'Washington DC to be precise.'

He hobbled to the chair and rested his crutches against the nearby wall as Phoebe closed the door behind him. His patient notes told her that he was thirty-three years of age, a smoker and had suffered a heel fracture as a result of a fall from a balcony at a party. Without wanting to pass judgement, she couldn't help but wonder if alcohol had been a catalyst for the injury.

'So, Evan, your referring doctor has noted that the fall took place one week ago and that the CT scan she requested has confirmed you have a fractured calcaneus— or, more simply put, a broken heel bone.'

'Yes, my doc said that I smashed it when I fell from Bazza's ledge at 'is bucks' night.'

'It must have been quite the party. When's the wedding?'

'In two weeks. We've been like best mates for ever, and I'm meant to be 'is best man, but I'm gonna give it a miss 'cos I can't get across the sand for the wedding. It's on the beach at Noarlunga. That's what 'is missus wants. So I gotta just watch from the road.'

Phoebe nodded. She had no idea where Noarlunga was, and she was struggling a little with his heavy accent and wasn't too sure she had understood everything, but she knew she would be able to clarify the details during her examination. What she *did* know for a fact was that a best man on crutches, sinking into the sand, would not auger well for a romantic beach wedding, so she silently agreed with the bride's decision.

'Well, let me look at your injury and see if I can at least get you mobile enough to be in the audience—even if it is standing on the side of the road.'

Phoebe slipped the X-rays and the CT scan on the illuminated viewer, switched it on and then donned a pair of disposable gloves while she studied the films. The specific nature of the injury was leading her to concur with the referring doctor that surgery would be Evan's best option.

Kneeling down, she removed his moon boot and began to assess the damage done to his foot during the fall. 'I will chat to you in a moment, Evan, about our options to restore function and minimise pain.'

'Yeah, I'm throwing back painkillers like I got shares in the company.'

'We don't want you to be doing that for any extended period, so let's find a solution,' she replied as she gently elevated his foot. 'Does that hurt?'

'Nah—but I just tossed back a couple of strong ones about ten minutes ago, so ya could probably remove me kidney and I wouldn't feel a thing.'

Phoebe smiled. She still hadn't caught everything, but understood enough to see the humour in his remark. Evan's was the thickest Australian accent she had ever heard, and she guessed he was a not a city dweller. Well, at least had not always been a city dweller.

'Did you grow up in Adelaide, Evan?'

'Nah, I'm from up north. Grew up just outta Woomera, on a sheep station.'

'I'm guessing that would have been pretty dry and hot. Does it get hotter up there than here?'

Evan laughed. 'This isn't *hot*, Doc. Hot's when it's fifty in the shade—or, as you folks would say, about a hundred and twenty degrees.'

'Oh, my goodness. I can't imagine being that hot. I think I would die.'

'Plenty do, if they're not bush-savvy,' he replied with a grin. Then, as she lowered his foot to the ground, he grunted with the pain. 'That did hurt a bit.'

'I apologise, but I just had to check if the skin on your heel is wrinkled—this tells me the swelling has subsided sufficiently to proceed with surgery.'

'No worries. So I'm good to go out there and make a time for the surgery, then?'

'Not so quickly, Evan…' Phoebe removed her gloves and disposed of them in the bin before she took a seat and began reading the referral notes, along with the patient details he had completed for Tilly. 'At your age, and with the extent of the damage that is indicated on the X-rays, I think you're a good candidate for surgery, but I can see here that you wrote down that you're a smoker.'

'Yep, but I can hold off before the surgery, and even a few hours afterwards. I've cut back heaps on 'em lately. What with the cost and all, it's sendin' me broke.'

'Actually, Evan,' Phoebe continued, looking directly at him with a serious expression on her face, 'you have to quit. Cold turkey, with no soft lead-in time, if we're to complete this in time for you to even be up and around to view the wedding from the side of the road.'

'Why?'

'Because smoking is harmful for wound and fracture-healing. I won't, in good conscience as a surgeon, consider you for surgery unless you stop smoking today.'

'That's a bit harsh, isn't it?'

'Unfortunately, Evan, I can't be gentle if you want me to operate and not compromise your health further. I need your vascular system at its peak to ensure the best results.'

'So say I give up—and I'm just puttin' it out there…not sayin' yet that I *will* give up—but say I do, when will you be operatin' and whatcha gonna do to me foot?'

'I could schedule the operation for approximately ten

days from today. The procedure involves cutting through the skin to put the bone back together and using plates and screws to hold the alignment. It's called an open procedure and it involves an incision over the heel. The incision can be likened to a hockey stick, or a large L, where the overlying nerve and tendons are moved out of the way. The fracture fragments are restored to the best possible position. Then I will place a plate and screws to hold the fracture in place.'

Evan shifted uncomfortably in his seat. 'Makes me shiver all ovah. So I'll be right under while ya doin' it?'

'If you mean under general anaesthesia—yes. You will be in hospital and asleep during surgery. We will also use a regional nerve block, which involves a local injection to help with pain control. This block will provide between twelve and twenty-four hours of pain control after surgery. Surgery can be a same-day procedure, or planned with a hospital stay.'

'So will I have a moon boot again afterwards?'

'Post-surgical dressings and a splint or cast will be applied, and you won't be able to put weight on your foot for at least six to eight weeks, until there is sufficient healing of the fracture. The foot will remain very stiff, and some permanent loss of motion should be expected. Most patients have at least some residual pain, despite complete healing. And, Evan, almost everyone who sustains a break of the calcaneus, or heel, particularly involving the joint, should expect to develop some arthritis. If arthritis pain and dysfunction of the foot become severe, then further surgery may be required. These fractures can be life-changing.'

'Hell, can anything *else* go wrong? I mean, I didn't know that I'd be in pain for ever and then get arthritis. Damn—if I'd known all this I'd nevah have taken Bazza's twenty-buck bet to walk on his ledge with me eyes closed.'

Phoebe used all her composure to refrain from rolling her eyes at the idea of risking life and limb for twenty dollars. 'There are always risks, but I would say that in your case, if you give up smoking immediately, the risks are outweighed by the benefits. What line of work are you in, Evan?'

'I'm a sparkie.'

'So you work with fire crackers?'

'Nah!' He laughed. 'Not a sparkler—a *sparkie*…an electrician.'

'Oh, I see.' She smiled at her confusion. 'Well, you will need extended sick leave to heal, and then you should be back to work without this affecting your capacity to earn a living in your profession.'

'So there's, like, no complications other than pain for the rest of me life and arthritis? Like that's not bad enough.'

'I can't say none, as there are always potential complications associated with anaesthesia, and of course there's infection, damage to nerves and blood vessels, and bleeding or blood clots. But I *can* say that in all of my time as a surgeon there has been none of these when patients follow my pre and post-operative instructions.'

'Like quittin' the smokes?'

'Yes, definitely like giving up cigarettes,' she replied as she completed the notes on her computer so that she could send a report to the referring doctor in an email. 'The most common complications are problems with the skin healing and nerve-stretch. Most wound-healing complications can be treated with wound care. Sometimes—and only sometimes—further surgical treatment may be required if a deep wound infection develops. But most times it is cleared up with antibiotics, and nearly all nerve-stretch complications will resolve over time.'

'So do the plates and screws need to be removed later on?'

'No, they don't need to be removed. They stay there—

unless they are causing pain or irritation. Then we can talk about removing them. But we'd make sure there was enough fracture-healing before even considering that, and I've not needed to do it up to now.'

'Let's book it in, Doc.' Evan sat back in his chair and looked down at his injured foot. 'Thanks, Bazza. Your harebrained idea's gonna cost me a hell of a lot more than twenty bucks.'

Phoebe nodded and then completed the paperwork, so that Evan could have the result of his bucks' night antics repaired.

Tilly had left and Phoebe was just finishing up some replies to emails and wondering where Heath might be when he appeared and answered her question.

'So, how was your day, Dr Johnson?'

Phoebe turned to see him leaning in her doorway. He looked as ridiculously handsome as always, but he seemed to have a sparkle in his eyes that she hadn't seen before. There was still a slight reservation to his manner, but now she understood the reason behind it and it didn't annoy her—in fact it was the opposite.

'Very nice, Dr Rollins. And I have tomorrow off, because apparently your father liked to play golf every second Friday and he has no patients booked in. So I'm looking forward to staying up late and having a sleep-in.'

Heath had been looking forward to seeing Phoebe again. All day he had had her in his thoughts. There were so many things about her that made him want to spend time with her. And she made him see life a little differently. He wasn't sure how long the feeling would last, but at least for a little while he thought he felt whole again.

'Then, since you have no curfew, would you like to join me for dinner? Not at my dad's or at Tilly's. Just you and me.'

'I'd need to pop home and change. Will it be like when we went to Hahndorf last week?'

Heath didn't want it to be anything like Hahndorf. He wanted this night to be so much more.

CHAPTER NINE

AFTER A QUICK SHOWER, Phoebe put on a pretty mint-green cotton dress and high strappy sandals.

'Finally ready,' she said, passing Heath the car keys he had left on the kitchen bench while he grabbed a cool drink and made himself comfortable on the sofa. 'Sorry I took so long.'

Heath looked at the woman standing before him and knew he would have waited for much longer. He loved being with her. And even being in her home brought a sense of serenity and belonging to him.

'I'm not in a hurry.'

And he meant it. He didn't want their time to end. He knew it had to. He would be heading back to Sydney in a few weeks but tonight he didn't want to think about it. He wanted to forget the past and not contemplate the future. He wanted for the first time in many years to feel alive in the moment. And he felt more than willing to break another rule.

Heath opened his hand to collect the keys and her skin brushed softly against his. He felt the warmth of her touch and his weakening willpower disappeared completely. He wanted more. He didn't want to wait any longer. He wanted Phoebe. Right there and right then. Gently but purposefully he pulled her down towards him.

'Why don't we stay here for a while? The restaurant isn't going anywhere.'

Phoebe swallowed, and her heart and her head began to race when she sat down beside him and the bare skin of her arm touched his. Their faces, their lips, were only inches apart.

Phoebe felt powerless to spell out the consequences and risks to her heart at that moment. Giving in to the feelings she had tried to ignore was imminent and she felt a pulse surge through her body.

She wanted Heath and from the look in his eyes focused so intently on her, she knew he did too.

'We don't have to go anywhere at all if you don't want to,' she said a little breathlessly.

He answered her with a kiss. And without hesitation she responded, and with equal desire her lips met his and her arms instinctively reached for him. It felt so right.

He pulled her closer and his hands caressed the curve of her spine, before climbing slowly to the nape of her neck. His lean fingers confidently and purposefully unzipped her dress, letting it fall from her shoulders to reveal her lacy underwear. He lowered his head and gently trailed kisses across her bare skin. She arched her back in anticipation and he stopped.

'Are you sure about this, Phoebe?'

Searching her eyes for permission to forgo dinner and seduce her for the rest of the night, he found his answer as she smiled back at him between kisses. He wasn't waiting a moment longer, and he led her to the bedroom.

He was not leaving before the sun rose. He didn't care that he was breaking another rule. He wanted to wake with Phoebe in his arms.

Phoebe woke from a beautiful dream. Then, feeling her naked body being held tightly in Heath's strong arms, she realised it wasn't a dream.

She couldn't remember feeling so happy. She felt as if

she had just come to life. Like a flower in full bloom on a perfect spring day. She had shed her fears and found something wonderful. It was as if before Heath had made love to her she had been merely existing—not living. Her body was still tingling as she felt the warmth of his gentle breathing on her neck, and she remembered the feeling of his moist kisses discovering her naked body.

She didn't want to stir and wake the man sleeping soundly beside her—the man who had made her feel more wanted than she'd thought possible. The security of being wrapped in his strong embrace was like floating in heaven. And she wanted to stay in heaven for a little while longer.

She closed her eyes and listened to the steady rhythm of his breathing. She drifted off to sleep again, knowing that she had made love with a wonderful man. A man who just needed help to heal. A man who had broken one of his rules when she'd met his son. And if he was there in her bed when she woke, then he would have broken another rule. Perhaps all that she had overheard in the changing room would now be in the past.

Phoebe heard the shower stop and moments later heard footsteps coming purposefully towards the kitchen, where she was preparing breakfast. She felt happier than she'd thought possible. And her breath was taken away when Heath appeared in the doorway in a low-slung towel.

His smile was borderline wicked.

And they both knew why.

'So tell me, Dr Johnson, how did I get to be so fortunate? What crazy man would make you leave Washington and head to Adelaide?' Heath asked as he moved towards her, kissed her neck gently, then picked a grape from the bunch on the table and slipped it into his mouth.

'Let's forget the man and call it serendipity.'

'For me it is—but for you I sense there was something a little more serious.'

'Let's leave it at serendipity—it has a nice ring to it.'

Heath was looking at Phoebe intently, a little concerned. 'Are you sure you don't want to tell me? He didn't hurt you physically, did he? Because if he did and I ever meet him I'll kill him.'

Phoebe saw how upset Heath had become. They had shared a wonderful, blissful night together, and she wasn't sure that Giles's name and his abominable behaviour should be raised, but she didn't want Heath to think it was more than it was—and after what he had shared she suddenly didn't want to hide anything from Heath. She didn't want to lie to the man who had shared her bed.

With a knotted stomach, she flipped the spinach-and-mushroom-filled omelette and mumbled quickly, 'It was a broken engagement that made me leave Washington.'

Heath's earlier admiring glance at Phoebe, in a short satin wrap with nothing underneath, suddenly became serious again.

'Seriously? You were engaged and you left him to come here?'

'We weren't suited.' Her response was matter-of-fact and somewhat awkward as she struggled with knowing how much to say and how to discreetly gloss over the embarrassing parts.

'How long were you engaged before you realised you weren't right for each other?'

'A few months. But we were two different people with completely different views on life and on the meaning of commitment,' she said, hoping that that would sum it up and they could move on to something more pleasant—like spending more time together.

'So just how close were you to getting married?'

Phoebe bit her top lip. He wasn't going to just walk away from this conversation. She knew it would sound bad, no matter how it came out. If she didn't tell Heath the entire story he might think her views on marriage were flippant—as she'd dumped her fiancé the night before the wedding—when he had lost his wife so tragically. But retelling the story of the bridesmaids sleeping with the groom would be humiliating.

She weighed up which was the lesser of the two morning-after-the-first-night-together information evils. Only telling him half of the story might scare him, but the full story might make him feel pity for her.

Her stomach was still churning and her heart had picked up a nervous speed. Neither was a great option, so she decided to omit the most debasing details.

'It was close to the day—but honestly it was for the best. Do you prefer your tomato grilled or fresh? I'm more grilled in winter and fresh in summer...'

'How close?'

Phoebe paused. Heath wasn't making it easy. He had been widowed, which was a tragedy, but she had been cheated on—which was pitiful. And the circumstances made it even more embarrassing. She had no option. She had to tell him the whole shameful story.

The pathetic bride-to-be who couldn't keep her man happy so he found love in the arms of another woman... or in her case women.

'Your omelette cook broke off her engagement the night before the wedding but I had good reason. Very good reason. But I did do it less than twenty-four hours before we were due to walk down the aisle.'

'I'm certain you had a very good reason. I wouldn't take you for the type to change your mind or your heart on a whim. Whatever happened, it must have seemed that you had no choice.'

Phoebe swallowed, and then fidgeted nervously. 'I *didn't* have a choice. It's an incredibly humiliating story... but, in short, I found out that my fiancé had cheated on me the weekend before the wedding. The best man told me and my fiancé didn't deny it. And to make matters worse—not that I thought it *could* be worse—it wasn't just the once. He cheated twice over the same weekend. But please don't feel sorry for me. It's pathetic and embarrassing and I really didn't want to tell you... But I didn't want to lie to you either...'

Heath crossed to her in silence, turned off the gas under the frying pan and spun Phoebe around towards him. He kissed her passionately and without another word scooped her up in his arms and carried her back into the bedroom. Gently he stood her beside the bed, undid the tie on her robe, slid it from her bare shoulders and let the silky fabric fall to the ground.

'The man was a fool...but *I'm* not.'

Heath stayed until just after eight, when he left Phoebe with a kiss at the door and the promise that with her permission they would do this again—very soon. He had a full day's surgery, but hoped to be home by six, when they would go out for the dinner he had promised her the night before.

Phoebe was so happy she could burst. She wasn't sure what the future held, but she had a very good feeling about it. Heath was so much more than she ever dreamt possible—as a man and as a lover. And she realised that if she had stayed with Giles she would have been cheated out of knowing true happiness.

Her body tingled when she walked past her bedroom and saw the bed with its sheets tangled from their early-morning lovemaking. And then she saw her dress on the living room floor and thought back to how he had carried her into the bedroom the night before.

As she soaked in a bubble bath she closed her eyes and thought back over everything that had happened. She thought there was nowhere in the world she would rather be this Christmas. Then she remembered the beautiful tree that was still waiting to be decorated, so she stepped out of her soapy resting place and wrapped herself in a fluffy white towel to dry off, before slipping on some shorts and a T-shirt and beginning the glorious job of putting up her very first Australian Christmas tree.

But first she needed to drag the boxes back out into the living room and then find just the right place for it...

It was almost an hour later that she'd finally finished. It was a huge tree, and filled a whole corner of the room, and the decorations were stunning. Red and gold baubles, tinsel, twinkling lights and hand-painted figurines. And there was also a miniature tree in the box. Perhaps her father had wanted her to have one beside her bed, but immediately she knew a better place for it. The practice—to brighten the faces of the patients.

She had keys, so she would drop it in later and surprise Heath and Tilly.

She stood back and admired the beautiful tree in her living room for a moment longer, and thought to herself how everything was finally right again in her world. Actually, more right than it had *ever* been. And she hoped in time that she could make things right in Heath and Oscar's world too.

The telephone rang as she was folding the cardboard boxes and putting them by the recycling bin, and when she picked it up she discovered it was Ken.

'I've looked over the paper we were discussing the other night, Phoebe, and I think I can shed some light on those questions you asked me. If you'd like to come over I can elaborate on those areas of research that you raised.'

'That would be wonderful. I can be there in half an hour.'

'Perfect.'

Phoebe changed into a blue and white striped summer dress and flat sandals. Her hair was back in a headband, away from her face, and she slipped on her sunglasses and climbed into a cab, stopping briefly on the way to drop the baby Christmas tree in to the practice. She put it on the reception counter and then locked the door again. She liked the idea of sprinkling the festive spirit around—particularly with her own newfound happiness.

She spent an hour talking with Ken, while Oscar watched his favourite cartoons. Ken explained the benefits of the new process that had confused Phoebe with its invasive and somewhat controversial approach.

'You're a natural teacher, Ken. You should think about doing more of that while you're out of action—and definitely when you're considering retiring in a few years,' Phoebe told him. 'You have a gift for explaining things in an engaging manner, and the medical profession can't afford to lose your knowledge.'

'That's very kind of you, and food for thought, but to be honest I'm not having much luck engaging with Oscar this morning.'

'Is everything all right with him? He is a little quiet today. Has he been watching television all morning?'

Ken looked over at his grandson. 'Yes, he hasn't wanted to do anything else. He's been a bit down in the dumps. It may have something to do with Heath's talking about returning to Sydney the other day. Oscar wants to stay here,' he replied as he lifted his leg to the ground. 'If only I could find a way to make that happen…'

Phoebe wanted them to stay too.

She looked over at Oscar and lowered her voice. 'Do you think perhaps it would be okay for me to take him into town for the rest of the day? We could have lunch, go to the museum—just get out of the house for a while.'

Ken considered her proposal for only a moment before he willingly agreed to the outing. 'I think that's a terrific idea—if you're okay giving up your day.'

'I'd love to—but only if you're sure that Heath will think it's okay? You know him so much better than I do. Should I call him and check?'

'He's in surgery all day. Who knows when he'll take a break and look at his phone? By the time you get his approval the day will be over. You have my permission as his grandfather and that's all you need.' He turned to Oscar. 'Hey, little matey—fancy the afternoon in town with Phoebe? She wants to take you to the museum, and I'm pretty certain there will be ice cream afterwards, knowing Phoebe.'

They both couldn't help but notice the little boy's face light up as he jumped to his feet. 'Sure would.'

'Then it's settled,' Phoebe announced, reaching for Oscar's hand. 'We're going dinosaur-hunting at the museum, and then we can head to the Botanic Gardens to have a late lunch—and that definitely includes ice cream. But we'll have to stop at my place on the way. I need to pick up a jacket as it might get a little cool out later, by the looks of those clouds.'

Phoebe called a cab while Oscar brushed his teeth. Then, as she was waiting by the front door, there was a knock. She opened it to find an elegantly dressed woman, her soft grey hair cut in a smart bob, with a lovely smile and what looked like a trifle in her hands.

'Is Ken at home? I just wanted to drop this off for dessert for the boys,' the woman said. Her voice was refined. 'I'm Dorothy. I live a few doors down.'

'I'm Phoebe—please come in.'

Phoebe held open the door while the woman entered with the large glass bowl filled with port-wine-coloured trifle. She could see the rich layers of peaches, custard, raspberries and cream.

'I'm sure that Ken would like to thank you himself.'

The moment Dorothy entered the house Phoebe could see that she knew exactly where to go. She moved down the hallway then turned left into the kitchen without any instructions. The woman wasn't a stranger. She looked as if she belonged there. But this was the first time Phoebe had seen her.

She followed Dorothy and saw her open the refrigerator and place the delicious dessert inside. Phoebe smiled. Perhaps Ken had a lady friend after all. He just wasn't sharing that information with Heath or the rest of the family.

While Phoebe waited for Oscar in the hallway, she overheard Ken mentioning to Dorothy that he'd had an epiphany that morning, after chatting with Phoebe, and how he might soon have more spare time, and then he said something about travelling to the Highlands of Scotland.

Oscar suddenly appeared, and with Ken's blessing they headed for the front door, with Oscar's tiny hand in Phoebe's.

'I love dinosaurs!' he told her loudly. 'The triceratops is the best!'

Ken smiled and waved from his chair. 'Stay safe—and have some ice cream for me!'

Dorothy just smiled. But Phoebe couldn't help but notice that it was a knowing smile, and she felt certain after the conversation she had overheard that Ken's visitor was a little more than just a concerned neighbour...

* * *

Phoebe asked the cab driver if he would wait outside her home while she ran inside with Oscar to get a jacket. She opened the front door and Oscar raced straight for the Christmas tree. His mouth was open wide and so were his beautiful brown eyes.

'That's an awesome tree.'

'Thank you. I think it's pretty special.'

'I've never had a Christmas tree. Aunty Tilly has one, but I've never had my own tree.'

Phoebe tried not to let Oscar see her surprise at his announcement. 'Well, I'm sure Daddy's busy—and it's a lot of work to put them up and decorate them.'

'I think it's 'cos they kind of make him sad. He gets really quiet when he sees one. So I don't ask for one 'cos I don't want him to be sad at home. But I helped Aunty Tilly with her tree the other day. Hers is really neat too, but not so big as yours. Yours is like the most *giant* Christmas tree maybe in the whole world!'

Phoebe smiled at his wide-eyed innocence. She remembered being only five and how wonderful it had been at Christmas time. Looking up at the sparkling lights and the baubles and the tinsel and thinking that their family tree was the biggest in the entire world.

'Maybe not the most giant, but I think it's one of the prettiest,' Phoebe said as they both stood admiring it.

'Sure is. Does it have lights too?'

'Yes, I'll put them on—but just for a minute while I get my jacket, because the taxi driver is waiting.'

A few minutes later, with the tree lights turned off, they were on their way to the museum. The short trip was filled with Oscar telling Phoebe he knew everything about dinosaurs, and she was happy to see him so excited.

An hour later, as they walked around the displays of giant skeletons, Phoebe discovered that Oscar *did*, in fact, know everything about dinosaurs—she was quickly learning so much about prehistoric times from her tiny tour guide.

Time passed quickly as they moved on to the Egyptian mummy collection, and Phoebe was quickly aware of how much Oscar knew about that ancient culture too.

'Daddy and I watch a lot of TV about this stuff, and he's bought me lots of books too. He's been reading me some ancient books too, from when he was a kid.'

Phoebe laughed. She wondered if Heath thought of his childhood books as 'ancient'. She felt a little tug at her heart as she remembered how Heath had not wanted her to read to Oscar. She'd put it down to him being very possessive. Perhaps being father *and* mother to Oscar had given him that right.

She just hoped that there was nothing more to it. She knew what a dedicated father Heath was, and how he doted on his son. She had nothing but admiration for how Heath had raised him, with equal amounts of love and guidance. Perhaps he didn't want their connection to change. He had every right to want to hold on to those special moments and treasure them.

'Shall we head to the park for lunch?' she asked, bending down to make eye contact with Oscar.

'Sure,' he said, and reached for Phoebe's hand.

She felt an unexpected surge of love run through her for the little boy. She had never thought much about children. It wasn't that she didn't want to have a family—it just hadn't been a priority. But now, feeling the warmth of the little hand slipping so naturally into hers, she knew it was something she wanted very much.

But it wasn't her biological clock ticking. She didn't just want a child. She wanted *Oscar*. He had crept inside her heart.

Just like his father had. Heath had restored her faith in
men. In the Australian heat, the ice around her heart had
melted too. She had not expected to find anything more
than a career change in her temporary home but she had
found so much more and it was all because of Heath. It
had not been without a struggle, but it had been worth it
and more to finally see him break his rules.

They wandered outside and discovered the weather had
turned from a lovely sunny day to quite overcast. It was
still warm, almost humid, with ominous summer storm
clouds looming.

'I think we'd better stay indoors,' she said, with disappointment colouring her voice. She looked up at the dark
sky and then back at Oscar protectively. 'I don't think
Daddy would like you to go home wet from the rain.'

'No, I don't think he would like that very much.'

Phoebe wondered what they could do. She didn't want
to end their day early, but she didn't think the nearby art
gallery would hold much interest for her little companion.

Then it dawned on her.

'What if we go to Santa's Magic Cave?'

'What's that?' Oscar asked with a puzzled expression.

Phoebe was taken aback by the question. She may be on
the other side of the world, but she'd assumed *every* child
would know about Santa's Magic Cave. 'It's where Santa
Claus comes every day in December, to meet boys and
girls and find out what they want for Christmas.'

'I've never met Santa.'

Phoebe was surprised further at Oscar's response. 'You
do know about Santa, though, don't you?'

'Yes,' Oscar said with a huge smile. 'I've seen him in
pictures and stuff—but not in his own cave. Where is it?
In the hills? Is it hard to find?'

Phoebe saw his curiosity was piqued, and couldn't help
but smile at his barrage of questions.

'No, it's not in the hills. It's right here in the city—in the department store.'

'Then it's not a real cave,' Oscar said in a five-year-old's matter-of-fact tone, a little disappointed.

'No, it's not a real cave—but it's Santa's workplace when he's not in the North Pole. And being in the city it means all of the children have a chance to meet him.'

'Not *all* children. *I* haven't met him.'

'Well, today you will.'

Phoebe didn't really understand why Heath hadn't tried to make Christmas a happy time for his son's sake, but she wasn't about to say that to Oscar. Heath had been through great sadness, but she hated to think that he would wallow for ever and never let Oscar experience this special family holiday. But it wasn't her place to question Heath. He was a wonderful man, and she assumed he must find the Christmas traditions time-consuming or awkward, without a wife to help with arranging dinner, presents and decorations.

She smiled to herself. *Could she be the one to bring Christmas into their lives?* And keep it there? Perhaps even take the pressure off Heath being both a father and a mother to his son?

'Today can be your first visit with Santa and you can tell Daddy all about it tonight,' she said as they headed for the pedestrian crossing, hand in hand. 'But first we have to have lunch—'

'And ice cream,' he cut in.

'Yes, Oscar, and ice cream.'

Lunch consisted of mixed sandwiches at a lovely café. Oscar loved the egg and lettuce, but sweetly screwed his nose up at the pastrami and avocado. Then, without any crusts left on the plate, they both had a double-scoop chocolate ice cream cone before they headed off to see Father Christmas.

Standing in line with all the other parents, Phoebe felt a bond growing with each passing moment she spent with Oscar. He was an adorable and caring little boy. Heath had raised him with impeccable manners. Without prompting he said 'thank you' and 'please', and was genuine in his gratitude.

He would one day grow into a wonderful young man—not unlike his father. And Oscar would be a young man Phoebe knew she would be proud to call her son. But she also knew that, no matter what her heart wanted, they were not destined to be together for much longer unless Heath changed his plans and stayed in Adelaide with his family.

Heath and Oscar would head back to Sydney in just over two weeks and her life would feel empty without them. It was a sad fact but the time she had spent with all of the Rollins men had gone a long way towards healing her heart.

And her faith in men.

'And what would *you* like for Christmas, young man?' Santa asked as Oscar sat on his lap on the large gold padded throne.

Mrs Claus was standing beside him, in a long red velvet dress with white fur trim on the collar and cuffs. She was giving each of the children a Christmas stocking filled with candy as they left.

'I would like to stay here, with Grandpa and Aunty Tilly and Uncle Paul, 'cos we don't have Christmas in Sydney. Daddy has to work, and we don't even have a tree 'cos they make him sad.'

'Daddy's very busy, so Christmas is difficult for him,' Phoebe said in a low voice.

'Well, you're lucky that Mummy brought you to see me today, then.'

'I'm not Oscar's mother—I work with his father...' she

began. 'Long story, but today is Oscar's first ever visit to see you, Santa.'

'Isn't that wonderful, Mrs Claus?' Santa said with a hearty laugh. 'So apart from staying in Adelaide, which I'm not sure I can arrange, what else would you like for Christmas this year? You *do* get presents for Christmas, don't you?'

'Yes, Daddy always gets me something. It's usually pyjamas or something. But if I can ask for anything…'

Phoebe could see that he was thinking long and hard about his answer. He was taking the question very seriously. Phoebe, Santa and Mrs Claus were all poised and waiting for the long list of toys they expected he would rattle off. As it was his first visit to Santa, Oscar would no doubt have a backlog to fill.

'I would like a bike helmet with dinosaurs,' he finally told the jolly man with his gold-rimmed glasses and a mane of long white hair.

'That's a very sensible present, to keep you safe while you're riding your bike. Is there anything else?' Santa asked curiously.

'No. You've got a whole lotta kids in line, and they'll want presents. I don't want to take too many and you run out. Then they'd be sad. The helmet's all I need.'

Phoebe signalled to Santa with a nod that the present would be bought.

'Well, then, Oscar, I think we can manage a bike helmet with dinosaurs for Christmas. And Mrs Claus has a lovely stocking filled with candy for you. I don't think I need to tell you to be a good boy—I think that you're a very good boy.'

Santa lifted Oscar from his lap on to the ground, and his wife held out a Christmas stocking for him to collect on his way past.

Oscar suddenly stopped and turned back to Santa. 'Santa—there's another thing I want.'

'Yes, Oscar.' Santa leant down. 'What is it?'

'I want Phoebe to be my mummy…'

CHAPTER TEN

HEATH CALLED IN to the surgery on the way home. He needed to check his list for the next day as he had an urgent request for a consultation on a colleague's mother, and had no clue as to his availability. As he unlocked the door, his heart felt lighter than it had in many years. He hadn't wanted to fall for Phoebe but he had and he had broken two of his rules in the process. He intended on breaking the third rule, of not sleeping with a woman twice, as soon as possible. Just knowing she would be near him at work made him smile as he walked through the empty waiting room. He knew he should be feeling on shaky ground as his rules had kept him safe, but with Phoebe he was beginning to feel he didn't need to protect himself.

But there had been a strange phone call from his father. One he would deal with when he got home. Apparently there was trifle in the refrigerator, his father wanted to retire and he wanted Heath to take over the practice. It had certainly been a day of major changes. Some he welcomed, but others Heath still wasn't sure about.

Heath thought his father had perhaps gone a little mad from being at home too long.

The cleaner was at the practice when he arrived, and he had piled all the wastepaper baskets in the centre of the reception area to be emptied. Heath didn't see them in the dim lighting and managed to kick them over. He could see the young man, busy in the surgery, with his headphones on, moving to the music as he polished the tiled floor.

He decided to pick up all the paper himself and then remind the young man on his way out to perhaps leave the bins in a safer place. There was nothing confidential—just general waste. Tilly was always careful that referrals with patient details were filed and that anything else of a confidential nature was put through the shredding machine.

For that reason he was very surprised to see the letterhead of another podiatric practice on a piece of paper thrown in with the general waste. It was unlike Tilly. She was more careful than that. He collected all the other waste and tidied the area before unfolding the letter properly to read its contents.

It wasn't Tilly who had thrown the letter so carelessly into the bin. It was Phoebe. The letter was addressed to her. And the letter wasn't about a patient—it was about her. It was the offer of a dream job. As an associate with the largest sports specialising podiatric practice in Melbourne. It couldn't have been more perfect with her qualifications and background.

And she had thrown it away.

His heart sunk as reality hit him.

This time she had thrown it away. But what if she didn't next time she received such an offer? And with her credential those offers would keep coming.

She had no roots in Adelaide, or even in Australia. She could leave at any time. And despite their night together there was no guarantee that she would remain in his life. Or in Oscar's. He spent nights with women and never felt compelled to remain in their lives. Why should she be any different?

She had come into their lives and within a few short weeks tipped them upside down. He could see Oscar growing closer to her with every day, and now his father had announced over the telephone that after speaking with Phoebe that morning he had decided to retire and consult part-time with the university. He had offered the practice to his son. And then he had told him about that trifle again. What was so damned important about a trifle?

Heath suddenly felt overwhelmed. His carefully organised life was going to pot.

As he tried to reconcile his life and find more reasons to return everything to the way it had once been he thought about Phoebe's ridiculous love of the Christmas season. It was completely at odds with his own feelings. In fact now he thought about it, everything was at odds with the way he saw the world. Phoebe was taking his life and without his approval making sweeping changes. Even Tilly had suggested a Christmas tree in their waiting room after hearing all about the glorious tree back at the Washington hospital.

It had to stop. All of it. Christmas was not something to be—

His thoughts came to a screaming halt when he saw the miniature Christmas tree on the reception counter.

Heath was struggling with the control he felt he was losing. Control of his life…and his heart. Looking at the crumpled letter in his hand, he knew he shouldn't feel safe any more. He never should have felt safe with Phoebe.

Phoebe felt as if she knew what true happiness was for the first time in her life. She was falling in love with the man who'd left her bed that morning, and she was already in love with his tiny son. He was the sweetest boy, and a tiny version of his father. Although not so battle-worn.

'What do you say to us buying a Christmas wreath for the front door of your grandpa's house?'

'Is that one of those green circle things with gold bits that you stick to a door?'

'Exactly. What if we buy one for Grandpa as a present?'

'Daddy doesn't like those things. He doesn't like Christmas much. So maybe no...' he said, in a little boy's voice but with the sensitivity of someone so much older.

She suddenly realised that behind his sunny disposition perhaps Oscar was battle-worn too. He just didn't wear it on his sleeve.

Phoebe thought about Oscar's wish all the way home. A wonderful maternal feeling she had never experienced before was surging through her and making her smile so wide and heartfelt. She wanted so much to be a part of the little boy's life, but she had never considered for a moment that he would picture *her* in such an important role.

His mother.

It was more than she could wish for, but she felt concerned for the little boy. He had never been able to enjoy a special time at Christmas, and she wasn't sure why, but she would chat to Heath and she felt certain they could work through it. Heath was a wonderful father—perhaps he just didn't see that what he saw as a silly holiday tradition was so much more.

To Phoebe, Christmas meant family.

And now she was beginning to feel as if Heath and Oscar were family too. It had all happened very quickly, but she couldn't help the way she felt.

She had never imagined when she'd left the sadness and indignity of her life in Washington that she would find anything close to happiness. She had just hoped for a respite. For time to find herself and put the pain and humiliation behind her. Love had only ever been in in her wildest dreams. Phoebe would have settled for a pleasant six months and never felt cheated for her efforts.

The joy that had become her life in such a short time was so unexpected. Heath was the most amazing man, and while she didn't know what lay ahead for them she felt certain it was something wonderful.

And he had the most adorable son.

Oscar was so sweet, and Phoebe had grown so fond of him. She thought that being his mother perhaps wasn't such a crazy idea. If it was what Oscar truly wanted, and Heath felt the same way, then one day in the future perhaps it would happen. Life had turned around, and Phoebe felt blessed as they arrived back at Ken's home.

Phoebe paid the fare just as she watched Heath's car pull into the driveway.

'Keep the change,' she said over the sound of the engine, and she handed the driver more than enough for the short trip home. The driver smiled and took off down the street as Phoebe caught up with Oscar.

She wanted so much to throw her arms around Heath and kiss him, but she thought better of it. She didn't want Oscar to feel that she was rushing to greet his father. She wanted any relationship they had to unfold slowly, and in a way that would make Oscar feel comfortable.

Her heart was light with the knowledge that he wished she could be his mother, but in her mind it was important that the little boy knew he would always come first with his father.

'Daddy, Daddy—guess where Phoebe took me today?' Oscar asked excitedly, and then without waiting for a response he continued. 'To the *museum*.'

'That sounds wonderful, Oscar. You *are* lucky that Phoebe spoilt you like that.'

Phoebe couldn't help but notice that Oscar hadn't yet told his father about Santa's Magic Cave.

'We saw dinosaurs and mummies and we had egg sandwiches.'

Phoebe was taken aback that still there was no mention of Santa.

Heath smiled a half-smile at Phoebe. 'Thank you for taking him out. That was very kind of you.'

Phoebe had thought that after the night they'd shared she would not be on the receiving end of a half-smile any more. Something had changed. She didn't know what, but she could tell that in the hours since he'd left her apartment the closeness he'd felt had cooled.

She hoped they could talk about it later. And she wanted to talk to Heath about Oscar too…

'I've put a roast in the oven,' Ken said as they all piled in to greet him. 'And afterwards there's trifle for dessert.'

'What's with the trifle, Dad?' Heath asked in an irritated tone.

Phoebe couldn't help but notice and assumed perhaps there were problems at the hospital.

'Nothing much,' Ken replied in a subdued voice. 'A neighbour dropped it in. They're a friendly lot around here. Someone's always coming by to say hello and check up on me. And I *love* trifle.'

Phoebe was confused that Ken didn't admit where the lovely treat had come from. For some reason he too was not telling Heath the whole story.

Suddenly she started to see that no one was really telling Heath how they felt, or what he needed to hear, they were all hiding parts of the story and telling him what they apparently thought he wanted to hear. Was Tilly hiding her feelings from Heath too?

'Can Phoebe read to me tonight?' Oscar asked his father as they were clearing the dinner table.

The roast had been lovely and the trifle divine, and Ken had had a big smile on his face as he'd eaten it.

Phoebe was clearly thrilled to be asked to read a story, and her smile didn't mask her happiness. But Heath wasn't thrilled. While Phoebe was a wonderful woman, and an amazing lover, he was more than concerned that she was bringing changes into their lives that he didn't think were for the best.

And he also realised that she might not be staying. Well not forever.

Everything was suddenly moving too fast for Heath to consider properly.

His son had never wanted his nanny to read to him. That was Heath's job every night. It was their special time together. It suddenly hit him that perhaps Oscar was becoming too fond of Phoebe, and he didn't want to see the little boy leaning on her when she could soon be gone.

He felt mixed emotions as he looked down at his son. Phoebe's life was in Washington, or wherever her work demanded. And his was in Australia. Oscar might be hurt if he saw more in Phoebe than she was able to give him. Or more than Heath felt ready to ask of her.

Adelaide was a dream. A wonderful dream. But it was one they could all potentially wake up from very soon. The way he'd woken up from the dream of a happy and long life with Natasha. It could all be over soon.

He needed to protect his son.

And himself.

'Phoebe's tired. She's been on her feet with you all day. Brush your teeth and I'll be there in five minutes.'

Heath continued loading the last of the cutlery and glasses.

'Please, Daddy, I want Phoebe to read to me—'

'Honestly,' Phoebe cut in with a smile in her voice. 'I'm more than happy to read to Oscar.'

'No, Phoebe. I will be reading to Oscar tonight.'

* * *

As Heath drove Phoebe home she decided to question him over his behaviour. The top was down on the car as they travelled into the city, but the fresh air was lost on Phoebe. She had something else on her mind.

'Is everything good between us?' she asked.

Heath took his eyes from the road for a moment. He saw the look on Phoebe's face and knew exactly why she was asking the question. 'I've had a long day and we can talk about it another time.'

'I think we need to talk about it sooner rather than later.'

Heath pulled up at the front of Phoebe's house. He wasn't sure how he felt, except that he was losing control by the minute. And although he wasn't blaming Phoebe completely, he knew she could never understand the way his life had to be.

'Come inside. We can talk about it for a few minutes. It won't take long.'

'Maybe we should,' he said as he climbed from the car and walked to the front door, before he added, 'But I'm not staying.'

He had been fooling himself to think they could see each other without complications or expectations. He had been swept up in the moment and had forgotten his rules and obligations. Rules that he had created when he'd lost his wife. Rules that he had been ignoring from the moment he'd met Phoebe. He needed to reinstate them.

Phoebe was surprised at the bluntness of his statement. But she put it down to his being tired and thought he might change his mind when he got inside. She turned on the light and Heath's expression grew even more strained at the sight of the huge Christmas tree.

'Didn't they have a bigger one?' he muttered sarcastically, then refused to look at it again.

'My father sent it to me. He thought it might brighten

my day. Oscar loved it today, when we called in. I think he wants to embrace Christmas but he knows it makes you sad. He doesn't know why any more than I do.'

It seemed so unfair to Phoebe that other little boys could share Christmas with their families but Oscar, at five years of age, was protecting his father. And she was worried what that would do to the little boy as he grew older. Would he think that his father missed his mother so much that he couldn't find joy even at Christmas? Would he think *he* was the cause of that? There were many widows and widowers out there who still managed to look for some joy in the world, she thought as she closed the front door.

'Oscar's fine.'

'He's wonderful—but do you ever think that you're stopping him from doing what most other little boys his age take for granted? Having Christmas—with a tree, and turkey, and presents, and laughter and the love of family.'

'That's a bit of a sweeping statement without basis, don't you think? He has presents, and we call home to say hello to my father around that time. Don't tell me he doesn't have Christmas. He does.'

'You call home "around that time"?' Phoebe asked, but they both knew it was a statement more than a question. 'You *acknowledge* Christmas, Heath. You don't celebrate it.'

'I don't want to celebrate Christmas. It's just a commercial holiday wrought by multinational companies to get families to spend up, and I won't be controlled as if I have no independent thoughts.'

Phoebe was not sure what was fuelling Heath's antagonism, but she needed to know. He had been so loving the previous night, and even in the morning, but now he seemed so bitter.

She was falling in love with a man who hated Christmas. And she had to know why.

'Christmas is about families, and love, and being to-gether. You can throw away all the advertising and the hype, but you have to see it for its true meaning and what a wonderful day it is,' she continued.

'It's not and never will be a wonderful day. It's a day I dread every year—a day I can't wait to see the back of. It's a day I need to get through, not celebrate. My wife died on Christmas Day, Phoebe. So don't tell me how I should feel about the day. It isn't and never will be a happy day for me.'

He didn't look at her. He looked at his hands and then at the floor. His jaw was clenched and his eyes stared blankly as he stood and began to pace.

'I'm sorry, Heath. I didn't know.'

Phoebe sat in silence for a moment, gathering her thoughts. She understood that losing his wife on Christmas Day had been incredibly sad, but she knew that he needed to move on and be the father to Oscar his wife would have wanted. If he saw the day with dread then everyone around him would see it the same way. As Oscar grew up he too would learn to dread the day he'd lost his mother and, knowing the facts as she now did, he might to some degree even blame himself. Instead of celebrating the woman who had given her life for him.

'You will never, ever understand. I see the way you make Christmas a big event. But for me, for everyone who knew Natasha, the day is filled with sadness.'

'Perhaps.' She hesitated for a moment. 'Perhaps because you're choosing for it to be a sad occasion. It doesn't have to be that way if you can look at it differently.'

'"Look at it differently"? What? Just pretend my wife didn't die and enjoy a perfect *Little House on the Prairie* Christmas? Life isn't like that. You can't make everything right in the world with tinsel and baubles.'

'No, but you can make Christmas a happy time for your son, and for your family and yourself.'

'It's not that simple.'

'It can be, Heath. But you have to *want* to make it happy—and you should try for Oscar's sake.'

'What do you mean? I'm a good father. I take care of him. I doubt that my attitude to Christmas is affecting him.'

'It *does* affect him. He's hiding things from you.'

'What do you mean?'

'Today we went to see Santa. Clearly I didn't know about Natasha's passing on Christmas Day so I took him to the Magic Cave but he couldn't tell you. Obviously he knew it would make you sad. He doesn't know why, but soon he will ask. I wanted to put a Christmas wreath on the door of your father's home as a gift, but he said no, that it would make you sad. He is taking on a role much too onerous for his age. What if one day, in some small way, he blames himself for your sadness and inability to enjoy life? That's a huge burden for a little boy.'

'It won't come to that. He knows I love him.'

'Of course he knows that—but he also knows that you're sad a lot.'

'And why do you care so much? It's not as if you will even *be* here next Christmas. You'll be gone. Back to Washington or somewhere else. I'm sure that Adelaide won't be able to compete with the offers of work that will arrive...or that you will seek out.'

'What are you talking about? I thought after last night and everything I told you that you'd know I'm staying here. If you want me to, I want to be with you—'

'I saw the letter from that sports practice in Melbourne,' Heath cut in as he leant against the doorframe in the kitchen.

'The one I threw in the bin?'

'The one you never told me about...'

'Because I wasn't interested in it.'

'Maybe the terms didn't suit you and you declined the offer, but you applied. They reached out to you. Forgetting what happened last night, didn't you think that as a common courtesy you should have told me you were looking around at other options?'

'But I applied a while back… Before I left the States. Before we even met. Before last night happened.'

'Before we had sex?'

'Before we made love.'

'However you want to say it…' He sniffed. 'There's some double standards here. You sit here and tell me how to raise my child, but you've never had a child. You tell me that Christmas is about family, but your family are on the other side of the world this Christmas. And you want to get close to my son and read him a bedtime story, and all the while you're looking for work in another city? I need to protect my son…from you.'

Phoebe felt a pain rip into her heart. There was nothing to protect Oscar from when it came to her. She loved the little boy. 'I'm not about to disappear. I would *never* run away and leave you or Oscar.'

'Stop it. I've heard enough. It seems to me that you want to change everything about the way Oscar and I live our lives. Well, we like it just the way it is—so I think *you* are what needs to change. You need to leave, Phoebe. It's for the best. For all of us, and especially for Oscar. I don't want him to get attached and then find overnight that you've taken off, despite what you say. I saw that letter. It was dated a few days ago and you had every opportunity to raise it with me.'

'I told you—it wasn't something I saw as important.'

'And nor is celebrating Christmas for me, so let's agree to disagree.' Heath had no emotion colouring his voice. It was suddenly cold and distant. Like a judge delivering a verdict. 'I won't have a temporary employee telling me everything that's wrong with my life. Take up that offer in Melbourne—it fits better with your qualifications anyway.'

'You sleep with me last night, then end our relationship *and* fire me the next day?'

'I think it's best if you step down. And one night is not a relationship, Phoebe. There is nothing to end.'

To Phoebe it felt like a death sentence to her heart.

She could see his lips moving but she didn't believe the words coming from them. He was telling her to go. Leave the practice and his life and take a job in another state.

She felt pain rip through her. They had shared the most wonderful night and he was trying to find anything as a reason to end what had barely begun.

'This isn't about anything you said. This is about your cardinal rules since your wife died. I know about all of them, and apparently you've broken two of them with me, but clearly you won't break the third. You never want to sleep with a woman twice.'

Heath swallowed and felt his jaw tick. It couldn't have been further from the truth. But if this would push her away and protect his son and himself, then he was happy for her to believe it.

'Fine—whatever. My one-night rule has been working fine for a long time, so there's no need for me to change it.'

Phoebe felt physically sick. Heath had just proved to her that all men were the same. She felt so many emotions building inside her. Anger, disappointment, betrayal and loss. But she would not take it lying down. She would not be told by a man what she should do with her life.

'Has your father agreed to this? He is, after all, my employer—not you!'

'Actually he's not. I am. You see, your talk with him this morning about how great he was as a mentor made him decide to retire and consult part-time at the university. He's asked me if I want to take over the practice. You have put me in the difficult position of uprooting my life in Sydney to relocate permanently to Adelaide, or watching him sell up. That is a lot of pressure that prior to your little chat wasn't even on his radar.'

'Stop being so angry! I'm sure it must have been on his mind, and it's wonderful news. It means you'll be near to your family and Oscar can see them...'

'Oscar is *not* your concern. You seem to be intent on changing everything about us. You want us to be one big happy family. Your way. That is *not* my way—and, again, if family is so important why is yours on the other side of the world? A little hypocritical, don't you think?'

The fairytale had just ended. He knew that a broken heart and humiliation had sent her away from her home-town and he was making her suffer both again.

He had played her for a fool.

'There's no need to come into work again. I'll cover your patients and pay you out for the rest of your contract.'

Phoebe didn't answer him. She didn't want his money. She had wanted his love and she'd thought she'd almost had it.

Refusing to respond to the words he had delivered in such a callous tone, she opened the front door, signalling him to leave. Her heart was breaking as she watched the man who had just shattered her belief in happily-ever-after walk past her. He suddenly looked different to her. Hand-some, still—but so cold. She was looking through a filter of disappointment and pain. The rose-coloured glasses lay shattered in a million invisible pieces. Heath would never look the same as he had that morning, when she'd woken in his arms.

'Please say goodbye to your father and Oscar.'

CHAPTER ELEVEN

'WHY ARE WE replacing Phoebe?'

'She's gone to Melbourne. She's taken up an offer with another practice. It's larger and it has a sports focus. You knew with her qualifications that it was always a risk she would move on.'

Ken searched Heath's face for a more substantial answer. 'Just like that? No notice? Phoebe's just upped and left us? That doesn't sound like Phoebe.'

'Well, I guess you never really knew her, then, did you,' Heath returned.

His anger wasn't towards his father—it was at himself and at Phoebe. He was battling his own feelings about what he had done. And about what she had told him about himself.

'How can you think you know someone in not much more than a few weeks?'

'I knew I was going to marry your mother after one week,' Ken said in a calming tone as he patted Heath gently on the shoulder. 'Some people you just know. And I thought Phoebe was one of those people....'

'She wasn't, was she?'

'There you go—getting all uppity again. I mean, what on earth makes a woman leave without any warning when only a few days ago she was happily accompanying Oscar to the museum without showing any hint of a woman about to defect. Not to mention I know you two were getting close. Perhaps think through what has happened, Heath. See if there isn't something you want to do or say to make her rethink her decision.'

Heath's jaw tensed as he recalled the visit that had triggered his need to send Phoebe packing. He couldn't allow a woman to get that close again. He might learn to depend on her and so might Oscar. It would turn them into a family. And then if something happened—if she left, how would he be able to pick up the pieces? He had been fooling himself to think she would stay forever. Her family, her life, they were in America. The letter was just a wake-up call and he felt grateful to have found it.

And even if she wanted to remain in Australia permanently, there was Christmas to consider. She loved everything about it with a passion equal to how much he hated it. Christmas was too painful and it always would be. Christmas belonged to Natasha and it had died with her. He couldn't bring it back to life. A piece of him had died that day, and he had tried but he just couldn't feel any joy about it. He couldn't be happy about a day that had ripped his world in two. He couldn't join the rest of the world in their merriment and trivialise Natasha's passing.

Phoebe would never understand. Just as his family never would. There was no one in the world who could understand.

Christmas was just too hard. He owed it to the woman who had given her life for Oscar to have more respect than to move on.

Before he'd met Phoebe his loyalty to Natasha had not been tested. But the moment Phoebe had fainted and he'd looked into her beautiful eyes as they'd opened Heath had been painfully aware that she would test him more than any woman ever had. Or ever would. But he wouldn't let himself fall in love with Phoebe. He had enjoyed her company, and against his better judgement he had slept with her. But falling in love was not on the table for him.

He had to be the father to Oscar that Natasha would have wanted. And he had to keep his heart locked away. And he couldn't do that if she stayed any longer. She was too easy to fall in love with. That was painfully obvious.

There was nothing he could do or say to Phoebe. He had to push her away. It was best for all of them this way.

Heath had patients on the two days since he and Phoebe had parted and each day he woke with less enthusiasm than the last. Tilly said nothing, but he could tell by the look on her face that she was just as disappointed as Ken—and a little more suspicious.

'Your three o'clock cancelled, but your four p.m. wanted an earlier time, so I've moved Mrs Giannakis forward. She'll be here in fifteen minutes. And I've rescheduled Phoebe's patients. You'll be working late tonight to get through them all, but they've been great and very understanding about the changes. You've obviously got a double patient load now, but I've been in contact with Admissions at the Eastern and we've worked out the surgical roster to make sure that no one is inconvenienced too much by Phoebe's sudden departure.'

'Good,' he responded, without making eye contact.

'You might have to put in a Saturday next week to do the interviews for her replacement. Dad did the shortlisting last night—there's three of them. I'll email them today, if you'll agree to do it on the Saturday. I don't think there's any other way. I can mind Oscar, so you and Dad can both be here.'

Heath shrugged. His mind was elsewhere. He hadn't even considered the interviews that needed to be set up. He had informed his father, who had obviously passed on the news to Tilly, but he hadn't put any more thought into it. His father must have moved on things very quickly. Which was best, since Heath's mind was on Phoebe. And on Natasha. And the mess he had made of everything.

Getting too close to Phoebe had been a huge mistake for both of them.

'I must say I didn't see it coming.'

'What?'

'Phoebe doing a runner. She didn't seem the opportunistic type. I know working for a huge podiatric practice with elite sportsmen and women is a great break, but the Phoebe I know would have given more notice and definitely not run off without saying goodbye. She seemed...' Tilly paused for a moment and put down her pen. 'I don't know—a better person, and more grounded than that. She actually seemed to *like* us, odd as we are, and I know Oscar liked her a lot. It's sad, in a way, and I'm surprised.'

'She doesn't owe us anything. She's from the other side of the world and she needs to make the most of these offers. We're just a small show in a small town. Why wouldn't she want to take up an offer like that?'

Heath knew as the words fell from his lips that Phoebe would never have run off for a better opportunity. He had forced her to take it.

'Perhaps there's more to it. Dad thinks there is.'

'You both need to get over it,' he said tersely as he looked over his day sheet, ticking off those patients he had already seen. He had to end the conversation. It made him uncomfortable and brought up feelings he needed to put to bed. 'There's nothing more.'

'So, Mrs Giannakis, how are you feeling today? I can see here that it's been two weeks since your surgery.'

As he slowly led the woman down to his consulting room and closed the door behind them Heath noted the relative ease with which she was walking for only two weeks post-surgery. Phoebe's surgical intervention had obviously gone well.

'It's still sore, Dr Rollins, but I can tell that it's improving a little every day,' she told him as she took a seat. 'Dr Johnson did a wonderful job.'

'Yes, Dr Johnson is a great surgeon,' Heath replied as he loosened the woman's padded space boot then slipped on some surgical gloves before he began to gently unwrap the bandage to reveal the site of the surgery. He admired the minimal surgical entry point and the exactness of the stitches.

'And she's so lovely. What a sweet disposition and bedside manner she has,' Mrs Giannakis said as she leant over to look down and watch Heath's examination.

'Yes,' he responded as he moved her foot slightly to check the return of flexibility.

'I recommended her to my niece last week. Stephanie's a professional netballer and she's always complaining about pain in her feet. She's seen a few specialists, but doesn't seem to be getting it sorted, so I wanted her to see Dr Johnson—but now Tilly's told me she's gone.'

'I'd be happy to see your niece,' Heath told her matter-of-factly.

'Of course,' Mrs Giannakis replied, still looking down at her foot and the slight mauve bruising. 'I'll still be recommending the practice, Dr Rollins, but I thought that being another young professional woman they would hit it off. And I know you would very quickly have found a large sporting clientele with Dr Johnson here.'

The rest of the day went similarly, with Heath seeing a number of Phoebe's patients and all of them speaking highly of her and their physical response to surgery testimony to her skill.

Heath wished his life was different, so that his reaction to Phoebe could be different. He felt powerless to change the way everything had turned out. He wished the manner in which he had ended things had been better, but that could only have happened if they had never become involved.

But they had.

She was irresistible and he'd overstepped the mark. He was angry with himself for leading her on. For letting her believe that there could be more, if that was what she was wanting. In hindsight, he hadn't set the boundaries early on, the way he did with other women. He had let his desire cloud his reasoning and rushed into something that would never last.

Could never last.

He wanted to turn back the hands of time to their meeting and not look into her beautiful eyes when he held her. He should have treated her as a patient who had fainted, checked her vital signs and not looked further. But he had, and he'd seen the most gorgeous woman. And then he'd got to know her more over iced coffee and realised that there was so much more to this slurping princess. She was warm, and sweet, and intelligent, and skilled. And then, when he'd taken her to bed...he'd lost his mind and his heart.

He would regret everything that had followed for ever.

Heath headed home, trying not to look in the direction of Phoebe's house. He took a longer, more roundabout route to avoid driving past the place where she had lived for those few weeks. He couldn't risk his reaction. What if her suitcases were being loaded into a cab? Would he screech to a halt and pull them from the trunk? Then pull her to his body, claim her lips with his and never let her go?

He couldn't. They had too many unresolved differences. Differences that they could never move past.

He turned left down another side street to take him around the square where she'd lived. Had she left? Would he be faced with a darkened house? Would he slow his car, look at windows with no soft glow from the lamps, and know that the love and warmth was gone?

With a deep breath he left the city and headed along the main road to his father's house. Back to his son.

Heath needed to travel to Sydney to give notice formally to the hospital there. He owed them that. He knew they would understand his need to take over his father's practice, but he wanted to let the Associate Professor and the hospital board know personally.

His flight left early in the morning and he planned on staying overnight. Tilly was happy to look after Oscar for the night.

He travelled light and the meeting went smoothly. While disappointed to lose his expertise, the Associate Professor and the board wished him well. There was little to do but return to Adelaide.

He didn't feel like socialising into the early hours with his peers over drinks, so he enjoyed dinner with three close friends and then caught an eight-thirty flight back to Adelaide. By nine he was at his father's front door.

As he opened the door he noticed that there were no lights on in the living room or out on the patio. He assumed his father had gone to bed early. As he walked past his room he could see a faint glow from under the door. It flickered like a candle. Why on earth, he wondered, was his father in bed with a candle burning?

He opened the door quietly, in case he had fallen asleep. He intended on putting out the candle for safety's sake.

What he didn't expect to see was a woman with grey hair cuddled up beside his sleeping father. Then he recognised her. It was Dorothy Jamieson from down the street.

She had been a friend of the family for many years. Her husband had died almost ten years ago.

'Don't worry, Heath, I'll put the candle out before I fall asleep,' she said quietly.

Heath was having breakfast the next morning when his father walked out very sheepishly. There was no sign of Mrs Jamieson.

'And you were planning on telling me about this little fling *when*, exactly?'

'It's not a little fling, Heath. Dorothy and I have been together for three years now.'

'Three years? Why didn't you tell me?'

'Because I was scared you wouldn't approve. You hadn't moved on from Natasha—in fact I know you still haven't. I didn't want to make you feel that I had forgotten your mother. I haven't, and I never will, but being alone won't bring her back to me. I have fallen in love with Dorothy and she loves me. We still have so much of our lives to enjoy. And we want to do it together.'

'So the trifle was made by Dorothy?'

'Yes. She knows I love her trifle, and she wanted to have an excuse to see me while you were staying here. I didn't expect you back until tomorrow, so I asked her to stay the night.'

'So you told me what I wanted to hear?'

'Perhaps. Don't be cross.'

Heath looked at his father and wondered if what Phoebe had said was the truth. 'Does Oscar want a Christmas tree?' he asked.

'Yes, he'd love one but he knows that Christmas makes you sad. So he won't ask for one.'

Heath collapsed back into his chair. Phoebe was right. Everyone was telling him what they thought would make him happy. He had made them into something they weren't and forced them to keep secrets from him.

He hated himself for what he had done. To his family and to Phoebe. She had been the bravest of all. She had stood up to him and told him what he needed to hear.

And he'd punished her for it.

'Anyone home?' Tilly asked as she stepped inside the front door with Oscar in tow.

Heath walked out to greet them. He was still in shock, and feeling more and more by the minute that he had lost the strongest, most wonderful woman he would ever meet.

'Hi, Daddy.' Oscar clapped his hands excitedly and ran to greet his father.

Heath picked him up and hugged him, then kissed his forehead. 'Did you have a nice night with Aunty Tilly and Uncle Paul?'

'Yes—but when is Phoebe coming over again? I miss her. I want to play Snap with her—and maybe we could go to the museum again or the pool. She's fun. I really like her. Don't you like her too?'

Heath's heart fell instantly as he listened to his son and studied the expression on his face. He lowered the little boy to the floor and took his hands in his. He wished he could give him the answer he wanted. But he couldn't. It was complicated in an adult way that Oscar would never understand.

He had broken the heart of a special woman. Phoebe was gone and she wasn't coming back. She would never be back to play Snap with Oscar again. Nor would they go to the pool or the museum. Heath had sent her away. Selfishly and blindly. For reasons that Oscar wouldn't understand.

'Phoebe's gone away to work.'

'When's she coming back?' Oscar asked, with his big brown eyes searching his father's face for the answer. 'I can do some drawings for her. Can you post them to her? Then she'll miss us and come back.'

Heath sat down and put his son on his lap. He knew the answer would not make him happy, but it was for the best. For everyone.

'Phoebe's not coming back, Oscar.'

'She's *never* coming back?'

'No, she needed to go away quickly.'

Heath saw his little boy's eyes grow wider, a little watery, and his lips tilt downwards.

'Too quickly to say goodbye to me?'

'Yes.'

'But I thought she *liked* me,' Oscar said with a furrow forming between his little brows. 'I thought she liked *you*.'

'She does like you, Oscar. She likes you very much.'

His actions had apparently made everyone sad, but Heath doubted it was a call that he could reverse now. Not even if he told her the truth. That he loved her.

'I guess… But it makes me sad for you, Daddy, 'cos you smiled so much with Phoebe. She made you happy and now you'll be sad again. I don't like it when you're sad.'

Heath felt his heart breaking. He had been so blind to what he'd had.

'Oscar, if you want we can go and buy a Christmas tree. Maybe it would be nice to put one up with Grandpa and—'

'No, I don't want one any more, Daddy. Santa isn't real and Christmas is stupid,' Oscar cut in, his voice cracking a little as he swallowed his tears.

'Why do you say that?'

''Cos I asked him to make Phoebe my mummy. And she left. A mummy would never leave me.'

Heath knew he had been a fool not to let Phoebe make changes to his life. They were much needed changes that everyone else had been too scared to tell him he needed to make.

He had no idea if she would ever forgive him, but he knew he had to try.

CHAPTER TWELVE

PHOEBE SAT STARING at her suitcases and at Oscar's cheerily wrapped Christmas present, standing by the door. Her landlord had kindly agreed to arrange a courier to deliver the dinosaur-patterned bike helmet to the little boy on Christmas Eve. She adored Oscar, and did not want him to stop believing in Santa Claus. His father could dress it up any way he wanted, but Phoebe still believed in Christmas.

Her tears had dried slowly as she'd packed her belongings over the three days since Heath had told her to leave. Regret filled her heart that she had so stupidly seen more in Heath and their relationship than there obviously had been from his standpoint. His one-night rule clearly still applied. She had broken the others, but that one still stood.

There was no regret that she had come to Adelaide. She had fallen in love with Heath and his son, and she believed in her heart that Oscar's innocent feelings for her were as real as her feelings for him. And then there was Ken. He was equally as lovable as his grandson, and she would never regret the time she'd spent with them both.

But allowing herself to fall for Heath would be a lifelong regret. And one she felt sure would haunt her waking moments for ever. She had completely fallen for the man who'd crushed her heart so easily.

Her airline ticket was booked. The destination wasn't

Melbourne, to take up the offer from the sports practice, although professionally it would have been advantageous to take on the role. Phoebe knew it wasn't what she wanted. She never had.

Nor was she heading home to Washington.

Instead Phoebe was heading to London.

'I don't know what to do!' Phoebe had cried into the telephone to Susy two days earlier. 'I thought Heath was the *one*. I feel so stupid for falling so hard, so quickly, but I've never felt that way about any man before in my life. How could I get it so wrong?'

'Because, like I said before, men are from another planet. They don't communicate in the same language. It may sound the same, it may even look the same on paper, but the emphasis is very different. It's like a completely different way of thinking.'

'You're right. He's just another playboy and he definitely played *me*. I should never have doubted my belief that all men are the same.'

'Why don't you come to London and spend some time with me? We can cry into a warm beer at the local pub and then, after a while, you can start planning the rest of your life.'

Phoebe had sat in silence for the longest moment. She had stupidly thought the rest of her life would involve Heath.

'Phoebs, don't go silent on me,' Susy had continued. 'It's a brilliant idea. I'm wrapping up a case now, and I'm due to have at least a week off, so the timing is perfect for you to get your sweet self over here. I miss you, and I'd love to spend time with you. I feel terrible that I couldn't get to Washington…'

Susy had paused as she'd realised that the last time

they'd supposed to catch up had been at the wedding that Phoebe cancelled.

'To witness my vows that never happened?' Phoebe finished drily.

'Sorry, Phoebs… I'm so insensitive.'

'Hardly,' Phoebe returned. 'It's just that your best friend's life is a series of unfortunate love stories. Only this one will be the last. I gave my heart completely to Heath—now there's nothing left for me to give another man even if I wanted to. I'm done.'

'London would be good for you, then. There are a million pubs and a nice fluffy bed in my spare room that can serve as shelter till you've healed.'

Phoebe was hurting more than she had thought possible and doubted she would ever heal, but she knew she had to listen to her father's advice and smile through the heartbreak until it didn't hurt any more.

'Okay, Susy—looks like you have a house guest. A miserable one, but you know that upfront. I'll book my ticket today.'

Phoebe was sitting on the sofa waiting for her cab and looking wistfully around the apartment that had held so many wonderful memories.

The night that Heath had stayed over was still only days before, and she could still feel his presence there. It was as if he might walk back into the kitchen with his towel hung low and tell her that the man who had cheated on her was a fool.

Now she knew the only fool was her, for believing him. For waking in his arms, making breakfast together, opening her heart and having him make love to her as if they were the only lovers in the world. For planning in her head the life and the love they would share together, wherever in the world that might be.

She had not dreamed for a moment that it was just a fling for him. A night like all the others he'd shared with different women.

She had never thought for a moment, as he'd held her naked body against his, that he knew it would end as quickly as it had started.

Her stay in Adelaide had been short and heartbreaking.

Her stomach was churning with nerves and hunger. She hadn't been able to eat for the two days since Heath had ended their relationship—forced her to leave and broken any chance of a future for them. There was plenty of food in the refrigerator, but as she stared at it her mind raced back to that morning when he'd walked out in his towel and she'd been cooking omelettes. Breakfast had been delayed as they'd been hungry only for each other.

Now she had no appetite. She had been too upset to think about food. There was no point cooking because she knew she wouldn't be able to eat. She hoped that on the plane she might feel differently. Or at least when she landed and had Susy's shoulder to cry on for a little while.

She felt more alone now, as she sat waiting for her cab, than she had when she'd arrived at the empty house all those weeks ago. Then it had been almost an adventure—an escape and a fresh start. Now she saw nothing that would ever fill the void in her heart…the hole he had made in her soul that she'd mistakenly thought he would fill with love.

Suddenly she heard a car pull up at the front of her home. Looking at the kitchen clock, she noticed that the cab was a little early. It didn't matter. There was nothing else for her to do in the house anyway so she might as well be at the airport.

She stood and crossed to the door. Her steps were shaky and her emotions like a tiny boat riding huge waves. An unexpected tear slid down her cheek and she wiped it away with the back of her hand as she opened the door without even looking up.

'My bags are there by the door,' she told the cab driver as she turned away. 'I'll get my handbag and coat and we can be gone.'

The driver didn't answer her, and suddenly his scent seemed familiar. She spun around. It wasn't a cab driver at all... Heath was standing in the doorway.

She froze for a second. Then the anger and pain that had been her only companions for two long days and nights found a voice.

'What do you want? Haven't you said everything there is to say? You couldn't make the message clearer or hurt me any more if you tried.'

'I'm so sorry, Phoebe. I've been the biggest idiot.'

'Don't do this, Heath,' she said, shaking her head. 'I don't want to play games. You made it clear how you felt. And I'm not about to waste a minute longer with you and your stupid rules.'

'I never paid attention to those rules once I met you. I just agreed with you so that you would walk away.'

Phoebe met his gaze. She wanted to look at the man who had shattered her dreams one more time. She wanted the image to burn into her heart so she could walk away and never be hurt again.

Her eyes were empty. She had cried the last tear on her way to the door.

'But why? What did I really ever do except try to make you and Oscar happy?'

'That's exactly what you did—and you did even more than that. You challenged me and stood up to me and told me what I needed to hear. When even my father was too scared to tell me what I was doing was wrong, you did.'

Heath moved closer, but he did not attempt to touch

her. He knew she was hurting and he knew he had caused the pain.

'I refuse to let it be too late. I'm here because I don't want you to leave. Not now—not ever.'

Suddenly there was the harsh blaring of a cab's horn on the street outside. The cab had arrived on time. Phoebe jolted back to reality. She was about to leave for the other side of the world.

'That's my transport to the airport.'

Heath swallowed hard as he looked over to see Phoebe's suitcases by the door. 'I'm so sorry I asked you to leave Adelaide.'

'*Told* me to, actually.'

'I was a fool.'

'I was too—to think that you actually cared about me.'

Her voice was flat. The bottom had fallen out of her world and she had no intention of letting him back in to hurt her again. He could not just arrive on her doorstep and expect to waltz back into her life.

'I can undo it if you'll let me. I'll fly to Melbourne and sort it through with your new employer. I'll find them a podiatric graduate. Please don't leave, Phoebe. Don't go to Melbourne. I want you here with me. I don't deserve you, but I will do whatever it takes to make it up to you.'

Phoebe drew a deep breath, suddenly feeling light-headed as her heart started racing. 'I'm not leaving for Melbourne, Heath… I'm leaving for London.'

She crossed the room in silence and, feeling a little unsteady, she picked up her handbag from the sofa.

Heath paused, momentarily stunned by the news. 'London? Why London? I thought you wanted to take up the position in Melbourne.'

'You assumed incorrectly. I threw that letter away because I didn't want the job. I told you—I applied for it be-

fore I left Washington, but the moment I met you and your
family I wanted to stay in Adelaide.'

Heath shook his head in disbelief at his own actions. 'I
wish I could take back everything I said that night.'

Phoebe stepped towards the door. 'Well, you can't.'

Her heart was still racing, her head was spinning, and
she needed to get away from him. Just seeing him again,
being so close to him made it hard for her to breathe. It was
hard to think clearly. She didn't want to hear the concern in
his voice. She didn't want to question her resolve to leave
and never look back. To walk away from the man who had
owned her heart but thrown it away. She felt overwhelmed.
Heath was pleading his case but she felt so confused.

She was confused by him, by his sudden appearance
and by the feelings that she felt welling inside.

She needed air. Her chest was at risk of exploding, and
she felt dizzy. The heat was stifling, her head was spinning and she realised the lack of food had taken its toll. It
was a recipe for disaster.

Without warning the floor lurched towards her.

And she fainted into Heath's arms.

Phoebe's eyes flickered as they opened. She looked up to
see Heath looking down at her, and felt the warmth and
strength of his arms wrapped tightly around her as he held
her against his chest. They were both on the sofa.

'What happened?' she asked as she tried to pull away
from the man she still unfortunately loved with all of her
heart but who she knew didn't love her. He had told her
to leave and she was still clueless as to why he was in
her house.

And why she was in his arms.

'You fainted…and I caught you,' he told her as he put
a glass of water near her lips.

She pushed it away. 'I don't need anything from you.'

'You need water—or you'll take two steps and faint again.'

Begrudgingly she sipped the water.

'Phoebe, I was a fool to treat you the way I did,' he said as he put the glass on the table beside them and gently brushed the stray wisps of hair from her forehead. 'I pushed you away because I was scared. You were like a change agent in my life, and I needed it and so did Oscar but I couldn't accept it. I didn't want to accept it. But I should have. I should have welcomed it, and thanked you for what you were trying to do. And I want to now.'

Phoebe inched away from Heath. She didn't know whether to believe him. She didn't want or need another ride on the same emotional rollercoaster.

'I just wanted to bring happiness into your lives—and Christmas. But you hate Christmas, and I understand why, but I wanted you to understand that you *have* to let go and let your son enjoy the day. One day you can explain what happened. But not now. He's too young to understand. He just needs to be a child.'

Heath nodded his agreement. 'I thought no one felt pain the same way and that I had to carry the burden alone.'

'I think that you are not giving anyone credit. Your father lost his daughter-in-law that day, and Tilly lost her sister-in-law. They would have felt it too. Not the same level of pain, but they would still have been hurting.'

Phoebe's words hit a chord with Heath. Simple words that made sense. He had been so tied up in his own grief that he had not considered theirs. In five years he had not looked through any filter other than his own despair. And now he knew that Phoebe knew him better than he knew himself.

'I just saw them all rallying around to help out with Oscar and they seemed to be fine. Their emotions were in check and...'

Phoebe shook her head. 'Of *course* they seemed to be in control. There was a baby to consider. If your family had fallen into a heap they couldn't have supported you through losing your wife or helped tend to your son. They were being strong for *you*, when they knew you couldn't be.'

'I never thought about it that way. I thought they were fine. *I* fell in a heap, and I had to get back up for Oscar.' His hands were raking through his hair as he relived the darkest moments of his life. 'That meant pushing away memories, but I didn't want to forget. I felt so torn about that day.'

'It's normal not to be thinking rationally.'

'The last thing I remember when I left the hospital the night Natasha died was the Christmas tree in the foyer. I wanted to pull it down—throw it to the ground and break it. It was so cheery, and my dreams had just died in my arms, and I couldn't understand what there was left to celebrate. It seemed so pointless and I resented everything about it.'

Heath drew a deep breath and stared straight ahead.

'My father drove me to Tilly's house and she had a Christmas tree up as well. It made me feel ill to see it, so I left and went home—and the first thing I saw was the one that Natasha had insisted on putting up a few days before she was admitted to hospital. Oscar was only five months old but she wanted us all to celebrate his first Christmas. She knew it would be her last. I swore that night, when I went home alone, that I never wanted to see another Christmas tree or celebrate the day again. There was nothing in my mind to celebrate about the day. But now I know that Christmas is about so much more than tinsel and trees—it's about family. It's about appreciation of those you have in your life.'

'Yes, and Oscar needs to know in his heart, as he grows up and discovers the day his mother passed, that you don't believe *he* was the cause of his mother's death and that Christmas was a day of joy for Natasha. A day she wanted to celebrate with him.'

Heath nodded.

'As he grows older he may feel that he robbed you of celebrating that day by being born. He may decide to take on your grief and resentment over the day. That's a heavy burden for a little boy to carry and a tragedy if he takes it on into his life as a man.'

Heath looked at Phoebe and understood why he had fallen in love with her. She was undeniably beautiful, but she was so much more. She had an enormous heart and a level of empathy and understanding that he had never witnessed before. And she saw life for what a blessing it was and made him want to be grateful for it.

'I thought if I ran away and pretended the day wasn't happening I could block out the pain.'

'I think you magnified your distress by trying so hard to ignore Christmas. It's everywhere. And every time you saw a sign it must have ripped your heart in two and made you hate it even more.'

'I do hate it,' he admitted. 'I can't understand how everyone can go on smiling and singing carols as if nothing has happened. It's the anniversary of Natasha's death, and every year I feel like I am drowning in memories.'

'Then stop fighting it, Heath. Embrace what the day meant to Natasha and how she would want you and Oscar to think of her—and the love that she wrapped around you both.'

Heath was silent for a moment as he looked at the woman he now knew for certain had claimed his heart. 'How did you become so wise?'

Phoebe looked away. She didn't think she was wise. But she knew that Heath was not the selfish playboy who had pushed her away. He was a man who hadn't known how to deal with the pain from his past. But she was hopeful now that he had clarity, and that he and Oscar would be okay. They could move forward and maybe even one day have their own Christmas tree.

The cab blasted its horn again and brought her back to reality.

'That's me,' she said, and she softly placed his hand back on his lap and stood up to walk away.

She understood his pain, but it didn't change anything. She had to leave. Heath would always hold a place in her heart but she needed more than she thought he could offer.

'I have a plane to catch. But I do forgive you and I hope we can always be friends.'

'I don't want to be friends, Phoebe,' he said, shaking his head. 'That is not why I came here tonight. I mean, of course I wanted your forgiveness—but I want so much more.'

'Heath. I'm leaving for London. This was a crazy dream, and we've both grown, but I think it's too late for anything more—'

'I won't let it be too late,' he cut in hastily as he gently pulled her back to him. 'You've never been anything other than loving and understanding, and I've been so consumed with fighting my feelings for you, and with the denial and grief and fear built up over the last five years, that I was blind to how much I love you. I was scared of loving you. *Really* loving you and then losing you. But love is a risk worth taking, and I know that now. I will never be whole without you.'

Phoebe stilled. *'How much I love you.'* Tears started falling from her eyes again. But these were tears of joy, and she let his hand gently wipe them away.

'I love you, Phoebe. I think I have from the first time you fainted in my arms. I don't want to spend another minute without you in my life.' Heath pulled her close to his hard body and kissed her mouth as if she was his life-line. Then, dropping to one knee, he continued. 'If you love me—*and* my dinosaur-crazy son—I want more than anything for you to be my wife. Phoebe Johnson—will you marry me and allow me to spend my life making love to you?'

Heath kissed her passionately, and when he finally opened his eyes they were on her. They didn't look anywhere else. Everything he needed was in his arms.

And Phoebe could see it and she had everything she had ever wanted too. She nodded. 'Yes, I will—because I do love you, and I love your wonderful son.'

EPILOGUE

'PLEASE BE CAREFUL, darling,' Phoebe said.

'Yes, Daddy, be careful. You're up pretty high.'

Balancing precariously on a ladder, Heath smiled down at his wife and son standing below. In one hand he held a large gold five-pointed star with the letter 'N' decorated in red crystals, while the other hand held on to the top railing.

'As soon as I secure Natasha's star on top of the tree I'll be finished.'

Heath's long arm reached over the top of the ladder and placed the Christmas star atop the ten-foot lush green tree that took pride of place in the living room. It was the same tree that Phoebe's father had sent for her very first Christmas in Adelaide. It was the tree that Oscar thought was the most gigantic tree in the world.

They had added baubles with their names on, handwritten in gold, which they had bought at the Christmas market their first Christmas as a family. And each year they had added more—including one for their beagle, Reginald, who had been rescued from the pound and now sat chewing his favourite toy while eyeing the new kitten, Topsy, who lay on the armchair. She was the most recent addition.

It was their third Christmas together, and Oscar was now eight. Each year Heath took pride in putting their hand-crafted remembrance of Natasha in place.

'Tilly, Paul and the girls are on their way over,' Ken announced as he walked into the room with sparkling fruit punch for everyone.

He placed the tray on the coffee table and took a few steps back to admire the festive decorations before he picked up the individual glasses and gave one to everyone in the room. Then he sat down next to Dorothy and she softly kissed his cheek.

'You know, at this rate, Phoebs, I'll be making an annual Christmas pilgrimage to your home Down Under,' Susy said as she sipped her chilled drink. 'This is my third, and it won't be too difficult to convince me to leave the snow behind to sunbathe and swim to the sounds of Christmas carols again next year—and the one after that. A white Christmas in England is quite spectacular, but I would never refuse the opportunity to exchange my Wellingtons for flip-flops.'

She looked down at her feet and with a huge smile wriggled her bare toes.

'Now all I need is an Aussie lifeguard to make my Christmas complete.'

'We're just glad you could make it again this year,' Phoebe said with an equally happy expression. 'We hope you can always share Christmas with us—and I'll keep a look-out for that lifeguard…then you might move here permanently.'

'You've outdone yourselves—all of you. Your home looks beautiful,' Phoebe's father said as he came down the stairs from the guest bedroom, carrying colourfully wrapped gifts he had pulled from the suitcases and handed them to Phoebe's mother, who was arranging them on the floor with the others already there. 'And I haven't seen a prettier tree ever,' he added with pride.

'It's the best, Grandpa John,' Oscar said as he dropped down cross-legged on the patterned rug, patted Reginald's head and then looked up with a toothy grin at the huge expanse of green foliage, sparkling lights and glittering decorations.

Heath climbed down from the ladder and folded it up against the wall. His smile grew wider as he reached around and gently pulled his pregnant wife against his chest. With a heart filled with love, he said, 'And it's all because of you.'

'No, not me,' she told him gently, with a smile in her voice. 'It's because you were ready to believe in Christmas again.'

'And love,' he reminded her with a kiss.

* * * * *